CAPTURED

Jasinda & Jack Wilder

Once again, this book is dedicated to all the men and women of the armed forces of the United States of America, past, present, and future. Thank you for your service, especially those who went boots down and didn't make it home in one piece, or at all. You are not forgotten.

THE LETTER

Thomas, my love.

I'm writing this in our bed. You're lying next to me, sleeping.

There's so much I wish I could say to you, but I know time is short. You ship out tomorrow. Again. I can't say it doesn't bother me. It does. Of course it does. It hurts every time. I act brave for you, but I hate it. I hate watching you lace up your boots. I hate watching you pack your bag. I hate watching you straighten your tie in the mirror. I hate how goddamned sexy you look in your uniform. Most of all, I hate kissing you goodbye, hate watching you turn around, your broad back straight as you disappear down the jetway. I hate that your eyes are dry when mine are wet.

I hate all that. I know I signed up for it when I married a Marine. I knew from the very beginning that you'd go into combat. I knew it, and married you anyway. How could I not? I loved you so much from the very beginning, from the first time I saw you, all those years ago.

You remember? I was visiting my brother at Twentynine Palms, and I saw you running with your unit. You looked right at me, and I knew in that very instant we were going to be together forever. You dropped out of rank, ran over to me. You kissed me. Right there, the gunnery sergeant yelling at you, in front of half the damn base. You didn't even ask my name. You just kissed me, and rejoined your unit. You got in a lot of trouble for that stunt.

I never thought I'd see you again, but you found me. You knew my brother, who was with me at the time. You asked him who I was a few days later. He said he'd let you have a shot with me if I was willing, but if you broke my heart, he'd break your face. You showed up at my hotel room dressed in civvies. You took me to Olive Garden, and we got drunk on red wine. We made love that night in my hotel room. You remember that night? I sure do. I remember every single moment.

Just like I remember every other moment of our lives together. Eight years. Did you know that? You ship out tomorrow, and tomorrow is the eight-year anniversary— to the day—of the first time we met, when you kissed me.

God, Tom. You know why I remember every single moment? Because for most of our eight years together, you've been deployed. Three tours in Iraq, and you are just about to ship out for your third tour in Afghanistan. I miss you, Tom. Every day, I miss you. Even when you're home I miss you, because I know you're always going to leave again.

But this time? This ship-out? It's been the hardest. It's so hard I can't take it. Can't stand it. I can't, Tom. I can't watch you leave again, knowing you could die. Knowing you might not come back.

You didn't say much about what happened with your friend Hunter, from your unit, when he went MIA, but I know it was painful for everyone. He came back, thank god, but you were a mess. You called me from the base. You were going crazy with worry. You thought he was dead. Your friend Derek had been injured, too. I remember all that. And I just...I don't think I could handle it if that happened to you.

Especially not now.

I've gone in circles over this a million times in my head. I've nearly told you so many times. But I just can't. It would make it harder for you to leave, and I know it's hard enough as it is. It would make it harder for me if I told you in person. You're going to be mad at me for not telling you. I know, and I'm sorry. But this is the only way that makes sense to me.

I'm pregnant, Tom.

I'm going to have your baby.

I wasn't sure at first. I thought maybe it was just the stress of knowing your leave was ending that made me miss my period. But then I took a test. Three of them, actually.

I'm pregnant. God, I'm pregnant. I'm going to have a baby.

Please come home to me, Tom. Come home alive. No matter what, you have to come back. I need you. Our baby needs you.

I love you so, so much, Tom. More than I'll ever be able to say. You'll be fine. You'll come back to me. To US.

Always, always yours,

Reagan.

P.S.: I hope it's a boy. I want him to look just like you.

CHAPTER 1

Derek

Eastern Afghanistan, 2007

THE HUMVEE STINKS OF SWEAT AND TENSION. I'VE GOT "Where the Green Grass Grows" stuck in my head. Some asshat had a Tim McGraw album on repeat for about two hours before I threatened to shove my fist down his throat if he didn't turn it off. He shut it off real quick, but the damage was done, and that goddamn song has been running through my head for the last three motherfuckin' days.

So now, rumbling down some dirt track through the middle of nowhere, I still can't get that song out of my head. I'm even *humming* the damned thing, and the guys keep ragging me about it.

I don't even *like* country music.

Barrett is sitting next to me in the back, and Lewis is driving. McConnell is up front riding shotgun. Our Humvee is the third in line out of four. We've been going across some of the flattest, driest country I've ever seen, but that's changing as we climb into a mountain range. Things are about to get hilly and serpentine, and that's when shit could get hairy. Which explains the tension.

It's the kind of gut-churning anticipation that, in my experience, always precedes something shitty and severely gnarly. You ain't got dick to do but stare out the window, and, this being Afghanistan, nothing's out the window except brown hills, brown dirt, and the endless blue bowl of the sky. And it's always right in the middle of this mind-numbing boredom that you get yanked back to reality.

I feel the Humvee tilt and hear the engine groan as we hit an incline.

"Look sharp, fuckers," Lewis barks. "This here is ambush country."

I thumb off the safety. My heart hammers. My stomach is a chasm with a river of adrenaline roaring at the bottom. Barrett is leaning back away from the window, hunched down to get a line of sight on the ridge rising around us on either side like the serrated edge of a rusty knife. I assume the same lookout posture, my finger resting outside the trigger guard.

Here in the foothills we're surrounded by naked rock, which is absorbing the sunlight and reflecting it back as baking heat. Higher up there'll be vegetation, but down here, it's just rock, bare stone thrusting up out of the hard-packed dirt. The ridges climb and fold into each other, shove together and knife apart, providing a myriad of little nooks and crannies, caves and caverns, places where a man with an RPG can lie down and be invisible from our vantage point. Which is exactly what I was told to expect. It's what the lieutenant expected when he got the orders to send us up to visit a couple of villages on the other side of these hills. He bitched up the chain about the mission, but the fuckin' brass knew damn well they were sending us through an area known for ambushes. They sent us anyway, and denied our requests for backup, air support, or any heavy armor. *In and out,* they said. *Just check out the reports of enemy activity in the area and come on back.*

Right.

The roiling of nerves turns to cold sweat despite the heat inside the vehicle. My chest is throbbing, my hands shaking.

"Lewis?" I say.

"What?" he barks. Lewis always barks. It's his natural state: aggravated, sullen, petulant.

"I got a bad feeling about this."

"Yeah, me, too," McConnell says, smirking at me.

"Can you pencil-necked dweebs quit quoting *Star Wars* for one goddamn second? I think I've got contact." Barrett's low, gravelly voice cuts through our chatter.

"Where?" I say.

He points out the window, high above our location. "Two o'clock. Way up there. It was just a flash of movement, but I know I saw something."

Lewis keys his mic. "Possible contact. Two o'clock high."

A voice comes back in our ears, Addison in the vehicle immediately ahead of us. "Roger that. I saw it, too."

I count the next sixty seconds individually—they pass like molasses in January. We drive past a low scrub bush on the edge of the road, a puff of wind-borne dust skirls, tires crunch, McConnell charges his M4, Lewis mutters "fuck" under his breath.

"*CONTACT!*" The scream comes over the radio, shrill, panicked. "GO! GO-GO-GO! He's about to fire—"

Whooooosh…BOOM!

RPG. Shitshitfuck. I hate that goddamn sound.

I feel the shockwaves of the RPG detonation in the ground beneath me, and—*CRUMP*—our entire Humvee is rocked by a second explosion, an IED.

My ears ring.

Hackhackhackhackhack—an AK-47, high. Two of them. Three. Fourfivesix separate reports.

Heat, someone screaming. *Crackcrackcrack… crackcrackcrack*—an M4 carbine from ahead and to my left. I smell smoke, and the horrible, unmistakable scent of charred flesh.

I throw myself out the door, land on my knees, and crouch behind the open door. Barrett slithers out of my door and hunkers down beside me as bullets *thunk* and *plink* and *pitpitpit* into the metal of the Humvee and the glass and the dirt. Ahead, a plume of gray-black smoke rises angrily, lit by flames. The first truck in the convoy hit an IED, and the last in line was blasted by an RPG, trapping the convoy in place.

Absurdly, I hear myself singing Tim McGraw under my breath, "corn poppin' up in rows…."

"Shut the fuck up, West," Barrett snaps at me. "I hate that fuckin' song."

"Me, too."

"Then why are you singing it?"

"It's stuck in my head, okay? I can't help it."

Lewis is beside us. "Cut the chatter, you two." He points ahead of us where Abraham, Nielsen, Martinez, and Okuzawa of Echo Company are crouched behind their as-yet undamaged truck. "We gotta get a line of fire up on that ridge. Get over to Echo and lay down some covering fire so Nielsen can get his SAW planted."

"Sir." I peek up through the window, see a flash of muzzle flash, wait for the firing to die down, then scurry forward to the edge of the truck.

I peer around the Humvee. Barrett is behind me, then McConnell, then Lewis. I'm always point, Lewis always last. I count...*one—two—three*...and then swing around the hood and bring my rifle to my shoulder. It jerks, and I barely hear the *crackcrackcrack* as I fire at where I saw the flash. The other three in my squad roll past me, Lewis hanging around the ass-end of Echo's Humvee and laying down fire. Abraham is firing over the hood, and Nielsen is unfolding the legs of his bipod, slamming down on the hood and drawing aim on the ridge where the contact seems to be heaviest. Bullets walk up the dirt toward Nielsen and hit the truck, and then he rolls around and drops to a crouch beside Abraham. I send half a dozen rounds flying, and then I hear a grunt, and watch as the muzzle flash stops abruptly.

"West, Barrett." Lewis points at each of us, and then at the burning wreckage ahead. "See if anyone's alive in there. Nielsen, cover them."

The SAW rips and echoes in short bursts, and Barrett and I run for the wreckage. It's burning from the front end. I slide to a stop in a low crouch, peer into the driver's side window. Nope. Blaskowski and Allen are both raw reddened messes. I leave them for now. Barrett is firing from around the ass-end, so I jerk open the passenger door. Silva is alive, bleeding from a gash on his forehead, and Glidden is moaning and clutching his stomach. I sling my rifle around my back, grab Glidden beneath his armpits, and pull. He hits the ground and screams.

"Sorry, buddy," I tell him. "Gotta get you clear. Can you move?"

"Ffffuck." He strains, his heels dig at the dirt. "Trying."

I pull him backward through the dirt toward the rest of Echo and my guys from Foxtrot. He's heavy, two hundred pounds plus full gear, but I get him behind the intact Humvee and leave him for Lewis to look at. I scramble back to get Silva, jerk him roughly from the Humvee. His head lolls on his shoulder, blood and dirt smeared on his face. His eyes are open but glazed, unblinking.

I shake him. "Silva!"

He blinks. "D? The fuck?"

"Ambush, buddy. You okay?"

He doesn't answer right away. "Head. It hurts. Can't hear." He stares past me, and something flickers in his gaze. He fumbles at his side for his rifle, brings it up, and fires. The barrel is less than six inches from my ear, and I'm deafened by the report. I clap my hand to my ear and scramble aside. Bullets snap and buzz, and I watch as Silva is hit: shoulder—neck—face. He goes down in a spray of blood, but the bullets stop, telling me Silva's bullets found an insurgent.

"Fuck." I glance at his dead body, and I'm frozen for a second.

Barrett is oblivious, his focus trained on the opposite ridge, adjusting his aim and firing, shift, fire, shift, fire. I register the sound of his rifle: *crackcrackcrack—crackcrackcrack…crackcrackcrack.*

The sound of Barrett firing brings me back to the present, and I plant my back against the door of the truck, chest rising and falling frantically, panic bubbling in my gut. It's an all-too-familiar feeling. Anyone who says they aren't scared in combat is a dirty fucking liar. I've been in combat more times than I can count, and I'm scared shitless every single goddamn time. Like right now. Silva was my boy. We pumped iron together all the time, sparred together, swapped dick jokes. Now he's fucking dead, and so are Blast and Allen and who the fuck knows who else.

Get it the fuck together, Derek. I shake myself, check the load on my magazine, and slam it home. Roll out, scan for muzzle flash, find a target, roll back. Pause. Swing out, fire. Bam, he's meat.

"WEST! BARRETT!" Lewis shouts.

I give him my attention. He signals for us to cross over and try to get up and around, giving the same orders to Martinez and Okuzawa for the opposite direction. He does a descending five-count on his fingers—*five...four...three...two...one*—and then the SAW is barking and echoing and ripping, Abraham and Lewis and McConnell all pouring fire onto the ridge. Barrett and I lurch out and scramble across the road, flatten against the rock face. Dirt crunches in my teeth. I pant, summon saliva, and spit the grit from my mouth. Barrett examines the terrain, and then points to a section where it might be possible to clamber up. He kneels and points his M4 up the ridge, and I sling my rifle on my back, heart hammering. I make it up about a dozen feet, and then the hill levels off enough for me to press back in a crouch, lean out, and wave Barrett up. I hear him huffing and scrambling, and then his head pokes up and I wait until he's on top of me.

We're two big men in full combat gear sharing a scrap of rock barely four feet wide, so we're forced to hug each other to stay balanced. Barrett grins, dirt on his face. "Kiss me, and I'll shove you off this rock, you pussy," he says in a low voice.

I put a foot on the escarpment and lever myself up. "Who the hell would kiss your ugly fucking face?"

"The hottest woman in all of Texas, that's who."

"Good point," I say with a laugh, because god knows he's telling the truth.

Reagan Barrett is fine as hell. She hosted a unit send-off party at their house outside Houston before we left for this latest tour. I'd suffered through years of Barrett's endless nattering about how beautiful and amazing his wife was and thought, like most guys, he was full of shit. I came to find out he was understating the case, if anything. But she's my buddy's wife, which means she's as off-limits as a woman can get.

Barrett nails my bicep with a sharp punch. "Hey, fucker. That's my wife."

"I was just agreeing with you, that's all."

"Well, don't."

"Fine. She's ugly as sin. You got a paper bag?" I'm glad for the banter, because it keeps my mind off the fact that I'm climbing up a rock face, essentially helpless, right into the waiting arms of the enemy.

"Asshole," Barrett mutters. "You know what I meant."

I'm out of sight at that point, and the sound of AK fire is getting louder. We're close now. This is a bad, bad idea. I could literally climb right into their laps, and my rifle will be slung behind my back. I hear Barrett climbing up behind me. Glancing up, I see that the rock angles in again. I climb up carefully, slowly. Peek over, see a lip running off into the distance. We're about fifty feet up at this point, and, by the proximity of the sounds, I can tell we're about to have a good old time with these Taliban fuckers.

I flop onto my belly, roll against the wall, rise to a crouch, and bring my M4 around. Barrett is up beside me, replacing his magazine and pulling the charging handle. We exchange glances. I nod and move forward as quietly as possible, which is stupid, since the sound of gunfire is loud enough to cover any sounds we might make, but it's habit at this point. The hill face bends away in a curve, and I crane my neck to see around it. Bingo. I do a quick count, turn back to Barrett, and hold up six fingers. He nods.

I key my mic and mutter into it. "We've made contact. Hold fire."

"Holding fire," Lewis returns. "Make it fast."

"Roger that," I say.

I suck in a deep breath, hold it, let it out. Shouldering my rifle, I edge forward inch by inch until I can hug the rock face on my left for cover yet still get a bead on the nearest target. Barrett, fearless bastard that he is, kneels on the edge of the lip so he can fire past me to my right.

Another breath.

Crackcrackcrack...one   down—crackcrackcrack... two down. Barrett is firing beside me, so, so loud. They're taken completely by surprise, and I hear M4 reports from the other side. Bodies bleed and fall.

We retreat around the curve, out of sight.

A heartbeat of silence, and then hell descends upon us.

Whooooosh...BOOM!

The Humvee behind which Lewis and the others are hiding detonates in a fiery blast. Black smoke belches, shot through with leaping orange flames. Debris and shrapnel rain down.

Fuck.

Barrett and I look at each other. We're boned, and we know it. Four of us are all that's left out of fourteen. And the four are split in half, with an unknown number of enemy between us. There's one intact Humvee, but it's sandwiched between three hulks of flaming wreckage, and the killzone is pinned down.

Barrett and I both exchange for fresh magazines.

"Martinez? Okuzawa?" Barrett mutters into his mic. "You boys alive over there?"

"Affirmative," Martinez comes back. "Both of us are intact. You and West?"

"Copacetic. Except that we're totally fucked."

"Yeah, except that little fact." This is Okuzawa, with his distinctively smooth, almost musical voice. "Plans, anyone?"

"We do, technically, have 'em surrounded," Martinez says. "One side will hit 'em and draw their attention, the other two'll come up behind and blast 'em."

"Sounds good," I say. "Who's hitting, who's drawing?"

Barrett glances at me, chews his lip, and then nods. "West and I will draw—you two pubes hit 'em. Give us a thirty count from contact. Pick your targets, boys."

"Oorah," I say.

"Oorah," the other three men respond in unison.

Barrett's hands clench and unclench on his rifle. A bead of sweat drips down his nose, and he wipes it away with a thumb. He draws a deep breath, blinks twice, and then nods at me. Rolls out. Rifle up, tucked against his shoulder, tactical crouch, inch forward on cat-silent feet. Fucker's always been the quietest of all of us, like some kind of goddamn ninja. I follow on slightly noisier feet. My breathing is slow and deep to combat the raw terror churning in my gut. I try to swallow, but my throat is dry. I blink the stinging sweat out of my eyes.

Barrett freezes, sinks to one knee, and hesitates with a single hand held up in a fist. Inches forward. Leans out a little. Inches forward. Lifts his hand again, flashes five fingers twice. Ten? Where are all these assholes coming from?

The answer hits me: from a cave, dumbass. This is Afghanistan.

I'm trying to contain my fear as Barrett adjusts his stance so he's hugging the rock face as much as physically possible. You'd think after all these tours, all the combat I've seen, that I'd be over the fear of combat, but shit, the fear is always there. You hear an AK go off, you feel your asshole pucker. You hear the *whoosh-BOOM* of an RPG, you eat dirt and break out in a cold sweat and hope the next one ain't coming for you. You want to live, don't you? 'Course you do. So you're afraid, every single time. If you're not, you're either crazy or a liar.

I'm neither, so I'm fucking terrified. But I know the drill: push it down. Ignore it. Do the job. Stay alive.

*Crackcrackcrack...*Barrett's M4 speaks, and the momentarily quiet air is cut with AK reports, shouts in Pashto or whatever dialect they speak here. There's a million damn languages in Afghanistan, and I can't keep 'em straight. Whatever the hell it is they're saying, they're plenty pissed, I can tell that much. I hear Martinez and Okuzawa open up, and the angry shouts turn to panic. I tap Barrett on the shoulder; he holds fire, and I leapfrog around him.

Fuck, there's a whole shitload of 'em. Coming down out of that cave like ants swarming out of an ant hill. I don't bother counting, just pour on the fire, watch one drop, two, three—they're twisting in place, firing wildly, looking for us, for where the bullets are coming from.

A whining *buzz-snap* of a bullet zinging past my head has me ducking involuntarily, backing up, spraying fire in three-round bursts. Barrett takes my place in front, but then swears and shifts backward.

"They're coming this way, buddy," he says.

"How many?"

"A fucking lot." He squeezes off another couple of rounds, then turns and jogs past me. "Go, dumbass! Go!"

I don't need to be told twice. Following behind Barrett has my back exposed, which I'm not a huge fan of. I pivot on my heel without breaking pace and walk backward, rifle up and hunting for a target.

There's one: *crackcrackcrack*—a burst of blood from a chest and the body falls, replaced by another. Drop him. Another; dropped. Shit, there's a lot of 'em. I hold down the trigger for a good dozen rounds, and each one hits a body.

Clickclickclick. Empty. I slam another magazine home, feel myself jerked to the side. Barrett shoves me against the rock face, leans past me, tosses a grenade.

CRUMP-BOOM!

Screams.

Stench of death, shit from ruptured intestines. Blood. Cordite. Charred flesh.

Smells that make my stomach clench every time.

Crackcrackcrack…crackcrack—

The bark of an M4 is cut off mid-burst.

"Martinez?" I speak into the mic.

"He's down. He's down. Shit, fuck, he's dead," Okuzawa gasps, panicked.

"You'll be fine," I say. "Just keep firing, Okie. I'm coming for you."

"You can't," he says, and then the line goes quiet.

I hear his rifle firing, firing, firing.

"They're right on top of me…." Okuzawa's voice is hoarse, low, panting. "Run. Just fucking run."

Moments later, I hear a shout, a curse in English, and then a grenade goes off.

Barrett looks at me, and his eyes are blinking a little too fast. His chest rises and falls too quickly. His jaw grinds. He's firing, swapping in his last magazine.

"I think we're fucked, Tom." I summon saliva and spit. My stomach is in knots.

"I think you're right, Derek." He nods down the rock face we scaled minutes earlier—minutes that feel like hours. "Get down there. Go. I'll cover you."

"The fuck you will—"

"I'm not asking, asshole."

Bastard.

I half fall, half slide down the nearly vertical surface. A jut of rock catches on my webbing, holds me up, and knocks the wind out of me. I hear Barrett up above, firing nonstop. I glance up, see him coming down after me. I unhook my gear from the rock and keep sliding.

Hit ground, stumble, run. The caravan of Humvees crackles in flames. I dart toward them, Barrett behind me, cursing me. I slide to a stop, roll Abraham's body over, feel guilty for ransacking his corpse for magazines, but I do it anyway. I grab his sidearm, tuck it into my gear.

Barrett is kneeling in the dirt behind me, and I hand him a magazine. I hear shouts and footsteps in the dirt. Terror churns in my belly. Seconds stretch out forever. Barrett is just as scared; I can see it in his stoic brown eyes. In the way he clenches and releases the grip of his rifle. In the grind of his jaw.

"Let's do this." He adjusts his stance, crouching to get his feet under him. Racks the charging handle of his rifle.

"Fuck," he grates through gritted teeth.

"Yeah."

"Ready?" He's breathing short and fast. He knows, like I do, that this is it.

"No." I brace the toe of my boot in the dirt.

"Too bad." Barrett meets my eyes in all the conversation we need. "One…two…three…."

On "three," he lunges out, and I'm on his heels. Firing over his shoulder. Bodies drop. Bullets snap and hum and buzz. Kick up dirt. Plink off the Humvees, crack into the rock. They walk toward us.

Slam into Barrett, twothreefourfive wet crunching impacts on flesh. He's knocked into me. I stumble backward, grab his webbing, and haul. He's gasping, kicking. I let him go, kneel in front of him, and unleash hell, a nonstop barrage of bursts. Empty my mag, slam another one in. Fuck, they're everywhere.

Sliding down the rock, running toward me, screaming, firing. Missing, mostly, but the bullets come for
me. Heat stings my cheek. I didn't even hear that one,
it was so close.

Something hot and hard explodes in my left shoulder. I'm knocked backward, another round slamming
into the same shoulder, only lower. My rifle goes flying, and I'm on my back beside Barrett, bleeding. I
palm my sidearm with my right hand. Lift it and fire
blindly.

Dirt crunches under a black loafer, wildly inappropriate footwear for this terrain. The shoe stops,
white pant leg fluttering in a hot breeze. The sun is
blinding, right overhead.

Barely noon, about to die.

The foot rises, swings back, kicks. My sidearm
goes flying.

A droplet of sweat trickles into my eye, and
through all the pain, all the fear, that drop of hot
stinging sweat in my eye is all I can fucking feel.

The body above the foot kneels over me. Dark
skin, pearly white teeth, thick black beard. Young,
mid-twenties maybe. Black turban wound around
his head, the end trailing over his shoulder. He grins.
Speaks, but I don't understand. I can't hear for some
reason. I just see his mouth move. He has an AK in his
hand, the butt planted in the ground, fist around the

barrel. He leans and stretches, grabs my pistol. Jabs my wounded shoulder with it, hard.

"You. Prisoner." He digs the barrel of my pistol into my shoulder again, so hard I cry out. "Fuck American."

I'm a goddamn POW. Fuck.

Nearby, I hear Barrett moan. He's still alive.

But for how long?

CHAPTER 2

Reagan

Outside Houston, Texas, 2007

Why am I peeling potatoes? I hate peeling potatoes. It's just me, so there's no reason to cook anything complicated. But I've had oven pizza and microwave meals a thousand times over the last few months, and I need something different. Thus, potatoes au gratin and chicken paprika. Besides, the mind-numbing tedium of peeling potatoes is something to do besides gnaw on the sense of impending doom that's been plaguing me.

Or, at least, that was the idea. The reality is that peeling potatoes leaves my brain with nothing to do *but* spin.

Something happened. Something happened. Something happened. It's all I can come up with. I won't allow myself to conjecture...or imagine. But I can't ignore this tension, this constant stress and prickling on the back of my neck, the tightness of my shoulder muscles. Something has happened to Tom. I know it.

The antique grandfather clock in the foyer goes *tock...tock...tock.* The faucet runs. Something creaks somewhere in the old farmhouse. The AC is out again, so it's hot as blazes in the Texas summer evening.

I hate this old house.

I glance out the window over the sink, and my gut clenches. A dust cloud announces someone coming up the long dirt road leading to the farm. I drop the peeler in the sink. Drop the potato. Turn off the faucet.

Breathe, Reagan. Breathe.

The visitor is still half a mile out, but I can't make myself move, can't make myself do anything but wait. After an eternity, I finally make out a low black car. An unmarked black sedan. Government.

No. *No.*

I wipe my hands on a towel, make my way on shaky knees to the front door. I shove open the screen.

Creeeeeeaaaaak...slam. There's an ancient ceiling fan mounted on the front porch, and it rotates half-heartedly, stirring the thick, hot air. I stand directly beneath it, waiting. Hands clutched together, squeezing.

The car rolls to a stop, and the engine is turned off. Then it pops and ticks. I forget to breathe again.

A car door opens; a tan pant leg descends to the dirt, a shiny black dress shoe. A body follows, tall, slim, straight. Buzzed black hair, mid-forties. Hard eyes. The insignia on the shoulder makes him an officer, but I can't remember which insignia means which rank. The driver door opens, and another officer steps out. This one is older, salt-and-pepper hair. They approach slowly, hats under their arms.

The older officer stops with one foot on the lower step of the porch. "Reagan Barrett?"

I nod. "Yes. I'm Reagan."

"I'm Sergeant Major Bradford" —he gestures to the younger man— "and this is Staff Sergeant Oliver. May we come in?"

I lean against the post, my knees giving out. "What happened to him? What happened to Tom?"

Sergeant Major Bradford's eyes soften ever so slightly as he ascends the steps. He taps the rim of his hat with a forefinger. "I think maybe we should speak inside, Mrs. Barrett."

I summon a breath, let it out. I step away from the post and turn toward the door, but my legs wobble, and I stumble. A hard but gentle hand supports my elbow, steadies me. He doesn't say anything, doesn't ask if I'm all right—he's here; therefore, I'm *not* all right. I steel myself, palm flat on my stomach as if to hold myself upright. I lead them inside to the formal sitting room just off the foyer.

"Would you care for some iced tea?" I ask.

"Sure, that would be nice," Sergeant Bradford says. "It's hot out there."

I pour three glasses and set them on a silver service tray.

It feels like I'm performing some kind of tradition.

Ice clinks, coasters are placed just so. Hats are set aside. I smooth my dress over my thighs. I wait.

"As I said earlier, my name is Sergeant Major Adam Bradford, and this is Staff Sergeant Travis Oliver. We're from Camp Lejeune." He clears his throat. "You are the wife of Lance Corporal Thomas Barrett?"

I nod. "Yes."

He verifies Tom's Social Security number, and then pauses to let out a small breath. "I'll get right to it, Miss Barrett. Your husband has been officially declared DUSTWUN, or 'duty station whereabouts unknown.' Which is military speak for—"

"Missing in action," I interrupted.

Bradford nodded. "Your husband was with his unit, traveling as part of a convoy assigned to investigate reports of Taliban activity in the eastern region of Afghanistan. The convoy was ambushed in the mountains." He pauses, blinks, looks down. This is hard, even for him. "When the convoy failed to report in or answer their radios, a small search force was sent after them. The—the remains of the convoy was located. There were sixteen men in that convoy, Miss Barrett.

Fourteen bodies were located."

I begin to sob uncontrollably. "Stop…please stop."

"I'm so sorry, ma'am. I hate delivering this news. This is—this is one of the worst losses of American military personnel in a very long time. I had friends in that convoy. Close friends." He pauses again, as if to gather strength. "There is still a chance your husband and Corporal West will be found. Search parties are out in force as we speak, and, given the number of lives lost, I know the units sent to find Corporals West and Barrett are doing so with extreme prejudice."

"Corporal West?" I ask, my voice faint. "You mean Derek?"

Bradford nods. "Yes. Derek."

I try to smile. "Those two were always causing trouble together."

He gives me the same effort in return. Neither of us are entirely successful.

"Yeah, they're troublemakers, that's for sure. They… it looks from the reports on the battle that I've seen that Derek and Tom—they…acquitted themselves well."

I sigh. "If you know Tom and Derek, then you know that's not a surprise."

Bradford bobs his head. "That's the damned truth." He ducks his head, breathes deeply, and then meets my eyes once more, steel in his gaze. "We'll find them, ma'am. One way or another, we'll find them and bring them home."

"Dead—dead or alive…you mean." My voice breaks.

He doesn't need to agree. "And we'll get the bastards who took 'em. You have my personal guarantee, Mrs. Barrett."

"I know, Sergeant Bradford. I know. But revenge won't keep my husband alive, and it won't bring him home."

The younger man speaks up. Oliver, I think his name is. "I know I don't have to say this to you, ma'am, but if the media should contact you, it's vital to the investigation efforts that you don't comment."

Bradford gives the younger officer a brief but scathing glare, then returns his attention to me. "We'll be in touch, Miss Barrett. When we find out anything, we'll call you, no matter what time it is."

"Thank you, Sergeant Bradford." I offer a small, faint smile to the other man. "And you, too, Sergeant Oliver. I know this wasn't an easy visit to make."

Bradford shakes his head. "It's always hard to make these visits, but I know Tom and Derek personally, and I was—I grew up with their lieutenant, Jonathan Lewis. We joined the Corps together after 9-11, and we fought in Desert Storm together. He was—he was like a brother to me." He blinks hard several times, squeezes his eyes shut, and then opens them again. They shimmer with emotion. "His wife lives in Dallas. I'm heading there next. That visit—that'll be hard."

"I'm sorry for your loss, Sergeant."

"Thanks." He stands up, straightens the lower edge of his uniform jacket, and places his hat carefully on his head. As he does so, I can see the emotion draining from his eyes. By the time I stand up, he's buttoned-up and hard-eyed once more. "We'll find them, Reagan. I promise." He hands me a business card with his name and rank and a phone number. "We'll be in touch, and don't hesitate to call if you need anything."

I can only nod and hold on to the back of the couch as the two men make their way out.

Bradford pauses with one foot on the second step and glances back at me. "I don't know if you're the praying kind or not, Miss Barrett, but...pray for those boys."

"I will."

"I will, too." He touches the rim of his hat in an old-fashioned gesture. "Good-bye, Mrs. Barrett."

I wave, my throat closing. I lean against the back of the couch and watch them drive away. When all I can see is dust, I let myself sink to the floor.

I sob. Choke, gasp.

I place both palms on my belly, which is just beginning to grow round. And I scream.

For me.

For my baby.

For my husband.

CHAPTER 3

Derek

Afghanistan, 2007

It's hard to swallow. They gave us water sometime yesterday, and a single piece of moldy pita bread the day before. Rice the day before that. Some gruel. No medical attention for either of us. I'm okay. I mean, my shoulder's fucked up, of course, but I was able to make some mud out of my piss and the dirt on the floor to cake onto the wound. It stopped the bleeding, mostly. I did the best I could for Tom. His wound is too big to do much for, though. His vest stopped the first couple of rounds, and he would've been fine, but the impact knocked him backward, exposed his belly, and he took three rounds to his gut.

Nobody ever tells you how long it can take to die from stomach wounds. Not just days, but weeks. My boy Tom is holding on, though. Stubborn fucker. I give him most of the food they give us. I want him to make it. He's got a wife at home. I got no one except for Mom and Dad and my little sister, Hannah, back in Iowa. They'll miss me. But that's not the same as leaving a wife at home. Leaving a widow.

Tom's in and out of consciousness. Honestly, the times when he's out are blessings. He's quiet then. When he's awake, he's groaning, trying not to scream as the stomach acid burns the open wound. He keeps clutching that letter. Unopened, unread. Saving it, I think. I'm worried if he waits too long to read it....

The door of the hut opens, bright sunlight outside making a silhouette of the form in the doorway. I tense, wait, watch. He doesn't speak, just leans in, grabs me by the shirtfront, and jerks me forward, up to my feet. I struggle to keep my balance, not bothering to protest. He pulls me out the door, jabs the barrel of his AK against my spine, barks a command I take to mean "walk," or "go." I move forward, blinking against the light. I try to make out my surroundings. Low huts, mountains in the distance, rocks, some larger buildings, glassless windows and open doorways. Other older, fallen-in buildings. Some that have clearly been destroyed by rocket or air strike. I don't see any people on the streets, so this is either a Taliban base of some kind, or a town on lockdown, the residents terrified of leaving their homes. Sometimes the two are the same thing.

I'm marched about three hundred yards from the hut where Barrett and I are being held, shoved through a doorway, stumble on rubble and bits of broken wood. The ceiling is so low I almost have to duck. It's dark, a single boarded-up window shedding light, a clear plastic bottle hanging from a hole in the roof acting as a makeshift light bulb. There's a battered couch on one wall, on which sit four men with rifles between their knees. Three wear turbans; one is bare-headed. There is a chair in the center of the room, facing a video camera mounted on a tripod. I can't help digging my feet in as I realize what's about to happen. The butt of the rifle hits my wounded shoulder, sending a lance of agony through me, eroding my ability to resist. So far we've just been shut in that hut and starved. Something tells me the fun's about to begin.

A hand grabs my arm, spins me, and shoves me into the chair. A space of ten seconds, and then the rifle butt crashes against my cheekbone, cracking it, splitting the skin. A fist against my wounded shoulder again. A fist to the stomach.

A long and thorough working-over, leaving me bloody and breathless with pain. Then, absurdly, they clean me up. Wipe the blood from my face, give me a sip of brackish water and a piece of bread. The bareheaded man shoulders his rifle and moves behind the camera, turns it on, focuses it on me.

"Name," he growls.

"Corporal Derek Allen West. United States Marine Corps." I rattle off my serial number and fall silent.

I tense, brace, expecting a full interrogation or more blows, but instead I'm merely led back to the hut, accompanied by two of the men. They shove me inside, follow behind, and grab Barrett by the arms, dragging him to his feet.

I lunge after them, cursing at them. He can't handle much more. If they beat him, he won't survive. I'm stopped by a rifle butt to the forehead, dropping me in my tracks. I see stars, head throbbing, but I scramble to my feet, blinking blood away, reaching for Tom.

Something cold and round touches my forehead, and a hand grips my shoulder blade, shoves me backward. "Shut up," a voice growls in thickly accented English, "or we kill. Not you. Kill him."

I go still, wipe my eyes with the back of my hand, and see that they have Barrett on his knees in the dirt outside the hut, an AK pointed at the back of his head.

Barrett is barely able to stay upright on his own, but he blinks and peers at me. Sweat beads on his forehead, drips down his pale face. "Stand...down," he says, panting for breath.

I sink to my haunches, then to my ass.

They haul him away.

I wait where I sit, bleeding from the skull, aching all over. Time is hard to measure, but it feels like twenty minutes before they drag Tom back to me. He's unconscious, his face a wreck. His stomach leaks bright red blood. They toss him at me, a heavy, bloody weight crashing against me. I take his weight, roll him onto his back. His shirt is dark and wet, caked with days-old dirt and dried blood, sticking to him. He moans, coughs.

Blinks his eyes open, finds me. "Letter?"

I stick my hand in his BDU pants pocket, find the crumpled, folded envelope. "Here it is. You gonna open it yet or what?"

He grunts, winces, and lets out a long moan. Breathes as deeply as he can, then licks his lips. "Read it."

"Sure thing, buddy." I sit cross-legged beside him and unfold the envelope.

I leave bloody fingerprint stains on the dirty white envelope, slide a finger under the flap. I wipe my hands on my pants in a futile attempt to get them cleaner than they are. My hands shake. I withdraw two pieces of thrice-folded paper. Yellow legal pad paper with blue lines. Neat, looping, feminine handwriting.

"*Thomas, my love,*" I read. Clear my throat and glance at him. "You'd better fuckin' appreciate this shit, man."

"Shut up and read." A hint of a smirk ghosts across his lips. "Been…saving this letter since we got back from…from leave. She gave it to me just before—gah, it hurts, man—just before I got on the plane. Been waiting."

"Why?" I ask.

"'Cause I always knew. I knew I wasn't making it home this time. Always had a feeling."

"That's stupid." I refuse to look at him. "You're making it home. We both are. The boys are coming for us. You know they are. All these fuckers are dead— they just don't know it yet. You just gotta hold on."

"Don't be a dumbass, D. You know better. Just read me my—my goddamn letter." He closes his eyes, breathes in slowly. Lets it out. "Just read it. Please."

"'*Thomas, my love,*'" I read again. "'*You're lying next to me, sleeping. There's so much I wish I could say to you, but I know time is short. You ship out tomorrow. Again….*'"

I read the letter to him slowly, scanning ahead. He keeps his eyes closed, listening. Soaking in each word. Fuck me. The raw love that bleeds through the words of that letter burns into me. The love makes my stomach twist, makes my eyes sting. It's so sweet and fucking romantic it's sick. And here the guy's dying. It should be me. He should get to go home to the girl. Not die here on the floor of some fucking hut in goddamn Afghanistan. And for what? What are we accomplishing here? I don't even know. I signed up to fight. To accomplish something. To serve my country. I signed up because I didn't know what else to do with my life. I signed up because a recruiter came to my high school in his dress uniform and looked so cool it made me want to be like him. Seemed like a better life than building houses with my dad in Bumfuck, Iowa. Yet here I am, a POW in Bumfuck, Afghanistan, with a dying buddy lying in the dirt next to me. And I can't remember why I'm here. What I was supposed to be fighting for.

And Tom? He's got something to live for, a woman who loves him like hell, waiting for him to come home. Except he won't.

"Read it…again."

"Play it again, Sam." I do a really bad fake James Cagney or whoever it was in that movie.

Tom laughs, which makes him cough and wince. "Idiot. That's…not the quote. It goes…'Play it, Sam. Play 'As Time Goes By.'" He blinks his eyes, licks his lips. "Reagan hates that movie. Her grandma…used to make her watch it with her every weekend when she was a little girl. Over and over. She made me—she made me watch it once. On leave, between Iraq and here. She watched it three times in a row with me."

"I don't even know which movie that is, honestly," I admit.

"*Casablanca.*" He turns his head to look at me with one eye open. "Now read the fucking letter."

So I read it again.

And again.

Eventually, he passes out.

He wakes up when the glow of light through the cracks of the door is golden, indicating evening. "Read the letter, Derek."

God, Tom. You know why I remember every single moment? Because for most of our ten years together, you've been deployed. Three tours in Iraq, about to ship out for your third in Afghanistan. I miss you, Tom. Every day, I miss you. Even when you're home, I miss you, because I know you're always about to leave again.

I read the letter to him again. Each time I read it, I feel guilty. Because I'm not reading him the whole thing. I can't bring myself to read the news at the end. I skipped ahead the first time I read it to him, and skipped from *I don't think I could handle it if that happened to you* to *Please come home to me, Tom.* I omit the reference to the baby, omit the *to US.*

I just can't tell him. Not now. He's unconscious more and more.

He makes me read the letter over and over, until it's all I do during his waking hours. Read the letter. Read the letter.

Eventually, after four days have passed, I can recite it word for word without looking at the paper. I stare at the words on the page—which is now brown and stained with dirt and blood and, yes, tears—and pretend I'm reading it. He knows it by heart, too. He mouths the words along with me.

We say the ending together: "I love you so, so much, Tom. More than I'll ever be able to say. You'll be fine. You'll come back to me."

And then Tom will pause every time, and whisper, "I love you, too, Ree."

A week later. He's almost gone. He'll wake up for an hour or two here and there. Gasp for breath. Groan. Now all he can do is mutter "letter…." It's all he has the strength for.

I read it, and I skip the news. I lie to him. I don't tell him he's a daddy.

I'm a coward. He deserves to know, but I just… can't tell him. I fall asleep, cursing myself for being a coward, for being a sick fuck. But I never tell him. Because it'll be too hard. He'll fight. He'll try to hold on, but…deep down, I know he's not gonna make it. He's gonna die any day now.

They leave us alone. Feed us every once in a while, just enough to keep us from starving. Tom has been refusing food lately. Telling me to eat it, that he doesn't need it anymore. So I eat it, because….

Because I still want to live. I still have hope that the guys will come for us. That they'll show up in the

Hueys and SuperCobras with guns blazing and take us home. Save Tom.

And then he'll kick my ass for lying to him about his baby.

But as the second week fades into the third, his wound going septic and stinking, my own getting infected and nasty, I just know the day will come when he won't wake up and ask for the letter.

Shitshitshit. I don't want him to die. I'd die instead of him, if I could.

Take his place at death's door.

Instead, I read the letter, and skip the last few words.

"Der…Derek." A whisper from the darkness.

I blink awake. "Yeah, buddy."

I feel his fingers digging in the dirt. "Going… now."

I take his hand. "Don't, man. We're going home."

"Liar."

I choke. "I'm here, Tommy."

"Reagan…you gotta get home. Tell her…tell her I love her."

"Jesus, Tom. Come on, man. You tell her."

"No." He squeezed my hand. "I won't. You know it. I know it. Bring her the letter. It's all—all I got to give her. Tell her it—kept me going."

"I'll tell her."

He coughs, weakly. "Tell her…she's my every-thing. Those words."

"I'll tell her."

"Swear."

I squeeze his hand as hard as I can, blinking away tears I refuse to shed. "I swear. On my soul, I swear."

"She has to know I went out thinking…of her. I held on…wanted—I wanted to go home to her. I fought for her. She has to know."

"She knows. I'll make sure." Something wet and hot trickles down my cheek. Not a tear, because I'm a goddamn U.S. Marine, and I don't cry. I haven't cried since second grade.

"Love you, brother."

"Fuck you."

"Yeah."

A long, long pause between breaths. A moan of pain.

"Love you back, Tom." I make myself say it, before he goes.

He squeezes my hand, a twitch of his fingers and barely that. A breath.

Silence.

Tears slip off the tip of my nose. He's holding the letter in now-limp fingers.

I fold the sheets of yellow paper, place them care-fully in the envelope. I rip a long, wide strip off my shirt. Wrap the envelope in the length of cotton, stuff it in my cargo pocket, and button the pocket closed.

I touch my fingers beneath Tom's nose. Feel for his pulse. He's gone.

"You're a father, Tom." The words come out, unbidden.

I hold his hand until they come back to feed us, see that he's dead, and drag his body away. I fight them then, because his body has to go home. She has to have something to bury. They took our dog tags for some reason.

They come back, later. Shout at me. Beat me. Take me to the room with the camera, but they have to hold a gun to my head to keep me still. But then I say what they tell me to say, because I still want to live. I have to now, because I made a promise.

I hide the letter in the dirt in the corner of the hut, in case they try to take it. Eventually they take my BDUs and hose me down. Shave my head, my beard. Put me in pajamas, or whatever the fuck it is they wear. Good thing I hid the letter, because I have it still. Buried in the dirt.

I whisper the words of the letter to myself, out loud, over and over.

You took me to Olive Garden, and we got drunk on red wine. We made love that night in my hotel room.

I lose track of the days. The weeks.

The months.

I repeat the words of the letter over and over again, every day. It's a reminder that there's somewhere other than here, something out there other than Taliban and dirt and the distant mountain peaks.

It's a reminder of my promise.

CHAPTER 4

Reagan

Houston, Texas, 2009

I'M SWEATING BUCKETS. IT'S A HUNDRED AND THREE degrees, and I'm chasing Henry the Eighth across the north pasture. He kicked the fence down and got out, and now I'm jogging through the prickly knee-high grass with a carrot in my hand, chasing a massive black Percheron through the blistering late August heat. I need to mow this pasture so I can move the herd. The eastern pasture is in desperate need of turnover. But between the baby, the thirty acres of hay that need baling, the dozen head of horses that need feeding, the house that's falling apart, and the fact that I'm only one woman trying to do it all…I just haven't had time. Hank, my nearest neighbor, is eighty years old and has his own farm to work, but he still makes time to help me. And thank god for Hank, because I'd be lost without him. His wife, Ida, watches Tommy while I work.

Tommy. God, that boy. Not even two yet, and so much trouble. So cute. So charming. So much trouble. Walking, talking, and getting outside when your back is turned, climbing onto the dining room table, climbing over the baby gate and getting upstairs.

He looks just like his father. Blond hair, brown eyes, devilish grin. Trouble.

I pause. I shouldn't have thought about Tom. My eyes sting with tears I refuse to let fall. Almost exactly two years, yet nothing. Sergeant Bradford calls me every once in a while to tell me they haven't given up, but it's hard for me to believe they're still looking for him after two years.

I shake the thoughts out of my head. "Henry! Come on, boy. It's too hot out here for this. Come and get the fucking carrot." I gesture with the vegetable at the horse, who stands six feet away, shaking his mane and stomping one foot to keep the flies away. "Easy, boy…easy now. That's it…just let me—" I hold the carrot out, the halter and lead rope in my other hand, inching toward him.

I'd just leave him out here, but there's even more fence down on this fence line, enough that he could get out completely if he were to find the gaps. Too much fence. Too much space. It's *all* too much for me. But it's land that's been in Tom's family for over a hundred years, and, aside from Tommy, it's all I have left of him. I can't sell it. And I don't know where I'd go if I did, or what I'd do.

So I do my best to hold on to the land, take care of the horses, plant the hay and the cotton, harvest it, bale it, sell it. But it's too much, and I can't do it all, and I sure can't afford to hire anyone to help. The barn is falling apart. The fence is falling down. The house is falling apart.

Everything is falling apart.

I'm falling apart.

Henry the Eighth whickers and dances backward as soon as I get within touching distance, bobbing his head and turning away. I reach for him, but he trots away again.

We repeat this for another twenty minutes, until I finally snap.

I curse, a sobbed sound of desperation, and throw the carrot to the ground, drop the halter, and fall to my knees. I breathe through it, keep it together, and then stand up slowly. "Fine, you asshole. Stay out here, then."

I wipe the sweat off my forehead and scratch the grass-tickled skin of my bare leg, and then I turn away and start walking. And, of course, I hear Henry behind me, huge hooves stomping. He nudges my shoulder and whickers again. I stop, and he puts his chin on my shoulder. That's Henry for you—asshole one minute, wanting affection the next. I turn and put my face against his hot, thick neck, wrap my arm around his shoulder. He stands there, lets me hold him. I let myself cry for a minute, holding onto a troublesome horse I've spent the last hour chasing. After a few minutes, I push it all back down and wipe my eyes.

Henry finally lets me halter him, and since we're a good half mile away from the gate, I clip the lead line hook to one side of the halter, tie the end of the rope to the opposite side, creating an impromptu set of reins. Henry is an amazing horse. Broke to ride and pull, and trained in everything from dressage to hunt to western and English, but he's got a streak of troublemaker in him when he's riderless. Put a rider on his back, however, and he's all business, steady, gentle, and trustworthy. I grab onto his mane with both hands and jump as high as I can, lying on my stomach across his back until I can get my leg over him. I adjust my seat, nudge him with my heel to get him turned in the right direction. A click of my tongue, and Henry sets off in a smooth trot.

We make it to the gate leading from the north pasture to the central run between house, barn, and the paddocks. Hank and Ida are waiting. Hank opens the gate for me and closes it behind me as I walk Henry through it.

"That boy makin' trouble for you?" Hank asks. Hank is tall and straight despite his age, his white hair still thick and his bright blue eyes clear and intelligent. His face is angular and lined like weathered leather.

I swing off and slide to the ground. "Yeah. He kicked down part of the fence and got out. I spent an hour chasing his stupid ass."

Hank pats Henry on the neck and takes the lead from me. "You oughta behave better, you big idiot. Sometimes I hate that we share a name, the way you carry on."

Henry the Eighth shakes his head and stomps a hoof, as if responding.

Hank just laughs and tugs the horse into a walk. "Come on, then, boy." To me, he says, "I'll put him up in the barn for now, till we can get the fence fixed. Think any of the others will try to get out?"

"Nah," I say. "The rest are too lazy to bother jumping it. He didn't knock the whole thing out, just enough that he could get over it. I'll fix it tomorrow."

"The hay's gotta come in tomorrow. I've got my grandsons coming in for the week. One'a them'll fix it for you."

I want to cry, thinking about how much work I've got to do, but I can't. I just nod. "Thanks, Hank."

He waves. "Yup," he drawls.

Ida has Tommy in her arms, and he's squalling like crazy, wiggling and trying to get to me. "He just won't calm down, Reagan. I don't even know what to do anymore. I've fed him, I've changed him, I've played with him…I think he just wants you."

I take my son from Ida, and he immediately quiets, lays his head on my shoulder. "Ma. Ma. Ma," he says. "Horsey." He points at the Henrys, off in the distance now.

I pat Tommy on his diapered bottom, swaying side to side out of habit. "Yes, baby. That's a horsey. That's Henry."

I can feel Tommy going limp and heavy. It's only eight-thirty in the evening, and he's had a long nap, but he's probably cried himself tired.

Smiling at Ida, I head for the house. "Thanks, Ida. I'll take him inside. Sorry he was so much trouble."

Ida, short and slim and seemingly too delicate for the harshness of Texas farm life, just smiles. "He's never trouble, dear. Sometimes he just misses his mama, that's all."

Guilt rushes through me. "Well, I'm out there all day. He never sees me."

Ida shakes her head and pats me on the arm. "You're doing the best you can, honey."

"But sometimes my best just isn't enough." I didn't mean to say that, but out it comes anyway.

"Give it all you got, and give God the rest," Ida says.

"I gave God all I had, and He took him from me." I'm fully aware of how bitter I sound, but I can't help it.

Ida leans in and embraces me. "I know, sweetie. I wish I had an answer for you. I really do."

I hug her back with my free arm, and then back away. "I know. Thanks again."

"See you tomorrow, then." Ida heads toward the dirt driveway where Hank is waiting by their ancient red F-150.

I take Tommy inside, wipe the dried tear tracks from his cheek as I set him in his crib, adjusting the ceiling fan to stir the air. The AC is on as high as it will go, but it's not up to the task of keeping this big old farmhouse cool. I watch him sleep for a moment, my sweet little boy, my reminder.

I hear a gentle knock on the front door, and my heart seizes. Hank and Ida have gone home, and if they were to come back, they wouldn't knock, having lived next door their whole lives. I couldn't think of anyone else who would knock on my door—not at this hour.

I close the door to Tommy's room and make my way downstairs. I pause in front of the door, hand shaking, not quite able to turn the knob. Finally, I summon the courage to open it.

"Sergeant Bradford." I step backward, opening the door all the way. "Come in."

He's in the dress uniform I remember Tom referring to as "blue dress D": a short-sleeved khaki shirt, tie, and belt, blue slacks with the red stripe down the side. Bradford steps in, back stiff, eyes automatically searching the room. He removes his hat as soon as he's inside, and suddenly seems hesitant.

"I know it's late," he says, his eyes sliding away from mine, "but I wanted…I had to come in person. I couldn't just call you."

My stomach twists into knots, and my heart stops beating. "They found him?" I don't dare to hope. Don't dare. Can't.

He nods. "Yes. A patrol received reports of a Taliban outpost with two white males being held prisoner. They searched the area and found—found where Derek and Tom had been held."

"Had been?"

"They'd been moved before our forces got there. But there was evidence they were there." Sergeant Bradford blinks, hesitates. Swallows. "They combed the area and they discovered—they found your husband. He's gone, Reagan. But they're bringing his remains home for burial."

I shake my head. Not in denial, but from the inability to accept what I'm hearing. "Tom…." It's all I can manage.

"I'm so sorry. I'm so sorry." Bradford touches my elbow.

"And Derek?" I swallow my tears. "Did they find him, too?"

Bradford shakes his head. "Unfortunately—or fortunately, no."

"What do you mean?"

"Just that they didn't find his body with Tom's, so he's likely still alive."

I don't know what to do, or how to be. My emotions are on so much overload that I can't even process them. "Oh," is all I can say.

"I know that's not a lot of comfort to you, though," he says as an afterthought.

I try to shrug, and manage to lift a shoulder. "No, it's good Derek's still alive. Hopefully he is, at least. He and Tom were close."

Bradford just nods. He shifts his weight from one foot to the other, turning his hat end over end in his hands. "I wish I didn't have to bring you this news. I dreaded it, honestly. But I felt I owed it to you to tell you in person."

"Thank you, Sergeant. Thank you very much."

"I'll be going. When Tom's remains are back on U.S. soil, I'll let you know, and we'll make arrangements for a burial. I can take care of it for you, if you want."

"That would be…helpful."

"All right, then. Anything I can do for you?"

I shrug, and it turns into a shake of my head. "No. I don't know."

"Well, I'm only a phone call away, if you think of anything." He hands me another business card.

He turns to go, and I find my voice. "Sergeant?" He pivots back, eyebrows raised in question. "Lieutenant Lewis's wife. How is she coping?"

He doesn't seem to know how to answer. "It's an impossible thing, Mrs, Barrett. I don't think you do cope. You just survive it, one day at a time. I wish I could say it gets easier, but it doesn't. My dad died in Vietnam, leaving my brother and me and our mom behind. I was just a little kid, but I remember Mom...." He trails off, shakes his head. "It was hard for her. Eventually...you'll find your way to okay."

He leaves then, and I stand with the front door open, smelling the promise of a summer rain.

Eventually...you'll find your way to okay.

Will I?

CHAPTER 5

Derek

Afghanistan, 2010

I'M WOKEN UP BY GUNFIRE, SHOUTS, AND THE SOUND of helicopters. Instantly, adrenaline rockets through me, supercharging me.

I've been a prisoner so long I'd forgotten anything else existed. My universe was in constant motion, never staying in any one camp for more than a few weeks, but I always managed to bring the letter with me, hiding it in my clothes. I don't know what they want with me, but they don't kill me, and they don't let me go. They use me in what I assume are propaganda videos, and keep me fed just enough to stave off starvation. They keep me in constant pain, too, with regular beatings. The gunshot wounds to my shoulder healed long ago, but they still ache sometimes.

I've tried to escape a few times. The last time, they beat me within an inch of my life. Took me weeks to heal from that one, and I think I nearly didn't. I'll try again, but I've gotta get my strength back first.

My mantra sustains me: *I know I signed up for it when I married a Marine. I knew from the very beginning that you'd go into combat. I knew it, and married you anyway. How could I not? I loved you so much from the very beginning, from the first time I saw you, all those years ago.* The letter. I repeat it over and over again. I wonder what it would be like to have that kind of love. I've never known. Never will know, probably.

I've had plenty of girlfriends. Gotten lots of ass on my short leaves. It's the uniform, and the fact that I ain't ugly. Or…I didn't used to be. Now, who knows? I haven't seen myself in a mirror in who knows how long. I piss in a hole, shit in a hole, eat ground meat and pita and thin gruel from a wooden bowl. Rarely see daylight. So I might be ugly now, my face misshapen from all the boot kicks and fist blows, nose broken a hundred times, cheekbones cracked, lips split, eyebrows mashed, scalp ripped. They shave me every once in a while. To keep the lice out, I guess. But they shave me, very literally, with a rusty razor, so it cuts me up, leaving scars.

They use a cane to beat me sometimes. Just a big stick, but it hurts like a bitch.

Pain tells me I'm still alive, and the letter tells me why I'm holding on. Why I don't just go nuts and make them kill me, I don't know.

You got in a lot of trouble for that stunt. But you found me. You knew my brother, who was walking with me at the time. You asked him who I was a few days later. He said he'd let you have a shot if I was willing, but if you broke my heart, he'd break your face. You showed up at my hotel room dressed in civvies.

Thundering gunfire. Assault rifles crackle, AKs bark. Helo rotors thump. Rockets *whoosh-boom*.

I tuck the letter between my belly and the pants. Flatten myself beside the door. Sure enough, the door is kicked open, and I see the flash of orange flame, hear shouts in Pashto, which I've learned a bit of now, simply through default: *"Kill the American! Shoot him!"* A figure swathed from head to toe, leaving only a slit for the eyes, appears in the doorway, wielding an AK. He doesn't see me at first, is confused, pivots, AK held at waist level. Idiot.

I slam the knife edge of my hand into his throat, grab the barrel of the rifle, jerk it up, knee to his groin, desperation making me inhumanly strong despite my near-starvation thinness. Head-butt to the nose, *crunch*. He goes limp for a split second, and I wrench the rifle free, slam the stock into his face over and over and over again, until the white cloth of his clothes and mine are both spattered in red. He falls against the wall, slumps to the ground. I step over him and go outside into the flame-lit darkness. Shadows within shadows, darting shapes in desert camo. The gray of near-dawn glows above the serrated mountain ridge.

Crackcrack…crackcrack…crackcrack.

Precision, coordination, merciless onslaught. Oorah, motherfuckers.

And then I realize it's dark and I'm wearing native clothes and carrying an AK. I tear the shirt off over my head, toss it to the ground. My pale skin is a flag now. Risky, but better than being accidentally shot by the guys coming to rescue me.

I see a turban and a brown rifle stock in a window, and I blast it. Run to the window, lean in, see two more faces and rifles. I drop them, too. No training here. Just vengeance, empty the magazine into dead bodies.

I twist at the sound of ghost-quiet footsteps in the grit. See night-vision gear, helmets, compact assault rifles.

Grin. "Oorah. Took you fucking long enough."

They don't respond. They just flank me, snatch the rifle from me, form a box around me, and march me through the burning rubble and bodies to the extraction point outside the village. One of them radios for pickup, acknowledging that they have me. Within seconds, rotors roar, and dust flies as a chopper descends. It doesn't even touch down all the way.

They escort me in, one on each side, rifles pointed out and down. A blanket is wrapped over my shoulders.

Airborne, adrenaline leaves me, and realization sets in.

I sob.

I'm free. I'm fucking free.

"You're safe, sir," a voice says. "We've got you. You're going home."

I don't even feel any shame as I bawl like a god-damn baby. Rest my head back against the vibrating wall.

"Tom. Did you find Tom? They killed him. I don't know where they put him, but they took him after he died. You have to find him. You can't leave his body here." I'm rambling.

"We found him, sir." The same voice, a young guy, maybe twenty at the most, sitting beside me, sharp-eyed, alert, fresh-faced.

I pat the cloth-wrapped letter, make sure it's still there in my pants.

Exhaustion hits, and I can't keep my eyes open. I feel myself leaning against the kid beside me, but I can't keep myself upright. He doesn't shift away. He lets me rest against him.

"How long?" I mumble.

"What, sir?"

"How long? How long was I gone?"

"You'll be debriefed in full, sir."

"Just fucking tell him, pinhead," someone else growls. "He deserves to know."

"It's twenty-ten, sir. You were a POW for three years."

Three goddamn years.

Tom's baby isn't a baby anymore.

I have to find Reagan. Give her the letter.

Camp Leatherneck. Home away from home. At least, it used to be. Now it seems alien. Familiar, yet foreign. The helo sets down, dust whirls, and my head spins. I should be overjoyed to be back, to be among my own countrymen, but…I'm nervous. Scared. There, I said it. This ain't combat, but I'm just as scared. More, actually. Damned if I know why, or of what.

Maybe it's the stares. Eyes follow me. A whole goddamn base of jarheads, and it feels like they're all watching me descend to the ground, blanket tossed aside to reveal how skinny I am. They see my shaved scalp and gaunt frame and haunted eyes. I know that's how I look. I caught a glimpse of my reflection in the windows as the Huey banked past the rising sun. Pale skin, sunken green eyes, thousand-yard stare. Used to have thick blond hair and a matching five o'clock shadow. Now all I've got is a nicked, scarred scalp shaved down to the skin. My jawline is pronounced, sharp, my skin sickly, the stubble on my head ingrown in places.

Hands grip my biceps, carrying me forward. I feel like a prisoner. Flanked by armed Marines, I'm marched across the tarmac.

"West?" a voice calls out from under a tent as I pass. "They fuckin' found you? Goddamn! Boys! They've got Derek!"

I pause, hunt for the voice. Billy Voss, Golf Company's heavy weapons expert. Big, black, and badass. One of the few guys who can hit the broad side of a barn with a SAW while moving. He ducks out from under the tent, all six-foot-six of him, and lumbers toward me. Wraps me up in a bear hug. My throat seizes, and I have to swallow the onslaught of overwhelming emotion. What the fuck is wrong with me?

Voss crushes me, then lets me down, and claps me on the shoulder so hard I stumble. "I can't fucking believe it, man. I never thought I'd see you again, brother."

He's joined by the rest of Golf Company: Hector and Isaiah and Deadly-Fredly and Spacey. They're all crowding around me, calling out my name, reaching for me, chattering too fast to catch anything, and my head is spinning and my heart is hammering and I'm sweating, stomach in knots, eyes leaking fucking sissy-shit tears I can't stop, and I just want to hide, go back into my hut in the darkness and the silence.

I should be laughing and joking and calling them names; instead, I'm hyperventilating and about to heave, except there's nothing in my stomach.

Voss sees what's happening, turns and bellows, "All right, y'all! Back off. Back off. Give the man some space. Ain't none of you got work to do?" He wraps a burly bare arm around my shoulder, his massive paw on my head.

I scrape the back of my wrist across my face, try to laugh off my mortification. "Sorry. It's good—good to see you, too, man."

He pulls me against him in another hug. "No shame in it, man. No shame in it." He lets me go, trots to the tent, calling back over his shoulder, "Hold up, hold up — I got something for you." Returns with a clenched fist. Grabs my hand in his, places two sets of dog tags in my palm. "Been holding onto these. They found 'em, along with—when they found Barrett. Yours and his."

My tags. Barrett's tags. My disbelieving laughter is part sob. "Shit." I blink, duck my head, and cough away the lump in my throat. "Thanks, Bill. You don't—you don't even know…just—thank you."

His voice is a low rumble. "I ain't even gonna pretend I know what you been through. But I'm here for you. All of us are."

"I—" Words stick in my throat.

"The medics are waiting for us," a sharp voice says. Captain Laughlin. "Reunions can happen later. As you were, Voss."

"Sir." Voss nods at me, returns to the tent where Golf is cleaning their rifles and readying their gear for a patrol. "Glad you're back, West."

My escort starts moving, and I'm compelled to go with them. In truth, I'm glad to be away from the guys. I ran a lot of patrols with Golf Company, spent a lot of downtime shooting the shit with Voss and Isaiah and Barrett in the gym. Seeing them…brings flashbacks of patrols, the clink of weights, Voss telling horribly racist jokes that none of us were ballsy enough to actually laugh at unless he did first. I touch the letter against my belly; it's still sitting under the waistband of my pants.

I'm taken to the medical facility. Most of my escort leaves, except one guy with a rifle held at rest—barrel down, butt up—eyes avoiding me, taking a place outside the door of the room. A jet takes off, rumbling loud, and then the room fades back to silence. A clock ticks. My heart thumps. I wonder what's next. A hospital stay, like I'm sick? Cycled back into active duty? I don't know. I can't remember what happens next, according to policy. I don't feel like a Marine. I feel scared, lost, overwhelmed, confused.

A doc and a couple of orderlies arrive. I watch the orderlies, young guys, barely more than kids, probably only been shaving a year or two. They stay by the door and wait for orders. The doc introduces himself, looks me over. It feels like a normal physical evaluation, which is sort of anticlimactic.

Then he starts poking and prodding, chest, lymph nodes, stomach, tugs the waist of the pajama pants down, sees the dirty sweat- and bloodstained olive-green packet. "What's this?" He grabs for it.

My fingers latch onto his wrist, and I shove him away. It's automatic. Nobody touches the letter. "It's nothing. It's a letter."

He's wary now, suspicious. "We have to check it out, Corporal West. Can I have it, please?"

It's totally normal. They just have to make sure it's clean, safe. But I can't give it up. I can't. I clutch the cotton-wrapped paper in my hands. The doctor reaches for it again. "We'll give it back, Corporal. You have my word."

I can't let go. Rage seizes me, unreasoning, blinding. Terror. Claustrophobia. The walls of the room close in. My chest is tight, as if iron bands are strapped around my lungs, preventing breath, preventing thought, preventing reason. I see the doctor's mouth moving, but hear nothing. The orderlies step forward, one to each side. They grab my arms. Someone is screaming and cursing. I'm thrashing, kicking, fighting. The orderlies are fucking strong for a couple of green little pukes. Something pokes my bicep.

Warmth floats over me, stealing my panicked rage.

I watch my fingers go limp, the shirt-wrapped letter tumbling, cotton drifting away, the envelope creased and wrinkled and stained with dark brown-red bloody fingerprints three years old. I struggle to stay awake, to get my letter back, but darkness is heavy and thick and—

I wake up in a bed. A real bed. It feels bizarre, after sleeping on a dirt floor or bare tile or concrete for so long. My head buzzes, and I feel fuzzy and muddled. Was the whole thing a dream?

No. I open my eyes and realize I'm in the isolation ward. Or what counts for it in this part of the world.

So much for cycling back to active duty.

I couldn't, even if they'd let me. I'm tired. Hungry. My arm hurts. I realize I'm hooked to an IV.

"You're severely malnourished and dehydrated," I hear a voice say. It's the same doctor, sweeping into the room. Middle-aged, buzzed military haircut, thick blond mustache. "Along with a whole host of bacterial infections, marked vitamin C deficiency…."

He takes a seat on a plastic chair. "But all that is easy to fix." He taps my temple gently with his pen, then my chest. "It's the psychological and emotional damage I'm most worried about."

I nod. He's right, and I know it. The freak-out over the letter proved as much to me.

"You're going to the San Antonio Army Medical Center for a while. They'll get you back to normal physically, as well as helping you reintegrate socially." He brushes a fingertip across his mustache. "You've been through a hell of an ordeal, Corporal West. You'll need time to heal, emotionally, mentally, and physically."

I nod again.

"In the meantime...." He reaches into the pocket of his lab coat, hands me my letter. "How in the hell did you manage to hold on to this all that time?"

I shrug. "I made a promise."

He nods as if he could possibly understand. "I see. Well, tend to your own well-being first, okay?"

"Yes, sir. I will, sir."

My own well-being. I don't even know what that means. I should be dead. Should've died with my unit. With Tom. Instead of Tom. But I'm here, and I feel nothing but lost and disconnected, as if all these totally normal people who were once my service brothers and sisters are a circle I can't penetrate, as if I'm an outsider looking in. Even hearing English is disorienting.

I find myself whispering under my breath: "I've gone in circles over this a million times in my head. I've nearly told you so many times. But I just can't. It'll make it harder for you to leave, and I know it's hard enough as it is. It'll make it harder for me if I told you in person. You're going to be mad at me for not telling you. I know, and I'm sorry. But this is just the only way that makes sense to me." The lie of omission. The truth I withheld from a dying man. The guilt burning like a hot coal in the darkest corners of my being.

"Tell her...she's my everything. Those words."

"I'll tell her."

"Swear."

"I swear. On my soul, I swear."

I hear it. Hear his voice. Am I crazy? Did the three years of captivity make me legit fucking crazy? Maybe. Probably. All I know is, I swore on my soul.

Fuck my own well-being.

I made a vow.

CHAPTER 6

Reagan

Houston, Texas, 2010

"I'm sorry, Mrs. Barrett, but we have to deny your loan application at this time. You simply don't have the minimum credit score or income requirements. Again, I do apologize, but those are the rules. I didn't make them—I just have to follow them." The banker is a young woman, maybe twenty-five, put-together, coiffured auburn hair, perfect makeup, slim pencil skirt and sensible blazer. Snooty, but polite.

I want to cry but can't give her the satisfaction. "I see. Well…thank you for your time."

"Thank you, Mrs. Barrett. Is there anything else I can do for you?"

I shake my head, let a wriggling Tommy slide off my lap to his feet. "No."

The young woman lifts her shoulders and clasps her hands in front of her, leans down toward Tommy, talking to him in that squeaky, shrill, horrible voice clueless adults use on children. "Would you like a sucker? Wouldn't that be nice?"

"Sucker!"

A sucker? Really? He's supposed to be asleep right now, and I was counting on him taking a nap on the way home so I could gather my frazzled emotions. And this bitch is handing him a basketful of Dum-Dums. He takes three, rips the wrapper off one, and shoves it in his mouth. Glee lights his features.

"I go' a thucker, Mama!"

"I see that, sweetie." I level a glare at the girl. "Wasn't that nice of her, to give you a sucker *without asking me first?* Sure was *thoughtful.*"

The girl makes an innocent *ooops, who-me?* expression.

"I go' four, Mama, see?" Tommy holds up the two remaining, wrapped suckers.

"You mean two, Tommy. One, two." I reach for them. "But I think one's enough, don't you?"

"No. How 'bout two?"

"How about one, the one you got in your mouth?" I take the two extra suckers, which elicits screaming and stomping from Tommy.

"NO! TWO! TWO!"

I could throttle the prim little banker bitch. Deny me a loan, my last hope for keeping out of debt, and then give my toddler a sucker?

"FINE." I give him the treats back, too close to snapping to argue or deal with his tantrum. "Fine, Tommy. Okay. Okay."

"Fank you, Mama. You so nice." He grins a purple sugar-slimed smile, tucks his little hand into mine.

I lift him up to my hip, carry him out to the truck, and strap him into his car seat. He's blinking hard, the sucker lodged firmly in his mouth, dripping purple drool from the corner of his mouth, which…yep, is now smeared all over my T-shirt. I drive home, the windows open to let some air into the superheated cab. The truck, a rust-and-blue 1972 F-150, was Tom's, rebuilt from scratch during high school. Hank's gone over the engine a dozen times to keep it running for me. He's patched up the AC more than once, but it cuts out more than it works.

By the time I make the hour-plus drive from downtown Houston back to the farm, I'm coated with a thick layer of sweat, and I stink. Tommy is dead to the world, the sucker stuck to his shirt, his face covered in a sticky purple mess, his fine blond hair pasted to his forehead. My little trooper, nearly three hours in a forty-year-old truck without AC in ninety-degree weather, and not one complaint.

All that, and I didn't get the loan.

I park the truck beneath the old spreading oak tree between the house and the barn, the best shady spot to park. The temperature in the truck drops immediately, and I wipe my forehead, cheeks, upper lip. I rest my head against the steering wheel, peeling leather sticking to my skin.

Let myself cry for a minute. Two. Three. When sobs threaten, I cut it off. Shove it down. Throw open the door and go around to get Tommy. I cradle him to my chest, head on my shoulder, the sucker dropping forgotten in the dirt and grass. I lay him on the couch and point the oscillating fan at him, and then I get a sippy cup of lemonade ready for him for when he wakes up.

Not knowing what else to do, I sit down at the laptop, an aging Dell purchased secondhand, and go through my budget. There's the twenty acres I lease to the Pruitts, and that brings in some. Meager income from the farm itself. Support from the Corps, also helpful. But none of it is quite enough. I sort through the bills, none of which I can pay.

The phone rings, sudden and jangling and jarring. Tommy stirs on the second ring, and then falls back asleep as I pick up the receiver. "Hello?"

"Mrs. Barrett? This is Sergeant Major Bradford. I wanted to share some news with you. Corporal Derek

West has been recovered, and he's currently at the San Antonio Army Medical Center for rehabilitation."

"You—they found him? Alive?"

"Yes, ma'am. We received some intelligence hinting that he was alive, along with a possible location. Recon units verified the intelligence, and a detachment of MARSOC Raiders went in and retrieved him."

I don't know how I'm supposed to feel about this. "Is he—is he okay?"

"He's been through quite an ordeal. Three years as a POW…he has some recovery time ahead of him but I think, in time, he'll be okay, yes."

"Should I visit him?"

"Actually, I think it's probably best to hold off for now. It'll take some time before he can fully reintegrate socially, and medical personnel feel he needs to remain isolated at first, and then they'll gradually introduce new elements. It can be very overwhelming at first, they say."

"That's understandable, I suppose."

"Yeah." An awkward pause. "Well, I just thought you'd like to know."

"Thank you, Sergeant Bradford."

"Of course. And, as always, if there's anything I can do, you have my number."

"Yes, thank you."

"Goodbye, ma'am."

"'Bye." I hang up the phone, trying desperately to sort through my thoughts and emotions.

Derek is alive.

I remember Derek West as a big, easygoing man with blonde hair, dark green eyes, and a quick, charming smile. He had a reputation in the unit as a lady-killer, which I could easily believe, being fantastically good-looking. Tom always described him as deceptively laid-back, always ready with a joke, no matter the circumstances, and fiercely loyal to his comrades-in-arms. Derek raised hell when Hunter Lee went missing in Iraq, and went AWOL with his unit to rescue him when the brass wouldn't send in a team. Tom admired Derek, and considered him closer than a brother, that special bond only men who have seen combat together can form.

Tom died; Derek lived. Tom came back in a body bag; Derek likely came back to wild media coverage, touted as a "returning hero." I doubt Derek himself would agree with that, but still.

I can't help wondering if Derek was there when Tom was killed. No one would tell me any details about his death, said they didn't have any information they were at liberty to share. I suspected they did have information, but just wouldn't tell me. Maybe Derek will tell me.

Maybe Tom had last words for me.

I can't follow that line of thought any further.

It hurts too bad.

Three months later

An autumn downpour soaked me to the bone as I struggled to replace a broken fence board on my own. Hank is busy with his own chores, his grandsons back up in Dallas for the school year, and so I'm on my own. I've got three massive slivers in my palms from pulling the old board down, and I'm having trouble holding up the new one while trying to get the screw gun in position.

I'm way, way out on the farthest northern fence line, nearly a mile from the house. My pay-as-you-go cell phone rings, the only way to reach me when I'm out of earshot. It's generally only used for emergencies, in case Ida needs something while watching Tommy. When it starts trilling in the cab of the truck, panic hits me. I drop the board and the screw gun, and run to the truck.

"Hello? Ida? Is everything okay?"

"Yes, yes dear. Everything is fine, I'm sorry to worry you. It's just that you have a visitor."

"A visitor?"

"Yes. A young man named Derek. He says he knew your husband."

"Derek? He's there? At the house?"

"Yes, he is. He's sitting on the front porch. I haven't let him inside yet. Should I send him away?"

"No, don't do that. Let him in. I'll be right there." I hang up the phone, grab the boards, and toss them in the back of the truck. The screw gun goes on the passenger seat, and I set off toward the house.

My nerves are on fire.

It's not until I'm parking the truck and heading up the stairs to the porch that I realize I've been outside in the pissing rain for the last hour. I'm soaked to the bone, my cut-off denim shorts and gray T-shirt pasted to my skin. I pull the wet cotton away from my stomach and chest, but as soon as I let go, it clings to my skin again. No point. I'll just have to face Derek looking like a drowned rat in a nearly see-through shirt.

I pull open the screen door and immediately cross my arms over my chest in an attempt at modesty. Derek is sitting at the kitchen table, sipping a mug of coffee, dressed in civilian clothes. Close-cropped military haircut, clean-shaved jaw. As soon as the door springs creak, he sets the mug down and rises to his feet. I halt in place, shocked at the change in him. He used to be fit, taut and muscular, his BDU T-shirts stretched across a broad chest and around thick biceps. His eyes were kind and full of good humor, although if you looked closely, you could see hints of the hardness of a combat veteran.

The man before me is…not quite gaunt anymore, but its easy to see he's not far removed from it. He still stands tall and straight, but the bulky muscles are dramatically lessened, and there's an unconscious hunch to his shoulders. The easy grin is gone, replaced by lips pressed together in a hard, thin line. His eyes are… distant. Haunted.

"Derek?" I step toward him, forgetting modesty, seeing only a man lost in the depths of pain and traumatic horror.

He inhales deeply, his eyes narrowing, blinking quickly. He has something in his hands. An envelope? Dog tags dangle, the end of the chain wrapped around his index and middle fingers.

"Reagan. I know this is a surprise…I should've called first, I guess."

"No, it's fine." I shiver, my wet clothes starting to make me cold. "But I need to change real quick. I'll be right back."

His eyes touch mine, start to flicker downward, and then move quickly back up. He closes his eyes as if berating himself, then turns away. "Sure, of course." His fist clenches around the dog tags, and the paper crinkles. I know what he has in his hands: the letter. I just know it.

And I'm not ready. Not ready. I need a minute to compose myself. So I jog up the stairs to my room, strip out of my wet clothes, rinse off in the shower, and dress quickly. I pull my damp blonde hair back in a twist and clip it up. Standing at the top of the stairs, I work up the courage to go back down, to hear what Derek has to say. To finally address the emotions I've worked so hard to bury for so long.

When I go down, Ida is scooping mac and cheese into a plastic bowl for Tommy. I pour a cup of coffee.

"Derek? You want to go out on the porch?" Derek is clutching his mug in both hands, as if afraid to let go. He's staring at Tommy as if seeing a ghost, and I don't think he heard me. I touch his shoulder. "Derek?"

He starts violently at my touch, jerking so hard his coffee sloshes onto his hands. "Shit!" He sets the mug down, and then glances at Tommy and stutters, "I—I mean, shoot. Shoot."

"Are you okay?" I reach for him, worried he burned his hands, but he shies away, subtly, but enough that I withdraw.

He grabs the mug again, shrugging. "Yeah. I'm just—yeah. Fine. Sorry about that."

I gesture at the front door. "Porch?"

He stands up. "Sure."

I precede him outside onto the porch, take a seat in one of the antique wicker chairs. Derek doesn't sit down. Instead, he stands on the top step, staring out at the rain-shrouded Texas farmland.

Eventually he speaks, not turning to look at me. "I don't even know where to start. What to say. I thought about it the whole way here from San Antonio, but…I just—I just don't even know." He inhales deeply, his shoulders rising and then falling as he lets the breath out. Turning, he extends his hand, dog tags swinging. "Here. One of the guys from Golf…I thought these were gone. They took 'em, when they captured us. I thought they were gone. Then when the Raiders brought me back—Voss had these. You should have them."

My hand trembles as I reach out to take the tags, warm from his hand. I stare at them:

BARRETT
T. M. O NEG
234 56 7890
USMC L
CHRISTIAN

I clutch the tags and fight for composure. "Th-thank you, Derek."

He shakes his head. Then he reaches into the back pocket of his dark blue jeans and withdraws a folded envelope. He turns to face me. His hands shake violently. He clenches one fist, transfers the envelope to his other hand, and clenches it, trying to still the trembling. I stand up, set my mug down on the floor, cross the porch to stand beside Derek.

"Is that…what I think it is?" I ask.

He unfolds it, stares at it rather than meet my eyes. Nods. "I—kept it. He gave it to me. To give to you. If I made it—if I made it back."

"All that time? You kept it—held on to it... through everything?"

He swallows; I can see his Adam's apple bobbing. "Yeah. I promised him." He's rubbing at the envelope with a thumb, rubbing at what are obviously bloody fingerprints. With what I can tell is a concerted effort, he looks up at me. His eyes are red, searching mine. "I swore—I'd tell you. You were—you are...his every-thing. I swore on my soul, I'd tell you that. Those were his last words. He wanted you to know he—he loved you."

I reach for the envelope, a tear trickling down my cheek. Derek, somewhat hesitantly, relinquishes it to me, but he never takes his eyes off it. It obviously has enormous significance to him. I touch the bloody fin-gerprint. I wonder if it's Tom's blood, or Derek's. Or someone else's. I won't ask, though. Gingerly, slowly, I open the flap and pull out the letter. It's been folded and unfolded and refolded a thousand times, creased and lined, dirty, the two pages molded in a curve, as if carried for ages against a body.

Thomas, my love.

I break down. I cry so hard I can't see.

"He—Tom carried that letter, unopened, all through the campaign," Derek says. "He wouldn't read it. Said he was saving it. Then…then our convoy was ambushed and—he got hit. They took us. He was in a bad way. Somehow they didn't find the letter when they searched us. I don't know why, but they didn't. He—I read that letter to him a hundred times a day. Day after day. Every time he came to, I'd read it to him. It kept him going. Kept—kept me going. After he—after Tom died, it was all I had. That letter, and my promise to find you. To tell you he tried, so hard, to hold on. That he loved you, and he wanted to come home."

"Derek…I don't even know how to thank you." I put the tags in the envelope with the letter and tuck it in my back pocket. I look up at him, and can't help but ask. "How—how did he die? I know I shouldn't—shouldn't ask. But—but I—"

Derek nods, and I'm not sure what he's nodding about. "He was wounded, in the battle. The ambush. Stomach wound. He held on for—for weeks."

"He suffered?" Stupid, stupid question.

Derek squeezes his eyes shut; his jaw grinds, fists clench. Turns away. "I—he…fuck. *Fuck.*" He stumbles down the steps, out into the rain, head bowed, shoulders arched, heaving. After a minute, he straightens, grinding the heels of his palms into his eye sockets. He takes a deep breath, turns, and comes back, damp from the sluicing rain. "Sorry. It was a bad situation, Reagan. I don't know what else to say. It was bad. I did my best for him, but there just wasn't anything I could—could do. I tried. He deserved…he should've been the one to make it. I think that every fucking day. It should be him here. Not me. So—so I'm sorry. So, *so* sorry. It should be him, but—but I couldn't save him."

"Derek, no. You can't think like that. I didn't mean—I'm sorry. I—"

He shakes his head and cuts me off. "I know. I know. But I can't *not* think that. It's true. It's all I *can* think about." He gestures at the letter. "You have that, and the tags. So…I'll go. See ya."

I follow him toward the steps and stop short of actually grabbing his arm. "Wait, how'd you get here?"

"Bus from San Antonio to Prairie View."

"How'd you get here from Prairie View?"

He digs a heel in the mud. "Walked."

"That's a long walk."

He shrugs. "I've marched farther carrying full gear. Don't mind it."

"Where will you go?"

He shrugs again. "I don't know. Somewhere. Anywhere. Iowa, maybe. They want me back at the Medical Center for more 'rehabilitation'" —he spits the word, bitterly— "but fuck that shit. Been there three months. Done with it."

"You can stay here."

He shakes his head. "It's fine. I'll walk." He starts down the steps. "Told you, I don't mind it.'

"Derek, don't be ridiculous—it's miles from anything, it's near dark, and it's pouring rain."

He stops, heedless of the rain beating down on him. "Why do you want me to stay here?"

I swallow and blink and hunt for words. "You—you were Tom's best friend. You came all this way to honor his last—" My voice breaks, and I have to start over. "To honor his last request. I can't—I *won't* just turn you out in the rain."

"All right. I don't want to inconvenience you." He jerks his head at the barn. "I'll stay over there."

"There's the couch, I could—"

"Not a good idea." He nods at the front door, where Tommy is visible through the screen, watching, listening. "I don't sleep well."

"Bad dreams?"

He shrugs uneasily. "You could say that."

"Okay, then. The barn it is. I'll bring some things over. Blankets, a pillow. There's a little workshop in the back. You can sleep there." I pause, and then ask, "Have you eaten? There's some leftovers—"

His voice goes a little sharp. "Reagan. I don't need any of that shit. I'm fine." He strides across the mud toward the barn. "Thanks for the hospitality," he says over his shoulder.

I let him go, sensing his need to be away, alone.

In the house, Tommy is leaning against the door-frame, watching me through the screen. His eyes are heavy, tired. I pick him up and cradle him against me.

"Mama?"

I kiss his temple. "Yes, baby?"

"Who guy?"

I hesitate. "He's…a friend."

Tommy lifts his head, leans back in my arms, peers at me. "Mama sad?"

Damned perceptive child. I blink, summoning a smile. "No, baby. I'm fine."

He doesn't believe me, clearly. He puts a hand to my cheek. "Kiss?"

I kiss his forehead. "Kiss." I tuck his head against my shoulder and carry him upstairs to his room, lay him down in his bed. "Time for bed, sleepyhead." He doesn't argue, and he's asleep within seconds, Buzz Lightyear clutched under one arm.

Back downstairs, Ida is drying the last of the dishes. She sets a plate in the cupboard, drapes the towel over the oven handle. She turns to me, eyes assessing. "That boy…he's very troubled."

"Derek, you mean?" I sigh. "He served with Tom."

Ida nods. "I saw a news program about him. A psychologist was saying that someone who's been through what he has…they never really recover." Ida rummages in my junk drawer, finds the tube of hand lotion and rubs some onto her wrinkled hands. "My Hank, he served in Korea, you know. He doesn't talk about it much, never has, really. But I know it still affects him. The things he experienced, the things he saw and did."

"Tom never talked about it, either," I say. "I asked him once. After his second tour in Iraq. He just told me there wasn't much to say. He did his job, and that was it. But I knew he was…protecting me. From the truth."

Ida nods, then glances out the screen door, watching headlights approach. Hank coming to pick her up. "Men will do that." It's clear she has more on her mind, but she just sighs and hangs her purse from her shoulder. "I'll see you tomorrow."

"Thanks, Ida." I lean in and hug her. "I don't know what I'd do without you."

She smiles at me, pats my cheek. "That's what family is for, dear. And you're family."

Tom's parents are both gone, his mother from cancer before I met him, and his father from a heart attack a few years after Tom and I married. My own parents are both alive, living in Tulsa. They never approved of Tom, and they've never forgiven me for eloping with him at nineteen. They've never met Tommy, and I don't think they ever will. So Ida and Hank are really my only family. Except Brian, my brother, a career Marine stationed in Okinawa. He visits sometimes, when he gets leave long enough to get back Stateside, which isn't often.

Hanks honks the horn, and Ida leaves.

The house is silent, and I'm finally alone. I pull the envelope from the back pocket of my jeans. Gather the dog tags in the palm of my hand, stare at Tom's name. Allow myself a few tears, wipe them from my chin.

"I miss you, Tom." I whisper it to the dog tags. "Why didn't you come back? You promised you'd always come back."

I can't look at the letter. I simply don't have the strength. I'll lose it if I read those words, written so long ago. If I imagine *him* reading them. If I imagine Derek and Tom, huddled together in some cave or whatever, Derek reading the letter over and over....

I should bring Derek some food. A blanket. A pillow. Something. But...I just can't. I can't face him. Can't handle seeing the ghosts in his eyes, the ache of memory in his posture.

A dirty secret: Sometimes I sleep on the couch, because I hate the memories that live in the empty expanse of my bed.

Another, dirtier secret: Sometimes the weight of loneliness is heavier than the weight of missing Tom.

CHAPTER 7
Derek

SLEEP IS IMPOSSIBLE. AT THE HOSPITAL THEY GAVE ME drugs to help me sleep. They were necessary, physically, because it's literally impossible to find rest. At best, I'll doze off, wake up sweating, screaming, panicked, reliving combat, imprisonment, beatings, torture.

I never told anyone about that, the torture. Not during debriefing, not to any of the psychologists or shrinks or doctors. The Taliban fuckers, they'd shove slivers under my fingernails, long jagged shards of wood, for no reason I could ever fathom. Burns, cigarettes or lighters. They broke the ring finger of my left hand. Kept re-breaking it, over and over again, day after day, until the pain drove me insane. If I'd had so much as a hunk of rock to hand, I'd have cut the finger off. Eventually they left the finger alone. I re-broke it myself and tried to set it, but it's crooked, hurts sometimes. Aches when it rains, shakes now and again.

The hospital made me crazy, too. Cooped up in a little room, a hospital bed, a window overlooking a parking lot. TV, tuned to sports, as if I cared. I used to care. Football. I loved football. Now? It's just irrelevant. I can't make myself care. I tried to watch Sports Center during the long hours alone in the hospital between rounds of physical therapy and head-shrinking. It seemed so stupid, so empty. So pointless.

The rain finally stops, and the clouds gradually clear as the hours of the night crawl by. I'm lying in an animal stall. I passed the first hour or so cleaning the stall out and laying down fresh hay. I checked out the workshop, but it was...it was a Tom space. Full of baseball memorabilia, NASCAR posters, a few of his old high school baseball trophies, a baseball signed by Nolan Ryan. The tools, the car parts. It's all Tom. He talked about this place almost as much as he talked about Reagan. He grew up on this farm, planned on phasing out of the Corps and going back to farming. Talked about taking apart engines with his dad and old Hank down the road. Riding horses across the pastures, breaking colts, and breaking his arm in the process once. He used to spend hours in the shop, getting away from the miserable reality of his dying mom. He always regretted that, not spending more time with her while he had her around, but it was always too hard for him, he said, to see her lying on the couch, skinny and sick.

So, yeah, I've never been here until now, but I know this place, this barn, the workshop. Hours and hours spent marching on patrol with nothing to do but talk to the buddy beside you, you relate all sorts of shit you never thought you'd talk about. For Tom, it was always this place. The land, the barn, the house.

I'm exhausted, sleepy. But when I close my eyes, I see Tom, clutching my hand, begging me to tell Reagan he loved her.

I told her, buddy.

I manage to catch a couple hours of fitful sleep before the dreams wake me. Dawn is painting the horizon with a gray-pink brush, visible through the open barn door. I rise, brush the hay from my clothes, lace the combat boots. Stretch the kinks out of my back and head outside. The grass is still wet, creating a pungent smell. It's early, probably barely five in the morning, but it's already warm.

The farmhouse is still and quiet. I can see into the kitchen from where I stand, no sign of movement. The farmhouse is a classic model of rural Texas style. Deep front porch, three steps up. Gables and eaves, white wooden siding in need of paint. Thick green grass around the sides leading to the backyard, where cottonwoods and willows surround a small green pond. Out in front of the house, there's a circle drive, gravel, a patch of not-as-green grass with a small maple tree in the middle of the island. The drive is a good three-quarters of a mile to the nearest road, which is only a slightly wider track of graded gravel leading away in a ruler-straight line. The barn is a huge building, faded wood, ancient peeling red paint. There's a good fifty acres in open pasture to the north and east of the house and barn, cotton to the south, hay to the west. The pastures are fenced, what must be miles worth of actual wooden fencing. Hell of a lot of upkeep, I think. Especially for a woman like Reagan. Alone. Plus a kid?

How does she do it all?

From where I stand, though, I can see a shitload of things that need doing. Several fence boards down, the steps up to the house loose and needing replacement, peeling paint all over the place. Getting toward the end of harvest season, and the hay and cotton need to be brought in, then baled and sold.

The sun peeks up over the horizon now, washing the land golden-red-orange. Open land, as far as I can see. Peaceful. Quiet. I can see why Tom loved it here. After the dead desert of Iraq and the often-barren terrain of Afghanistan, the miles of crops and lush green pastures of Texas are a welcome change. I'm not at peace, but as near as I can be. In this moment, at least.

I'm restless, though. Hungry. Worn out from dodging dreams.

I spy some boards sticking out of the bed of the rusting blue pickup truck. Crossing the yard, I peek into the truck bed. Some fifty new planks of treated wood, a big box of screws. Screw gun in the cab. The keys…under the sun visor. I start the truck and aim it toward the section of fence in most need of repair. I yank off the hanging, broken slats, tossing them aside. Screw the new board up. Repeat. Repeat. Move down the line, replacing boards. The sun rises fully, heating me until I shed my shirt. It's tedious work, but it keeps me occupied. There's a vertical post rotting through toward the north end and, conveniently, a new post and a shovel in the truck bed. Pulling the old post out has me grunting and cursing, but I manage it, dig the hole deeper, replace the post and fasten the boards to it. I steadily make my way along the fence line that divides the north pasture from the east, which, thankfully, is mostly intact.

I'm sweating profusely and wrestling with a stubborn fence slat and a stripped screw head. I don't hear her approach until she's right beside me.

"Derek, what are you doing?" She's got a Thermos of coffee and a paper plate piled with scrambled eggs, toast, and bacon, all covered with plastic wrap.

I move away from her. She's too close—makes me nervous. She smells good, some faint perfume. I risk a glance at her as I finally wrench the old board free. Hair the color of sunlit honey, loose and brushed to a shine, hangs in waves around her shoulders. Eyes a pale blue, just a shade darker than the color of the sky above. She's wearing a red V-neck T-shirt, jean shorts, shin-high black Bogs for the mud from yesterday's rain.

I lift up the screw gun. "Fixing the fence."

"Why?"

I shrug. "Needed doing. I was up."

"Did you sleep okay?" She shifts from side to side, eyes flicking nervously. "I should've brought you a pillow last night. I'm sorry I didn't. I just—by the time I got Tommy in bed…."

It's a lie. I can tell by the way she won't look at me. I remind her of Tom. What she lost. I'm here and he's not, and the lie covers the fact that she couldn't bring herself to see me again.

I shake my head. "Don't worry about it. Slept worse places than on fresh hay." That statement ends up being way more loaded with meaning than I intended.

She does a duck-her-head-and-nod thing, lets a thick pause hang between us. "You should eat," she says eventually, lifting the plate.

I take the plate from her, take a seat on the lowered tailgate of the truck. "Thanks."

There's a metal fork on the plate, held in place by the plastic wrap. I peel away the Saran wrap and dig in, forcing myself to eat slowly. My instinct is still to wolf the food down as fast as I can, but I don't let myself. I have to do everything I can to distance myself from being a captive. I might have hated the gradual reintegration program the military doctors forced on me, but I recognize the necessity of it. I'm not okay. I'm not comfortable around people. I have flashbacks. I get violent when I'm startled, suffer bouts of rage that don't make any sense. Little things. Like that board just now. If I hadn't gotten it off….

I don't go there. I have to learn control.

I take careful, measured bites, chewing slowly and thoroughly. Hold the fork like a civilized man, between my index and middle fingers and thumb, rather than in my fist. Reagan slides up onto the tailgate beside me, and my chest tightens. It's hard to breathe. I stop eating, turn and look at her. She's on the far side of the tailgate, leaving a good foot between us, but it's still too close.

People get close to me and I tense, expect violence subconsciously.

She unscrews the top off the Thermos, pours black coffee into the top, hands it to me. I take it, careful to keep my fingers away from hers. Sip the coffee. It's thick, black, strong. She just sits quietly while I eat, and, slowly, my tension fades. I know, mentally, she poses no threat, but my reaction to people, to anyone, is automatic, unconscious. I can't help it, no matter how hard I try.

When I finish the huge mound of food she brought, she takes the paper plate, folds it up, tosses it deep into the bed of the truck. I hold onto the fork, poke my fingertips on the grease-shiny tines. Silence, long, awkward, delicate. She lifts one hip, produces the letter. I glance at her, see the chain of the dog tags against her tanned neck. My gaze focuses on the letter.

She's going to ask me a question.

"He didn't read the letter until you and he were—" She cuts off, won't say the word.

"Captured," I fill in for her. "No, he didn't."

She doesn't respond, but seems troubled. "And by the time you read it to him, he was already" —another pause where she has to summon the word, force it out— "dying."

I can only nod. I think I know what she's getting at. And I know for a fact I absolutely cannot handle this conversation right now. Not now. Maybe not ever. There are some truths that are too potent to speak of, too damaging to reveal. To guilt-freighted to see the light of day.

I hop off the truck, toss the fork into the bed. "I should go." I grab my shirt from the cab. "Thanks for breakfast."

"You—you don't have to leave, Derek. I'm sorry I asked. I know it can't be easy for you talk about… what happened. I just—"

"You have questions. Shit only I can answer. I get it. It's fine. But some stuff…there's some shit I just can't talk about yet. I'm sorry." I shake my head. "I should go. I don't belong here. This is his place."

I'd forgotten my scars. I can feel her eyes on me, on my shoulder, on the twin puckered and pinched scars. Doctors say I was insanely, incredibly lucky to have survived my wounds. Movies make it look like a "real hero" can take bullets to the shoulder and keep going, act like it's nothing. It's not like that. I should have had surgery. Could have lost the arm. Could have bled out if the bullets had hit an artery. Any number of *could've* scenarios, but somehow I pulled through. There's a loss of motor control, even still. You get shot, you're damaged. Plain and simple. But mostly, I'm fine. I forget the scars are there, especially when I'm alone, and then I was focused on my discomfort at being around Reagan. Now she sees the scars. Her eyes move, search. Find the scars from Iraq, shrapnel scars to my back and legs from the grenade. Cut on my bicep where a bullet sliced me, rescuing Hunter.

That grenade really did almost do me in. That was luck, too. Fortunately, the corpsman got to me pretty fast, patched me up and got me to a field hospital. Lost a lot of blood, took some time to heal, but no lasting damage, cycled back to active duty soon enough.

That was then, this is now. Now? I won't be going back. I can't. Won't. I'd rather fucking die than ever lift a rifle again. Than ever see another Afghani face.

I shrug into my shirt, covering the scars.

I don't want to leave; I like it here. Texas is peaceful, quiet. Open. I feel like I can breathe out here.

But I have to get out of here: Reagan is a potent presence, reminding me of Tom, of the letter. Of the self-serving lie. I see her, and I hear the words of the letter. *Thomas, my love....*

Shit. I think I whispered those words out loud. She heard; she's looking at me, staring, eyes curious, shocked, brow furrowed.

"What...what did you say?" she whispers.

"Nothing." I stop breathing, hoping she'll let it go.

I've mostly stopped reciting the letter, but it still comes out sometimes. The words are burned into my soul, and I just can't help it. But she can't know that. I feel this odd, penetrating shame about it. Like I stole something sacred of hers, of Tom's, like I appropriated something private.

I move away, stepping through the tall grass at the fence line. I walk as fast as I can, my fists clenched. I concentrate on slowing my breathing. I focus on each step, each breath, on the blades of grass, the grain of the wood, the boards sliding past like train tracks. There's the driveway. Finally. Duck through the lower and middle rungs, jog toward the road. Flee.

Run. Lungs burn, heart pounds. Legs hurt.

God, I'm so fucked up.

The blue Ford rumbles up behind me, past me, brakes squeal. Reagan kicks open the door, leaves it open, crunches through the gravel toward me. "Why—Derek, why'd you run like that?"

So many questions, none of which I can or will answer. "I don't know. I'm messed up, Reagan. Obviously, I'm not—I'm not good to be around. You have a kid. I don't belong here. I did what I came to do. That's it."

She drags a hand through her hair, a light, hot breeze ruffling the honeyed waves. She's agitated. At a loss for words. "You have nowhere to go."

It seems like a non sequitur to me. "So? Not your problem."

"Tom would've made sure you were taken care of. That you had somewhere to go. I can't just let you wander away alone like this."

"Tom's dead." It comes out flat, harsh.

She flinches. "I know that."

I scrub my scalp, inch-long buzz tickling. "Sorry. Shit, I'm so sorry. That came out wrong."

She shakes her head, turns away. The sun is heating up. Dandelions at the side of the driveway sway in the breeze, send white seeds tumbling. "Look, how about this: I need help. On the farm. The fence you fixed? I've been meaning to fix it for months, but I just can't get ahead enough to do it. There's so much to do and I—I just can't do it all. And you have nowhere to go. You were like a brother to Tom, and that means— it means you have a place here."

I don't know how to answer. She's not family, but I don't think I can go back to my own in Iowa. My parents wouldn't be able to handle me like I am now. They visited me at the Army hospital in San Antonio. But I was so obviously fucked up that they didn't stay long. They said I'd always have a place with them, but…I knew better. It'd be uncomfortable at best. My nightmares would keep them up. They'd want to help, and there is no help. They never really understood why I signed up for another term, and I couldn't adequately explain it. I just knew Barrett and McConnell and the rest were all going to Afghanistan, and I wasn't about to let them go without me. So I re-upped and went back into combat.

And now look at me.

"Fine," I say. "I'll stay for a couple of days. Help you get some shit done."

"I won't ask you any more questions. I promise."

I feel my left hand trembling. I squeeze to stop it. "Don't make promises you can't keep, Reagan."

Reagan

He won't sleep in the workshop. Won't say why, just says he feels more comfortable in the stall. Hank had an old Army surplus cot stowed away, so I set that up in the stall with a pillow and a couple of blankets, a camping lantern. It's odd, knowing he's out there, in the barn, when I'm trying to sleep. I feel guilty, wishing I had better accommodations to offer him than a barn. But I don't. There are only three bedrooms in the farmhouse: the master, Tommy's room, and the third bedroom. But that third one...it's Tom's, from when he was a kid. When he joined the Corps out of high school, his parents left it the way it was, so he'd have something familiar to come home to, I guess.

Tom and I got married a month before he was scheduled to deploy to Iraq for the first time. He'd finished his infantry MOS training and was rotated home before shipping out. We'd kept in touch while he was in California, via letter and phone call. When he got his leave papers, he hopped the first train to my hometown of Tulsa, showed up at my front door unannounced. Dressed in his finest blues, he took my hand in his, dropped to one knee, and proposed with a white gold and cubic zirconium ring worth maybe a hundred dollars. My parents were standing behind me, furious. I said yes, pulling Tom to his feet and leaping into his arms, wrapping my legs around his waist and kissing the ever-loving shit out of him, right there in front of Mom and Dad. Since clearly my parents weren't going to be a part of a wedding, Tom waited on the front sidewalk while I packed two suitcases and called us a cab. We took a Greyhound bus to Houston and had a courthouse wedding. We spent three nights in a hotel in Houston, fucking like jackrabbits. Finally, we made our way to Tom's family's farm outside a tiny place called Hempstead. His dad stood on the front porch, waiting for us, a huge man in dusty jeans, a dirty white T-shirt, and Caterpillar boots. He was broad, thick, carrying a beer belly and wearing a bushy blond beard, staring at us with dark eyes. Tom dragged me up the porch steps and stopped in front of his father.

"Dad," Tom had said, "this is my wife. Reagan."

Carl Barrett just grunted, nodded at me, and said, "Welcome to the farm. Y'all can take the spare bedroom. Just don't keep me awake at night." He then brushed past us on his way to his tractor, swigging from a flask.

He died a little more than two years later, but I'd spent those two years while Tom was in Iraq getting to know Carl, learning to love him like a parent. He was gruff and taciturn, but he was always kind to me. I'd grown up on a horse ranch, so I wasn't out of place on the farm, and Carl appreciated the help I gave him.

When Carl died, I'd made all the arrangements. Tom came back for the funeral, and again between each tour for a few months at a time. Once he was back almost a year before they shipped him back to Iraq, and that was, honestly, the best year of my life. Farming with Tom, riding the north pasture with him, making love in the tall grass, our tethered horses grazing nearby. When he was gone, I learned to manage the farm by myself for the most part, with a lot of help from Hank and his bevy of grandsons.

All that time, in eight years of marriage to Tom, and the three years since, the bedroom where Tom grew up has stayed the same. Gathering dust, except when I can summon the courage to clean it. I know for a fact Derek won't stay in there. He wouldn't be able to set foot in that room. I barely can.

Derek has been here for a week. He's repaired every single foot of fence, fixed the porch steps, and he's now working on painting the barn. He works like a man possessed, up and working before dawn and staying out until past dark, sometimes working by the light of the truck's headlights or the lantern. I usually end up bringing food out to him. He refuses to eat with Tommy and me. He avoids Tommy like the plague, actually. Won't go near him, won't talk to him. If Tommy's around, Derek vanishes. I've stayed true to my word and haven't asked any more questions, although they're burning a hole inside me. There are so many things I want to know.

Today, I'm driving the tractor, towing the baler up and down the last few rows. It's near dark, and I'm itchy with sweat, exhausted, ready to collapse. And then the tractor quits. Rumbles, slows, then dies. It's been on its last legs for years now, and this isn't the first time it's quit on me. I want to scream. Cry. But I don't.

I hop down, stomp through the lowering darkness, cursing under my breath, trying to find a center of calmness. The barn is a hulk in the darkness, the shape of a ladder visible against one side, part of one long side wall ready to be painted. I don't see Derek on the ladder. I hear the creak of the well pump out behind the barn, assume he's back there washing the paint off his hands. There's a refrigerator in the workshop, and it's got another one of my dirty little secrets in it: a secret stash of beer. I never drink at the house or around Tommy. But sometimes, after a hard day's work, I sneak in here, sit at the workbench, and drink a cold beer. Sometimes two, before I head up to the house.

I need one today.

I pull open the fridge, grab one, and pop the top on the bottle opener mounted to the workbench. I plop down on the stool, hold the sweating bottle to my forehead for a second, then take a long swig. I don't think twice about pulling up the hem of my T-shirt and wiping the sweat off my forehead. So, the shirt is up, my entire torso bared, when I hear a step and a creaking floorboard. I drop the hem and catch Derek's gaze at the same time.

He was looking at me.

He backs away. "Sorry. Sorry. Thought I heard someone in here, and I came to check it out." Scratching the back of his neck, he turns away.

"It's okay." It's not. I felt his gaze on me, on my tight red sports bra, my sweat-covered stomach. I don't know how I feel about it, how he feels about it. Or what I'm supposed to say, or do.

"Everything okay?" he asks. "You don't usually come in here, that I've seen. In the last week, I mean."

I shrug, take a drink. "The tractor broke down. I keep some emergency keep-myself-sane beer in here. I was almost done baling the hay, and now it'll be days before Hank can fix the tractor, so…emergency beer."

"I can take a look at it in the morning if you want." He's determinedly not looking at me. His gaze is on the floor, on the Little League and high school baseball trophies.

Silence.

"Want one?" I gesture with my bottle.

He hesitates. "Um…sure. I guess."

I take one from the fridge, open it, and hand it to him. He holds it, stares at it for a long, long time.

"It's just beer," I say, confused by his reaction.

"Yeah, I know. But I haven't had a drink in…a long time. Since before."

"I'm sorry, I wouldn't have offered if—"

He waves. "No. Nothing like that. It's not a problem. It's just been a long time." He lifts the bottle to his lips, takes a small, measured sip. The look of rapture that crosses his face is priceless. "God, that's good. I'd forgotten how much I liked beer."

A few minutes pass in a not-entirely-awkward silence. Derek stays in the doorway, standing.

"There's another stool, you know," I say. "You can sit down."

He eyes the stool, crosses the room, pulls it out, and sits on it. It doesn't escape my notice that he moved it so he wasn't too close to me.

He's not wearing a shirt. I can't help eyeing his torso, his scars. He's gained weight in the last week, put on some muscle, a little much-needed body fat to cover the bones. He's not anywhere near where he used to be, but he's not gaunt anymore. His hair has grown out, and he's let the beginnings of a beard cover his jaw.

He scratches at his scalp, at a scar on his head. He notices me watching, drops his hand. "An old scar," he says. "It itches sometimes."

"How did you—" I start to ask, then cut myself off. "Sorry. Never mind."

He swallows some beer, sets the empty bottle down. "It's fine. They kept my head shaved when I was a prisoner. Except, they weren't exactly gentle, and they didn't always use very sharp razors."

"God, that's horrible."

He shrugs. "Nah. It was probably better than getting lice or something."

There's an element in his words hinting at much, much worse. I'm torn between offering him another beer and the worry that I might be introducing a potential problem. I know I want another one. I open one, glance at him in question.

He takes it, sips slowly. "Thanks."

"Yeah."

Another long silence. Derek sighs, runs his palm over his scalp, and looks at me. "Go ahead and ask."

"Ask…what?"

He shakes his head and shrugs. "Whatever. I can't promise I'll be able to answer, but I'll try."

What do I most want to know? I stare down into the thin scrim of suds in my bottle. "The letter. He carried it with him for almost a year, without reading it?"

Derek nods. "Yep."

"Why?"

"Well…he said he was saving it. For when he needed it the most."

I watch Derek closely. He's struggling with something; his jaw is grinding, his fingers are tensed around the bottle. The ring finger of his left hand is visibly crooked. Where the other four fingers curl naturally around the glass, the ring finger sticks out as if it doesn't work properly. His hands are shaking, the golden lager in the bottle rippling.

"A year." I don't even know how to phrase my next question. "If he didn't read the letter, then he never… he never knew. Until the end. About Tommy, I mean."

"I—he…" Derek seems to be having trouble breathing. He's blinking quickly, and his shoulders are hunched as if expecting a blow. "He loved you. He loved you a lot."

That doesn't answer the question. I know avoidance when I see it, but Derek clearly isn't capable of this conversation right now.

He swallows a long swig of beer, then lurches to his feet, sets the half-finished bottle on the workbench, swaying on his feet. "Shit. Shit, I'm dizzy. Used to be able to put away a twenty-four pack on my own. Now I'm fucked up on two beers? Jesus."

He stumbles, puts a hand on the workbench to steady himself. His legs seem about to give out. I stand up, set my beer down, and move toward him. His eyes are closed, squeezed tight, his mouth moving as he's whispering something I can't hear. He sways, tilting off-balance. He's going to fall.

I reach out slowly, tentatively. Touch his shoulder. "Derek?"

His skin is hot to the touch. Hot and hard and soft at all once. I'd forgotten what male skin feels like.

He jumps at my touch, his eyes flying open wide, nostrils flaring, every muscle tensing. He stumbles a step backward, away from me, blinking as if seeing double.

"It's okay, Derek," I murmur in the low, soothing voice I used on a spooked horse. "It's okay. Just breathe. Relax. You're okay."

"Not okay. Not okay." He's staring at me, at my outstretched hand.

Me touching him isn't okay, or he's not okay? Both, maybe. I don't know. All I know is he's tilting away from me as if spooked by my proximity, as if the sight and smell and reality of me are too much to handle. I know he's acting hammered on two beers. Not even two, one and half, really. He's about to fall backward, so I have no choice but to put my shoulder under his armpit and wrap my arm around his waist. Even shrunk to a third of his former bulk, Derek is a big man. Six foot three if not more, broad shoulders, long legs, thick, heavy arms. I'm a strong girl, buff from a lifetime of farm work, but it takes all my strength to keep Derek on his feet.

"Come on, Derek. Let's get you lying down, huh?" I say.

I've got his mouth near my ear, and I can definitely hear him whispering something, but I can't
make it out. I half-carry him out of the workshop,
down the hallway between the stalls. The smell of hay
is pungent, layered over the more faint odor of cow
manure from Ilsa the milk cow, who is out to pasture right now. The single bare, dangling incandescent
light bulb in the workshop sheds just enough illumi-
nation that I can see which stall he's claimed as his
own. The hay is flattened on the floor and piled up in
one corner. Several old blankets are spread across the
hay in the corner, with the pillow I've given him on
top. The camping lantern sits against the wall near the
pillow. There is nothing else. The cot is folded up and
leaning against the wall. This man, this brave combat
veteran, this PTSD-plagued ex-POW, is sleeping on
the hay in my barn like a vagrant. There's something
very wrong with that.

Derek grabs the upright of the stall door, pulls
away from me, collapses to his knees, and falls onto
the hay, crawling toward his pillow. He fumbles at the
lantern, finds the knob, and turns it on, shedding a
white glow.

"You shouldn't be sleeping out here on the hay,
Derek. It's not right."

He rolls to his back, and his gaze fixes blearily on
me. "It's fine. I'm fine here."

"You deserve a real room. A real bed."

He wobbles his head back and forth. "No. I don't. I had a bed at the hospital. I hated it." He blinks rapidly, lays a hand over his eyes. "Spent three fucking years sleeping in the dirt. There was the one place they had me in, an old school, I think it was. Put me in a closet. Bare concrete. Got damned cold at night. Gave me sores on my hip and shoulder. After that, I was thankful for the dirt floor. Kept me in a cave, too. That sucked. Cold and dark. Every sound I made echoed. My breathing echoed. Drove me fucking nuts. I'd stop breathing until I passed out, just to make the echoes go away. Swore I could hear my heartbeat sometimes. Total silence is fucking unnerving." He lifts his hand, stares at his palm, squeezes his fingers into a fist, and releases it and stares at it some more. "The hospital was its own kind of hell. I was basically a prisoner there, too. Here, I can breathe. I can see the sky. I can get up and move around when I want. I can walk out the door and keep walking. Nobody will stop me, give me orders, or yell at me. I might've been among my own countrymen in the hospital, but I didn't feel free. Felt trapped just as much as when the Taliban had me."

He levels a look at me.

"And, trust me, Reagan, you do *not* want me in your house. I don't want to be there, and you wouldn't want me there." He goes quiet for a moment. "Maybe that came out wrong. It's not that I don't want to be in your house, or around you. It's not that, it's just...."

"I get it. As much as anyone can, I get what you're saying. It's okay."

He widens his eyes, blinks, and shakes his head. "Can't believe how fucked up that little bit of beer made me. Guess it was a bad idea."

He stretches, shifts, and the jeans ride low on his waist, bare a hint of the "V" of muscle, curls of body hair. I can't look away. I should, but I can't. Guilt assails me. I shouldn't be looking at Derek like that. At anyone, but especially him, especially when he's so fragile, emotionally and psychologically. Not fragile— that's not the right word. Unstable, maybe. Raw, healing. Wounds to the body heal faster than those within.

I rip my gaze away, stare at the floor between my feet. "Do you need anything? Can I get you anything?"

"I'll be fine. Just need some sleep."

The moon is a high bright sliver, shedding silver light on the grass. There's a lamp suspended from the power line stretching between the house and the barn, casting a broad circle of orange light on the gravel drive. I stop beneath it, stare back at the open barn door, at the faint glow of the lantern. My work boots crunch in the gravel, and the only sound is crickets, a few frogs somewhere far away. An owl hoots. The streetlight buzzes.

I don't want to go in. I don't want to talk to Ida. I don't want to crawl into my empty bed.

I do, though. Ida can tell I'm not in the mood for conversation, so she bids me a brief farewell and waits for Hank on the front porch. I strip off my sweat-stiff clothes, pull on a long T-shirt over my bare skin. As soon as my eyes close, I'm seized by a visual memory of Derek stretching, the hint of places on his body I have no business thinking about.

Yet, I do. I wonder. And when I finally fall asleep, I dream.

CHAPTER 8

Derek

THE WORLD SPINS. EYES CLOSED, EYES OPEN, IT MAKES no difference. I plant one foot on the floor, and the spinning lessens a little. Eyes open is better, though. Not because it helps the spinning, but because every time I close my eyes, I see her. The black T-shirt lifted up to wipe the sweat off her face, revealing a tight red sports bra, the tan, muscular stomach. Hipbones above low-rise jeans.

She's a tiny thing. Barely five-five, maybe a buck-twenty soaking wet. Packs a hell of a lot of curve on her tiny frame, though, and I shouldn't be thinking about her like this. Shouldn't. Can't. It's so wrong, on so many levels.

She's Tom's widow.

But no matter how forcefully I remind myself, I still can't get that vision of her out of my head. Red

Reebok sports bra, plump and stretched. Taut stomach flexing as she moves.

When she touched my shoulder, I nearly lost it.

No one has touched me since I've been back Stateside. I can't handle it. The last time a physical therapist tried to grab my leg to test my flexibility, he ended up with a broken nose. They learned after that to leave me the fuck alone. Tell me what they want me to do, but keep their damned hands off me. Hands bring pain. Touch means ache and agony. Touch flashes me back to being chained to a metal chair, a fist wrapped around my ring finger, bending it slowly and inexorably backward until it snaps. Touch flashes me back to hands shoving my face against the wall, a dull razor being dragged across my dry scalp, stuttering and slicing.

When Reagan touched me, I don't think she had any clue how close I came to lashing out with my elbow. Her touch was lightning. Sudden, and striking me with instant heat. Her fingertips only, on the round part of my shoulder, a gentle, hesitant touch. And then she pressed her body up against mine, held me up somehow, and carried me to the stall. It shouldn't have been possible, but that woman is *strong*. And all I could smell was citrus shampoo in her hair, the sweat on her body.

Fuck.

Eventually sleep comes, but I have a dream. A different one this time. Not the cave or the splinters or the beatings or Tom dying, but a dream about Reagan. The image of her lifting her shirt. Only in the dream, she peels it off and steps toward me, her hair loose.

And then I wake up.

I fall back asleep and have the same dream.

I manage to sleep till just past dawn, and then the dream drives me out of the barn. I don't bother with a shirt, since the day is already warm. Plus, it's the only shirt I've got with me. I uncap the paint can, gather the rollers and brushes, hike up the ladder. Roll, dip, roll, dip. Gray turns to pink, then orange, and I finish one side of the barn with the first coat. The old wood is porous and thirsty, so it'll take several coats. I start on the other side, get a third of the way done, and run out of paint. Descending the ladder, I find Reagan waiting for me, holding out a plate full of food. French toast, fried eggs, sausage. The woman can *cook*.

When I finish eating, I glance at her. "I ran out of red paint. I'll need several more gallons to finish the barn. Some white for the house. Unless you want the house a different color. It's so faded and peeled away that at this point it can be any color you want."

Reagan tilts her head. "I hadn't thought about that," she says. "Maybe a dark green?"

I shrug. "Sure. Green it is." I hand back her stoneware plate, the fork rattling across the surface. "I'll wash up and head into town."

I angle toward the back of the barn, where the old red well pump is located. This is where I've been washing myself.

"Oh, my god," Reagan says, surprise and consternation in her voice. "I'm a horrible person."

I stop and turn back. "The hell you talking about?"

"You've been using the pump all this time, haven't you? You've been here a week, and you haven't had a proper shower." She glances at my jeans. "And you don't have any extra clothes, do you? God, I can't believe myself."

I shift from foot to foot. "Wasn't sure where I was going except here, so I didn't bring anything. Don't have anything to bring anyway. I'm cool."

"It's not cool," she says. "Come inside and take a shower." I hesitate, and she moves behind me, shoves at me. "Get."

I get, if only to get away from the fire and uncomfortable intensity of her presence. She follows me up onto the porch, moves past me, and opens the screen door, which slams behind me. I have trouble moving past the foyer. There's a formal sitting room to the right, a stairway directly opposite the front door, a small den with hardwood floors overlaid by a thick rug, a couch under a window on one wall, a TV on the opposite wall. A doorway leads to the kitchen, and I can see it's painted yellow with white tile on the floor. White cabinets. Twenty-year-old appliances. There's a round four-person brown wood table, set with clear glass salt and pepper shakers, Tabasco sauce, and A-1 sauce.

My nerves come back. The cause of my problem is sitting on the couch, drowsy, staring at the TV. Towheaded, with eyes exactly like Tom's, wide and brown and deep. He's damned adorable. Gotta be around three by now. Clutching a plastic cup with cartoon characters of some kind on the side, a bright red sippy lid. The TV blares, and I can see little mermaid creatures with huge heads singing a song about going outside.

He's the lie I told...or didn't tell, more like.

When Reagan asked me about the letter and if Tom had known about his kid, I freaked. I couldn't answer. Reagan deserves the truth, and I'm not sure I'm man enough to give it to her.

"Derek?" Her voice is quiet, right beside me. "He's just a little boy. He's not gonna—I don't know. You act like you're—" Clearly, she's hedging around the issue. Doesn't want to say right out that a three-year-old won't hurt me, that I'm acting scared of a kid. She kneels down. "Tommy? Can you come say hi?"

The little boy slides forward off the couch in a weird, slinky maneuver. He toddles over, clutching the cup under his arm, then stares up at me. "Hi." He points at the TV. "Guppies."

I look at the TV. "Guppies?"

He puts the cup to his mouth, takes a long drink, making a whining, gurgling noise from the lid. "Bubb' Guppies."

I turn to Reagan for translation. The corner of her mouth is curled up in a smirk. "The show he's watching. It's called *Bubble Guppies*."

"They don't look like guppies. They look like big-headed mermaids."

She snickers. "I know. It doesn't always make any sense, but he loves it." She points at the TV. "Take a look."

Now the little mer-kids are singing about going camping. There's a fire, made of bubbles. All underwater. They're swimming around, sort of, but clearly the show has set the laws of physics aside.

"Weird," I say.

The kid is just staring at me. He puts his cup down on the floor, raises his arms over his head. "Up."

I take him by the hands, my big mitts engulfing his tiny little fingers. I lift him up, set him down. Reagan laughs again. "No, you big dolt. He means pick him up. Like, *hold* him."

I don't want to. This kid is the reminder of my guilt. But he's leaning against my legs, arms extended upward, chanting, "Uppy, uppy, uppy."

"I don't know how to hold a kid. Do I have to hold his head up or whatever?"

Reagan snorts. "Oh, my god. He's *three*. He's not a baby. Just pick him up by the armpits. He'll do the rest."

"Why?"

This has her at a loss. "He wants to be picked up. I don't know. It makes him feel better, I guess."

I lift Tommy up by the armpits, holding him at arm's length. He somehow manages to crawl across the empty space and cling to my torso, hugging my waist with his legs. His head lies against my shoulder. This is the most bizarre sensation I've ever felt. He's clinging to me like a monkey, his breathing going steady and deep. Some strange instinct has me tucking my arm under his butt to support him, and he goes limp within seconds. I just stand there, holding the kid, as he falls asleep. His arm flops loose, dangling at my chest.

I turn in place and look at Reagan. "Now what?"

She smiles, a strange, almost dreamy smile that I'm not sure how to interpret. "Just lay him on the couch."

I hold the back of his head with one hand, my other arm beneath his knees. I lay him down on the couch on his back. He sprawls out, mouth open, snoring.

The old woman—Ida, I think her name is—stands in the kitchen, flour on her hands, watching. Her surprised expression probably matches my own.

Reagan heads up the stairs. "Come on—I'll get you a towel."

I follow her, staring at the stair treads rather than her ass, which is where my gaze wants to go. She leads me into the master bedroom. There's an antique queen bed with a metal wrought-iron frame, a five-drawer bureau on one wall, and a three-drawer bureau with a mirror on the other. I steadfastly refuse to think about the fact that I'm in her bedroom.

Reagan darts ahead of me into the bathroom, yanking a white bra off the floor. "Shit. Sorry. No one's ever in here but me."

She opens the lid of a wicker hamper, tosses the undergarment in. I catch a glimpse of panties, jeans with one leg inside out, and another bra—the red one from last night—twisted and inside out, along with T-shirts and balled-up white ankle socks. It's a strangely intimate thing, a woman's laundry. I look away, at the sink. That's not much better. Makeup, trays of powder and tubes of lipstick, a bunch of other stuff I can't identify. None of it looks as if it's been used in a long time. There's a curling iron, a blue brush with black bristles. Several hair ties in a pile at the corner of the sink, strands of long blonde hair still attached. There's a package of tampons on the floor by the toilet. Can't look there. Two damp towels hang over the railing of the shower curtain.

This is, without a doubt, the most feminine space I've ever entered. I'm intensely uncomfortable, hyper-aware of Reagan beside me, smelling fresh and clean, and my thoughts jolt to the red sports bra, to the fact that she stripped it off and tossed it into the hamper. The bathroom still smells faintly of a recent shower, that vague damp smell that is equal parts steam and shampoo and something else indefinable, the smell of a bathroom after a shower.

After an awkward moment, Reagan bends over at the sink, opens the cabinet beneath. There's that ass again, round and taut and facing me, a reminder that this is a beautiful woman and I'm in her bathroom, in her private space, and she's off limits. She straightens, hands me a thick rust-colored towel.

"There's shampoo and soap in there, obviously." She points at the shower. "I'll see if I can find you some of—some clean clothes."

"Thanks. I can wear these. It's fine."

She pinches the denim over my thigh between her finger and thumb. "Don't be ridiculous. Those pants are caked with dirt." She visibly steels herself. "I've got a couple bins of Tom's clothes in the attic. They should fit."

"You don't have to—"

She shakes her head, cutting me off. Her voice is hard, brusque. "They're just clothes, Derek."

She's gone then, and I wait until she's out of the master bedroom before nudging the bathroom door closed and stepping out of my jeans.

The shower is glorious. High enough that I don't have to duck or do the limbo, a hard stream of hot water. The shampoo is a little girly-smelling, but whatever. I'm clean, and it's an amazing sensation. Showers at the hospital were short, usually either tepid or scalding, and the showerhead was so low I had to basically sit down to fit under it.

I soak for a long time, until the water goes lukewarm.

When I get out, there's a pile of jeans, T-shirts, socks, and boxer shorts on the bed. I put on the clothes, except the underwear. I'll be damned if I'll wear another man's underwear, no matter whose they were, or how clean.

Just no. No way.

When I head downstairs, I see that Reagan is writing a list. She doesn't look at me. "Ready? Let's go. I need some groceries from town anyway, so we can go together." She glances at Ida. "We need anything from town, Ida?"

Ida shrugs. "Not that I can think of."

"We'll be back as soon as possible."

Ida ruffles Tommy's hair. "We'll be fine here, won't we, bub?"

Tommy just smiles and goes back to his PB-and-J. Reagan kisses him on the top of the head, and then heads for the front door. She's avoiding my gaze now, and suddenly seems more uncomfortable around me than before. Maybe it's Tom's clothes. Or it might be something else entirely, something I can't begin to fathom.

All I know is, I get a whiff of citrus shampoo and something vanilla as she sweeps past me on the way to the truck. The smell of her makes me dizzy in ways I don't dare examine.

Off limits, Derek, I tell myself. *Off limits.*

Reagan

He's off limits, stupid woman, I berate myself. *You can't think about him like that.*

He'd shut the door to the bathroom before getting in the shower, but he didn't realize that the door has a tendency to come unlatched and swing open a few inches. I only meant to put the clothes on the bed and leave again, but I was arrested by the glimpse of him I got through the partly open door. The shower curtain is clear plastic, hiding nothing, meant only to stop the water from spattering on the floor. For one brief moment, I got a look at all of him. He was facing me; eyes closed, head back, running his hands over his head to rinse off the shampoo. I couldn't swallow past the lump lodged in my throat, couldn't think and couldn't look away.

Derek West is gorgeous. I can admit that much. The weight he lost and is slowly regaining only serves to heighten the angular beauty of his features. It's been so long since I've seen a man.

Four years, I think. The last time I saw a naked man was the night before Tom shipped out for what would be his final tour. Since then, it's been just me, Tommy, and Hank and Ida. I waited for Tom, and then waited for news, for official word. And then when I got it, I mourned. Long, and deeply. I grieved for my dead husband. Keeping the farm going, staying out of debt, keeping food on the table and my son cared for takes everything I have, takes every spare moment of my life, and then some. Other men never even crossed my mind.

And then Derek West shows up, and shakes my whole world.

His help is so gratefully appreciated; I've been running this farm by myself for a long, long time. I drive the tractor, bale the hay, plow the rows, plant, harvest, weed, spray. Fix fences and feed the horses, keep their hooves trimmed, and worm them and ride them—not as often as I'd like, but every once in a while—as well as mow the little patch of grass behind the house.

I'm a strong, capable, independent woman. But that doesn't mean I don't want and appreciate the help of a man.

I blush as I precede Derek to the pickup, trying my best and failing to erase the image of his naked body from my mind.

Derek is a *lot* of man.

Again I shake myself, forcing those thoughts from my mind. Think of my shopping list. *Eggs. Bread. Milk. Juice. Cinnamon. Vanilla extract. Bacon. Sausage. Ground beef. Fresh veggies. Pasta.*

It doesn't help. He's in the passenger seat, smelling clean. I steal a glance. The skin around the back of his neck is still beaded with moisture. His hair is darker when it's wet, long enough now to curl at the edges. It sweeps across his forehead, blown by the wind coming in through the open window.

His left hand rests on his thigh, on the dark-wash jeans. Those were Tom's favorite pair. *They're just clothes,* I tell myself. I glance at Derek's hand, at the crooked ring finger. "What happened to your finger?" I ask, by way of conversation.

Okay, so that's a shitty opening gambit.

Derek tenses, and I know I've asked a bad question. "It was…broken. A couple of times."

I twist at the leather of the steering wheel. "Shit, Derek. I'm sorry." I can tell by his reaction that it's something that was done to him, something he doesn't want to talk about.

He shrugs. "You couldn't know." He laughs sardonically. "Talking to me is kind of like walking though a minefield. You never know which step will cause an explosion."

"And I seem to have a knack for missteps, I guess."

"Not your fault. There are a lot of land mines, I guess." He is silent a moment, curling and straightening that finger. "It won't close all the way. They broke it, and then every couple days, they'd break it again. Keep me in pain, I guess. Never really knew why—they never wanted any information from me. Not that I really had any to give. They did it just to do it, I guess. They kept it broken for…I don't know. I lost the ability to track time after a while. A couple of weeks, probably. Eventually they lost interest in the game and left the finger alone. But it was so fucked up I had to re-break it myself and try to set it. Of course, I didn't have a splint or anything, so it didn't set right."

I cover my mouth with my hand. "God, Derek. That's…that's horrible."

"Yeah, it wasn't fun."

I trace the crooked path of his knuckles with my index finger. "Does it still bother you?"

He shrugs. "Yeah, sometimes. The usual broken-bone stuff. Aches when it rains, that kind of thing."

I shouldn't have looked at his hand, shouldn't have touched him. Now that I'm looking, I see other scars. Shiny burn scars, smooth to the touch in contrast to his strong, weathered hands. Some are round, some oblong and misshapen. Something tells me they're not accidental burns. I glance at him, see that he's watching me touch his various scars. I withdraw my hand; turn my attention back to the road.

"Those weren't accidental, were they?" I can't help asking.

"Nope." He clams up after that, and I'm not about to ask any more questions. A few minutes of silence, and then: "You know, you've done an incredible job, keeping that massive fucking farm going on your own."

I attempt a half-hearted smile. "Thanks. It's been hard—I'm not gonna lie." It feels good to say that out loud.

"I bet it has been. It's a big place. Lots to do."

"Yeah."

"Not many people could've done it, I think. Kept going, the way you have." I'm not sure whether he's talking about the farm anymore.

"Not much choice. Give up, or keep going, you know? Those were my only choices. And once Tommy was born, it's turned into a routine I can't get out of. You just…get up, do what you have to do. Don't think about the next day, or the huge list of things still to be done. There's no time off on a farm."

Derek hangs his arm out the window. "War is the same, in some ways. Do what you gotta do. I don't think about it too much, and I try not to think about what I've done, or what the pencil-dicks up the chain are gonna ask for next. You just…do the job. Patrol. Keep your eyes peeled, watch your buddy's back. Obey orders and keep your head down. Try to have some fun when you get a few hours of liberty."

He rests his head back on the seat, stares off into space, at the trees lining the road. "It's funny, I haven't thought about life as a Marine in a long time. I don't feel like a soldier anymore. For…so long, it's what I was. It was my identity: Corporal Derek West, United States Marine. Now? I don't even know anymore… who I am, *what* I am."

"Are they going to try to make you go back? I mean, are you discharged?"

"I don't know, officially. I *do* know I won't go back. Fuck that. Fuck the Corps. Fuck Afghanistan. Fuck war. They'll have to drag me back in cuffs. And I wouldn't survive the first SNAFU. I'm twitchy. Jumpy. I'm in horrible shape." He shakes his head. "No. I'm not going back."

"I don't blame you." Another long silence. "I never wanted to be a farmer. I grew up on a horse ranch in Oklahoma. Middle of nowhere, just like here. I hated it. I wanted to move to a big city. Phoenix, or Austin. Even New York City. I wanted to be a chef." I'm not sure where that admission came from. I've never told that to anyone.

Derek glances at me, head lolling on the seat. His eyes are the green of moss on a tree, dark and cool. "Yet here you are. Why?"

I shrug. "I loved Tom. This is where he wanted to be. He loved this land. His father farmed this land, his grandfather. His great-grandfather. That farmhouse is the second one built on that spot. The first one burned down in nineteen twenty-three. And Tom? He just...identified with the farm, with Texas, with being a farmer. He wanted to see some of the world before he settled down, though. He wanted to *do* something with his youth, I guess. I mean, he watched his father, who grew up on that plot of land and never left it, never left Texas, or even traveled any farther than Galveston."

"Well, Tom saw the world, all right. Iraq, Germany, Afghanistan, Morocco."

This was news to me. "Morocco? When did Tom go to Morocco?"

He grins, remembering. "Me, Hunter, Tom, Blast, and Abraham, we took a trip together. This was when we were stationed in Baghdad, early on in the second go-around. We had four days of liberty, so we hopped a plane to Casablanca. Raised some serious hell. We all got written up for that. Barrett and I pulled latrine duty for two weeks because of that trip." Derek's voice breaks. "Me and Hunter, we're—we're the only ones left alive of our entire unit. Everyone from the original Foxtrot…they're all dead. Most of 'em—most of them died in the ambush."

I can't just not respond, but I don't know what to say. "Have you seen Hunter? Since you've been back?"

He nods. "Yeah. Him and Rania came by the hospital. Spent a few days with me. They're having another little girl." He pauses to think. "Should be due in a couple of weeks."

"They're doing well, then?"

"Yeah. Real good. Hunter works on a road crew, Rania is a nurse at a hospital."

Suddenly, we're at the Home Depot in Brenham. It's a strangely domestic experience, buying paint and fence rails and a few other odds and ends. Then it's on to the Brookshire Brothers for groceries. Even more domesticity. Wandering up and down the aisle, a cart with one wobbly caster, Derek strolling beside me, casual conversation about idle things: Baker—Hank's aged and zany Blue Heeler—chasing a rabbit through the north pasture, barking madly and tripping every third step because he's game in his hind leg; Henry the Eighth and his endless search for loose fence rails to knock down so he can get to the greener grass on the other side; anything but Tom, anything but the war.

I haven't gone grocery shopping with a man since Tom's ten-month leave between tours. It's a strange feeling, having someone around who's not Hank, Ida, or Tommy. I catch myself watching him, staring at the way his shoulders move when he walks, the remnants of an unconscious hunch. The long swing of his legs, the way he clenches his left hand every so often, wiggles the ring finger. Holds his hands low by his thighs and shakes them to stop the trembles. The way his eyes are always scanning, hopping from person to person, assessing, and noticing when someone comes up behind us. Derek notices everything, missing nothing.

We're tossing the bags into the bed of the truck. A souped-up pickup truck full of rowdy teenage boys roars into the parking lot, pounding rap music thudding from the speakers, shouts and laughter and curses. There are three or four boys in the bed of the truck, shoving each other and laughing, standing up as the truck squeals to a stop one row over. One of them has a cigarette in his mouth, and he's leaning toward his buddy, nudging and laughing, holding a hand out, demanding something.

The other boy hands the object over, and I hear him say, "If the fuzz show up, I'm out of here. Just sayin'."

"Pussy." The kid with the cigarette dangling from his lips puts one foot up on the rim of the truck bed, pulls the cigarette from his lips, and holds it to the item cupped in his hands. "Go, go!" he shouts, hopping down, reaching up to grab his friend's hand and jerking him down, pushing the rest into a run, tossing what I now realize are firecrackers a few feet away.

Derek noticed the kids show up and dismissed them, busied himself with tying a bungee cord through the loops of the plastic grocery bags and fastening them to the rungs on the bed liner. He misses the exchange with the firecracker. Before I think to alert him, the firecrackers go off.

CRACK!

At the first explosion, Derek is down, kneeling on the far side of the truck, back against the tire.

Crackcrackcrackcrack—

When the rest of the firecrackers go off, Derek identifies the sound and straightens to his feet. He's shaken, pale. "Fuckin' firecrackers? Jesus." He grips the metal rim of the truck bed, braced and clearly struggling for composure.

I don't think twice about putting my hand on his back, rubbing in slow, soothing circles. "You okay?"

He tenses at my touch, but doesn't move away. "Embarrassed." He barks out harsh, deprecating laughter. "Ducking for cover at some goddamn firecrackers like some green fuckin' rookie."

"It's a natural reaction—"

"Just get me the hell out of here. Too many people." He pushes away from the truck, rounds to the passenger side, and gets in, staring out the window.

I point us home. After fifteen minutes of stony silence, I risk a hand on his knee. He glances at me in question. "You have nothing to be embarrassed about, Derek," I say.

"My heart is still hammering. I'm fucking sweating and shaking. Look at this." He holds out his left hand, which is shaking violently, until he squeezes it into a fist, resting the fist on his thigh.

I cover his hand with mine. "The last time Tom came home, he was here over the Fourth of July. We went down to Houston, and we had this great dinner, took a walk through Memorial Park. Went to the Miller Theater for the fireworks show. I didn't even think about it—how the fireworks would affect him. He played it tough, you know how he—how he *was*" —I have to emphasize the past tense still sometimes— "but he was a mess through the whole thing. When they started shooting off the cannons, he couldn't take it anymore. He took off, and I found him in a men's bathroom, sitting in a stall, just about hyperventilating. He wouldn't let me in, so I crawled under the door to be with him until it was over."

"Sounds about right."

Both of us pretend that my hand isn't still on his. I pretend that my heart isn't rabbiting like a teenage girl's, and I pretend not to notice that his hand still shakes every once in a while. He, in turn, casually unclenches his fist, relaxes his hand on his leg. He pretends not to notice that my fingers somehow, on their own, slip between his own. I pretend like it's totally natural and normal to drive the rest of the twenty-mile trip with only my left on the wheel, even through the turns.

I pretend to myself that I'm not disappointed when the drive is over and I have to pull my hand away.

He, like a typical man, carries almost all of the grocery bags into the kitchen in a single trip, bags draped along his forearms, three or four clutched in each finger. He slams the tailgate closed as I grab the gallon of milk. He stops, one hand on the tailgate, his eyes meeting mine finally. "Reagan?"

I rest the milk on the bumper. "Yeah?"

"Just…thanks. For understanding. For not making me feel like a pussy."

I smile at him. "You are literally the farthest thing from a pussy, Derek."

He ducks his head and nods, not really agreeing, more acknowledging my statement. "Well, thanks." He smacks the side of the truck with a palm. "Guess I'll finish the barn now."

I watch him go, and for the rest of the day I'm fixated on the memory of his hand under mine.

CHAPTER 9
Derek

THE NEXT MONTH IS A STRANGE, AWKWARD DANCE. Reagan and I partially avoid each other, and partially seek each other out. I can't erase the feel of her hand on mine, the gentle way she has about her. But it's because of that inability to forget something so simple as almost-but-not-quite holding hands after my minor freak-out that I avoid her. I avoid her after we each finish the day's work. She's always sweaty, dirty, and sexy. It drives me fucking nuts. Her shirt sticks to her chest and stomach, her shorts molded to her thighs and ass. Her hair hangs limp and tangled and sweat-pasted to her forehead and the back of her neck, her tanned skin flushed. I can't not look at her, so I avoid her until she's cleaned up. But that usually means she ends up bringing supper out to the barn, or leaving it on the kitchen table for me after I come down from the shower.

She's never come right out and asked me to eat with them, so I don't. It would be weird, sitting at that round table with Hank, Ida, Reagan, and Tommy, like some kind of faux-family unit. I haven't sat down to a real dinner at a real table in years. Growing up in Des Moines, we weren't a sit-down dinner family. My dad worked construction and was never home for dinner. My mom was a teacher, and she wasn't home much after school. Hannah and I would usually just make PB-and-J, grilled cheese, or Kraft Macaroni, and eat it in front of the TV, watching Nick at Nite. There were holidays, of course, but those were fucked-up formal affairs. Nana and Pop would come in from D.C., Pop and Dad would drink too much Johnny and get in an argument. Nana and Mom would sit in icy silence, while Hannah and I pretended not to notice, pretended to like Mom's shitty pumpkin pie. We'd usually end up escaping the house, Hannah going to her friend Marybeth's, me to Hunter's. That only worked until Hunter's folks died when we were in high school, but at that point we had our crew of football buddies, and we'd steal forties from the Seven-Eleven and play pickup football in the empty lot.

So, yeah, I don't do sit-down dinners. I sometimes sit in the open door of the haymow, feet dangling out over space. I can just barely see through the front window straight through to the kitchen table. Reagan sits on the left side of the table, Tommy beside her closest to the den. Ida beside him, and Hank opposite Reagan. They're not blood relations, but they're a family. Ida spends her day here, watching Tommy while Reagan works. Hank's farm is a good bit smaller and more manageable, so he gets his chores done and then helps Reagan, although since I've been here, we haven't needed his help as much. I've actually ended up at his place a few times, helping him. We don't talk much, Hank and I. Don't need to. He's an old soldier; he gets it.

Although, one evening Hank and I are spreading hay in his barn, and he rests on his pitchfork, glances at me. "You got a plan, Derek?"

I hate that question. I ask it of myself every day. I shrug. "Not really."

"Probably will need one, eventually." He nods his head in the direction of Reagan's farm. "That situation yonder. Ain't gonna last forever."

I nod. "I know."

"Reagan is a strong woman, but she's been through a lot." He goes back to pitching hay. "She ain't got much more she can give."

I blow out a breath. "I hear you, Hank."

"Do you?"

"Yes, sir."

He nods. "Just so we understand each other."

He wasn't warning me off. There's nothing to warn against. I'm just helping out until I sort my shit out. But I do need a plan. Somewhere to go. Something to do. It's obvious I can't stay here forever. It's not my place. Not my family.

But....

I don't want to go.

I like it here.

I wave off Hank's offer of a ride back to the barn, choosing to walk through the gray-blue of twilight. In this part of Texas, half a mile away is considered a close neighbor, so it's a decent walk, but a peaceful one. Crickets sing, swallows dart, and bats swoop. An owl hoots somewhere. Churned soil and bits of root and stalk from the hay harvest are underfoot. The soil gives off a pungent smell, still warm from the day's heat. I walk and watch the stars prick the sky, twinkling to life one by one, until suddenly there's a hundred and then a thousand and then too many millions to count.

The stars were one thing I could count on when I was a prisoner. Afghanistan is a wild, rugged, rough, unforgiving land. Huge skies, vast lifeless plains, high bare mountains, and sharp rock peaks. The stars are bright and numberless. If I could see them, they gave me hope. Cracks in the door, high windows, distantly seen from deep within a cave. I would try not to breathe too loudly and watch the stars come out, watch them brighten and move and fade.

Now the Texas stars are something I can latch onto, some kind of continuity in my life. There were bright stars growing up in Des Moines. Impossible millions in the desert of Iraq. Countless billions in Afghanistan. Now here are those same stars, equally bright and innumerable. Something to anchor me while I struggle to find my way in this confusing post-war, post-captivity life.

Watching the stars instead of where I'm going, I end up off-track. Instead of the barn, I find myself angling past the house, walking behind it. The grass is a dark swath before me, separated from the harvested fields by a fence, which I duck under. There's a pond back here somewhere. There, behind the trees. Oak, cottonwood, a few willows. A short dock, just barely visible through the branches of the trees, is barely a ten-foot length of aged wood. I can see it from my vantage point on this side of the pond.

I duck beneath a low-hanging oak branch and push through the still strands of a willow. I strip my boots and socks off, roll my pant legs up and sit, dangling my feet in the lukewarm water. I watch the waxing half moon reflect on the gently rippling water, soaking in the silence and the peace.

I close my eyes and drowse, for how long I don't know.

My senses prickle, and I open my eyes. Reagan stands on the dock, limned in silver starlight. I'm obscured by the willow strands, and I watch as Reagan sits on the dock, slips off her shoes and socks. The pond is barely a hundred feet across, so I can see her clearly, bare feet, toes wiggling. She stands up, turns to glance at the house, watching, listening. A pair of headlights backs away, turns, and vanishes; Ida and Hank are going home.

Reagan is motionless, watching the house. Listening to make sure Tommy is asleep, I assume.

After a few moments, she seems satisfied.

My heart seizes and my mouth goes dry and my hands curl into the grass at the pond's edge; she unbuttons her khaki shorts, unzips them. Lets them fall to the dock.

I should go. I should look away. Alert her to my presence.

Asshole that I am, I do none of those things.

I watch as she grabs the hem of her shirt, arms crossed, and peels it off. White bra, red underwear. Long, strong legs. Taut stomach, muscular arms, slim shoulders.

God, so beautiful. I can't look away; I'm caught up, hypnotized.

She just stands there in her bra and underwear for a few minutes, breathing, staring up at the sky. Counting the stars, maybe.

Eventually, she pushes her underwear down past her hips and steps out of them. She reaches behind her back and unhooks her bra, shrugs out of it, sets it on top of her clothes. She's naked, stunning, breathtaking. Her breasts are full, round, pale in the starlight. I can just make out the peak of one of her nipples in silhouette. She presses her palms to her stomach, smooths her hands upward, lifts her tits and rubs the undersides before letting them fall with a beautiful bounce.

A toe lifts and scratches at her calf; she tugs her hair out of the ponytail and shakes it out, running her hands through it. Another moment of hesitation, then, stretching her arms high above her head, her buttocks tensed, her boobs swaying, she spears forward in a nearly horizontal dive.

When she's under the water and out of sight, I let out a harsh breath, scrub my face. "You're an asshole, Derek West," I tell myself out loud.

But, my status as a grade-A dick established, I don't get up, I don't leave. I know I should, but I'm greedy for another glimpse of Reagan's nude beauty. Even the guilt burning in my soul can't make me move.

The water ripples, and her head pokes up above the water on the far side of the pond, hair slicked back, shoulders peeking and flashing as she swims. The pond is clearly more of a swimming hole, deep by the looks of it. She reaches the far bank and holds onto the grass with one hand, running her other palm over her scalp and down her face.

And then she ducks under the water again and is out of sight once more.

Reagan

Skinny-dipping late at night after Tommy's asleep is another of my dirty little secrets. It's relaxing, freeing. Exhilarating. Refreshing after a hard day's work.

Today, a swim is especially welcome. The day was hot, the work endless. My skin itched from dried sweat, and I'd been looking forward to a quick dip from the moment I woke up. Ida left, Tommy went to bed and fell asleep. Derek was nowhere to be found after helping Hank with his barn chores for the evening, so I assumed he was in my barn, doing whatever he does in there.

Except, when I broke the surface just beneath my favorite part of the pond, near the willow tree, there he was. Bare feet dangling in the water. His eyes wide as I came up for air.

I gasped, ducked back down, and held onto the bank. "Derek. What—what are you doing?"

"I—um. I ended up here. Thought I'd sit by the water for a minute." He stared down at the grass. "Then you—and I couldn't—I'm a dick. I'm sorry, Reagan. I'm just an asshole."

He lumbers to his feet, turning away. Now that I'm over my shock at seeing him, the rest of my emotions are hard to decipher. Irritated at his gall, yes. But also… not as mad as I should be. Not as offended or indignant as I should be. More intrigued than I should be. A lot more unwilling to let him walk away than I should be.

"Wait." I put both arms on the bank.

The pond is actually a manmade swimming hole. Just a big hole in the ground, a good twenty feet deep with no real slope to it.

Derek stops, one hand on the trunk of the willow, but he doesn't turn around. "Yeah?"

"You watched me?"

He hangs his head. "Yeah." He turns slightly, glances at me over his shoulder. "You have every right to hate me."

"But I don't."

He lifts his head in surprise, turns a little more. "You don't?"

I shake my head. "No." My throat catches, but I force myself to keep going. "I actually have a confession to make. That first time you took a shower in my bathroom? I brought you the clothes—I should have told you, the door doesn't latch, and it kind of swings open a little. I accidentally saw you showering."

"Accidents happen," he says. "I kept watching, even though I knew you didn't know I was here. I just watched, like a pervert."

I'm blushing furiously, heart hammering. "Yeah, well, I didn't exactly look away right away, either."

He's silent for a moment. "Oh."

"Yeah." I look at him, and our eyes finally meet for the first time. "So…I'm sorry, too. Guess this makes us even."

I don't know how to interpret the look in his eyes. Curious? Nervous? There's desire, too. His eyes touch mine, and he doesn't look away. I wonder what he sees in my gaze? My emotions are rampant, confused. Curiosity and nerves, surely. The same veiled, pushed-down hint of desire, like banked coals beneath a thick layer of ash.

He abruptly turns away again, takes two fast steps toward the house. "I'll go. Let you finish your swim."

My tongue betrays me. "Don't—maybe you don't have to go."

I'm lonely. Tired. My heart is heavy from long-carried grief. Weighted by sorrow. Thick with loneliness. Coated in a tough hide of self-reliance.

It's late, and my ability to resist the things boiling within me in regard to Derek—things I've been ignoring for weeks—is weak. The knowledge that Derek is not someone I should get involved with fades to black. It's still there, of course. It never goes away. He's my husband's best friend. My *dead* husband's best friend. He was there when Tom died. He's a soldier, a damaged, unstable combat veteran with a complex case of

PTSD. I'm in no position to help him, or to take on his issues. My own life is hard, with no relief in sight. I'm saddled with a farm I never wanted, raising a child alone, left to handle my grief as best I can, left to cope the best I can.

And in the middle of all that is Derek, handsome and troubled. Yet he's taken a huge load off my shoulders simply by assuming work I've never had the time to get to, doing the things that are simply too hard for Hank or me. And…his presence reassures me somehow. He's an enigma, often silent, going off on his own. I never know how he'll react to some things. Never know what will send him into himself, memories raging in his eyes. But despite all that, I'm drawn to him. Drawn to his silences, drawn to the ghosts in his gaze, drawn to the stillness in him. There are times, when the troubles in his soul are more distant, that he can be totally still, entirely present in the moment in a way that pulls me to him with the inexorable tug of gravity.

Like now—he's not looking at me, but I can feel his awareness of me. The air between us is fraught and alive with tension and chemical combustion, sparking like a live wire. He saw me naked. Watched me strip.

I'm inviting trouble, and I'm fully aware of it. But I allow the words from my lips anyway: "Swim with me."

Slowly, he pivots in place, and this time his eyes go to my shoulders, the hint of heel and calf and thigh as I kick to float horizontally on the water. "Swim with you?"

I nod.

He swallows hard. "I shouldn't."

I don't answer, just meet his gaze and watch him decide.

My heart thuds in my chest, and my nipples tighten as he stares down at me, then grasps the hem of his shirt and peels it off. He's put on a good bit of muscle over the last two weeks. A lot, actually. I think he's working out in the barn. He has to be to have built that much definition in his arms and abs. There's that "V" of muscle, making it clear he's not wearing anything beneath the jeans.

The moment becomes a tableau, a challenge almost. Will I look away? Will he turn away? This moment feels definitive, delineating the path before us.

I return my eyes to his, staring up at him, making my choice. He hesitates with his hands on the button of his jeans. Unsnaps them. Puts finger and thumb to the zipper, his eyes so dark green in the night as to look black, not wavering from mine. Lowers the zipper. I blink and keep my focus on his gaze.

He pushes the denim down, steps out, standing naked in front of me.

I have to look.

Holy fuck.

I blush scarlet and wonder if he can see the flaming redness of my cheeks, if he can hear the pounding hammer of my heart. He's a very...blessed man. The glimpse I caught of him in the shower hinted at his size, but the huge, hard reality is something else entirely. It's been so, so long since I've seen a man's erect cock, and I'm powerless to look away.

He dives into the water, slicing in past me, splashing me. I kick off the bank and dive under the surface, kicking and pulling at the water. I dive down deep, until the water gets cold and my eardrums tighten, and then I kick to the surface. I emerge less than a foot from where Derek is treading water, waiting for me. His eyes go to my chest, then up to my eyes.

There's nothing to say.

He swims away, and I pace him. We go back and forth a few times, side by side. I stop in the middle of the pond, turn to my back and float. I can feel Derek's eyes on me, on my breasts and stomach and thighs.

Moments pass in silence, Derek floating somewhere to one side, each of us lost in our thoughts, lost in the myriad stars above, lost in wondering exactly what's going on between us. The only sounds are the frogs and crickets and the occasional splash of a hand or foot as we float.

I roll over, tread water, and find myself inches from Derek, at his right side. He's floating on his back still, eyes closed. I can see the dusting of hair on his chest and stomach, the bullet scars on his shoulder. Hipbones, a small thin white line of a scar across his right hip, high, near the stomach. The thick thatch of curly pubic hair, his cock, now at rest and floating and swaying with the swish of the water. He kicks gently with one foot, waves at the water with both hands. His right hand brushes my thigh. The brief, accidental touch sends a bolt of lightning through me; I blink, inhale, and there's a splash, and Derek is there, eyes hot and darkest green and searching mine. I'm sucking in deep breaths, my chest swelling, breasts rising and falling, floating in the water.

Our legs kicking to keep us afloat, he reaches out through the water, and his palm finds my waist. I inhale sharply at the long-forgotten sensation of male touch on my skin. His fingers curl into my flesh, and the barest pressure is enough to tug me toward him. The tips of my boobs touch his chest; he's leaning back, and I'm leaning toward him, he's swimming backward, and I'm swimming forward. There's no chance of resisting. I find myself on top of him, my arm around his neck somehow, my legs kicking between his.

This is such a huge mistake. I'm crossing a line, falling over some edge from which there is no return.

I feel the thick soft presence of his dick at my belly, hardening and lengthening.

Oh, god, why am I allowing this to happen? We shouldn't be doing this.

But his hand is low across my back, just above my butt, and my eyes and his are locked, and I'm so completely unable to look away, pull away, swim away, or do anything except feel his body beneath me, hard and strong and intoxicatingly male. The bank approaches, and in a move I don't understand and can't quite follow, Derek is twisting in the water, his hands going to my waist, legs kicking powerfully, and he's lifting me out of the water. I land in the soft cool grass beneath the willow tree, the long dangling strands undulating in a warm breeze with a quiet susurrus.

My legs wrap around his torso, holding him to me. My arms snake around his neck; he's supporting himself partially out of the water with the strength of his arms alone.

His face is level with mine, his mouth slanting, closing in. "Stop me," he whispers.

I exhale, my palm touching his jaw, and I close the distance between my lips and his.

God, god, god.

Lips alone, at first. Meeting, moving, melding. Then his tongue and mine venture out in the same moment, touch and tangle. Things jangle in the back of my head. Warning flags flap and klaxons blare, but they're stilled and silenced by the taste of his mouth, by the solidity of his waist between my legs, his stomach pressing teasingly against my damp aching core, that long-ignored part of me.

Oh, there've been any number of times over the years when my fingers have eased the ache in the long nights alone, but that is so, so inadequate. Dreams and fantasies cannot begin to compare to the heat and strength of a man's body against your flesh, of his mouth on yours, his chest hair tickling and scratching, his stubble scraping your upper lip and chin as you kiss and the way you can feel his muscles rippling and shifting as he begins his conquest to possess you.

When he arches his back and hovers over you, palm beside your ear, breath on your cheek, in that moment, all those sensations fade to background beauty, because the sole focus of your existence is the thick hard presence of his cock against your softest place, and you feel yourself wet and warm and ready for him, aching for him, needing him, needing to feel that perfect soul-swelling fullness, the completion of being joined.

A breath and the slightest shift of muscles are all that stand between us.

My hands are on his back, on his shoulders, caressing and smoothing in circles, pulling, sliding from shoulder blades to the broad expanse of his back. Balance shifts, and I fall backward to the grass, blades pricking my shoulders, and my hands find the hard swell of his taut ass. He's above me, still kissing me, totally out of the water now, one knee between my thighs. One hand supports him, planted in the turf beside my face, the other sweeping up the curve of my waist to my breast, sagged to the side by gravity.

They were once high and firm, my tits. Pregnancy swelled them, milk stretched them, nursing changed them. There's a moment of discomfort, embarrassment, self-consciousness. That moment is erased by his palm against the weighted side of my boob, lifting it, caressing it reverently.

His mouth leaves mine.

Descends. Lips touch my clavicle.

"You are…so beautiful." His words float up to me, make me swallow hard against the sudden glut of emotions charging through me.

I haven't felt beautiful or feminine in so, so long. Four words, a heartfelt compliment, the wonder rife in his tone making it clear he means it down to the depths of his desire. Four little words, and I'm wrecked.

The moment of rapturous forgetting is ruined.

Tears explode, sudden and furious. One moment I'm caught up in the sensuous slide of skin on skin, of Derek's hands and mouth, and the next I'm sobbing uncontrollably.

"Shit, shit." Derek rolls off me, lying on his back in the grass beside me, hands pressed to his face. "Shit,

I'm such a selfish asshole. I'm sorry, Reagan. I'm so sorry. I shouldn't have let that happen."

He starts to rise, but I, incapable of speaking, can only shake my head and roll toward him, stop him with a hand to his chest. "Don't—don't." I choke the words out. Suck in a deep, steadying breath and try again. "You didn't—it's not—"

He sinks back to the grass, staring at me in confusion. I'm rubbing at my face, trying to breathe, trying to stop, but now that I've opened the floodgates, it's all coming out, years and years' worth of pent-up misery and sorrow and loneliness and weakness. All I can do is wriggle toward him, rest my cheek against his chest and cry. Horrible, ugly tears. Endless, endless. Derek doesn't speak, doesn't ask questions. He just cradles me in the sheltering warmth of his arms and strokes my hair away from my face. He doesn't shush me, or tell me not to cry, or act awkward or uncomfortable. He just holds me, and that, truly, just makes it so much worse. Because it's exactly what I need, and I can't take it, can't handle him being so sweet and understanding when he doesn't even comprehend the depths of what I'm feeling.

Hell, *I* don't even fully comprehend my own emotions, so how could he?

We're both still nude, but that somehow fades. The warm air is thick and humid and smells strongly of impending rain. The sky is dark, stars blotted out by rolling clouds. His hands brush back from my forehead, down my cheek, tucking flyaway wisps of hair behind my ear, and his thumb touches my cheek, slides across my cheekbone. I sob again, because that, unbeknownst to Derek, was Tom's favorite gesture of affection.

Which thought only serves to remind me of what nearly happened just now. That I nearly had unprotected sex on the bank of my pond with my dead husband's best friend.

I manage to quiet the flood, wipe my eyes with the heel of my palms. I suck in slow, steadying breaths and tilt my face up so I can see Derek's. "I'm sorry," I say. "I just—"

"Needed to cry. It's okay. I get it."

"Yeah, but that's not it. Not totally. I just haven't felt…I don't even know how to put it. I haven't felt beautiful in a very long time. I haven't felt like a *woman* in years. I'm a mom. I'm a farmer. I'm a widow. I'm a lot of other things. But since Tom shipped out, and even…even before then, through all his deployments, I haven't felt like a woman with desires and needs. I haven't felt wanted or beautiful in so long, and when you told me you thought I was beautiful, I just…I guess I kind of lost it, because it felt so strange, so foreign. And…so incredible. But then I started crying, and I've been holding so much in for so long, you know?"

He nods. "I know about holding shit in, at least. And I know it doesn't work. You gotta get shit out. I've told you things about what happened over there that I haven't told anyone else. The shrinks and doctors and everyone else wanted me to just open up and tell 'em everything, but I just couldn't. It was too new, too fresh. And they didn't really give a shit—they were just doing their job." He holds onto my shoulders, arm across my back, and the sensation of being held is so deliriously heady that I have to close my eyes and breathe through the wave of overwhelmed neediness. "As far as the other stuff? Not feeling like a woman? I think I get that too. I wasn't a man, you know? I was a prisoner. A victim. Name, rank, and serial number. I was reduced to the drive to survive. Then I felt guilty that I *did* survive. That's still there, in fucking spades, but whatever. Now I'm still figuring out what I am, what I feel like. Who I am. And feeling like a man again? Like a real man? That someone wants around, that someone needs or feels desire for? That's some powerful shit."

I nod. "Yeah, it is."

A long, warm breeze sends the willow fronds waving, and then a low distant growl of thunder rolls over us. Rain hisses, stray drops hitting our faces and bodies, rippling the surface of the pond in a million concentric spreading circles. Neither of us moves.

The rain doesn't really touch us, and the sound of it is peaceful, soothing.

Seconds of silence turn to minutes, each of us lost in our own thoughts and the rain falling in wind-blown waves across the water.

"Reagan?" His voice is low and deep. I turn into him, my body pressed against his. "You *are* beautiful. You should know that. You're a hell of woman. You're beautiful, and you are wanted. I know I'm not supposed to feel that way about you, but fuck it. I do. What just happened between us, it probably shouldn't have. But it did, and I guess I'm asshole enough to not feel sorry for it. Guilty, yes. Confused, a little. But I'm not sorry. I felt more alive just now than I have in…in a long motherfucking time."

I have to breathe and swallow and blink a few times before I can respond. God, I'm so emotional. "You're not an asshole, Derek." I lift up on an elbow. My boobs drape against his chest. I steady myself with a palm to his heartbeat. My eyes meet his, and I let him see the turmoil in my soul, let him see whatever he can see. "I didn't just *let* that happen, okay? I'm not just…I don't know…complicit? That feels like the right word. I *wanted* that to happen. I took everything you were giving and gave it right back. So quit hogging all the guilt, would you?"

He chuckles. "All right, I guess you can have some of it." His hand slides down my bicep. Down my waist. Cups the extreme lower edge of my back, just above my butt, as if he's contemplating caressing me there, but chickens out.

I want him to touch me, and I'm scared of what will happen if he does. I feel both in equal measure. "Derek?"

"Hmm?"

"What's happening? Here, between us."

"Hell if I know." His palm ascends to my shoulder blades, his thumb rolling over the back of my neck, and then his touch moves back downward again, and he gets closer to my ass this time. "Something wrong? Something right? I don't even know."

That's not what I want to hear. "Derek...I need—I can't handle the confusion. I can't handle not knowing. I've been—I've been in charge for so long. I've been strong and decisive. Made the hard decisions, for myself and for Tommy. All alone, making this farm work." I'm enjoying this far too much, and I simply cannot move away from his touch. No matter how much I know I should, especially considering what I'm saying at this very moment. "I can't be in charge of this, too. I don't *know* what I want. I don't know what's right or wrong, and I don't even know how to decide."

"You need me to be strong for you. You deserve that." He pauses for a long moment. "You also deserve honesty, so I'll tell you I'm just not sure I have that. I don't know what's right or wrong any more than you do. Less, maybe. You've got me tripping on my own hormones, desires, and needs, and I'm not sure I've got what it takes to…I don't even know. Either give you what you need and deserve, or walk away. I don't know what this is, and I don't know what to do about it."

"Derek—"

He keeps going. "And you deserve better than that." Long sigh. "Better than a fucked-up mess like me."

Women find confidence attractive. That's a fact. And I'm no different. But there's also something about vulnerability, and something about the kind of strength it takes to admit to vulnerability.

He sits up, and I'm forced out of the shelter of his arms. What does it say about me that I don't want to leave this place, this moment? I don't want to leave the rain and the pond and the man beside me.

"Where are you going?" I ask.

He draws his knees up, wraps his arms around them. My traitorous eyes follow the broad lines and curves of his shoulders; my fingers touch each of the hundred tiny cuts and scars that crisscross his back.

"One of the first things you learn in rifle school is that if you can't pull the trigger, you have no business holding the weapon. When it comes to combat, that lesson is vital. And…somehow, right now, that lesson feels like it applies to what's going on between us. Does that make any sense to you? I don't know how to say it any better."

I sit up, cross-legged, wrap my arms around my torso. "Yeah, it does, I think."

"I'm not...how do I put it? I'm not pushing you away. I'm not making a decision. I think we each just need to figure out what we're thinking and feeling and what we want and what this is." He stands up, and my eyes follow the shifting of his buttocks, the ripple of his back muscles. He turns slightly, and my gaze is drawn to his dick, long and thick and dangling, swinging. He blows out a breath. "Fuck me, Reagan. How am I supposed to think straight when you look at me like that?"

I rip my gaze away. I stand up. "I'm sorry. I just— you're beautiful, too, Derek. You are."

He shakes his head, grins ruefully. "Put some clothes on. Go home and get some sleep."

I cover my breasts with my palms, take one last long lingering look at Derek, at his body, at the obvious war in his eyes, and then make myself turn away. I ignore the prickling heat of his gaze following the sway of my butt. Pretend I'm not putting more lilt into my walk just for him. Face away from him as I stand on the dock, step into jeans and my T-shirt, gather up my bra, underwear, and shoes and socks.

Don't look back. Don't look back. I make myself walk away, heart hammering. My body wants me to drop the garments from my arms, race back, crush myself to Derek and take his tongue into my mouth, taste the salt on his jaw and feel the rasp of his stubble, demand his hands everywhere. My soul aches, swells. Confused, emotionally fraught, full of things I never thought I'd feel again: wonder, need, desire, passion, tenderness. Things I thought had died with Tom. Things my heart and mind keep telling me *did* die with Tom. And, as I cross through the grass and enter the kitchen through the back door, I recognize the conflict within myself. Those things truly did die with my husband. I buried them when I took the folded flag. Each cracking report of the twenty-one-gun salute buried them deeper and deeper. And my conscience tells me they should stay buried with him. Yet my body and heart and mind tell me other things, feed me conflicting reports. This is new, right? I'm not pretending like my love for Tom is the same thing as I'm feeling for Derek.

I'm allowed to move on, right?

Or is that a betrayal of my love for Tom, my husband, the father of my sweet, perfect son?

I vowed to love and remain faithful to Tom in sickness and in health, till death do us part.

Well, death parted us.

Now what?

CHAPTER 10

Derek

I DON'T SLEEP THAT NIGHT. NOT A WINK. EVERY TIME I close my eyes, I see Reagan, stripping. I feel her body sliding wet and soft and warm against mine. I taste the sweetness of her lips. Feel the silk of her breast in my hand. Even silk isn't so soft, so delicate, so lush and lovely as her skin.

I close my eyes, and I hear her sobbing, broken and miserable and confused.

I close my eyes, and I feel her core throbbing against me, feel the dampness of her opening and the strength of her thighs as they wrap around my waist.

I close my eyes, and my heart thuds crazily. My body aches. My cock throbs, pulses, hurts.

Hours before dawn, I find myself stumbling out of the barn into the dew-damp cool, jeans pulled on but not zipped or buttoned. I'm gasping for breath, chest aching, heart pounding. Visions of Reagan in my head. My body is on fire. I round the back of the barn, plant my hands against the wood wall of the barn, head dangling between my shoulders. Trying to banish the thoughts of Reagan, the image of her trim waist and full tits, the warm heat of her mouth on mine, the sound of her breath.

I can't.

The images coruscate in my mind, and I'm a raging ball of need, of pent-up desire.

I lick my lips and taste her skin. Close my eyes and see the need in her expression. I tug my dick free of my pants and clutch the painfully hard length in my fist. Stroke slowly, eyes closed, forehead to the barn. I picture Reagan standing on the dock, back arched, tits thrust out as she stretches. Picture her as she walked away, taut, round ass swinging. Feel again her legs around my waist, hands circling my back and finger-nails scratching my ass.

Heat builds in my groin, urgency.

I'm a few short seconds from letting go when I hear a footstep behind me.

"Derek?" Her voice is timid, hesitant.

Reagan

I can't sleep. Guilt and need war within me. I ache. Derek's body is all I can think of. His muscles. His firm skin. His mouth on my chest, his palm cupping my breast. His cock, so big, so thick and hard and pressing against me. I can't sleep for thinking of him.

I pull on a pair of boxer shorts—Tom's, claimed as comfy lounge wear years and years ago—and a T-shirt. I check on Tommy, who's lying sideways across his bed and snoring, Buzz on the floor. Tiptoe outside, barefoot in the dew-damp grass, to the barn. I find Derek's spot empty, blankets rumpled as if lain in and abandoned. Check the rest of the barn, but I don't find him. Exit, circle around to the back, wondering where he could've gone. Rounding the back of the barn, I call his name quietly. I don't know what I'm looking for, what I think I'll say or do when I find him, I just know I'm driven by something deep inside me.

I stop dead in my tracks when I see him. He's leaning against the barn, jeans open, cock in his hand. His posture is tortured, hunched, tense. His fist is moving on his length, and he's growling under his breath. He halts when he hears my voice.

His eyes meet mine. Neither of us moves. My gaze travels, against my conscious will, down to the open "V" of his jeans, to his thick, straining cock. Fluid is beaded on the tip. He was about to come. My body is somehow moving toward him. I don't know what I'm doing. What's happening. He straightens, hands reaching for the button of his pants.

"Reagan, I—"

What am I doing? What the hell am I doing?

I'm reaching for him, that's what. Not taking my eyes off his, my fingers close around his cock. He gasps, his eyelids flutter. He groans.

"Jesus Christ, Reagan." His words are pitched so low I can barely hear him.

I slide my fist down his length, and he shudders all over.

"I was thinking of you," he admits. "I was jerking off, thinking of you. You're so fucking beautiful, so fucking perfect, I can't handle it. Can't — oh Jesus, oh, fucking hell, that feels good — I can't stop thinking about you. I haven't slept at all, because I keep feeling you, thinking of you. Fuck…I keep wanting you."

Slowly, I plunge my fist around him, lifting, twisting my palm around his tip, sliding back down. He pounds a fist against the barn with a dull thud.

He was thinking of me? He couldn't stop thinking about me? He was masturbating…to me? Why the hell is that such a turn-on?

"Tell me…." I whisper, pausing, my fist clenched around the root of him. "Tell me what you were thinking."

"Your legs, around my waist. Your tits. How you tasted. The way your lips felt when we kissed. How— how wet and hot your pussy felt against me." He growls deep in his chest. He moves, and I'm pressed back against the wall of the barn. "Your ass. Your eyes. The way your hands felt when you touched my ass."

"I was thinking of you, too." I lean into him, eyes closed, press my lips to his cheek, whisper in his ear. I squeeze his cock. "Of this." I place my other hand around his body and slip it under his jeans, raking his ass with my nails. "Of this."

"God, Reagan...."

I stroke him once, slowly, tip to root. "I don't know anything. I don't know — right or wrong, good or bad — I just know I couldn't sleep, either, because I couldn't stop thinking of you. I ache all over."

"Me too. Everything is on fire." His palm touches my stomach, over my shirt.

His fingers lift the hem, find my skin. I suck in my belly instinctively as his fingertips slide down. Under the elastic of the boxers. Through the thick thatch of my pubic hair. I've had no reason to trim there, not for a long time. He seems unaware or uncaring, so I hold in my apology for another time. I whimper as his long middle finger carves a path between the lips of my vagina, then curls in. A desperate breath as he drags his finger in a circle around my clit. My knees are weak, my lungs shaky and shuddering. His touch is fire; his touch is perfect. I'm kindling, and the catalytic heat of his touch ignites me. I stroke his length, gasping as he draws faster and faster circles around my throbbing clit. I suck in a whining whimper when he slicks a single finger into me, deep. Then adds a second.

Clouds part, and moonlight shines bright silver.

A frog trills.

Derek groans in my ear.

His cock pulsates in my fist, and I feel his hips drive, thrusting his girth through my grip. I wrench my eyes open and look down between our bodies. See his hand between my thighs, fingers moving, forearm muscles rippling as he caresses me into paroxysms. I can't help but moan, both at the feelings he's drawing from me and the way his iron-hard straining cock feels in my hand, soft yet hard, sliding through and pulling back as he starts to thrust unconsciously. I watch the pre-come bead on his head, smeared into my hand. My thighs shake and tremble as his middle and ring fingers curve in and find the upper, inner ridge deep inside me and rub it, his thumb pressing against the rigid and juice-wet button of my clit. His moving fingers make a sucking noise that should be embarrassing but is somehow unbearably hot.

"Fuck, Reagan. Fuck. I'm so close. I'm gonna come. It's gonna be messy."

"Me—me, too."

His other hand leaves the barn wall, and he's thrusting up into my fist, off-balance and demanding and urgent. He reaches up under my shirt and finds my boob, cups it, kneads it. My turn. I reach into his jeans and palm his tight, heavy balls, squeeze gently. He groans and loses his balance, tipping forward, into me. I take his weight and let him press me up against the wall.

"Derek…oh, god, Derek."

"Right—right now. Ohhhhhh, oh, fuck. Oh, god." He thrusts, a slow grind.

I open my eyes, which I don't remember closing. I grip his cock tight and stroke hard and relish down to the darkest corners of my soul the way his dick feels in my hand. Fascinated, I watch as the tip of his cock squeezes up and out of my fist. He spasms, and a thick white stream of semen spurts over my hand. Cupping his head with my other hand, I stroke him root to tip hard and fast, watching the jizz seep out between my fingers, hot and sticky and wet as he gushes again and again, cursing, and whispering my name.

And through it all his fingers inside me never slow, never stop. He thrusts his fingers into me, pulls them out, smears my juices onto my clit and circles, circles, and while I'm watching him come into my hand, I'm right there at the edge, whimpering, hips fluttering. He shoves his fingers into me again, and somehow that draws it out of me. I bite my lip to muffle a shriek, lean my forehead against his chest, and watch his cock thrust, smear his come down his length and keep stroking him, feeling my thighs tense as a rocket of intensity shoots through me, every muscle spasming, another breathless scream leaving my lips. I thrust my hips at him, grinding my pussy against his fingers. Arch my spine to press my throbbing tit into his hand, my entire body writhing, his fingers twisting and pinching my nipples, palm cupping my core, heel against my pudendum, fingers inside me, ring finger against my taint, pinky and index finger buried in the flesh and muscle of my inner thighs, hand working and moving.

"Ohgodohgodohgod, Derek, yes, fuck, yes...*oh... god*...." My inner muscles clench and spasm, and something wet squirts out of me and over his hand.

He keeps going until I'm limp against him, batting his hand away because I can't take any more; I'm too sensitive to be touched.

"Jesus Christ, Reagan," he mumbles against my shoulder. "I've never come so hard in my life."

"Me, neither," I admit.

He removes his hand from between my legs, and I let him go as well. A little reluctantly Derek pulls me toward the water pump, gets a jet of water going. We weave our fingers together, my essence coating his hand, and his mine, smearing on our palms, merging. The well water is bitterly cold as he moves our joined hands under the stream, scrubbing us clean. I untangle my hand from his, get a palm full of water and splash it on his crotch, washing away the mess.

"God, that's cold," he laughs.

We're both sort of clean, although his jeans are damp where the water splashed onto them. My boxers are wet from the well water, too, and there's come on my shirt, and on his belly. I work the pump handle, get my hand wet, and wipe the streak of semen off his stomach.

A good few minutes after orgasm, and his cock is still semi-rigid and thick.

Derek backs away from me, tries to button his jeans, but they won't close around his still-fading erection. He abandons the effort, leaving them open. I honestly don't mind.

I dry my hands on my shirt, and look up to see him stalking toward me. I back away from him, unblinking, putting my hands on his chest. I don't push him away, though. God, no. My back to the wall, I stare into his eyes. He presses against me. Shameless in my need for contact, I lift my shirt so I can feel the warmth of his stomach and the still-thick but softening ridge of his penis against my belly. His hands brace against the wall on either side of my face.

His mouth descends, his lips slant across mine. I lift my palms to his jaw, hold him close and kiss him. Caress the back of his neck with one hand, tangling my fingers in the short, soft hair there. God, his kiss is drunk-making. Slow and tender and sweet and hesitant.

I feel him thickening. Already? Jesus. His kiss deepens, his tongue demands mine. I give it, willingly. Taste his tongue, his mouth. Scrape palms against the beard growing on his jaw. And then he breaks the kiss, breath shuddering, hands clenching into fists against the barn wall, pushing. But he can't seem to actually move away.

He's panting, chest heaving. Eyes shut. "You'd better go."

"Why?"

"Because if you don't…." His eyes open, and those deep, mossy pools drill into mine, piercing, rife with need and intensity and sincerity. "If you don't, I'm gonna take you up against this wall, right here, right now."

Not good. Not good. That should have me turning tail and going inside. But instead, it only makes my thighs quake and my core tighten and grow damp. I want that. Damn me, I want it.

"I came out here looking for you, Derek. I didn't expect…*this*…to happen, but like you said at the pond earlier, I'm not sorry it did."

"But Reagan, we shouldn't—" he begins.

I interrupt him, two fingers against his lips. "Derek, shush. I thought that, too. I think it still, in some ways. But I had some other thoughts, too, while trying and failing to sleep. I thought, 'why not?'. Why can't we, why *shouldn't* we? God, there are so many reasons, I know."

He smacks his fist against the wall, making me flinch, and rolls away, puts his back to the wall next to me. "What are your reasons?"

"I'm a widow. I'm—I'm still grieving. I still miss Tom. I still think about him. I still wish he were here. I'm sorry, Derek, I know that's not what you—"

"No, it's exactly what I think, too. I wish he were here, too. Every—every fucking day, I think that. I wish he were here instead of me. He didn't deserve to die. He should've—*fuck*—it should've been *me*." He shoves his fists into his eye sockets. "I miss him, too. Damn it—" He slides down the wall, shoulders shaking.

I pivot and kneel in front of him, taking his wrists in my hands, and pull. He resists. I pull harder.

"Look at me." I can't overpower him; I'm not trying.

He lets me tug his hands away from his face, but turns his head away to hide the fact that tears are slipping down his cheeks.

"Derek, no. No. *Look* at me, goddamn it!" He slowly, grudgingly turns to look at me, blinks, scrubs at his face angrily, embarrassed. I hold his wrists and lock eyes with him. His are bloodshot, tortured. "I don't wish that. I don't. Yes, I miss him. Every fucking day I miss him. I loved him. I *still* love him. I'll always love him. I wish he were here. But I don't wish that you'd died instead of him. Yes, I want him back. I'd give anything—*anything*—to have him back. But he's not—he's not coming back. You're here, and he's not."

"And I'm sorry for that."

"That's not what I meant."

"I know. But it's true. I'm sorry I lived and he died. I'm sorry I'm not him."

"Damn it, Derek! Stop it! You lived! You don't have to feel guilty about that!" I shout.

"But I do!" he shouts back. "Okay? I do. I feel really fucking guilty because I lived and Tom didn't. His last request was that I tell you he loved you, to give you that letter." He blinks, and another tear falls, brushed away. "And I did. I should've left. But I didn't, and look what's just happened? Look what I just did."

"*We*, Derek. Look what *we* just did. It wasn't just you. I came out here, and I touched you first. And, yeah, part of me feels guilty." He winces, but I keep going. "I'm so torn, so confused. Because I—I *want* this. I want *you*. I can't help it. Part of me says I shouldn't, part of me says this is…wrong. I feel like I'm betraying Tom. Like what we just did together is a betrayal of his memory. It's as if wanting you now that he's dead is cheating, or…god, I don't know…like it's making less of what I had with Tom. And I feel guilty, too, for not feeling guilty enough. Because I'm still not sorry. I enjoyed it. You said it earlier: just now, I felt more alive than I have in so, *so* long. And I want it again. I want *more*. I want to touch you again. I want you to touch me again. I want to kiss you and—fuck it, I'll say it—I want to have sex with you. When you said you were about to take me up against the wall? I wouldn't have stopped you. Because the other part of me says that Tom is gone. He's gone. And don't I—don't I deserve happiness? Am I supposed to mourn him forever? I'm *lonely*, Derek! I've been lonely for eleven fucking years! I married a Marine, and he was gone more than he was home for the eight years we were married, and I've been even more lonely since he went missing and died, because I knew he wasn't coming home this time. I was faithful to him, Derek. Every day he was gone, I loved him, and I was faithful. I stayed true to him, and welcomed him home and never made him feel guilty for always having to leave. I loved him with all that I had for *eight years*, even though he was gone all the time, and then he was fucking *taken* from me!"

I sob, choke it down.

"He was taken from me," I say again. "And I mourned him. For three years I grieved. I kept going, and I raised his son. Ran his family's farm by myself. Did everything I was supposed to, and more."

"Reagan—" he begins.

I talk right over him. "When do I get something for *me?* When do I get happiness? When do I get to be selfish? I'm angry, Derek. I'm angry at Tom for dying. And I'd be lying if I said I hadn't felt angry at you, too, for living instead of him. But I can't change what happened. You lived, and he died, and I'm left to pick up the pieces. And I'm lonely. I'm horny. I'm scared. I'm tired. I feel old and frumpy and ugly. I'm sweaty all the time. I haven't put on makeup in months. I barely ever even shave my legs because there's been no reason. There's no one to see, no one to care. The only TV I watch are kids' shows. And I'm usually too tired at night to even masturbate. Until you came along, I felt dried up. Empty. Alone." I swallow hard, blink. I let go of his wrists and sink to my butt in the damp grass.

"And then you—you started making me feel like a woman again. And I—I *like* it. Even if it is a betrayal of Tom, and that just makes me feel worse. Because I just keep asking myself, 'Why can't I have something for myself, just this once?' And you—you make me feel so good. You look at me like I'm beautiful, and I *really* like feeling beautiful again. I like it," I whisper, struggling for control now myself, "and I don't want to give it up."

"You *are* beautiful, and you don't have to give it up. You aren't alone." It's his turn to take my hands in his, pull at them. Pulls me toward him, lifts, and I'm on his lap, cradled against his chest as dawn begins to touch the night sky with gray. "I like the way you make me feel, too. Like I'm a real man again. Like I'm more than just the soldier with scars and PTSD and a sackload of psychological damage. Like I'm more than just the fucked-up ex-P-O-W. Like I'm someone who can do something right. Like I can make you feel good, like I have something to give. Like maybe I can overcome my issues and be normal someday. Like— shit. Like I could be someone somebody could— could care about."

My heart breaks for him.

"Someone already does care, Derek." I say it through sniffles.

As fraught and tense as things are between us, I find myself drowsing. His skin is warm, and his arms make me feel protected. I nod off, then jerk awake when I hear the screen door creak. Somehow, while I was sleeping, Derek carried me to the house.

"Derek?" I mumble.

"Sshh. Sleep."

"Tommy—"

"I'll take care of everything. I want you to rest."

He carries me upstairs, nudges my door open. Sets me in my bed and covers me with the blankets. I feel his breath on my cheek, and I blink my eyes open, grab at him. "I care. I'm the someone."

He smiles. "I know."

"And you're beautiful, too."

I can't stay awake anymore. I should. He doesn't know anything about kids, and Tommy will need breakfast and the tractor is hard to start and....

Sleep claims me. I surrender.

CHAPTER 11
Derek

I SET HER DOWN AND COVER HER WITH THE BLANKETS.
Watch her fall into slumber. Watch her features relax.
She curls her hand by her cheek, mouth slack, knees
drawn up beneath the blanket. I should go. Leave the
room. Leave Hempstead. Leave Texas. But I don't.
Instead, I take a seat on the floor in the doorway, one
foot propped up against the opposite post, watching
Reagan sleep.

I'm woken up by a finger tapping my shoulder. I
start, jerk awake. Tommy. "Hey, buddy. What's up?"

"Mama?"

I stand up. "Mama is sleeping, bud."

He glances past me, at Reagan. God, I shouldn't
have followed his gaze. Her T-shirt is hiked up; she's
twisted in the bed with the blankets shoved down

around her knees. I'm afforded a delicious glimpse of underboob, waist, the angular beauty of her hipbone. God, so fucking beautiful. I turn away, back to Tommy.

"I hungry," he says.

I nod. "You're hungry, huh?"

"Yeah."

"Me, too. Let's eat, then." I head down the stairs, but he doesn't follow, so I stop and look back at him. "You comin'?"

"Uppy." He extends his arms.

I hesitate, then pick him up like last time. He clings to me with his legs, one arm on my shoulder. So weird, me holding a kid. I don't know jack shit about kids or this little guy in particular. Nonetheless, I told Reagan I'd take care of it, so I will. I mean, it's one three-year-old for a couple of hours. How hard can it be?

"So," I ask him, "what do little snots like you eat for breakfast, huh? Cheerios?"

"Can-cakes."

I just stare at him. "Can-cakes? What the hell does that mean?"

"Can-cakes. See-up."

I take a guess. "Pancakes and syrup?"

He grins. "Can-cakes! See-up!"

I frown. "Dude, I ain't made pancakes in fifteen years." He seems to be catching my drift, because his face screws up like he's gonna cry. I hold up my hands. "All right, all right. I'll do my best. Hang on, give me a minute."

He sits in his little booster that's strapped to the kitchen chair, wiggling his little butt. I spy a cookbook on a shelf above the stove, and flip through it. I find a recipe for pancakes and discover that, amazingly, and perhaps not surprisingly, the kitchen is stocked with all of the ingredients. Plus coffee, which allows me to actually function on three hours of sleep.

And, amazingly, I actually manage to get the batter put together, a griddle heated, and some pancakes made. They're about two inches thick, just this side of burnt, and enormous. Tommy doesn't seem to care, though. I slather the flapjack liberally with butter and syrup, cut it up in pieces, and hand him a fork.

Holy shit, that kid can eat. And holy shit, that kid can make a godawful mess.

He's got butter in his hair, all over his PJs, on his hands...syrup is literally everywhere. I suppose, in retrospect, I probably should've helped him eat it, but I didn't think of it. Besides, I was hungry too.

I find a box of wipes under the sink in the half bath, and I use at least half of the box cleaning him up, and another half of a roll of paper towels and a bottle of Windex cleaning the mess off the table, the chair, the booster seat, the floor. Eventually, things are clean...ish.

I look at Tommy, who is sitting on the floor smashing a Tonka truck into a white, red, and green airplane that has eyes and a mouth and is wearing a cape. Weird.

"Okay, dude. Now what?"

He hands the plane to me. "Play."

So I sit and play. And you know what? It's kinda fun. I make airplane noises, fly it around. I make it do Cuban eights and make machine-gun noises. Tommy giggles, so I do it again. And damn, the sound of that kid laughing hits me in some part of my heart that I didn't know I had.

Reagan

I wake up smelling pancakes and coffee, and the sound of Tommy giggling hysterically. I get out of bed, change clothes, tie my hair back, and put on some deodorant. As I head downstairs, I stop halfway down, before I'm easily visible. I see something that brings tears in my eyes, and leaves my heart clenching in a really, really weird and scary way.

Derek is sitting on the floor, a cup of coffee within reach. He's got Tommy's El Chupacabra toy, and he's pretending it's a dog, barking at Tommy, chasing him around the kitchen.

Tommy has butter in his hair.

His pull-up is on backward.

He's happier than I've ever seen him.

The front door is open, and Ida is standing on the porch, watching, and she seems as stunned as I am, her hand across her mouth, eyes wide. Her gaze meets mine, and we exchange stupefied, emotional expressions.

This just made everything that much more impossible to figure out.

CHAPTER 12

Derek

LATE ONE NIGHT I'M WORKING ON THE TRACTOR, replacing the starter. I'm no mechanic, but I can figure shit out with enough time and cursing. Three days have gone by since that night at the pond—and behind the barn. Jesus, I can't get that out of my head. The sounds she made as she came. The feel of her fist around my dick....

I get hard just thinking about it.

But there haven't been any repeats since then. We've been...not quite avoiding each other, but taking a little time and space. It's remained unspoken, but we both needed it. We also both need time and space to absorb what happened, and to understand what it could mean. What's going to happen in the future.

All I know for sure is, I can't stop thinking about her. Not just about her naked, fucking glorious body, or about making her come. Yeah, I think about that nonstop, 'cause, duh. But about what she said that night. How she wants something for her. And I want to do something for *her*—something to make her happy, just for her.

So after the tractor is fixed, I walk over to Hank's. He's sitting on his porch, sipping at a Natty Ice, reading a battered, dog-eared Tom Clancy novel.

"Hank?"

He looks up, nods at me. "Derek. What can I do for you, son?"

"Reagan. She's here all the time. I thought…I wondered if you think she might want to take a day off. Do some sort of girly day-out kinda shit." I swallow hard and shift from foot to foot. I'm playing my hand here. I look him straight in the eye and let him read me. "I don't know anything about that shit. So, I kinda need help, I guess."

Hank just stares at me for a long time. "Growin' a heart in there, are ya?" He chuckles. "About damn time."

I shrug. "Guess so. Any ideas?"

"Women, they like to get their hair done. Manicures, pedicures. That kinda thing."

The screen door squeaks and bangs, open and closed, and Ida comes through with two beers. She hands one to me, but I wave it off. After the incident at the barn, I haven't wanted to drink again. That scared me.

"Linda from church," Ida says, "her daughter owns a day spa up to Brenham. I can ask about a gift certificate for a pampering package."

"How much?" I ask.

Hank and Ida exchange looks, and Hank nods. Ida smiles, saying, "Don't worry about that."

"I couldn't ask you to—"

"You ain't askin', son. We're offering. Just say thanks and get on with you."

You don't argue with a man like Hank. "Thanks, then."

"I'll call Linda in the morning," Ida says.

I head back to the barn. Sleep is getting a little easier. The nightmares still wake me up most nights, but they're starting to fade. They never lose their potency, but I'm learning to deal with them. Wake up, breathe. Do pushups, sit-ups, squats, lunges. I get back to sleep eventually.

I spend the earliest hours of the next morning replacing the ladder up to the hayloft. Ida finds me in the barn and calls out to me. I descend, wiping the sweat off my face.

She hands me an envelope. "This is the gift certificate. It's for a haircut and color, a manicure and pedicure, and a facial. She'll enjoy it, I think. I know

I would." She smiles at me, pats the top of my hand. "This is a sweet gesture, Derek."

"She deserves a day off," is all I can think to say.

"She sure does."

It's late evening before I finish the various projects I've got going. I'm washing up at the pump when I hear Reagan behind me.

"Would you eat with us? Tommy and me? I made lasagne."

I swallow hard. Shrug. "Sure."

Dinner is a weird thing. I don't know what to say, or how to act around Reagan. Tommy provides most of the conversation, chattering at me and smearing lasagne everywhere. I allow myself one small half-glass of red wine, which makes me feel warm and loose. Tommy nods off right onto his plate, making us both laugh. Reagan wipes his hands and face, and then carries him up to bed.

While she's gone, I clean up. Cover the leftovers with foil, wash the plates in the sink. Dry them, put them in the cupboard.

Reagan comes back into the kitchen. "You didn't have to clean up."

I shrug, drying the forks. "You cooked. You shouldn't have to clean up, too."

She sits at the table, sideways on the chair, facing me. "So, I was wondering if tomorrow you'd mind helping me in Tommy's room? It's still decorated for a baby, and I want to paint it. Update it a little for him."

I pivot and put my backside to the sink, pull the envelope containing the gift certificate out of my back pocket. "I'll handle that tomorrow myself. In fact, I'll take care of the rest, too."

She's confused. "What? Why?"

I hand her the envelope. "'Cause you won't be here."

She opens it, reads the gift certificate. "What is this? I don't understand."

"It's a day off, Reagan. Sleep in late. Head into Brenham and spend the day at the salon. Sit in the park and read a book. Whatever it is you feel like doing." I'm nervous, talking too fast.

She doesn't say anything for a long minute. "Derek, you didn't have to—I don't need—"

"The gift certificate and day off was my idea, but Ida and Hank...Ida's friend Linda's daughter owns the salon." I rub my upper lip and try to sound casual. "You deserve a day off. Hell, you deserve a fuckuva lot more than that, but this is what I could make happen. You work too hard. And you deserve something just for you."

She won't look at me, staring down at the gift certificate, at her feet. "Derek, I don't even know what to say." She glances at me, then away, clearly struggling against emotion. "It's too much. I wouldn't know what to do with myself for a whole day."

"I'm sure you'll figure something out." I point at the envelope. "I don't know if it says so on there, but Ida told me that'll get you your hair cut and colored, plus your fingernails and toenails done. And something else. For your face. A facial, maybe? Just have fun. Relax a bit."

She's still for another moment, and then she launches herself at me. Arms around my neck, body flush against mine. We both hold on to each other, a tense, passionate hug. And then she sinks against me, the tension bleeding out of the embrace. And now I'm just holding her. She's soft, warm, smells of hay and horse and feminine sweat. I inhale her scent, memorize the feel of her in my arms.

She pulls back just slightly, staring into my eyes. Her palm splays across the back of my head, her other hand clutching my neck. A moment passes, another. And then she tilts her face, presses her mouth to mine and leans into me. Her boobs are crushed against my chest, her hands pulling me closer and closer to her, as if she can't get close enough. At first I manage to keep my arms across her waist, in the safe zone. But then she parts my lips with her tongue, and one of my hands slips down, cupping the swell of her ass.

She moans, a murmured outbreath, and my other hand joins the first, and I've got the firm, perfect feel of her round ass in my hands. I've dreamed of this ass—dreamed of feeling it in my hands. I've woken up hard and aching and wishing for this perfect ass. Somehow I'm exploring the fullness of it, squeezing, kneading. I'm amazed that she's letting me do this, here in her kitchen. Her palms slide down my shoulders, down my chest. Our kiss breaks, and she lets out a sigh, curling her fingers into fists in the fabric of my shirt, either to hold me in place as if I'll try to get away, or to maintain her own balance.

"I only meant to kiss you to say thank you," she whispers, her breath huffing on my lips. "But now I can't stop."

"I dreamed about you the other night." I'm not sure why I'm saying this, or what I hope to accomplish. My mouth seems to be working independent of my brain. "About your ass."

She laughs, leans her head against my shoulder. "You dreamed about my butt?"

"Maybe. Yes. It's so perfect. I've been wanting to feel it. I dreamed about…well, this, basically. Kissing you. Making out with you, and getting my hands on this." I squeeze, lifting the bubble of muscle and flesh.

"Well, you've got it now. Is it…does it live up to your expectations?" She sounds hesitant. Unsure.

"It shatters my expectations," I say, truthfully. "It's beyond perfect. I don't want to let go."

"Really?"

I glance at her. "Why do you sound surprised?"

She shakes her head. "I don't want to talk about my stupid insecurities right now. It'll ruin the moment. I just want to kiss you again."

Stupid insecurities? What is she talking about? I don't get it. But I let it go, slide my lips over hers, teasing her mouth with mine, pulling away when she leans in to deepen the kiss, darting close to nip at her lower lip. She unclenches her fists, slips her hands around my back, tugs up the hem of my shirt and connects with my skin. Skims her palms up my back, mashing her lips to mine and demanding more of my mouth, my tongue. She rakes her nails along my spine, then flattens her palms and wedges her hands under my jeans, against bare skin.

She sucks my tongue into her mouth, clutches my ass with clawed fingers, moans into my mouth. I need more. I lift her light frame, sliding her up my body. She clings to me, her legs encircling my waist, her arms around my neck. One arm holds onto me for balance; the other palm goes to my cheek. My hands have ideas of their own, one palming her butt, the other going up under her shirt, grazing her flat stomach, cupping her breast over her bra. Tongues tangle, we break for breath, mouths merge once again. I've got the tail of her T-shirt in my fist, dragging it up. She tugs her head free, presses her body against mine, hands roaming my shoulders and chest. She rips off my shirt.

I release the hooks on her bra, a breath, two, and she's topless in my arms, her hot flesh sliding across mine.

Holding her, I walk into the den, then set her on the couch. I crawl over the arm to kneel with my knee between her thighs, one foot on the floor. With my palm on her side, I slide my hand up her ribs. Her tit fills my hand, just barely more than a handful. Softer than anything I've ever felt.

I taste the salt of her skin behind her ear, on her throat, down the slope of her breast. Her nipple slides between my teeth, and she's moaning, arching her back. Clutching the back of my head with one hand, roaming my back with the other. Reaching between our bodies, she finds my zipper. Buttons are unsnapped. God, god, her hand is warm and small around my achingly hard dick. Sliding so slow and deliberate, making me crazy. So hard I'm leaking, moments from coming already—just like a damned teenager. Her perfect tit is in my mouth, and her hand is caressing my cock, her breath moaning in my ear.

A floorboard creaks above our heads. Reagan stills. "Wait. Wait." She places both palms to my chest.

Silence.

But then she looks at me. "We keep getting carried away."

I lean back, and she sits up, but doesn't cover herself. "Yeah, we do," I say. "One taste of you, and I just…can't stop."

"Me, too." She's wearing jeans with a hole above one knee and she picks at the frayed white threads. "I like getting carried away with you. I do. But I'm not—I'm not on birth control. And I don't have any protection. So we can't let it go too far. No accidents."

I run my hand through my hair. "God, you're right. I haven't even been thinking of that." I touch her knee through the hole in the denim. "Is this what you want? With me? I don't want to just get carried away. I don't want it to be an accident. I don't want you to feel guilty. Or to regret it."

I can't help letting my eyes roam from her face down to her boobs. She follows my gaze, looks down at her own chest and cringes. She covers herself. Stands up, rounds the end of the couch, and finds her clothes, faces away, pulls a shirt on braless. I fasten my pants, move up behind her.

"Did I say something wrong?"

She shakes her head. "It was dark before. We were caught up in the moment. Sometimes I feel okay about myself. But now, with the lights on, you looking at me? All I can think about is that my tits aren't as high or firm as they used to be. They sag. I've got stretch marks on them, and on my belly from carrying Tommy."

"I just see you." I'm behind her, holding onto her arms. "You're beautiful, Reagan. In the light, in the darkness. All the time."

She shrugs. "Thanks. You're sweet." She turns, looking up into my eyes. "I hate feeling like I have to make a decision about this. I want to be able to just… let what happens, happen. I want to give in and not think about it. But I can't. I have Tommy to think about. I want you, Derek. I—I *need* this with you. It's been so long since I felt the way you make me feel. You make me forget the stretch marks and the stress and the loneliness. But…what about Tommy? What if he gets attached to you? How long will you stay? What will I tell him? You can't just live in my barn. If we did this, if we…I don't even know how to say it. If we fuck…if we make love, whatever phrase you want to use, if we do that—*I'll* get attached. I'll want you in here. With me. In my bed. And what if you don't stay? I can't take another heartbreak. Not yet. Maybe some-day I'll be strong enough to risk getting hurt again. But I'm scared. Because you're…you're a soldier. What if you change your mind about going back? What if they make you? I couldn't send another soldier off to war. I couldn't. I won't. And what if—what if we do this and I'm not good enough? What if I don't satisfy you? What if a woman with a kid isn't what you want? I've been thinking about this nonstop. Over and over and over. What if, what if, what if…."

"Reagan, I—"

"You could say anything right now. Reassure me. You'd mean it, too, I'm sure. But you could change your mind. Things change. Feelings change. And yeah, I want you. You want me. We have this insane chemistry, and you make me feel things…such amazing things. And I want more. I want all of it. But I'm scared, Derek. I'm scared of feeling guilty. And—it's been so long since…my last time, with Tom. I'm sorry to bring him into this right now, but you need to know what I'm feeling. It's been so long since my last time with Tom, I barely remember it. I'm forgetting him, Derek. And that scares me. It hurts. What he looks like, what he felt like. What *we* felt like. And I'm scared that if I keep letting this happen with you, that it'll—it'll be better. Than before…than with him. And what would that say about me? He was the love of my life, Derek! I loved him…so—*fuck*." She sucks in a sharp breath, an almost-sob. "I loved him so much. And I don't want to feel like I didn't. It's so damned complicated, and when I think about it, try to figure it out, I just get more confused and mixed up. I think sometimes maybe you should just go, because then things would go back to the way they were. The farm, Tommy, Hank, and Ida. Tommy would grow up, I'd get old, the end. But I…I don't *want* that. The way things were sucked. I think about you going, and something inside me just…resists it. I don't like it.

And when I'm with you, not even doing anything, just being *around* you, it's easy to feel like…like it would be okay. Like it could work out."

I stay silent, let her think, let her talk. Absorb.

She tugs at the hem of her shirt, making the outline of the tips of her breasts and her nipples stand out. I can't help looking once, and then return my gaze to her face. She searches my eyes. "I wish I could be the kind of girl who can do casual sex. It'd make this easier. I want you. I'm crazy with wanting you. But I can't do casual. I just can't."

"Can I say a couple of things?" She nods at me, and I take a moment to breathe deep, let it out, formulate what I want to say. "I can't give you some reassuring speech about how to deal with grief. I don't know what to say about that. I'm fucked up over it, too, honestly. Losing Tom, losing—shit—watching twelve of my buddies get fucking slaughtered. Watching Tom die. Being a prisoner of war. It fucked me up. I may never be normal again. So…I don't have any reassurances about forgetting him. Because I can only remember him the way he was at the end. And that—it blows, Reagan. I'm glad you don't have that. I'd be happy if I *could* forget him. Sometimes, I think, you just have to…accept that you're gonna feel like shit. You miss him. You forget him sometimes. I want to think that's natural. It's your heart healing, your mind helping you past the hurt. I don't know. I know none of that is making you feel any better, and I'm sorry. But I know you loved Tom. He knew you loved him. But I want to think that Tom would want you to find…peace. Happiness. He wouldn't want you to be alone, or to suffer. Or to be miserable."

I have to pause and gather my thoughts. Sometimes you just have to put it all out there, good or bad.

"I know you've got a lot to think about, as far as this thing between us goes. It's complicated. It's not just sex. You said you can't do casual…well, neither can I. I used to. A lot, actually. It's all I did. I wasn't really a very great guy in that regard. I chased tail, and I got a lot of it. But it was all casual. I never got close to any of them. I mean, how could I? I'd have a couple of weeks, maybe a month. I told myself it wouldn't be fair to the girl to act like it meant anything but fun. Why start something I couldn't finish, right? But I'm not that same guy anymore. I'm a fucking mess, Reagan. I've got damage. Baggage. Nightmares, survivor's guilt, all sorts of complex psychological bullshit. And how could I ever saddle anyone with all that? I could go somewhere and probably get a girl to take me back to her place, but as soon as she saw my scars, as soon as she wanted to make small talk, I guarantee you most girls would run screaming. I couldn't tell some innocent little hipster city chick who's never left Houston about being tortured by the fucking Taliban. I couldn't tell her why I still wake up in the middle of the night crying and screaming. She wouldn't get it. How could she? I'm too messed up to play the games I used to play. So…I can't do casual, either."

Silence again.

Reagan opens her mouth to speak, but closes it again. She looks at me in the eyes and sighs. "I have to ask you something, Derek. And I…I need an answer. It's about the letter."

Fuck. My hands are shaking. I turn away and pace the length of the kitchen. Sink into a chair, elbows on my knees, head hanging. "That letter kept me sane. I read it to him so many times I had it memorized. I still do. I think…I think I started to feel like—not like it was meant for me, but…I don't know. Something about how much you loved him, how obvious it was in the letter, it gave me hope. I would…not read it, but say it to myself. Recite it, I guess. After Tom died, when I was cold and hungry, after they kicked the shit out of me, or broke my finger or whatever. That letter kept me going, over and over and over again."

I look at her, keep my eyes on hers, unblinking. "*Thomas, my love,*" I say. The words come easily. "*I'm writing this in our bed. You're lying next to me, sleeping. There's so much I wish I could say to you, but I know time is short. You ship out tomorrow. Again. I can't say it doesn't bother me. It does. Of course it does. It hurts every time. I act brave for you, but I hate it. I hate watching you lace up your boots. I hate watching you pack your bag. I hate watching you straighten your tie in the mirror. I hate how goddamned sexy you look in your uniform. Most of all, I hate kissing you goodbye, hate watching you turn around, your broad back straight as you disappear down the jetway. I hate that your eyes are dry when mine are wet.*

"*I hate all that. I know I signed up for it when I married a Marine. I knew from the very beginning that you'd go into combat. I knew it, and married you anyway. How could I not? I loved you so much from the very beginning, from the first time I saw you, all those years ago.*"

Reagan is crying silently, staring at me. Neither of us looks away. She covers her mouth with her hands.

I continue: "*You remember? I was visiting my brother at Twentynine Palms, and I saw you running with your unit. You looked right at me, and I knew in that very instant that we were going to be together forever. You dropped out of rank, ran over to me. You kissed me. Right there, the gunnery sergeant yelling at you, in front of half the damn base. You didn't even ask my name. You just kissed me, and rejoined your unit. You got in a lot of trouble for that stunt. But you found me. You knew my brother, who was walking with me at the time. You asked him who I was a few days later. He said he'd let you have a shot if I was willing, but if you broke my heart, he'd break your face. You showed up at my hotel room dressed in civvies. You took me to Olive*

Garden, and we got drunk on red wine. We made love that night in my hotel room. You remember that night? I do. I remember every single moment. Just like I remember every other moment of our lives together. Eight years. Did you know that? You ship out tomorrow, and tomorrow is the eight-year anniversary—to the day—of the first time we met, when you kissed me. God, Tom. You know why I remember every single moment? Because for most of our ten years together, you've been deployed. Three tours in Iraq, about to ship out for your third in Afghanistan. I miss you, Tom. Every day, I miss you. Even when you're home, I miss you, because I know you're always about to leave again. But this time? This ship-out? It's the hardest. So hard. I can't take it. Can't stand it. I can't, Tom. I can't watch you leave again, knowing you could die. You might not come back. You didn't tell me much of what happened with your friend from your unit, Hunter, when he went MIA, but I know it was painful for everyone. He came back, thank god, but you were a mess. You called me from the base. You were going crazy with worry. You thought he was dead. Your friend Derek was injured, too. I remember all that. And I just...I don't think I could handle it if that happened to you."

I stop. Swallow hard. Force the admission out. "I—every time I read Tom the letter, I stopped there. I skipped to the very end. Where you said you love him. I read the letter to myself first, before I read it to him. He could barely move, and he couldn't read it on his own. He was too weak. So I read it. And…when I saw" —my voice breaks— "when I read the news… about you being pregnant, I panicked. He was dying. I knew he was dying. He knew he was dying. And I just—I couldn't tell him. Every time I read the letter, every time I got to that part, I couldn't do it."

She's pale. Shaking. Eyes wide. "What? Derek, no. What are you saying?"

I squeeze my hands into fists. I say the hardest words I've ever spoken in my life. "Tom never knew. He died not knowing you…not knowing—" I clench my eyes shut. I can't finish.

"He—he didn't know?" She's whispering. Her voice is thin, reedy. "He didn't know about Tommy? He died…he—he didn't know he was a daddy?" Tears, fat wet drops sliding down her cheeks.

"Yeah." I can't look at her. "I'm sorry, Reagan. I just…couldn't."

"How could you?" A whisper at first. Then she's lunging at me. I'm standing, and she's hitting me, slapping me. "*How could you?* He was a father! He deserved to know! God…god…."

I catch her hands. "He was fucking DYING, Reagan!" I shout. "He had three bullets in his stomach. His stomach acid was eating his fucking flesh from the inside out. We were in a hut in the middle of nowhere, surrounded by Taliban. I was wounded. We were getting beaten every other day. It took him fucking *weeks* to die, and I had to watch! I watched my best fucking friend die. I held him in my goddamn arms and fed him my own food, what little bit they gave us. He'd pass out, and when he woke up, he'd ask for the letter. 'Read the letter, D. Read the letter, D. Derek, the letter.' He could barely speak toward the end. He was in so much pain, and all he could think of was you. If I'd told him you were pregnant…? He held onto that letter, unopened, for months. He carried it on dozens of patrols. It was like a good luck charm for him. If he'd just read—just read the goddamn letter… but he didn't. And I couldn't tell him. I was too much of a coward. I was too scared. Too hurt. Too weak. I couldn't handle how that would make him feel, when he couldn't do a damned thing about it. All he could do was die."

She's sobbing, bawling, collapsing onto the floor and covering her face with her hands. I kneel beside her, touch her shoulder, but she shoves at me. "Leave me alone! Just…please. I need to be alone."

"Okay." I stand up. Turn away. "I'm sorry, Reagan."

She ignores me, and I leave her there, crying on the floor of her kitchen.

CHAPTER 13

Reagan

THE HOUSE IS SILENT WHEN I WAKE UP THE NEXT morning. I glance at my alarm clock: 9:30 a.m. I haven't slept in this late…ever. I sobbed myself hoarse after Derek left. Crawled, literally crawled, up the stairs and into bed. I cried myself to sleep.

I push away the storm of thoughts and emotions raging inside me and tiptoe downstairs. There's a note on the kitchen table:

Reagan, dear.

Tommy is with me at my house. My granddaughters are over for a few days, so he's going to spend the day playing with us. Don't you worry about a thing. Go, have yourself a wonderful day.

Ida.

Oh. Right. My day off.

The envelope with the gift certificate is on the table. I head back upstairs, take a shower, brush my hair and shave my legs and underarms, trim myself in other places. Head outside into the hot early fall air. I hear noises from the barn and look up to see Derek, shirtless, on the roof of the barn, scraping at the roof. Shingles tumble to the ground and fall in a pile. Hank is there on the ground, giving orders to three of his older grandsons, who are shoveling the mess into a huge red dumpster and carrying square pallets of what I assume are new shingles up the ladder onto the roof. Derek sees me, stands up straight, leaning on the tool he's using to scrape at the shingles. Even from here, I can sense his turmoil. He doesn't wave; he just stares at me.

I can't deal with him right now. I just can't. So I wave. Hank, his grandsons, they all wave back. Derek just stares at me, and then goes back to scraping.

I blast the radio on the drive up to Brenham and refuse to think about anything. I find the salon easily, and an effusive red-haired woman a few years older than I am welcomes me. She introduces herself as Sandy and hands me a mimosa and helps me into a stylist chair, and starts chattering volubly without pausing for breath about my hair and how much fun I'm going to have. Her enthusiasm is infectious, and I'm soon laughing with her, telling her to do what she wants, just nothing crazy. Not too short, no weird colors. She waves me off and starts snipping. I watch as she clips a few inches off the bottom, leaving it just above my shoulders. After that, she goes through my hair again, adding layers and shape to it.

She says I don't need any color, that my natural honey blonde is just perfect the way it is. So I'm hustled to the manicure station, where I'm given the royal treatment. Hand massage, clip, file, painted a deep plum. Same for my toes. Then they give me a long, luxurious facial, leaving my skin tingling and feeling cleaner than ever.

Sandy looks me over and nods. "Lovely. Just lovely. But you still seem a little tense. Since it's so slow in here today, how about I throw in a massage? Lisa is just the best. She's got a light touch, but she can really get those tricky knots out."

"I've never had a massage before," I say. "I guess I—"

"Then it's settled. Right this way!"

The massage is probably the best thing I've ever felt. I'm jelly by the time Lisa is done, feeling more relaxed than I thought possible. I leave them as big a tip as I can afford, thank them, and leave. I find myself at a coffee shop, listening to quiet folksy music, sipping at a big mug of hot tea.

Thinking about Derek.

How angry I was. Rightfully, to my thinking. But then...I think about Derek, what he said in his defense. And I understand. It doesn't make it any easier, knowing that Tom never knew. That Derek intentionally kept it from him.

And then I think about how close I've come to having sex with Derek, three times now. How am I supposed to reconcile my wide extremes of emotion? Guilt, lust. Grief, need. Confusion and clarity.

Clarity?

I know for a fact that the next time I'm alone with Derek, there won't be any stopping us. I'm no clearer on my emotions, no clearer on how I'm supposed to reconcile the love I still feel for my dead Thomas with the need I feel for Derek. It's not just physical, although that plays a huge part of it. It's a need for a companion. A need to banish the loneliness. He's here, and he understands, as much as anyone on earth can, where I'm coming from emotionally and mentally. Just like I understand him and why he's drawn to me. He knows I know the toll combat takes on a man. He knows I'm strong enough to fathom what haunts him. He doesn't have to pretend to be fine around me, because I *know*.

But then all the what-ifs crop back up. Will I still get attached if Derek and I have sex? Hell, I'm already attached. And Tommy? What if this keeps going? I bring Derek into my bed, and Tommy finds him there in the morning? How do I explain that?

I huff in frustration. No matter how many times I go through this in my head, I get no closer to an answer. I want him, and I want to let myself go, let myself have it. I have a few moments of *it'll turn out fine*, but then all the what-ifs clamor in my head, and I start thinking I should end it.

But my heart and my body clench up at that thought.

I just don't know what to do.

I think about going home, but end up at the grocery store instead. Since I'm all the way out in Brenham, I might as well get some things while I'm here. I had my pampering, and it was nice. Now back to reality. I feel spoiled, though. I'm going to want that again.

I end up in the pharmacy section of the store, in front of the condoms. Looking. Knowing, if I get them, we'll use them. Probably a lot of them. But I'm no closer to knowing the right thing to do, so doesn't that mean I shouldn't let it happen? But then, who am I kidding? Unless I make him leave, it's going to happen anyway.

I grab the smallest box. I toss it into the cart, then stop and pick it back up. I find a bigger box.

I hear a voice from beside me, a woman about my age with a baby in a carrier in the front of the cart. "If you're not sure," she says with a grin, "it's probably best to get the *big* box." She grabs the largest box from the bottom shelf, tosses it into my cart, and sashays away, cooing at her baby.

She's probably right. I cash out, head home, stopping in Hempstead for a few boxes of pizza.

When I finally park the truck under the tree, I see that the roof of the barn is almost done, and Derek, Hank, and his three grandsons are all sitting on the front porch, drinking bottles of water. They are all sweaty and laughing. I hand them the four boxes of pizza, watching in amazement as the first box is emptied within seconds, the second vanishing not long after. I shake my head and laugh.

At least until I catch Derek's eye. He's watching me, and I can see that he's biding his time. Expecting something from me. A conversation? I don't know.

I start carting the groceries into the house and find Derek helping me. We get the dozen or so bags inside, and he starts putting them away.

"S'posed to be a day off," he points out.

I shrug. "It was, and it was amazing, actually, so thank you. But there was no reason to be out there and not pick up a few groceries while I was at it. We were getting low on a lot of things."

He stacks the cans of soup in the pantry, puts the bread away, the milk and juice. Pasta, pasta sauce. Eggs. He gets to the pharmacy bag and quickly sets my carton of tampons aside, along with the aspirin and toothpaste. He holds up the box of condoms, finds my eye. Just stares at me, curious.

I shrug. "Can we…can we talk about it later?"

He sighs. "I packed. I thought…after last night, what I told you—" He sets the box back in the bag, along with the other pharmacy items, and sets the bag aside. "I figured you'd want me to leave."

"I—"

Hank comes in at that moment, grandsons trailing behind him. "Well, that was a hell of a day's work, wasn't it, boys?" He slaps two of the boys on their backs. "Well, we'll be heading back now, Reagan. Thanks for the pizza—it really hit the spot. Derek, we'll see ya in the morning, finish that roof off."

Derek nods. "Thanks for the help, y'all. Made it a hell of a lot quicker."

Before I can grasp what's happening, Hank and the gang are out the door, tromping down the porch steps. I set down the bag of frozen chicken and run after them. "Hank, wait! What about Tommy? Should I go and get him?"

Hank turns. "Didn't Ida tell you? Lizzy and Kim want to do a sleepover. Tommy has spent enough time at our place that he'll be fine. Figured you might as well finish the day off with a night off." The boys are heading across the field, roughhousing as they walk like boys do.

Hank takes two steps back toward me. "Reagan, sweetie. I been where that boy in there is now, or close enough, and my Ida, she's been where you are exactly. All's I'll say is, life ain't meant to be lived lonely. You gotta move on. You don't ever forget. Not totally." Hank touches his left bicep in an unconscious gesture; I've seen that arm, seen the tattoo of his unit I.D.— battalion, company, platoon—surrounded by six military serial numbers. "True for him, true for you."

"But what if—"

He shakes his head, speaks over me. "No. That never got anyone any-damn-where. You can ask 'what if' till you're blue in the face. You won't get anywhere with that. You either risk, or you don't. Up to you." He wraps me up in a bear hug and keeps going. "Nobody can tell you what Tom would have wanted, or would want. Nobody can tell you what you should or shouldn't do. You don't answer to anybody 'cept yourself. And little Tommy, maybe, when he's older. But he's a good boy. He's loved. You're loved."

"Thank you, Hank. For all these years of…everything. Thank you."

He clears his throat, speaks gruffly. "Family takes care of family."

He lets me go, pats me gently on the arm. "Go on now."

I go on. Derek is sitting at the kitchen table, the last box of pizza in front of him, two slices folded over together in his hand. I sit down opposite him and take a slice. We eat in silence, sharing a can of Coke. When the box is empty, Derek puts it with the other empties, washes his hands. Straightens the dishtowel. Fidgets.

He's waiting for me, and I'm scared to open it all back up.

He waits another few heartbeats while I continue to chicken out, and then he does it for me. "I should've told him. I know that. Guilt over it has been eating me alive this whole time." He rubs his forehead with his thumb, not looking at me. "All I can say is I'm sorry. It doesn't change anything, but I'm sorry."

"No one can fault you for it, Derek. I sure don't." He looks up at me, surprised. "I'm hurt, and I'm angry. But I'm not really angry at you. More at the world in general. But mostly I'm angry at Tom for just not reading the damn letter when I gave it to him. We talked on the phone, wrote other letters, and he never asked about it, never referenced it. I was scared he was…I don't know. Mad at me for getting pregnant, maybe? It was an accident. We'd said we were waiting till his term ran out.

"I was so hurt, so confused as to why he never asked how I was doing with the pregnancy, how I felt, nothing. Not a word. So I never said anything, either. I didn't want to make things harder for him, didn't want to let him know I was upset. I didn't want to distract him, you know? I figured he'd come home, and we'd sort it out. I loved him, he loved me, and we'd work the rest out. I was trying to be a supportive soldier's wife. And then I got the news about the ambush, that you and he had gone missing, and… then they found his body." I shrug, as if the rest is self-explanatory.

"Soldiers? We're superstitious. He carried that letter as a talisman. For luck. I carried my favorite baseball card. Hunter had this little pocketknife. All the guys had something. For Barrett, it was your letters, especially that one." Derek leans against the stove, watching me, but his gaze is still hooded, cautious.

"I don't want you to go, Derek." I stand up, taking a step toward him. I don't touch him, though, because that's just too dangerous. "I can't come up with any other answers than that. I can't answer any of the what-ifs. I'm scared of getting hurt. This whole thing is big and confusing and frightening, but the one thing that seems clear to me is that you're here now, and that I feel better when you're around."

Derek and I stand face to face, not quite touching.

"Where do we go from here, then?" he asks finally.

"I don't know." I've been thinking so hard, processing, sorting through my emotions, thinking of Tommy, of Tom, of the farm, of right and wrong and good and bad and what I want versus what's best, and I'm just fried. I don't want to decide.

I want *him* to decide. I want someone to tell me what to do, rather than having to be the one who's strong and decisive and in charge.

"Come on," Derek says. "Let's go for a ride."

He takes me by the hand, and I follow him willingly. I let him tack up Henry the Eighth and Mirabelle, the bay quarter horse. He lifts me up into Henry's saddle, and climbs onto Mirabelle. I follow him as he trots ahead of me, out to the north pasture. When we're through the fence, he clicks Mirabelle into a canter. I'm beside him, and I realize that this is exactly what I need. The wind in my hair, Henry pounding the grass beneath me. Sunshine, Derek, freedom. We canter across the pasture, dismount, and go through the small gate separating my property from the Lovitzes', remount on the other side. The Lovitz property is truly massive, four hundred acres of farmland, and another two hundred acres of woods. I've ridden through their forest from time to time, and I follow Derek along the tree line to the trail running north and east through the woods. Under the foliage, we walk the horses. Words are unnecessary.

Thirty minutes later, the trail opens up in a clearing. Derek dismounts, extends his hand to me. We unsaddle Henry and Mirabelle, tie them to a tree branch with a nosebag of grain. Derek lays the saddle blankets side by side on the grass in the middle of the clearing, in the sunlight.

My heart is suddenly pounding.

He's lying there on the saddle blankets, arms crossed beneath his head, staring up at the clouds as they twist and shift and pass.

"C'mere." He holds out one arm, inviting me. "Quit thinking, quit worrying. Just lie down with me and watch the clouds."

I lie down, and his arm curls around me, holds me against his left side. My head rests on his chest, and I can hear his heartbeat, faint and steady.

"Your hair looks beautiful." He takes my hand in his, examines my fingers. "These, too."

I shrug, still feeling absurdly nervous. "Thanks. I enjoyed the spa. It was really relaxing. Thank you."

"I just had the idea. Hank and Ida made it happen."

"They've got Tommy for the rest of the night," I say, apropos of nothing. Or perhaps not. Maybe it is relevant. I'm trying not to think about it too hard, because I'll start overthinking it again. Or maybe I'm already overthinking things.

"Reagan?"

"Yeah?"

"Quit thinking."

I laugh, a gentle snort. "I can't. I'm trying, but I can't."

He rolls, and suddenly I'm partially pinned beneath him. He's looking down at me with his moss-green eyes searching, piercing, seeing into me. His hair is blond and thick and falling across one eye, a little too long. He's got a beard, grown long enough to be soft to the touch now. He's put on muscle; his T-shirt sleeves stretching out once again, shoulders broad and chest thick. His arm is beneath my neck; his hand is clutching my shoulder, weight on his elbow. His other palm touches my cheek, thumb caressing the corner of my mouth. He traces the line of my lips.

For reasons I can't even begin to fathom, I bite his thumb.

"Ow." He pulls his thumb away and fits it to the tiny hollow beneath my lower lip.

"Sissy." It's more of a breath than a word.

"Reagan?"

Whisper in response. "Yeah?"

His face descends, his words a murmur as his lips touch mine. "You're breathtaking."

"I—"

He cuts me off with a kiss. Kisses me breathless. Pulls away, speaks before I can. "All of you, who you are. You're stunning."

"So are you."

He grins and shakes his head. But his eyes, dark and perceptive, see that I'm still wondering, still worrying, and the smile fades. "Tell me what you want. Just for you. Not for Tommy. Not for Tom. Not for me. Not for Hank or Ida or the farm. Just for you.

Reagan—what's your middle name? I don't even know."

"Olivia."

"Reagan Olivia Barrett. What do you want for *you?*"

My answer is immediate. "To forget. To not be in charge. To give in and not think about the consequences. To just...even for an hour...not have to worry."

His hand cradles the back of my head, his fingertips massaging my scalp. "You want to feel. To get lost."

"Yes," I sigh.

"I think I can do that."

"But what about—" I'm cut off by his lips. He steals my breath, eats my words, and leaves me dizzy.

The kiss goes on, and on. It doesn't deepen, only continues. Lips scouring, moving, tasting, demanding, giving and receiving. I breathe into him, accept his breath. I slide my hands onto his shoulders, explore the hard muscles there. I wonder how long you can kiss and let it remain only a kiss?

He flicks his tongue into my mouth, and I gasp at the sudden intrusion. My gasp breaks the kiss. Instead of crushing his mouth to mine to continue it, he shifts downward, touches his mouth to my jaw. My head tilts back, baring my throat. Another kiss, lower, near the hollow at the base. I hold onto his shoulders, my eyes closed. Birds chirp, trees rustle. The late after-noon sun bathes us.

His palms brush my T-shirt up, baring my stom-ach, my ribs. Bra. Then my shirt is off, and it's broad daylight and I'm self-conscious, nervous. What if he doesn't like the way I look when he sees all of me, bare in the light? What if—

My thoughts are scattered by his mouth on my ribcage, his palm on my side, warm and callused and strong. I feather my fingers through his hair and remember to breathe, but I can't because his lips stut-ter across my skin to the opposite side of my torso, sliding and kissing down to my waist. He kisses my belly. Above my navel.

Worry returns.

"Not there, Derek, don't—" He pauses, looks up at me. Then back down to my waist, my belly. I slide my hands over the stretch marks. "I'm sorry. I'm just weird about them. They're not sexy."

He narrows his eyes at me, glances down at my crossed hands. He shifts back on his elbow, withdraws his hand from beneath my head. I watch him, worried I've turned him off. So much for an hour of forgetting. But then his fingers close around my wrists, both of them. His grip on my wrists is gentle but implacable iron. Slowly, deliberately, he moves my hands above my head, ignoring easily my attempts to fight him. When my arms are stretched out, held in place by his strong hand, he adjusts his position beside me. I cling with both hands to his thick wrist and palm, squeezing with all my strength, insecurity and fear and exhilaration warring within me. I don't know what's he's going to do. I'm bared to him now. But not totally. The waistline of my jeans hides the worst of my pregnancy scars.

And yes, his free hand smooths over my stomach, finds the button of my jeans. Unsnaps. Lowers the zipper. I can't swallow, can't breathe. He pinches the denim over one thigh and tugs down. My hip is bared, the elastic of my underwear pulled with it. He repeats the process on the other side and lowers my jeans down over my hips.

"Kick 'em off." He touches a kiss to my rib, just below the underwire of my bra.

"Derek, I'm—no, I—"

"Do it, Reagan. Please."

Slowly, hesitantly, eyes squeezed tight, I hook my big toe in the cuff of one leg, lift my knee to draw my leg out. But then I chicken out and start fighting him, tugging at his grip on my hands, trying to cover my stomach by curling my thigh up, twist away. He's too strong. Gentle, but strong.

"*Reagan.*" His voice is whip-sharp, cutting through my struggles. I open my eyes and look at him. "You're beautiful."

Before I can protest or agree or whatever would have come out of my mouth, he's kissing me. Jesus, the man can kiss. His lips are soft and skillful, moving against mine so my breath catches and my heart swells and my body heats, and then his tongue delves into my mouth and slides across my tongue, sweeps over my teeth, and he pulls away, draws his tongue over my upper lip, my lower lip, and I'm left breathless.

I'm still partly twisted away from him, my jeans half on, half off. His palm slides over my stretched buttock, sweeping over the curve, cupping my thigh and grazing downward. I register it only as pleasure. He does it again, and I moan at the heat of his palm on my flesh, and then he moves his hand to the other side of my butt, where my jeans are still half on. He slides the denim off me, and his kiss steals away my breath, my protest, and I don't even think to be nervous because his hand is caressing my skin, moving over my thigh, up my back. I'm twisted awkwardly, turned away from him, but he's kissing me, and I'm locked into the kiss so my neck is twisted back.

I want more of his touch. His touch I like. It's the scrutiny that unnerves me.

I roll into him, and he takes my weight on top of him, still gripping my wrists so I can't escape, kissing me and deepening it, turning it heated and needy. I moan and struggle against his grip, wanting to touch him. He doesn't relent; instead, he tugs me fully onto his chest. I can feel his heartbeat under me and his hard-on at my core. His mouth is demanding and relentless and insistent on mine, and I'm powerless to do anything but give in, give him all he's demanding of me and beg for more with whimpers in the back of my throat. Oh, god, his hand. On my spine between my shoulder blades, nails scraping down my flesh. Pausing at my bra strap. Unhooking it in one deft move. Brushing the straps from my shoulders. Guiding my arms out, and I willingly cooperate, not knowing why or how, but only that he's eliciting desperate compliance from me. Lift up my torso enough for him to slide the undergarment out and set it aside. Now I'm lying completely on top of him clad in only my panties, and he's still kissing the ever-loving life out of me.

He's tongue-fucking my mouth.

God, I love it.

Oh, shit. Ohshitohshit. He's rolling with me and I'm on my back, and he's still got my damn hands pinned above my head, except now his mouth has finally left mine and he's kissing down my throat to my chest, between my tits, cupping one to bring it to his mouth and sucking my nipple in, and I actually squeak with surprised need. With ecstasy. I soften. I melt, and then I moan and moan and moan as he crosses my sternum with tongue-laving kisses and finds my other boob, suckling that nipple with equally passionate attention.

He moves down my body, kneeling between my thighs, holding my wrists over my chest now.

"Derek?" I don't know what I'm asking, only that I'm pleading with him.

I'm scared and I'm needy and I'm on fire and I'm nervous and I'm self-conscious. My core trembles. His eyes are on mine, unwavering and intense. He gathers a handful of the front of my underwear, a pair of deep crimson silk, high-cut bikinis, and drags them slowly and deliberately down, removing them the rest of the way.

"Lift up for me, sexy."

"Sexy?" It's part question, part protest.

But yet, I'm lifting up—my hips are off the saddle blanket to let him pull the silk the rest of the way off.

"It's not a strong enough word." His eyes are still on mine, unwavering all this while.

Now that I'm totally naked for him with the evening sun streaming through the trees and bathing me in golden light, his eyes rove downward. They search me, take me in totally and completely, head to toe, up and down and up and down. Perhaps more than anything he could ever say to me, the best motivation for me to realize my own beauty in his eyes is being able to watch his zipper tighten and tent out, watching his nostrils flare and his breathing deepen, his tongue wetting his lips in anticipation.

Being told you're beautiful? Unless you never hear it, it can quickly become cheap. Any guy desperate for sex will tell you you're beautiful. Friends or family will say things like, "oh, well you're a beautiful woman, so…", and it just becomes part of you, people telling you you're beautiful. I know what I look like. I'm beautiful. Fair, attractive, proportioned features. Curves, nice eyes, thick hair. Whatever. That doesn't mean I don't have my insecurities. I dare any woman who has carried a child to tell me she's never, *ever* felt insecure or self-conscious about her stretch marks. Some use oils and lotions and yoga to get rid of them, some don't. I haven't. Haven't had the time. Some learn to own them, to rock bikinis and strut their stuff on the beach. Good for them. That's just not me.

And really, it's not like I'm paranoid about it. It's less about the stretch marks and more about the fact that I've not been looked at as a sexual creature in so long that it's unfamiliar and scary. It's about the fact that I only had two partners before Tom, both short-term, awkward, teenage romances. Then I was with Tom, and only Tom, for the rest of my life. And he was gone for most of our marriage. Meaning, there have been many long periods in my life without sex. Tom was my best friend and my husband, so it was easy with him. He knew me, he got me. And even still, I'd be nervous the first time after he was back on leave.

So now, with Derek staring down at me, I'm rife with insecurity and nerves.

Yet Derek's expression…it reassures me. He's nervous, too. And looking at me, he's clearly attracted to me. His gaze rakes over me, takes in my breasts, my thighs, my stomach, my core, my eyes, my face. My lips. And with the way he looks at me, the appreciation so apparent in his eyes, I feel beautiful. I feel wanted.

I feel sexy.

He lets go of my wrists. "Leave 'em there, okay?"

I nod. I don't question. He smiles at me. Licks his lips again and touches his lips to the side of my boob, the underside, my rib. My stomach. And then, ever so gently, ever so deliberately, he kisses each mark on my stomach. Each blemish, each gap in the tautness of my belly, he kisses. He draws his tongue up, pressing his lips over each…and every…one.

I'm crying by the time he's done. He didn't have to say a thing, but his meaning was clear.

I let my tears fall, tears that are soft and gentle, appreciative and thankful. He looks up at me, his chin on my hipbone. "Okay?"

I can only nod. My heart rate ratchets up between one second and the next, though, because his gaze slides away from mine, over my body once more, down between my thighs. Hooo…shit. No insecurities here. I did Kegels and all those other exercises to keep things tight down there, so I feel fine about myself in that area. What I'm feeling right now is just raw nerves. He's moving, his hands sliding over my hipbones, trailing down through the trimmed "V" of hair—*I wonder if I should have shaved it for him?*—his finger sliding over the seam of my opening. I tremble. Exhale. Keep my eyes on him, hands above my head as requested.

A finger inside me. His mouth on my stomach, then my left thigh, then the softness of my inner leg, near the knee. All of that is within the bounds of what I was anticipating. I close my eyes, thread my fingers together, and sigh at the soft, wet feel of his mouth on the crease of my thigh where hip meets leg.

I don't expect his tongue sliding up my opening. I gasp out loud, eyes jerking open, knees closing around his shoulders. "Derek! What are you—?"

"Tasting you."

"But I'm—" I don't even really know what my protest was going to be.

"Sweet as sugar and twice as nice." He caresses my inner, upper thighs, gently parting my legs. "Now relax and enjoy it."

This Derek, the slightly bossy one? I *really* like him. I offer up a token resistance, nervous about my taste, my smell. Whether I'm groomed enough for him down there. Whether he expects me to return the favor, because I'm not sure I'm ready for that just yet, either. My token resistance, a stiffening of my legs, has him taking my ankle in his hand, placing it where he wants it. Namely, over his shoulder. Then the other. My knees are wide apart, spreading my vag open for him to see all of me, every fold and crease and wrinkle. My ass is almost off the ground, my knees hooked over his shoulders.

"I feel ridiculous like this," I mutter.

Derek doesn't answer. Not right away, at least. He glides in, palms sliding up my thighs, back down. Around my hips to cup my tautened ass, and then I'm subsumed by sensations. His tongue on my clitoris. A long, thick finger sliding into my opening, diving in, exploring, circling, curling. His tongue, sweeping and swiping and stabbing and spearing and tasting. I moan—I can't help it. It's a breathy, erotic sound in the quiet forest, a long, drawn-out "*ohhhhhh.*" And my hips drive up, demanding more of him. Because holy god Jesus, does this feel amazing. So good. So, so, so good. His tongue is strong and relentless, finding a slow circling rhythm around my clit, which is throbbing and thick with sensitivity, each touch of his mouth and lips and tongue shooting rockets of ecstasy through me. I'm tingling from my toes to my scalp, my fingers grasping my own wrists, then stealing down in disobedience to feather through his hair and hold him in place, clutching him against me, greedy for more.

He adds a finger inside my pussy, curling up against that perfect spot, rubbing back and forth in a gentle thrust. "Now how do you feel? Is it ridiculous still?"

"Derek…god, please…."

"Please what?"

"More, Derek. More. Don't stop."

"Keep talking, gorgeous. Tell me exactly what you want." He licks me, a fat wet swipe of his tongue up my opening, ending with his stiffened tongue dragging against my clit.

"Ooohhh-*ohhhhh*-fuckinggodyes…more. Do that again. Your mouth, right there. Please." I might not be making any sense, but clearly Derek likes what he hears.

He growls in his throat and dives back in, repeating the move with his tongue. Again and again. And each time, the pulsations of explosive heat roll low through my core up to my belly, tightening my muscles and making my skin scream, and each time, they get stronger and hotter. His two fingers inside me drive relentlessly into me, a slow, rhythmic, thorough fucking of my insides, his fingertips sliding and pressing against that ridged area of so-tender, so-sensitive skin, and with each fuck of his fingers I go slightly mad, my hips rising and falling, driven to unbridled ecstasy by his tongue and his fingers.

I'm moaning nonstop now. Who *am* I? This is a new me. I've never been vocal. Not like this. Not loud enough to shock my own ears. Not these high-pitched whimpers that turn into mini-screams and quiet shrieks.

And, just when I'm on the verge, hovering on the trembling edge of detonation, he changes it all up. He shifts my body upward, his shoulders sliding between my thighs to throw them wide open, and his mouth travels up my belly, slick juices on his chin smearing against my diaphragm. I'm insane with need now, growling at him, squeezing him with my legs, thrashing beneath him, shoving at his head. But those motions immediately still as his mouth finds my nipple and sucks on it, teeth worrying at it, mouth flattening it, fingers of one hand pinching and twisting my other nipple, cupping my tit and kneading it, thrumming the nipple, strumming and scraping with his fingernail.

And his other hand...please fuck yes...yes, it goes between my legs. Middle, index and ring finger slide and slip against my saliva-slick folds, my own essence throbbing out of me, his fingers dipping into my channel and smearing the pungent juices of my desire and need over my trembling folds. He presses and circles. I moan. He releases the pressure, leaving a light touch, the pads of his fingertips barely touching my clit. They circle around the sensitive nub without actually touching it. And I scream.

Volcanic heat floods through me; my thighs shake and my gut tenses and my eyes clench shut and my toes curl. I rake my fingers down his back, and my hips are rising and falling, lifting and sinking, seeking his fingers in rhythm with his touch, which does not relent, doesn't speed up or slow down. He just keeps the pressure, the pace, and it drives me wild as I come with a frantic detonation.

And then he's down there again, between my thighs with his lips suckling my clit and his fingers driving into me, and holy shit I'm coming again, both of my hands on his head pulling him against me, driving into his mouth with my hips.

I'm fucking his face.

And he's going wild over it. He's moving his tongue against my clit in a feverish pace, driving my orgasm to heights I hadn't thought possible, his fingers sliding into me slow and deep.

When the riot of ecstatic madness fades a bit and my shrieks have quieted and my hips have stilled, he takes to licking me slowly once more, his tongue sliding up the drenched opening of my pussy to flick gently against my clit. This is, in its own way, just as crazy-making as the fast and furious explosion. It sends shuddering aftershocks through me, potent waves of clenching heat that have me making a sound in low in the back of my throat that I can only describe as primal.

He's made me come twice, come so hard I'm limp and gasping and close to tears of stunned, frenzied, pleasure. And he hasn't even taken his shirt off.

Suddenly, I feel desperate for him. Hungry for him.

Fuck dignity or decorum. Fuck being ladylike. I want Derek, and he's here with me, doing incredible things to me. I want him, and I'm going to have him, consequences be damned.

I wonder if he knows what he's done to me?

CHAPTER 14

Derek

I'M SO HARD IN MY JEANS IT HURTS. IT PHYSICALLY hurts. Reagan, goddamn...the woman is the most erotic being I've ever seen in my life. So responsive, so alluringly beautiful and unaware of it in a maddening kind of way. Maddening because she's drop-dead gorgeous, hard-working, patient, kind, and generous. She's not insecure, not self-conscious except about that one particular thing on her stomach. Those aren't unattractive. They're part of her. And she is, from head to toe, the sexiest girl ever, so fucking hot she's a fantasy. She has a potty-mouth at times, which I find attractive. I like a woman to talk dirty, to say nasty things to me. And when I make her scream, it gets me so hard I could come in my jeans like some little thirteen-year-old kid seeing tits for the first time.

Speaking of tits, hers taste so good, feel so soft in my hands, against my lips. She's a C-cup, unless I miss my guess, not that it matters, because, like all of her, they're perfect. Big enough to hold, grip, and knead and overflow my hands. Softer than silk or satin. Firm. Thick, sensitive nipples surrounded by lush dark pink areolae.

She's gasping beneath me, sucking in desperate breaths as she comes down from two intense and vocal orgasms, and I'm just staring at her, soaking in her beauty, memorizing every single inch. Her thighs, pale and strong. Angular hipbones, padded with curves. That dip, there at her hips. Her ass, round and high and firm.

And…Jesus, her pussy. That pussy. So tight and wet and sensitive. Each touch of my tongue drove her wild. Going down on her wasn't just to get her off, to make her lose control—it was an homage. It was worship of her body, her slick, deep sex, her pink delicate labia and her small, hard, sensitive clit.

I'm kissing her mouth and she's breathing into me, pulling away and holding my head and looking at me with these pale sky-blue eyes hot with passion, emblazoned and emboldened with need and searching me, penetrating into my soul, wet with emotion and melting with affection. She kisses me, leaning up, and then she falls back. Her hands are on my ears, sliding down to my cheeks, holding my jaw. One hand on my cheek, thumb at my lips, the other feathering through my hair and caressing the nape of my neck with her fingertips in a way that has me wanting to melt into her, wanting to purr like a cat and beg her to tell me how to please her. It's a gentle, affectionate gesture that is almost too heady, too soul-shakingly tender for me to handle.

She lifts up on her shoulder blades, neck arching, to kiss me, I thought, but no. Not a kiss. Her tongue touches my chin, my upper lip. She's licking her essence off my mouth, and holy fuck is that hot. So hot.

She's pawing at my shirt. "Too—too many damned clothes."

Ripping at it impatiently, she pulls it up over my skull, but it's stuck with my face in the opening. I *am Cornholio!* The joke flits through my head, but I don't say it. I shrug out of the shirt, toss it aside.

"Better?" I ask.

She shakes her head. "No. Mmmm-mmm. Not better. Not enough." She reaches between us, fumbles at my zipper. "Pants. No more pants."

I like this Reagan, this demanding, voracious, hot-eyed vixen. I feel like I broke down some wall inside her, broke through her reserves or her fear or her nerves or whatever, knocked down those walls to bring out a sex-starved demon.

I go for the button-snap of my jeans, but I'm not fast enough for her. She shoves at me, knocks me to my back. Kneels beside me and jerks my jeans down. I lift my butt up, and she's got them off. I'm commando, and she's gasping, panting, sighing as I lie naked before her. I like that moan, that sound of appreciation, the way her eyes light up and her nostrils flare and her lips curve up in a smile at the sight of my rigid cock. I lie still, knowing if I move a single muscle I'll have her on her hands and knees in front of me, driving into her.

I'll have her like that sometime soon. Oh, yes. I'll have her in the hay, a blanket beneath us, her tits swaying and her sweet ass spread wide open for me, thick round flesh and muscle cushioning me, taking me balls-deep in her tight pussy. I'll bend her over her bed and up against the wall of the barn out back where she first fondled me into coming all over both of us. I'll have her everywhere and anywhere.

But this? Here and now? This is about her. Not me. It's about showing her that I can't fucking breathe for wanting her, that her desires, her need, her desperation are all I care about, that giving her exactly what she wants, what she needs, is my only focus. That she's worth the whole goddamn world, even if all I can offer her is my fucked-up self.

So I lie still, moments from spooging on myself because she's so fucking hot, her lips swollen from kissing me, glistening and moist and parted, her tits hanging heavy and lush and luscious, her thighs opened just enough to give me a teasing glimpse of her pussy, of the curls of pubic hair that I'm glad she didn't shave totally. I lie still and wait for her to take what she wants.

She reaches out hesitantly, her eyes on my dick, tongue-tip tracing her lower lip.

"Anything you want," I say. "Take. Demand. I'm here, and I'm yours. I want you to be happy."

She blinks and looks me in the eye. "I'm torn. I want you inside me. I want to come while you're inside me." My cock twitches because I want that so bad I can feel it. But I stay still and listen. "But I want to make you feel as good as I felt."

She wraps her fist around my cock, runs her thumb over my tip. I tense and close my eyes, and tighten up all my muscles.

I used to be able to hold back until I wanted to let go. I used to have almost total control. Not any-more, unfortunately. That kind of muscle control is the use-it-or-lose-it kind. I'm trying to act confident and in control for her, because she wants to forget—she wants to just abandon herself to feeling for a while, and I know I can give that to her. But this is totally new for me, too. On so many levels. It's been a long time since I've had this. It was a good year and a half in Afghanistan, which is a hell of a dry spell.

There was leave, sure. Liberty, and whatever. Some fine-ass chicks on deployment, too. But our company CO frowned on that kind of fraternization because it just causes trouble in most cases. Which I totally got, having seen buddies hook up with girls from their company or others, and when spats happened, as they inevitably will, it made shit messy. So I avoided that, a rare display of restraint in that department for me, really. And as for the local talent? No. Leave it there. Just no. Too dangerous, if it existed at all. So that long dry spell, plus three years as a POW, plus the three months in rehab? I'm so sex-starved as to be dangerous to humanity.

And I've changed. That, more than anything, is the biggest issue. I'm not the same guy who shipped out to Afghanistan. I used to bag 'em and tag 'em. Take what I wanted and split. Oh, I was attentive to how the girl beneath me was feeling, because it just feels better and is more fun if she's a willing and eager participant. Make her feel good, you'll feel good. And I was good at making 'em feel *really* damn good. Now? I'm worried I'm not good enough for a fucking goddess like Reagan. I'm worried I've lost my touch. I'm worried I'll have some kind of flashback or freakout and ruin things.

That's inside.

Outside, I'm trying to play it cool.

Except, she strokes me. Once. Twice. Her petite but strong hand sliding down my length, burying at my root. Drifting up. Light touch, palm grazing. Cupping over the head, squeezing and rolling. I crane my neck to watch, and fucking hell it's erotic as shit watching her touch me. Her hand is small, makes my cock look that much bigger. She can wrap her fist around me, fingertips barely meeting, both hands on me, sliding hand over hand, and there's still cock spilling up over her hand. She's doing that hand-over-hand thing, and I fucking love it. I love the downward slide of her hands, the constant touch and pressure.

And I'm groaning. Fisting my hands in the saddle blanket to keep still. Sweating, trying not to hump her fist.

"You better stop that, or this'll be over before it starts," I end up having to say. "I'm trying to hold back, but...god, that feels good."

"You made me come *really* hard, Derek. It felt so good, it was...almost too good. I almost couldn't take it."

"So I did something right at least."

She ignores me. "And it's been so long since I've done anything like this, but I want to make you feel good, too."

"No, this is about you, Reagan."

She shakes her head, pausing with both hands around my dick, just the bulbous head sticking up over the top of her fist. "No. I want…Derek, I want this to be about us."

She glances at me, offers me a shy smile. Strokes me again, hand-over-hand, and I have to seize up again, *think about not coming, don't look at her, think about the sky or the trees—*

Nope. That's not working. She's got my sac in one hand now, cupping gently, rolling and squeezing so softly, massaging. Middle finger extended down past my balls, massaging there. Fuck, I can't hold it.

"Reagan…."

"Sshh." She's sliding her fist up and down my length. Driving, pumping. Relentless. "Give it to me. Let me have it, Derek. I want it. Let me see it."

"What?"

"Your come."

"Shit, Reagan, I'm right there. I can't hold back. I can't stop it." I'm gasping, and I'm totally in her control now.

I want to come. Need to. I'd do anything she asked of me right now, if only she'd let me come.

"Good. That's what I want." She slows her strokes. "This is your turn."

She pulls my cock away from my body, stretches it. Grips tight and grinds her fingers down my length, and I growl. I force my eyes open, and I'm glad I did. She's so lovely. So hot. Hair the color of pure honey draping over one shoulder, skin tanned and flawless, breasts swinging as she leans over me.

Oh, god, she's going to. God, I hope she does. I'm selfish, so selfish. I want her mouth around me. I shouldn't; it's too soon for her to give me something like that. But I don't have the self-control to stop her as she bends over me, her silken boobs sliding against my ribcage and over my stomach, pressing against me as she puts her face to my hip. She's watching herself stroke me into orgasm.

"You're so goddamn sexy, Derek. You are. I hope you know that. You're not just handsome—I mean, you're that, too, but you're sexy. You're gorgeous." She's going slowly, my cock stretched out to keep me from coming, sliding up and down so, so slowly it's making me insane. But I listen, and listen well, because I really need to hear what she's saying to me. I need the reaffirmation, too. "I don't know if I'm allowed to use this word this soon between us, but…I *love* your cock. I love the way it feels. I love the way it looks in my hands. So big, so thick. It's straining, isn't it? Does it hurt yet?"

She twists her neck to glance at me.

I gasp, swallow hard. "Yeah, it hurts."

"You want to come?"

I nod. "Fuck—fuck yeah. God…*damn*, Reagan. What the hell are you doing to me? I want to come so bad."

"I'm doing what you did to me, hopefully." She takes my dick in both hands now and pumps me up and down, hard and fast, still straining away from my body. "Where? Where, Derek? Where do you want to come? Tell me."

"Anywhere."

"In me? On me?" I look into her eyes. She's getting a rush from this; her pupils are dilated, and her breath is coming fast.

"How—shit, shit, I'm so close—how am I supposed to decide?"

She slows, shifts closer. I can feel her breath on my cock. "Like this?"

"You…if you want to…." That's what I want, so bad, but I wouldn't ask her.

I used to tell girls to suck my dick all the time, and they would, but Reagan…she deserves better, deserves more, deserves to be treated like fucking gold, get what she wants, make herself happy.

Her cheek is on my stomach, over my navel, and she's got her slim little hands around my cock and going so slowly, and I'm seriously about to beg her to let me come, because I'm still just barely holding back, and I can't anymore. God, yes. Yes. She lets my cock go flat against my stomach. She cups my balls in one hand, massaging them with her warm, gentle palm. Strokes me hard and fast near the top, short hard strokes, and I'm done.

"Reagan, Jesus, Reagan...."

"You're coming?"

"Uh-huh...."

"Hard?"

"Fuck...*so* hard."

She moans, a murmur in her throat, and slides her face away. I come, a gushing explosion that has me juddering and shuddering and grunting. I feel the stream jet out of me, hitting my stomach. She lifts my cock and takes me into her mouth for the second surge, and she's not stroking me, no, she's caressing me, soft, slow, gentle caresses of my length. Reagan is taking just the head of my cock between her lips, and it's just too good to believe, that she's doing this to me.

"Oh, god, Reagan, fuck, oh, my god."

"Mmmm."

And then I'm out of her mouth, the air cool on the wetness of her saliva and my come coating my cock, and she's still slicking her hand down my length, up over the tip, smearing the juices and stroking until I'm helpless to do anything but curl up and arch my back and thrust my hips, groaning. I feel a third gush of come splash out of me, watch it cover her fingers and drip down her knuckles. She grinds her fist down to my root and takes me in her mouth again, sucking until I feel myself clench again and let go with one last, small surge.

And then she's sliding up my body and cradling her head against my chest, still gently and idly stroking my cock. "I can't believe how much you came," she says.

"You do something to me," I tell her. "You make me crazy. Make me so hard."

"You do the same thing to me." She buries her face in my skin. "I can't believe I did that."

"What?"

She squeezes me. "This. With my mouth. I wasn't going to. I didn't think I wanted to, or—or didn't think I was ready. But I felt you, felt how close you were, and I liked it. I liked knowing I could make you feel that way. And I liked how your cock looked and felt. I liked touching you. Tasting you." She giggles into my skin, and then turns so her voice isn't muffled. "I remembered how hot it was when I made you come behind the barn, and I thought maybe…. I was nervous. Could you tell?"

"You didn't have to," I tell her. "This was supposed to about you, making you—"

"I didn't have to. I wanted to." She looks at me. "Could you tell I was nervous?"

I shake my head. "No. All I knew was how fucking incredible it felt. And how hot you are."

Somehow, for reasons I can't guess at, there are no more words needed between us right then. She rests her hand on my chest, the other pillowed between her face and my chest. I'm holding her close, grazing her back, waist, and ass. My other hand goes out from beneath my head, and I find her hand. We thread our fingers together on my chest and hold hands, listening to the birds and the wind and our heartbeats.

Reagan

I'm drowsing, but I'm not sleepy. I'm content. Sort of. For the moment, at least. That was fun, doing that to him. I liked it. I liked the power I had to drive him crazy. To give him such intense pleasure. And it was for him, to make him feel good. It was also for me. Cutting loose. Doing things I never thought I'd do again. Giving in to my deepest desires. It made me feel free and alive and potent.

That was only the very beginning, of course. I'm still aching inside. My core aches. I came twice, but it wasn't enough. I need more. So, so much more.

But for this moment, I'm loving being held, being outside in the golden afternoon sunlight. Being this close to Derek, his heart thumping faintly under my ear. I don't know how much time passes with us just lying here like this. I don't know, and I don't care. It's quiet and calm and pleasant.

But down deep, beneath the warm, buzzing layer of contentedness and muzzy happiness and self-satisfaction, there's a burning. A fierce ache. I'm impatient.

Needy. Desperate and frantic. It's like a kind of panic. My sex drive is coming awake, igniting, coming alive, having been buried for so long. I've gone a long time without, and I've pushed down my urges, but no more. I feel a leviathan within me, swimming up to the surface from the dark depths, and this time it will no longer be denied.

I *NEED* more, and I won't stop until I'm sated.

I can't help myself. I let go of his hand and untangle our fingers. My eyes blink open, and I shift so I can look up at him. Watch him and see the effect I have on him. His penis is draped over his thigh, flaccid, curling to one side a bit. His eyes are on mine, hooded and waiting. I force myself to do this slowly, even though I want him inside me NOW, but I don't even know if he has a condom. I sure don't. I wasn't thinking about that when we left the house, although I should've.

Damn. Now that I'm thinking, my brain won't shut off. "Derek?"

"Hmmm?"

"Should we head back? I don't have a condom."

He grins. "I was being maybe a bit hopeful, but I brought some."

"Some?"

He stretches, snags his jeans, gropes in one of the back pockets. Pulls out a string of four packets.

"Wow. So when did you put those in your pocket?" I think back, wondering when he could've done that.

Not that it matters, because I'm grateful he did. I like it out here, and I don't want to go back yet.

"When you went out to talk to Hank." He pauses to think, then resumes. "Just…I didn't bring you out here just for this. To have sex with you. You just seemed so upset, so confused, that I figured you'd want to get away for a bit. So I thought we'd just come out and talk, cuddle or whatever. But I grabbed the condoms because I thought maybe—fuck it…because I *hoped* we'd eventually do this. And I wanted to be ready if and when we did."

He brought *four* condoms, but was ready to just cuddle? God, what a man. "I'm glad you thought of it."

I'm stuck in a conundrum now. I want him, but I don't want to make the first move. I don't want to be the aggressor. Taking over earlier was fun, and it was something I needed, I think, just to find that part of myself. But now? I want the bold and dominant Derek back. But I don't want to say so. I want him to just…*know* what I want and give it to me. Not fair of me, probably.

Maybe I'll give him a little hint. Besides, I'm eager to touch him some more. I trace my index finger along the curve of his softened dick. At my touch, it responds, and what happens next is fascinating. I trace the length again, following a seam in the skin, and his cock flinches. Hardens, rolls off his thigh as if alive, thickens, straightens. I graze the tip of it with my thumb, touch the tiny hole and scrape just inside it with my thumbnail, then follow the groove beneath the head.

Within seconds, he's at half-mast.

I look back up at him and find his eyes on me, watching my hand as I fondle him into erection. I smile at him, take his tightening girth into my palm and stroke him once. I blink up at him, the picture of innocence.

"God, Reagan. How can you be so fucking sexy?"

I just shrug. He shakes his head as if he can't believe me, as if to say, *Damn, girl.*

Somehow, with no warning, I'm on my back, his dick still in my hand. But he's above me, leaning over me, his body pressed against the length of mine. He's still beside me, though, not really on top of me. But he will be. Oh, boy. Please? I hold my breath in anticipation as his hand finds my boob, caresses, fondles, massages. Tweaks my nipple erect. The other. I'm not panting yet, but I'm breathing kinda hard through my nose. I don't move. I've got his cock, but right now I'm really just holding on to him for something to hold on to, and because I like his dick. But right now, this is totally his show. I'm just waiting with bated breath as he moves his hand down my stomach, pausing to trace lovingly—yes, lovingly—those marks I was so nervous about earlier. How silly of me. He can no more get enough of me than I can of him, and he can't take his eyes off me, can't keep his hands off me. How could I have thought Derek would find any part of me unattractive?

I let out a relieved, anticipatory gasp as his long middle finger finds my folds. I let my thighs slide apart, draw my heels up to the backs of my thighs and let my knees fall apart, wantonly inviting him to do as he wishes with my body. What he wishes, it seems, is to tease me. For the next several minutes, he fondles and fingers every part of my pussy, but he doesn't let me find a rhythm, doesn't let me have the rush of thrill. He just touches me, and as soon as I start to moan, start to pant and let my hips grind, he does something else. He slides his finger inside me, curls and thrusts, and I groan, lift my hips off the ground, and then his touch is moving to my clit, circling, flicking, circling, flicking, and I want him to either circle or flick and keep at it, but he won't, and I'm getting loopy with needing him to stop teasing me and just let me come. But he doesn't. He's got his mouth on my tits, all over them, not just the nipple, either, his tongue sliding up the mounded flesh to trace around my nipple, licking my areola, taking a mouthful of my boob and suckling, then spitting it out and moving to the other side.

And all the while, he's growing harder and harder in my hand. But I don't move, don't dare fondle him, because I'm going to be jealous this time. I want all of that inside me; I want to feel him unleash inside me, and I want to milk every last drop, every spasm. So I just hold him and try to be sane.

Sanity is a losing battle. I'm mewling and growling as he slides two fingers into my opening, then three, fucking me with them now, in out in out in out in—curl, *scraaaaape* against my G-spot. I'm writhing up off the ground, into his hand. God, yes, he's still doing it, that three-finger fuck, and I'm gyrating against his hand, shamelessly grinding in my quest for orgasm. I'm there, right there. Oh, fuck, oh, fuck.

"Yeah, talk to me. Talk dirty. Say all that nasty shit that's in your pretty head."

I said that out loud, huh? Okay, then. "God, yes. Yes. Derek, yes. Yes, Derek. Like that. Oh, fuck. Harder!"

I get it harder. Faster. Three fingers deep inside my pussy, his knuckles crushing into my ass and my taint, thumb along the inner crease of my thigh, pinky teasing my back entrance.

I'm a virgin there. I wonder if I should tell him?

Not yet.

The edge is there, sudden and massive. I'm riding a wave, fucking his hand. "I'm coming, Derek! I'm coming!"

And he jerks his hand out and my pussy clenches, throbs, seizing up in protest. "NO! Fuck, Derek! Please…." Yeah, I'll beg. Absolutely I'll beg when I'm that close.

He takes his time sliding down my body, kissing all the way. The edge still looms, but it's receding, shrinking. Yet I can feel it…deepening. Intensifying. My hands go immediately to his head; my fingers thread into his hair and greedily pull his face to my pussy.

"Yes, yes, YES!" I'm eager. God, am I eager. "Eat me, Derek."

"Oh, fuck, Reagan, I love it when you talk like that. Such a sweet mouth, talking so dirty." He speaks into my folds, his breath hot on my flesh.

"It wasn't so sweet when it was on your cock, was it?" Is that my voice, flirty, seductive, playful?

"Yes, god, yes, it was. So sweet. Just like this pussy. So sweet."

"Is it really sweet?" I wonder out loud.

He lifts up, slides his middle finger into my pussy, draws it out. Leans up over me, and I feel his dick bobbing and swaying and brushing against my inner thigh. Oh, just a little higher. But no. Not yet. I'm waiting for him, for how he wants it. I'm waiting for him to take me, to show me what he wants, to give me what I need the way I need it. He hasn't failed me yet. I'm blinking and breathing and panting and picturing all the ways Derek could take me, and then I feel his finger at my lips, smell myself.

"Taste."

Instead of obeying him right away, I smear the tip of my middle finger on the tip of his cock, through the leaking pre-come, press my finger to his mouth. "You taste too, then."

I open my mouth and take his finger in, licking, tasting my essence, musky, a little sour and a little sweet, slightly tangy. He lets my finger past his lips, and his tongue slides between my fingers, and god, is that erotic, us tasting our own juices on each other's fingers. I remember the way his come tasted, salty, smoky, and thick.

And then he's back between my thighs, his palms pushing my legs farther apart. I drape my knees over his shoulders and hook one ankle over the other. I'm not letting him go till I come this time.

He starts slow, just a slow circling around my clit. Then faster. And then I'm whining in my throat, and my hips are involuntarily lifting up. At which moment he adjusts tactics, still teasing me, it seems. Parting my folds with his thumbs, spreading my labia open, and driving his stiffened tongue into me. Tongue-fucking me. Oh, my, oh, my, oh, my. How delicious, how dirty. He shoves his tongue into me, withdraws, does it again. And again. And then the next time, instead of withdrawing, he laps up between my folds and takes my clit in his mouth, and sucks it in, deep, hard. Suckles. Draws it out, stretches the sensitive skin and lets it free with a pop. Tickles it with the tip of his tongue, then begins a new series of long slow fat licks, pressing in hard. This one has me gasping, grinding against his mouth.

"Please don't stop. I need—"

He pulls his mouth away just long enough to breathe a question. "What? What do you need?"

"Come...please, let me come."

"What do you say?"

"Please?"

"Nope, not it. You already said please."

"Fuck, Derek. I can't—can't handle games. I'm too close."

"There it is."

"Fuck?"

"Yeah, baby. Fuck."

If that's the magic word, I'll say it a bazillion times, as long as he lets me come. "Fuck, fuck, fuck, *fuck*."

And then he's kneeling between my thighs, lifting my knees so they're against my stomach, spreading me apart. Takes my hands one at a time and places them behind my knees. "Hold on like this."

I'm on my back, a breeze blowing, cooling my bared core, cooling the dampness between my thighs. I hold onto my legs, pull myself open wide. Lift my head and look, watch as he traces a finger ever so carefully down my opening, up, down, teasing, playing, plying my folds. He swipes at me with one finger. *Pleaseohpleaseohplease*.... Two fingers....

"One more, Derek. One more. Please...."

A third finger, and then he's sliding them in. "Like this? You like it like this?"

"F-ff*fuck* yes. Yes."

A slow penetration at first, that's all I get. But that's okay; it takes me a minute to open for him, to take those fingers. Curl, caress. Deep inside, then pull out, sliding in, curling on the drawing out, scraping that G-spot of mine. In this position, all I can do is take it. I can't move, can't grind into it the way I want to. Turns out there's no need. He knows what I want somehow, knows that I can't take any more teasing. He ramps up his intensity, speeds up the tempo of his fingers inside me, driving in and out with a loud sucking noise, and I'm groaning, moaning, whimpering, his head curled up between my arms.

"Eyes open, Reagan. Watch yourself come."

He puts an arm across both my knees in a bar, holding my legs up and back, and I can let go and crane my neck forward, watch his three wedged fingers sliding in and out, curled slightly, forearm muscles rippling, driving in and out so hard and fast my thighs and ass quiver with the impact of his hand.

And there's the edge again, the sense of impending detonation, something welling up inside me hot and hard and huge and powerful, moving within me, expanding and growing. I'm making sounds nonstop now, mewls and whines and groans and primal grunts and other noises I don't know the words for, all of them ripped out of me by the force of the climax spreading throughout me.

I'm ripped apart. Split in a million pieces by a white-hot spear slicing through me, clenching my core with an iron grip, clenching so hard I can feel it actually tightening around Derek's fingers, and I'm caught up in it, drawn aloft by a kaleidoscopic wave of blasting ecstasy so sharp and so potent it hurts. I feel something inside me break, burst. I'm screaming so loud birds flap and take wing, and Derek is unrelenting, still fucking me with those three curved fingers, and I'm still screaming through gritted teeth, sobbing. All the muscles in my core squeeze, and I feel all the gathered wetness of my arousal gush, squirting all over his hand, and my eyes are open and watching it happen, watching gelid white cream spurt onto his hand.

And still he fingers me, slower now. Milking every cranking wave, spasm after spasm, each one making me shriek high in my throat until finally he pulls his fingers out and lets me come back down.

I let go of my legs and sprawl out, gasping for breath with burning lungs. "Jesus, Derek. Jesus." I lie for a moment, panting, tremoring.

I crack an eyelid, and he's just kneeling there, watching me. His cock is so hard it's nearly purple. He's still got my cream on his hand, and when he knows I'm watching, he takes himself in his hand and smears it all over himself. He grimaces, grinds his teeth. I reach out, free a foil packet from the string of them, rip it open with my teeth, and pull the condom out. I roll it between my fingers to figure out which way it goes, then put it on his tip. Hand over hand, I spread it onto his length.

I pull him to me. Grab his neck, hang on, and pull myself up to kiss him. Desperately, I kiss him. Devour him, tongue, lips, and breath. Suck his breath into my lungs, wanting to be closer, wanting to be more enmeshed with him. He slides his knees between my thighs, and I hook my ankles around his waist. Tugging, insistent.

His palms go to the blanket on either side of my head, his face centimeters from mine, his breath on my lips. I'm still quivering from my orgasm, still jelly, still gasping. Yet now I've finally got him where I want him most, the tip of his cock nudging at my entrance. He's shaking, too, from holding back, probably. From working so hard to give me an orgasm like no other.

Our eyes meet. We've been building up to this, dancing around this, avoiding it and wanting it and playing for it, and now it's here. I've dreamed of this, wondering what it would be like, fantasized about it. I know he has, too.

I hold off for another moment, enjoying the anticipation.

I reach between our bodies, grip his shaft, and guide it to my opening, slide him in. And oh, my god, oh, my fucking god, his cock is inside me, and it's the greatest thing I've ever, ever felt, so perfect, fitting exactly, filling every crevice inside me. He's sliding deep, no hesitation, slowly gliding, shoulder and chest muscles rippling, stomach tensing, hips flexing. I love the flex of his hips, the way his buttocks go concave on the sides as he moves into me, the way his biceps swell as he supports his weight above me, the way his body pushes me into the soft ground. I love how blue the sky is above us, cloudless and clear, and nearing late evening.

I spread my palms on his back, one between his shoulder blades and the other on his ass, cradling him against me.

He touches my cheek. "Tears?" he questions in a whisper, his finger coming away damp.

I shake my head; I didn't know I was crying. "It feels so good, I can't help it. God, Derek, so perfect. You feel so perfect."

"That's because this is perfect." His brows lower and his eyes widen as he moves into me, such a long slow wet slide in that it takes forever, a perfect forever just for him to fill my pussy with his cock the first time.

"Oh, oh...." I love even the sound of my own voice, the erotic breathlessness of it, how the way I moan spurs him to pull back and almost out, pause, and glide deep once more.

I bite his shoulder, so overwhelmed by the feel of him inside me that I don't know what else to do but bite him and take him deep and rock with him and whisper his name.... "Derek...."

Derek

She says my name on an exhalation, and it's like a prayer.

I'm a total mess, an emotional wreck, overcome by how she feels, how tight she is, how wet and warm and silk-smooth. Her hips move flush against mine, and I stay deep, hip to hip, thigh to thigh, loving the slide of body against body, the way her flesh feels against mine, how the depths of her squeeze my cock, how her walls clench around me. Her eyes never leave mine, at least until she latches onto my shoulder with her teeth and bites down. It's not a gentle bite—oh, no, she's got a hunk of my shoulder between her teeth and she's bearing down, groaning, writhing against me, both hands now on my buttocks and pulling, pulling. Her heels are around my ankles, and now she lifts them, slides them up my calves and thighs, grips the backs of my shoulders with her hands and wraps her legs around my waist. This opens her up for me, and I delve deeper into her. I thrust like this for a few moments, palms planted, hips driving.

And then I need more. I need to go deeper.

I lean forward, into her, resting on her for a split second as I get a hold on her thighs and push them back. I find her ankles and hold onto them. Angle backward to get on my knees between her legs. This stretches my dick downward, but that's good. Draw this out a bit. She scoots down toward me, and I get the soles of her feet planted in my armpits, splitting her sweet, gorgeous pussy wide open. Now I'm as deep as I can go, and I hold onto her calves and start moving.

"Play with your tits, Reagan. Lemme watch you."

She grips her boobs and massages them, then takes her nipples in her fingers and pinches, twists. "Fuck yes, just like this. I love it. You're so deep, so big."

"You like my cock?"

She moans through her teeth, then wrenches her eyes open. "God, yes, Derek. I *love* your cock. So big inside me. It hurts so good."

I'm moving, sliding in, groaning with each thrust. "Fuck, Reagan. Fuck…so tight. Oh…fuck."

"Yes, fuck me. Please fuck me. Harder, Derek. I need it more. I need it harder."

How am I supposed to deny that? I fuck harder. Drive in hard, pull out soft and slow, and then slam deep, and she gasps at each impact, her mouth wide open, eyes wavering on mine. Each thrust is harder than the last as I near climax, heat burgeoning inside me. Her tits bounce every time my hips slap into her ass, and I'm mesmerized by the way they jiggle and jounce. God, she's so beautiful. Have I told her that yet?

"God, you're gorgeous, Reagan." I say it in time to my thrusts. "So…fucking…beautiful. So…fucking…sexy. God, I can't—I can't handle how perfect you look, just like that."

"More."

"More?" I ask. How can she take more?

She slips her heels over my shoulders so her thighs are flush to my pectorals. "Come here. I can stretch farther."

I lean over her, slowly stretching out her thigh muscles until her knees are pressed against her chest and I'm so deep it should be impossible, so deep it should be illegal. She takes all of me and asks for more. How is this woman real? But there she is, hair splayed around her face in a halo, blue eyes blazing with need and arousal and satisfaction. She's a dream, the seductive exotic erotic fantasy of female perfection, everything I could ever have even thought a woman could or should be and then some. I didn't know it could be like this, didn't know it could be more than sex, didn't know it could feel like some part of me has joined with her, beyond the physical, like some tangible corporeal aspect of my soul has merged with hers.

God, that scares the shit out of me. I'm going to freak the fuck out later, because I just don't know what to do with this shredding surge of immense emotion, such intensity of feelings beyond the rush of sex, beyond the chemicals and the flesh.

Now, though, I focus on the rhythm of our bodies. On the crush of my shaft sliding so deep, deep, deep into her. The way she accepts it into her and clings to my neck with her thighs in a silent plea for more. I focus on the way she's watching me without blinking, refusing to look away or miss a single second. I focus on the shiver of her lips, the way her tongue flicks out and tastes the salt sweat on her lower lip. She whimpers, and I drive in. Moans, and I pull out. Shrieks on her exhalation and sobs on her inhalation, which matches the pattern of my driving hips.

I think of some stupid phrase from the couple of times as kids my mom tried to make me go to church: "and they shall become one flesh." Never made a damn lick of sense to me, my whole life.

Now it does.

My body is hers, and hers is mine. I know exactly what she's feeling, what she needs and wants. She's close, and so am I. All the sex I've had in my life—and there's been a *lot*—I've never had a mutual orgasm, never come at the exact same moment as the girl. But now I know, deep down in my soul, that when Reagan and I come, it will be simultaneous.

And it will shatter both of us.

Reagan

I'm wrapped up around him. Legs clinging to his neck, thighs clutching so hard I think I must be choking him, my hands holding onto his forearms beside my ear, my breath and his matching, lips so close but not touching, eyes locked and unwavering. And god, he's so deep inside me, filling me so full. Whatever is happening here between us in this clearing is something I've never felt before, and that has a thread of panic weaving through my thoughts, but I ignore it, bury it beneath the fervor of my need, the burn of my arousal, the flames of his passion and mine fanned hotter and hotter until all is ablaze, my skin on fire, my core going nova, his cock throbbing, my pussy clenching so hard I know he feels it, and I know he knows what that means.

We need no communication. Even as I think, *I can't take it like this any longer,* he's sliding my feet over and off his shoulders and I'm wrapping them low around his waist. He's above me now, his weight on mine, and I'm clinging to him with my heels locked around his ass, which flexes iron-hard as he pistons into me, slow and steady and rhythmic. Arms around his shoulders, a hand on each of his shoulder blades. I claw at him, heedless of how hard. He knows that clawing of my fingers down his back means I need more, need it harder and faster, and he gives it to me just like I want it. I feather my fingers through his hair at his nape, because I know it drives him absolutely wild. And it does. He buries his face in my neck and, thank god, now I can move properly. I can fuck him back, fuck up into his thrusts, take him deep and give it back harder. I hold his head, cradle his skull, loving his breath on my breast, forehead, on the slope of my tits.

We're lost to each other in this now. Whatever it means, whatever this becomes and wherever it goes between us, this is the culmination of so much buildup, so much emotional devastation and mental turmoil and physical anguish, so much need and desperation and heated foreplay, and it's exploding between us, through us, melting parts of my identity to his, our souls forming anew, parts of each of our essence becoming a xenolith within the substance of the other in some metaphysical ouroboros. He moves, and I move with him, breath and breath and breath, moan and hum and groan and curse and plead. So close.

His grunts of exertion are beautiful to me.

I put my mouth to his and devour his lips, eat them. I drink his mumbled plea of my name: "*Reagan....*"

The syllables drawn out—*Reeee-gannnn*—

And I match him with the whispered song of his name as we merge and merge and merge: *Derek... ohDerrrrrek.* I don't need to swear, don't need to call out to God or to pant out the social epithet "god," because in that moment, in that timeless time when I've abandoned myself to him, to this, to us, despite the blasphemy it might be, in this moment with Derek, he is God, all the god I need.

We come.

We detonate sun-hot, my shrill shriek harmonizing with his feral roar. His cock is a driving force within me, squeezing between the clamping walls of my core, and yet nothing is more potent than our orgasm. It's neither mine nor his, but *ours.* It lasts and lasts, his groans and sighs matching my screams and whimpers, mirrored and tasted with kisses that miss mouths, lips found and tongues tangling even as we both moan and shift together, writhe together, his hips pounding into mine, my ass lifting clear off the ground to slam my pussy into his thrusting.

After an eon of metamorphic climax, we slow and pant together, and finally he must slip out of me, and

I take all his weight onto me, love the exhausted collapse of him onto my breast. I cradle his head still, kissing his forehead. His fingers trace idle swirls on my boobs and sternum and nipples. He shifts aside and removes the condom, ties the end in a knot, and tucks it into a back pocket of his jeans, starts to move off me.

"No," I murmur, pulling him down onto me again. "I like it."

I wasn't going to say "like," but I've thought that troublesome, tricky other word too often in the course of this experience with Derek.

So he stays, stubbornly letting a portion of his weight slide off me, though his head remains on my breast, his leg thrown over mine.

Holding him like this is its own kind of heaven.

CHAPTER 15

Derek

SOMEHOW IT'S DUSK. DID WE DOZE? IT DOESN'T matter. She seems to like the way I'm lying half on top of her, even though I have to be heavy. At some point, she starts weaving her fingers through my hair past my ear, over the top of my scalp. I could very seriously purr when she does that.

Her fingertip touches my chin; I lift my head and look into her sky-hued eyes. "I'll go ahead and be the first to say it...whatever *that* was"—she pauses, for effect or to gather her thoughts, and to brush my hair out of my eye and trace from temple to jaw—"it was the most—I don't even know."

I swallow hard. I was half-hoping I'd imagined it. The ramifications are scary. "It was unlike anything I've ever experienced before," I admit.

"No kidding." She lets out a sigh that is part laugh, buries her nose against my forehead. Inhales. "I'm glad it wasn't just me."

"What *was* that, then?"

She lifts a shoulder in a shrug. "I don't know." A moment passes. Several. She kneads the muscle of my shoulder. "Can we go back?"

I have a tripartite emotional reaction to her words. I think she's talking about what just occurred between us, and I'm relieved that she wants to go back, too, but I'm also devastated that she might want to take it back, and then I think, with a thrill, that she wants to go back so we can do it all over again.

And then I realize that she means literally, physically, go back to the house. Go home? Is that right, for me? Is that my home? Do I have a home? Yet another epiphany hits me—this one more frightening than the others—and it's that her home, the farm, the barn, this little remote scrap of Texas, is the closest thing to home I have, that I've ever had since joining the Corps right out of high school.

"Yeah," I say. "Let's go."

We saddle up the horses and ride back ho—ride back to the farm. The horses seem to know where they're going, which is good because I sure as hell don't, and I'm not the greatest rider. I can stay on a horse, but not with any great skill. We make it back to the barn in what feels like half an hour, unsaddle the horses, and let them loose in the east pasture. I put the saddles and tack away. By this time it's dark, and my heart and mind are whirling in mad circles. I don't know what's going to happen now, or what to expect. Or what I want. I'm scared of what I'm feeling. I'm scared of what I'm sure Reagan is feeling. I'm not sure I'm ready for what just happened, for the intense bond that was just created between us.

Until today, it was a dance: an attraction and a mutual emotional need drawing us closer and closer, creating chemical reactions in the form of sexual fervor. It was all of that, yet clearly it was more, a subtext I, at least, didn't anticipate being woven under the surface of our interaction. And now that we've consummated it, our relationship has somehow grown, deepened, expanded, and it scares me. I don't know if I'm ready for it, if I'm capable of it. If I'm man enough for what Reagan needs and deserves.

Do I assume we're going inside the house?

I'm standing in the open door of the barn, staring out at the fading reddish-purple-orange of the setting sun behind the house. Reagan is behind me. I feel her move closer. Feel her press up against me, chin on my back, arms circling my middle, hands flattening against my chest.

"Derek? What happens now?" Guess she's just as confused as I am.

And here I thought sex would simplify, or at least clarify, things between us. Turns out it only deepened the shades and shadows of all the gray areas, making the tangled web joining us more complex.

I owe her my strength. Decisiveness. Or, failing that, I owe her a modicum of honesty. "I don't know. What just happened between us, Reagan, it was…a lot." I place my hands over hers, because for some reason touching her in any way makes it easier to let the honesty tumble out. "I don't know what to make of it. What to do with it."

"Are you scared?"

This feels like going into combat, when you feel fear and know you have to face it, admit it, and gut through it, man up and deal with shit despite it. "Yes."

She ducks under my arm, slides up the length of my body, and looks up at me. "I am, too. I wasn't expecting that." She runs her palms up and down my chest. Her eyes are so soft, so understanding. "Explore it with me? Please?"

Reagan steps away from me, backward. Toward the house. Holds her hand out to me. I don't think I have any real clue what I'm agreeing to, but I take her hand anyway, and we walk side by side to the house.

Each moment is a vignette, a tableau: my boots crunching on the gravel; a glance sideways at Reagan, her honey hair swinging and tossed in the breeze, the subtle bounce of her tits as she walks; a thick shred of white cloud shaded dark by coming night, hanging low over the house; our feet clomping on the wooden porch steps; the screen door creaking open, a pause, a *slam*.

I follow her up the stairs. Watch her fine ass sway from side to side with each step. I glance at the generations of framed photographs lining the wall of the stairway, photos ranging from sepia tone and black and white to washed-out '70s to the '90s, Tom as a kid, his official Corps photo. One of Reagan and Tom and Tom's dad. Look away from that one. Twinge of guilt. I stop, and I'm staring at the photo of Tom, Reagan, and Carl. Must've been just before Tom shipped out for the first time, after he and Reagan eloped. They're both so young, just kids. Reagan realizes I've stopped following her, and she turns back.

"I see that photo every time I come up these stairs," she says. "And it hurts every time. But I can't bring myself to take it down."

"Good-looking son of a bitch, wasn't he?"

"Yeah, he was."

What am I doing here? What did I do? That's Tom's wife coming down the stairs, concern in her eyes. His widow.

Shit.

I'm not breathing, shaking all over, sweating. Panic attack. Haven't had one of these in a while.

"Derek?" She's on the step above me, touching my cheek with a tender hand. "Breathe, baby. Look at me. Look into my eyes."

I find her eyes, so blue, so blue. Palest blue and wide as the Texas sky. But I still can't breathe. Find myself sinking to the step, mouth open and trying to find oxygen, blinking too fast, seeing double, fists clenched and shaking.

I see Reagan, see her mouth moving. Hear nothing. Ceiling, wall. The photo, the fucking photo, fucking Tom and a young, slim, bright-eyed Reagan with flaxen hair a lighter blonde than it is now and an arm around Tom and her hand on his chest, big burly beefy Carl with his arm across both.

Then I can feel Reagan's hand on my back, scratching and smoothing and circling, start to hear sounds, words, distorting and cohering into her voice.

"…Rek….Derek? Talk to me. Please, please come back. Breathe. I'm here. You're okay."

I shift, roll. I see her eyes again, scared and worried. "I need to sit up." I'm lying down, falling, sliding down the stairs, an edge of one of the steps in my back. "Help me sit up."

Reagan moves down past me, takes my hands, and helps me to a sitting position. She sits on the stair below me, sideways. A tear slides down her cheek. "Are you—are you okay now?"

I'm still gasping for breath and sweating, but the attack has passed. "Yeah. I just need a second."

She wipes at her face, rests her cheek on my knee. "You scared me, Derek."

"Scared myself. It just…hit. No warning."

"The photo triggered the panic attack?"

I deliberately stare down at her, anywhere other than the photograph. "Yeah."

She reaches up for it, takes it off the wall. Holds it. Stares at it. Another tear. She wipes them away.

No. That's hers. Her family. Her memory. I have no right to let my weakness force her take it down. I tug the photograph free from her hand, make myself look at it. I see her, see him. Remember him as he was, in the good times. Easy smile, bawdy jokes. Constantly talking about Reagan, how he can't wait to get home and see her. I see him lying on his bunk, writing her a letter. I block the wave of flashbacks that threaten and hang up the photo where it belongs, nestled among the others.

"Derek, it's fine. You don't need to—"

"No. If you take it down, do it for you. Not me. This is your home. Your place. It's…Tom's place. His photo belongs here. You deserve better than to let me—my moments of weakness like that force you to…to change things."

"Wait just a damn minute, Derek." Her voice is strong now, and she takes my face in both hands, forcing me to look at her. "That wasn't a moment of *weakness*. It was a panic attack. And, yeah, this is where Tom grew up. But—goddamn it. I didn't want to think about this. Fuck, this is hard. Tom is dead, Derek. He's gone. I miss him. You miss him. But… we lost him. That stupid fucking war took him from us. And we just…we have to keep living without him. You lived and he didn't, and don't you dare feel guilty about that. There was nothing you could do. And…I don't know how to even put this. He's gone and I loved him, and I'll always miss him. There will always be a part of me that belongs to him. But I'm glad you lived. I'm—I'm glad you're here. I'm glad you came and gave me the dog tags and the letter, and I'm glad you stayed. You've made my life better since you've been here, Derek. I've mourned him. I've grieved him. But until you arrived, I wasn't healing. I wasn't even trying to. I was stuck. I don't know what's happening. Here, between us, I mean. It scares me, I don't mind admitting. But it is happening, and I can't deny it. And—I want to know more. I want to see what it is. I don't want to be lonely anymore. I don't want to feel…trapped. Stuck. Lost in between what was and what is, maybe."

What am I supposed to say to all that? "I'm not sure what to do about the guilt. Telling me not to feel it doesn't make it go away. But…for the first time since the Raiders snatched me out of that village, I feel…

alive. Like I'm *someone*. Like life can mean something to me. For my entire adult life, all I knew was combat. The Corps. And then I was the POW, and since then I haven't known…I *don't* know—who I am? *What* I am? Being here, working on your farm. Spending time with you…it's given me something." I duck my head, gather up the courage to speak the deepest truth I can muster into words. "It's not the farm, really. It's *you*. You've given me that. But even *that* comes with guilt. Because it still should be—should be *him*."

"But it's not, Derek. It's not him. It's *you*." She's crying openly.

I'm close to it myself.

"What the fuck do you do to me, Reagan? My whole fucking life, I'm a typical dude. Heavy shit happens, you feel it, but that's it. You don't cry. I don't cry. But since I've known you, I've spent more time crying like a fucking sissy than in the whole rest of my life." I sniff and breathe and blink hard. It doesn't work. "Shit."

She scrambles to her feet, climbs onto my lap, and buries her face against my chest. She wraps her arms around my neck and clings so tight it hurts, but it's comforting, having her close, having her crush me, feeling her weight on my lap and her tears staining my shirt. I don't feel judged.

"You know what I think?" she murmurs into my cotton shirt. "I think it makes you stronger, that you're able to cry. I think it makes you *more* of a man. Feelings are human, and you have them. You're allowed them."

"Even the guilt?"

"How are you *not* supposed to feel that?"

"It sucks, though." Something wet trickles down my cheek, dripping into her hair.

She twists, looks up at me with her cheek on my heartbeat, and wipes her palm across my face. Does it again and again, and not once does she look at me as if she thinks less of me for crying like a damn girl. She just keeps wiping each droplet away, her own tears sliding down and mixing with mine.

I don't know exactly what I'm crying about. Everything. Combat. Losing buddies. Losing Tom. Being a prisoner. Survivor's guilt. Guilt that I'm glad I'm alive, even though Tom isn't, and Abraham isn't, and Okuzawa isn't, and neither are Lewis or McConnell or Nielsen or Martinez or Silva or Blast or Allen.

And I'm crying, too, I think, because I'm relieved. I've been holding all this in, letting it out unwillingly, usually ripped out of me by Reagan and the things that pass between us.

The stairs are hurting my ass. I slide my arm under Reagan's legs and stand up with her. I carry her into her bedroom. Lay her on the bed, move in beside her. Somehow, she's on top of me, and she's kissing me. I taste salt, and I know she does, too, on my lips. We're kissing and crying, both us. Her breath in my mouth and on my lips and her tongue sweeping over mine steals my tears, my breath, everything but my awareness of her.

Hands push and pull at clothes. Skin emerges slowly. Kisses merge into kisses. I've got her breast in my mouth as she straddles me, her hands planted on my chest, head tilted back, spine arched to push her nipple against my lips. Her hips writhe, but I'm still wearing my jeans, and so is she. She's grinding on me, and we're both breathing in rasping gasps. She moves away, tugging her nipple from my mouth with a *pop*, jerks open my fly, and pulls down my jeans, traveling down my body, mouth touching my stomach, navel, hip bone, thigh, knee. She gets stuck at my boots, glances up at me in amused frustration, fumbles with the laces. She reaches up with one hand and palms my cock, strokes me, then returns her attention to removing my boots. As soon as she has the laces loosened, I kick them off and she's ripping at my socks, pulling my jeans off over my feet. Tossing them to the floor, then diving after them, snagging them up. Pulls the string of condoms from the hip pocket. Rips one free. Stands up, facing me, shucking her jeans in record time. Those panties, god. Dark red silk. Cut high up over her hips, the silk making a deep "V" to cup her pussy. The silk is damp over her opening, darkened with moisture.

Eyes locked on me, she hooks her thumbs in the elastic waistband, pushes them down, steps out. Her palms smooth over her belly, as if she's contemplating covering herself, but she doesn't. She just stands there, hands at her sides, chin high, hair loose and tangled, a bit of grass in it, unnoticed. She's owning her body, owning her beauty. And *fuck* it's hot, watching her deny the insecurity, watching her claim her self-iden-tify as sexy, powerful. She pops one hip out, lifts her chin a bit more, tongue-tip licking her lip, and then her hand hovers over her thigh. Palms the flesh there, then dives into the slight gap between her legs. Gasps as she drags her fingers up between her thighs, touch-ing herself. One brief circling touch, and her knees buckle and she whimpers. I sit up, swing my legs off the bed, reach for her. Grab her hand and pull her close, position her between my legs. Lean in and flick her nipple with my tongue.

Trace the opening of her pussy with my fingers. "Open up," I say.

She shuffles her feet to either side until they're shoulder-width apart. She rests her hands on my shoulders as I delve up into her with two fingers. So wet, so hot, so tight. I groan and lave my tongue between her breasts, gathering the wetness of her arousal on my fingers and smear it over her clit. She falls forward against me, grasps my cheeks, and lifts my face up for a kiss. But the kiss stutters and fades as she moans with my ministrations, her mouth hanging open against mine, forehead to forehead, gripping my jaw with both hands and groaning.

No games this time. Bring her to climax as fast as possible, circling her clit and delving into her tight channel in an alternating pattern. She shrieks as she comes, leaning into me, riding my fingers, knees dipping, hips gyrating.

When the climax fades to shudders, she opens her eyes, and her usually clear blue eyes are clouded, hooded. She pushes at me, shoves me forcefully to the mattress, climbs up on me. She finds the condom, rips it open. Rolls it onto me. I'm in an awkward position, lying back on the bed with my feet on the floor, but Reagan isn't waiting, isn't going to let me adjust. She leans over me, palms on my chest, kisses me and raises her ass. I gasp into her mouth as she reaches between us, guides me to her opening, and sits on me. Impales herself on me, letting out a growling moan as I fill her.

Reagan's eyes are feral, her mouth open, lip curled, low groans escaping as she grinds her ass against my hips, rolling my cock inside her, moving in circles and then side to side, getting me deeper. She gets her knees under herself, spreads her thighs wide, and holy fuck, am I deep inside her. Her fingers are clawed into my chest, raking my pecs. She bites her lips and stares down at me, grinds on me. Side to side. Side to side, working me in and in until I'm as deep as I can physically get, and then she starts moving in circles, around and around, stretching her abdomen to widen the circle her hips circumscribe. The circling grind has me wanting to thrust, but she's pressing down so hard I can't—all I can do is let her have her way with me.

And then she abruptly lifts up, raising her ass off my hips, hesitating at the apex, the tip of me just barely inside her. Slams down so hard our hips crash together.

"Fuck...*yes*...." she growls.

She lifts up slowly this time. The feel of her labia sliding slick along my cock drives me wild, has me trying to thrust up, but she pulls away, shakes her head.

"Unh-uh." She hovers like that, teasing us both. "Not yet."

Reagan flutters her hips, biting her tongue and lower lip, fucking just the tip of my cock in quick rolling thrusts.

I'm groaning and cursing. "Fuck, fuck. Oh, god, Reagan, god. Give it to me." I grip her hips and hold on, try to pull her down, but I can't. She resists, leaning forward and continuing the small shallow fucks.

"You want it?" she demands.

"Yeah." I pull at her again. "I need it."

"What do you need?" Slower, shallower, the head of my cock held delicately between her labia, thighs flexing to slide me a quarter-inch in, then out again. Tantalizing.

"You."

She shakes her head. "I want to hear it, Derek." She walks her hands down my chest toward my stomach, angling my cock toward my feet in gradual increments as she finds her balance on top of me. Then she plants her palms on her thighs, lifts up off me in what has to be a precarious and difficult position to hold. "Please? Tell me what you want me to do to you."

Playing for control, huh? I cup her perfect tits, pinching her nipples between the middle and ring fingers of each hand. "What—god, you're gorgeous—what do I want you to do?"

"Yeah, tell me. So I can do it."

"I want you to take what you want. How you want it."

She lets her head hang back on her neck. I'm stretched out so far it aches. Strains. She takes my hands, one at a time, threads her fingers through mine, and we shift her balance onto our joined hands. Reagan tilts her head forward and leans over me, and I'm supporting the weight of her upper torso on my hands. Her tits hang, sway, thick tan nipples hard, begging for my mouth. I lift up, lick her nipples, each in turn, and then fall back onto the mattress.

"I want…this," she says, and sinks down, burying me deep, deep inside her.

"Fuck, yes."

And then she's moving, letting me take all of her weight on our joined hands, and she starts rolling her hips again. She gasps, moans, lifts up, then sinks down. Grinding on me, she rolls my tip through her labia. Seeking what she needs. Her tits bounce and sway with each movement, and I love watching them. Love even more staring between our bodies at my sex-slick cock sliding up into her, watching her pussy take me in and out, in and out, watch the way the lips of her pussy flatten and stretch as I drive in, watch the juices drip and coat me, smear me, on her, on us both.

She's gushing wetness, and fuck, *fuck*, is it hot watching us. She's watching, too. And loving it just as much.

Reagan finds an angle, tilted forward slightly, lifting her hips to pull me out, then canting her hips forward and sinking down and grinding backward hard to get me deep, using my cock to hit her G-spot. Once she finds the zone, she falls into a rhythm, and I don't care if my arms are trembling, if my forearms ache and my biceps shake, I'll hold her like this until I give out. I groan and thrust with her, working my hips up to match the way she angles down to drive my dick against that perfect spot, and she's shrieking now, "*oh, oh, oh, oh,* fuck yes, Derek, godyesoh*fuckyes*...." shouting, thrusting onto me hard and fast, and our hips crash together, bodies meeting with a *slapslapslap* and a delicious wet sucking noise and she's screaming and I'm grunting and bellowing as I feel her pussy tighten, feel her pistoning motions grow frantic and shuddering. The tempo slows, but now she's drawing me out slowly and slamming me into her *hard*.

And then I feel it. Watch it. Her face screws up and her eyes squeeze shut, and I'm taking all of her weight now and thrusting for both of us, fucking into her as hard as I can, still trying to hit her just right, and she's trying to move, too, but she's lost all sense, all rhythm, all capacity to do anything but sob and scream breathlessly.

Reagan collapses onto me, gasping for breath, sucking in shuddering, sobbing breaths, still holding my hands, my cock still buried inside her.

When I think she's regained her breath, gotten some composure, and I've had a chance to push down my own heated near-climax, I squeeze her hands. "Reagan?" She lifts up her head, hair a curtain, eyes wide, pupils dilated, lips parted. "My turn."

"Oh, god."

I roll her onto her back, give her all my weight for a brief moment, push into her, feeling her walls spasm around me. A couple slow, gentle thrusts, just until she starts to move with me. And then I pull out entirely. Lean down, kiss her hard, and shove my tongue past her teeth, take hers into mine and taste her beautiful mouth. Break the kiss, shove my hand between the bed and her body to cup her ass, roll her to her stomach. She crawls forward, away from me, toward the head of the bed. I follow her. I grasp her ankles and pull her back toward me. She cranes her head over her neck to watch me, eyes wide, mouth open. Tucks her knees beneath her.

"Yeah, baby, stay just like that." I caress the globes of her ass. "Look at this ass. Fuck, I love your ass. So round and soft and perfect…." I palm her cheeks, spread her wide, lift the heavy flesh and muscle, let it go with a lush bounce.

She's watching me as I kneel behind her, playing with her ass, my cock standing tall and achingly hard. Watching me, stilled, waiting, breathing in long sighs.

Anticipating.

Reagan

I'm totally incapable of moving or breathing. I'm waiting, barely breathing. His rough tender hands massage my buttocks, kneading the muscle, and then his fingers slide into the crack and part me, spreading me open. My heart hammers. I should tell him.

"I've never…oh-oooooohgod—" I'm stopped as the fingers of his left hand dip between my legs and find my clit, caress me there with feather-soft touches, his left hand still on my ass, fingers spreading me wide. "Back there…never—never done anything."

"Jesus, Reagan, don't fucking tempt me. I'm just looking at you. I want to see every sexy inch of you." He licks his lips, flicks his eyes to mine, back to my butt. My breath huffs out, I suck in oxygen, and then lose it again, and even my heart stops as he touches the pad of his middle finger to my puckered, tensed hole. "Never been touched here, huh? Never felt this? Hmmm?"

I can't look at him, can only hang my head between my shoulders, shake it, grunt a negative.

The tip of his finger is barely touching me back there, but I'm frozen in place, every nerve ending in my body heated like an electric live wire. I couldn't move if I tried, and I don't even try. I let out a whimper, as the slightest increase of pressure has me tensing even tighter, fearful exhilaration rocketing through me.

"You like this? I'm not even touching you, and you're coming apart."

"I—I'm scared," I murmur into the blanket.

"Don't be scared, Reagan. God, I'd never do anything to hurt you, never, never. Tell me no. Tell me to stop."

"Stop."

Immediately, the breath of pressure is gone, and his hand is skimming over my ass cheeks, and the pressure of his other hand on my clit increases, making me forget what just almost happened, what

I almost let him do. His caressing hand never stops, moves over my back and cups my butt, one side and then the other, over and over, down to the backs of my thighs and up again, as if he couldn't ever get enough of touching me like this. I could take this all day, let him touch me like this forever, never quite come and never get tired of it, never get enough of his ravenous appetite for touching me.

Somehow, his gentle circling of my clit with his left hand turns into the three-finger fuck, that thing he does that morphs me into some ravening orgasmic monster. Except this way, on my hands and knees in front of him, his hand is palm-down, the curve of his fingers pointing to the bed, and of course this has his fingers scraping even more accurately against that place I'm thinking about as my *Jesus-fuck* spot, because "G-spot" isn't nearly descriptive enough a term. Plus, it has me saying that, over and over again, "Jesus...fuck, oh, god, Jesus, Derek, Jesus-fuck, that feels good."

I'm not a church-goer or a believer by any means, but neither am I a habitual blasphemer, nor even usually very vulgar. But Derek does something to me, has this way of pulling just the most vulgar, blasphemous things from me.

Four or five thrusts of his fingers, and I'm coming with firecracker rapidity: *oh-oh-oh,* coming and coming and coming, and now he's got that tender, erogenous place where leg meets hip in his right hand, strong fingers holding me hard, left-hand digits still inside me, getting me up and up and up, driving in so hard I'm almost lifted off the mattress, and I'm exploding—

"OH, FUCK!"

That's me, screaming as he jerks his fingers out of me and shoves his thick, iron-hard cock inside me in one smooth move, grabbing my thigh with his sticky fingers and pulling me against him. I'm pulverized by the feel of him inside me like this, and *holy SHIT,* I'm still coming, and he's so fucking big, stretching me to a blissful burn with his girth and pushing deep with his glorious length.

He holds my hips in place as he pushes in, then shoves me forward, and I move for him, crane my neck to watch him kneeling tall and gorgeous behind me, thick blond hair a riotous mess, moss eyes blazing, pecs flexing and abs tensed, V-cut rippling, thighs like trees, scars glinting in the moonlight. I'm glutting on his beauty. Gorging on the image of him up there behind me, spine straight, so tall and muscular, plowing into me, teeth white as he peels his lips back in a hissing sigh. He moves slowly, drawing out and pushing in glacially, just holding my hips for the moment.

I wonder what I can do in this position to drive him wild, what his button is like this? If I can reach him with my hands, I know the hot button is to feather my fingers through his hair. If I'm riding him cowgirl style, it's to grind on him like I'm trying to forcefully merge our bodies together. If he's above me in the missionary position, he goes manic over my legs squeezing his waist and my fingernails raking down his spine. But like this? I don't know. I'll have to find out.

The next time he draws out, I lean forward, and when he starts his inward glide, I bend my spine down toward the mattress and push back into his thrust. He growls and his nostrils flare, and he grinds into me when his hips meet my buttocks, an intense and visceral reaction. But not quite it. I move with him like that, rolling back into his movements, watching him, devouring him with my eyes.

When next I dip my spine and lift my ass to drive it down and back onto his driving cock, I squeeze with all the Kegel-strong force I can muster with my inner muscles. I clamp down hard, gripping his shaft with my walls as he slides home.

He growls deep in his throat like a predator, snarling like a lion, pulls back and tightens his grip on my hips and pounds into me so hard my ass quivers with the loud slap of impact, and I shriek with the ecstatic surprise of it.

Yup, that's it.

Oh, fuck, is that ever it.

He's primal now, a lust-maddened savage, our bodies meeting with jarring impact, my body rocked forward on the bed, his cock cramming deep, shoving home again and again, and each time I shift forward, wait, rock back, squeeze hard around him, and each time he growls and grunts and curses.

I started out just trying to make it better for him, already having orgasmed so hard I cried, but the intensity of this is breaking something open inside me, his massive cock hitting me deep and hard, and I'm feeling something well up inside me, something hot and billowing like wildfire and aching with volcanic pressure. I'm totally enthralled by the sound of his voice enjoying me, the feel of his hips slamming into my ass, shaking me all over, my body jolted forward by each powerful thrust, my throbbing pussy taking all of him, taking the force of his fucking, and I'm still aching, still desperate for more, still clenching around him and driving back into his fucking cock, his big thick straight beautiful cock.

And I'm begging him for more. "Oh, please, oh, please, don't stop, Derek, please don't stop…oh, god." I think I'm actually choking on my own bliss, caught up in the whirling maelstrom of my own exploding orgasm, forgetting to squeeze and then remembering, and now I don't have to remember because my body is clamping down out of my control, my pussy squeezing his cock so tight it has to be painfully tight, barely able to move.

He falters, groaning a sigh. "Reagan, oh…fuck.…"

Pound,

Pound,

Pound,

POUND—

Is that me screaming wordlessly, deafening, crazed? Yes, it is.

His hands jerk me by the hips, his head falls back on his neck, and I'm twisting to watch, watching him come, watching him take his own pleasure in me, feel a raging thrill of pride that I can do this to him, give this to him. He slams home once more, and I'm hit without warning by yet another seizing tremoring orgasm, my vagina squeezing him yet again, and he's growling and roaring as he comes in synch with me,

and I'm watching this happen, watching him,

loving him—

No, no, no, I didn't just think that, didn't just realize that. Nope.

But I did. Oh, god, I did. And now the thought is out there, I can't push it away, and dammit, I can't deny the veracity of it, because I'm a melting, soul-swelling, heart-soaring wreck watching him finish, watching his sex-god body sheen with sweat, thick muscles swelling and rippling.

He releases me, and I fall forward, hide the frenzied fearful mask of emotions in the blankets. But then he's beside me, turning me, taking me against his chest, cradling me, our panting for breath synched, my head on his heartbeat so I can every thud of his heart—*thumpthumpthumpthump*—and it matches the tempo of my own so exactly I actually panic. I attempt again to ignore what I'm feeling, distract myself by reaching down and carefully stripping the condom off his still-hard penis, toss it onto the bedside table and stroke his length, watching a few last beads of come form on his tip, smear them away with my thumb, taste them.

"Holy—holy shit, Reagan. Holy fucking shit."

I can't answer, because if I do, something entirely too much will tumble from my careless lips.

Maybe he senses something. He has to, because he's rolling into me, over me, his mossy eyes searching mine, and oh, no, oh, god, no, I can't hide it, can't hide the sudden rush of emotions so suddenly and intensely emancipated within me. He has to see it in my gaze, in the wet waver of my eyes, the melted-in-to-liquid blue-hot passion I'm feeling for this man, for Derek.

It's just the sex, though, right? It has to be just the sex. It's really intense, really good. "Good" isn't enough of a word. Rapturous. An agony of ecstasy. Nope, still not good enough. There are no words for what I'm feeling, for how he makes me feel, for how caught up and swept away I am when we join. It's only been twice. We've been together twice. Fucked twice. And it was amazing, yeah. Word-stealingly incredible. He does things to me, draws reactions from me I didn't know I was capable of.

But it's not *that*.

I had the love of my life. I married him. He died a prisoner of war from wounds received during combat with the enemy. I buried him. Flinched at every deafening *crack* of the twenty-one-gun salute, dressed in a somber black satin-and-lace dress that was a family heirloom, passed down to me from four generations of women, all of whom wore it to bury the men they loved.

I had my love, and he was snatched away.

I'm not allowed another love, am I?

I'm not allowed to have my torn, battered, broken, and lonely heart sewn shut and repaired and filled by another man. I'm not. I'm just not.

And it's not even that, really, which has me spinning. Allowed or not, I can't deny, simply cannot manage a denial of the bare, raw facts of what I feel for Derek in this moment. No, love or not, I feel it. It's there, and it's real. It's the fact that it's somehow, impossibly, *more*. Bigger and deeper and more sudden than what I felt for—than what I felt before. And how is that *possible*? How does that happen? So suddenly, so shockingly fast? I mean, it's not like it just appeared here between us, here in my heart and soul. Nothing in life is instant, nothing with humanity happens instantly and in a vacuum, without buildup.

I knew, from the moment Tom came jogging up to me and kissed me without warning, that I loved him. That I would love him, and that I would marry him. I waited for his arrival at my front door with gleeful anticipation. I was overjoyed. Swept away by him, by how handsome he was in his uniform. Each new exploratory touch had me over the moon. It was new and beautiful, and he was my whole life. And I knew it would be that way from the very beginning. Then time passed, and I only got to see him for a few weeks or months out of the year, if that much, but the way I felt for him never changed. Grew, yes. But it grew from absence. And it was tempered by a deeply hidden bitterness that he always had to leave, bitterness I never gave voice to, not once. Bitterness I never even thought about around him.

This, for Derek, is something wholly new, and totally different. It's not gleeful. It's not giddy or fun.

If loving Tom was flying with the earth spread out beneath us, then loving Derek is a terrifying suspension over a bottomless chasm. It's feeling your desperate fingers clinging to a scrap of dirt, feeling the dirt crumble and give way, it's the slow inexorable grip of gravity pulling you down, down, down. And then feeling something catch you, some silent winged creature the size of all the universe, invisible but present and carrying you across the chasm, up and up and out over the depthless beyond, into something very like infinity, but you cannot grasp infinity, not truly, so you can only focus on the sense of speed, on the ripple of galaxy-massive muscles, and you don't know where you're going or how long it will take or anything at all except *him*, beside you. Holding your hand. Clutching you close throughout the black nightmare-plagued nights and beyond the lonely endless fathoms of solitude that is the misery of widowhood. And *he's* real. He, at least, is slippery flesh and sweaty muscle and breath and eyes and memory of sun-golden light on taut skin, pink-red lips wet with our mixed saliva, kiss-swollen lips. He's the knowledge of what you want, what you need, and he's the one who's there, giving it to you, more and more, and such things you never knew were so integral to your continued existence.

"Reagan?"

I never looked away from him, never moved my eyes from his, but I was lost for a moment, drifting in my thoughts. His chest presses to mine, my boobs flattened against his chest. I sweep my palms over the backs of his shoulders, wait for him to speak. He's thinking, summoning words. And I need to know what he's going to say.

I won't admit to it first, because if I never say it and it turns out he doesn't want what I want, doesn't feel it, too, then I can bury it deep and cover it with miles of dirt, erect the walls of solitude once more.

I'm swallowing hard against my fear, searching his eyes, waiting.

"Reagan, I've—I've never felt...like this before." He draws a deep breath and lets it out. "I don't know, I'm not sure if you felt...if you're feeling what I am. Maybe I'm imagining all this."

I breathe out a disbelieving laugh. "Derek, god. Look into my eyes, look at me, *really* look at me, and tell me you don't see it. Tell me you don't feel it coming from me."

He laughs, too. "I see it, Reagan. But I'm scared I'm imagining it. And...I'm not sure I know what to do with it." He hesitates, struggles. Opens his mouth, closes it.

Gently, gingerly, tenderly, sweetly, I kiss him. Slow, shallow, encouraging. Break away with a sighed breath. He lets out a laugh, a small, unsure, boyish sound. Derek ducks his head and touches his forehead to mine and breathes in. Deep, sucking in a huge lungful of air. I'm on my back, staring up at him, and I can't help it, can't help letting my hands cup his backside, closing my eyes briefly in pleasure at the cool, taut hardness, how perfect it feels in my hands. His hair hangs across one eye, and I brush it away with a finger and return my hand to his ass.

"Reagan…god. Why is this so hard?" He lifts his head, his eyes roaming, searching, wavering. He swallows and sighs, tries again. "I've never loved anyone before, Reagan. I don't know how."

"You're doing just fine so far," I tell him. "And I don't know what to do next, either. So let's just…figure it out together."

"Together."

"Together."

He collapses onto me, making me *oof* from his weight, and we laugh together as he rolls with me so I'm crooked into his shoulder. I crawl up against him, nestle every part of my body against his, draping my leg over his thigh so my core is brushing against his leg, my arm across his torso, hand resting low on his belly, just above his crotch, my breast smooshed against his ribcage.

"You really want that with me? Whatever this is?" He sounds more confident, but still a little disbelieving.

"Yes! Yes, I do. I really do." I kiss his collarbone, the only place I can reach without moving. And I'm so, so content right now I don't want to move.

Our breathing slows, and we sleep.

CHAPTER 16

Reagan

WAKING UP IS BLISS. IT'S A SLOW RISE TO THE SURFACE. I'm warm, cocooned in softness. I send out tendrils of awareness, and almost sigh in relief as I feel Derek behind me. I am held. I let myself drowse back under, warm and content.

Float.

Not quite awake, not asleep.

I have a smile on my lips, let it play wider and wider as I get closer and closer to being fully awake. Take stock: I'm a little sore between my legs, but that's a *really* good thing. I'm on my left side, facing the window. Sunlight streams in through my open window, bathing my eyelids in a yellow glow. Derek is behind me, snoring softly. I'm curled up, his knees nestled against mine. I can feel his dick between my ass cheeks, and I like that. I also like his hand low across my belly, his wrist resting on my hipbone.

I feel him take a deep breath and let it out, wiggle a little. He's waking up, I think. I keep still and silent and wait, content in his arms, loving the feeling of being spooned. As I open my eyes, squint against the light, watch a sparrow hop on a branch of the oak tree outside my window, I feel Derek stirring.

His hand is the first thing to move, sliding up my stomach. He's still mostly asleep, I can tell, but he finds my boobs anyway, cups one, and holds it. I smile wider at the feel of his palm on my tit, scratching my nipple. I close my eyes and just sink into sensation. Enjoy the feel of his broad hard body behind me, sheltering me. His hand, sleepily holding me.

He stretches, and I hear him swallow, murmur, moan muzzily.

Oh, my. Something *else* is waking up. Thickening, hardening, spreading my buttocks apart as it burgeons fully erect. And just like that, I'm wet between my legs, biting my lip and wiggling my butt against his front. Sliding his girth between my cheeks, exploring the feel of it. Wondering how it would feel to let him touch me back there. Let him *inside* me back there. Still a scary thought, but not so much as before. I like *this*, after all, his cock between my ass cheeks, sliding, gliding. I angle forward on the bed, tilt my hips back toward him, and now, Jesus, now his thick massive hardness is brushing right against my rear hole. Oh, god. That's nice. Really nice. Really good.

"*Fuuuuuuuuck*, Reagan..." he groans, his voice sleep-thick. "What a way to wake up."

"Unhhhh..." is all I can manage to say.

His voice is at my ear, waking up now, whispering. "You're a dirty girl, aren't you, Reagan? You want that. You know you want it."

"Yeah," I whimper. "I do. I want it."

He's letting me move. And god, am I moving. Writhing my ass up and down his length, pressing back to get more pressure on me where I want it, where I'm scared to want it, scared to get it. It's not close enough, though. I can't get him close enough. He's not actually touching my asshole with his shaft. Then, kissing my shoulder, he pushes his knee between my thighs, and I lift my top leg. Turn my head to find his mouth waiting, hot and wet and his tongue is sliding against my teeth, and I'm reaching down between my thighs, finding the silk-wrapped steel of his cock. Mewling high in my throat, needing him. Taking him in. I have no thought for anything but him, but completion in him. Feeling him behind me, body flush against my back. His groin burying into my ass, his cock sliding into my pussy, sliding in, merging with me, hot and thick inside me, filling me, stretching me. Oh, the burn of stretching open for him. I'm wet, soaked for him.

I reach behind my head and clutch his face, thread my fingers into his hair the way he loves, moaning in affirmation at his powerful hands clutching at my tits, fondling them, tweaking them. Gasping into the kiss as he finds my clit with his fingers, and we're moving together, bodies meeting in perfect unison, finding a flawless rhythm together.

"Reagan, *god,* Reagan."

"Yes, Derek. Ohhhhh. *Oh…yes.*"

Strong, fast, powerful, unending thrusts, bodies meeting, sighs merging, kisses sloppy and groping and wet, hands roaming and clutching.

His movements faltering with fervency even as I'm gripping his hand that's digging between my thighs, and I'm shredded apart and gasping.

Derek rolls and takes me on top of him, my back to his front, and I'm coming and he's coming, and I feel the jetting hot wet gush of his seed, and it makes me come even harder, come so fucking hard I nearly bite through my tongue, breathless, mouth falling open in a silent scream. He's still coming, grunting in my ear, thrusting up, pressing down on my clit with his fingers, holding me down against him even as he fucks up again and again and harder and harder, shooting thick spreading wet heat through me, and I come again, or come still, gripped by wave after wave of spasming exhilaration, and I can actually feel his cock thickening and throbbing as he comes yet more, whispering my name,

"Reagan, Reagan...my god, Reagan." Kisses behind me ear and thrusts again, grinds against me, and I squeeze, milking every drop of pleasure out of him and thus out of myself. "I *love* you, Ree."

He said it. *Ohmyfreakinggod, he said it.* And he called me Ree. No one's ever called me that. Except—

I shake that thought away. "I love you, Derek." I reach back for him, find his cheek, his nose, his mouth biting my thumb and letting go. "Oh, oh, I love you."

"How? God, how do I love you so much?"

"I don't know, but I do." I spoke as if I was him, answering him from the unity of he-is-me-is-we.

It's not until we're motionless at last and he's still hard inside me but softening and slipping out that either of realize what we just did.

I speak first. "Derek? We just...."

"Yeah."

I think fast, calculate. "It's the end of the month, so I shouldn't be fertile. It should be okay." I'm just saying that to reassure him and myself both, even though it's true.

"I'm sorry, I never even stopped to think." His voice is harsh, self-deprecating.

I roll, twist, and lie on top of him, looking down at him. "Derek, don't. I didn't, either. And I'm *not* sorry.

Don't take back what we just experienced together." I bury my face in his neck. "You meant it, didn't you? You weren't just saying it?"

His arms go around my back, holding me close. "I meant it, Reagan. I *swear* I did." He swallows hard. "That's not something I'd say without really meaning it."

I lift my face, touch my nose to his, stare deep into his green eyes. "And so did I. That was…what I just felt with you—there's never, *never* been anything like it. So I'm not at all sorry it happened." I feel everything inside me swell, feel impassioned blazing love. "It's going to be fine. You and me together, right? Just—just stay with me. Don't run."

"I'm here. I'm not going anywhere."

"Promise?"

"I promise."

I kiss his cheek, just below his eye. "Then it'll be fine." I roll over, slip off the bed. I feel him watching me, and I add some slinky sashay to my walk. "I'm gonna take a shower."

I make it into the bathroom, get the shower running, and sit on the toilet and pee. And that's when the worry hits me. The *one* time Tom and I had sex without using a condom, I ended up with Tommy nine months later. I've never been on birth control because it makes my hormones go wacky. I'm regular as clockwork without them, and my periods are usually not too bad. And Tom was gone so much, there was just no point. I wasn't having sex, and I didn't need the birth control to regulate anything, so there was just no need. Of course when Tom and I conceived Tommy, I was at my most fertile time of the month. He was at the tail end of his leave, and we were drunk, and then...oops.

But just now, with Derek? God. So...fucking... intense. I never thought about it, never even considered it. I just *needed* him. *Had* to have him. Nothing else mattered, or even existed. And yeah, I'm a little worried I might have another little oops on the way come...June or July, if I'm counting right. It's late September, so—yeah. June or July.

But no. No. That's not happening. It'll be fine. Something tells me that would be more than Derek can handle. Right now, at least.

I do my best to push those thoughts away, to stay positive. It'll be fine. We'll be more careful in the future. Turns out, though, that "the future" might be a little sooner than I anticipated. I shampoo my hair, rinse, lather conditioner in. Scrub myself, head to toe. Oh. Oh, god. Yeah, that's a *lot* of come sluicing out of me, even *after* peeing. Keep washing, don't think about it. I don't even register the door opening, or the rings of the shower curtain scraping. All I'm aware of is the nearly scalding water on my back, and then hands on my waist. Lips on my clavicle. I smile and sigh, lick shower water off my lips and slide my arms around him, smooth my hands from his shoulders down to his ass and back up, tilt my head back and lean out of the stream, letting it hit him.

Mmmmm. He's hard again. Already. Jesus, the man has, like, *zero* refractory period. Lucky, lucky me.

He groans low in his throat as I clasp my hands around him. Get him harder, get him ready. Then grab the shower gel and my purple scrubby-poof, get him soapy. Neck, shoulders, chest. His eyes close, and he lets me wash him. Back, thighs, ass. Pay special attention there, get him *really* clean. Smile up at him, love the way his wet hair is slicked back against his skull, the way water beads and drips down his chest.

Ooops, how did I get down here, on my knees in front of him? Wash him here, too. All over. Nudge his thighs apart and make sure his balls are extra clean. Scrub the poof up and down his cock, over the tip, all around. He's staring down at me, eyes hooded, and I can see he's half-hoping I'm about to do what I absolutely am about to do. Half-hoping, yet also clearly worried it's just too good to be true. Scrub his length again, then cup my hands under the stream of water hitting his chest, splash him to rinse the soap off. Take his tightened sac in my palm and his cock in my other hand.

"Reagan?"

I tilt my head and look up at him. "Derek?"

"What—um, *ahem*—what are you doing?"

I plunge my fist down around him, then back up. Slide my palm over the thick, broad head, caress the opening with my thumb. He likes that a lot. He squirms, squeezes his eyes shut, and opens them again.

I shrug. "This."

Stroke with a feather-light touch downward, and at the same time I part my lips and take him into my mouth. He tastes clean, like nothing but skin. As I lean forward to take him deeper into my mouth, my sopping-wet hair flops down around my face. His hands slide past my cheeks and gather my hair up. Piles it onto my head, tangling his fingers into the thick mass. Tugs, just a little, as I draw my mouth up around him. When I twist my fist around his girth and slide my touch up and down, up and down, faster and faster, bobbing on him, he lets out a sighing groan, and his grip in my hair tightens.

This is new. I'm not sure what to think, honestly.

Obviously, I've gone down more than a few times before now, but it was only with—I can't think his name, won't, not now, not in this situation—and *he* would hold as still as possible, hands on my shoulders, squeezing to let me know when he was close. He would let go quietly, a slight groan, a gentle nudge of his hips. He was…careful with me. Polite. Considerate.

Derek is different. He's gripping my hair tightly enough that the roots at my scalp twinge, but it doesn't quite hurt. He applies gentle pressure as he moves into my mouth. His hips flex, just a little. Not quite an actual thrust, but almost. And…I don't mind it. It's the same brand of *I think it might be hot but I'm scared to give into it* as my hesitant exploration of letting him touch my asshole.

Everything with Derek is different, a little scary, yet it always ends up being amazing.

I lift my head, turn my face to look up into his eyes. Keep stroking him, slow and soft. "Let go, Derek. Don't hold back."

My heart is hammering, nerves welling up within me. I'm not sure I know what I'm telling him to do to me, or if I'll like it. I'm putting a lot of trust in Derek to not do anything that will hurt me or make me uncomfortable.

He just looks down at me, eyes heavy-lidded, jaw flexing and shifting. He's breathing heavily, and his stomach muscles are tensed. I massage his balls, let my middle finger extend down the length of his taint. Press. Extend a little farther. Dare. His eyes narrow, and the grinding of his jaw quickens. Stroke him, fingers barely brushing his taut flesh. Keep my eyes on him as I slide my palm up over the head of his dick, cup and squeeze, twist, squeeze, keep the tightened grip as I stroke down. He exhales heavily, an almost-groan. As the tip of his cock peeks up over the edge of my hand, I take more and more of him into my mouth, pulling his length away so I can retain eye contact.

"Oh—oh, fuck."

"Mmmmmm." I hum around his cock, slide my tongue over him, taste the leak of pre-come.

His eyelids flutter, his head falls back on his neck. He claws his fingers deeper into the wet, tangled mess of my hair and pulls my head down. Gently, slowly, but insistently. Giving me room to demur, but making it clear what he wants: Deeper. So I take him deeper, letting him push me down, open my throat. Taste his skin on my tongue, feel him at the back of my throat. Pump at the base of him, massage his taint. Back off, suction my lips around his head, my fist clenched beneath my mouth.

And then Derek starts to thrust. Gently fluttering his hips, sliding his cock between my lips, through my fist. Fucking my mouth. He pushes at me, ever so gently, as he thrusts.

"Mmmmm," I hum, encouraging him. He likes this, and I love his pleasure, love feeling him lose control. "Mmmmhmmmm…."

"Ohgodohfuck, Ree…so close."

"Mmmhmmm."

He fucks faster now, through my fist, and I taste pre-come strongly now. He's groaning with each flex of his hips.

A thought floats through my head. Earlier, in the forest, when I swallowed his come, I loved making him lose it, making him come. Feeling how crazy I had him. But I could do it without actually swallowing, which I don't mind but isn't my favorite. I much preferred watching it happen, watching the little hole at his tip spasm, watching the thick stream jet out, hit his skin. I liked watching him come onto my hand, behind the barn. And now, having him right there on the edge, I have to figure out where to have him come. Not in my mouth, I decide. I don't really like that. I never really have, I'm realizing. I've always swallowed—not out of obligation, because I did enjoy giving pleasure, just as I am now—but because that was just the way you did it. Less mess, for one thing. But…I'm in the shower with Derek. What better place to let him make a mess, to try something new?

Derek is thrusting hard now and groaning, and I'm bobbing up and down on him, taking him as far in as I can, tasting him, feeling him. He's close. So close. He tugs my hair twice.

I spit him out of my mouth, look up at him, stroking him hard and fast, pumping him greedily. "Derek…watch."

His flexing hips falter, and his eyes flick open and fix on me, on my fists sliding hand-over-hand down his length. I feel his testicles tighten, spasm. Tilt his cock toward my body, arch my back, tits out. Grip him up near the head and pump. He groans, and his hips push, grind him into my hand.

Now.

He comes, a white flood of thick seed splashing onto my chest, hitting my tits and sliding down, washed away. I keep pumping him, milking him, and he comes again, another jet spurting onto my skin. He grunts and fucks into my hands, and I speed up the tempo of my hands on his cock. This time, I cover his tip with my fingers and we both watch the come seep out between my fingers, and I stroke him, smearing it on him, and then another short burst drips out of him, onto the tub. He doesn't come anymore, but I keep stroking him until he pulls out of my hand and grabs me by the shoulders, lifts me up. Plasters me against the wall of the shower and kisses me, the water going lukewarm on our bodies.

I pull away, smile at him, find the poof on the floor of the tub and squeeze the suds out. I wash his softening cock again, and then he takes it from me and lathers up my front, gently scrubbing each of my boobs and in between, underneath, lifting each one. We each rinse off, and then he takes a moment to shampoo his hair.

We get out, and he dries me off, and I do the same for him. He runs his fingers through his hair instead of combing it, leaving it messy, while I brush my teeth and my hair. We do all of this in a companionable silence, although I can feel him questioning why I did it that way. I'll wait for him to ask. We get dressed, him in the same clothes as yesterday.

Which raises the question….

"Derek?"

He tugs his shirt down, glances at me. "Yeah?"

"I think you should go get your stuff."

He frowns, misunderstanding. "Oh. Um. Okay."

I laugh. "No, Derek. Not go get your things and leave, go get your things and bring them in here."

"You're…sure?"

"Yes. I'm sure." I wrap my arms around his middle in a hug. "I just made you promise me to not run, didn't I? I want you here. With me."

He hesitates a few moments, thinking. "Okay. If you're sure you want that." He frowns down at me. "I still have nightmares, sometimes. Bad ones. Not as many, recently, but…they still happen."

"Did you have one last night?"

"No," he says. "But last night was special. I slept with you last night. Like, sleep-slept. That's a first for me. I never—before, with anyone else, I'd just leave when I—when we…when—"

I make a face. "Really? You'd just leave?"

He seems upset by my reaction. "Yeah. I guess I wasn't a nice guy then. I'm not that guy anymore, though."

God, I hope not. "Did you like it? Sleeping in my bed with me?"

He grins. "It was…magical. Hope that doesn't make me sound like a pussy, but it was really amazing. I loved it. Just holding you. Waking up with you." His grin widens. "Especially the way you woke me up."

I cling to him, scratch the beard on his jaw. "I liked that, too. Loved it. Having you wake up beside me." Kiss his chin, nip at his jaw. "Making love to you first thing in the morning."

I run my hand on his jaw again. I like the beard. Tom was always clean-shaven, being in the Corps. "Say it again. I want to hear you say—"

I don't have to finish. He's cupping my cheeks in his big strong rough hands. "I love you, Reagan."

CHAPTER 17

Derek

TWO WEEKS. THAT'S HOW LONG HEAVEN LASTED.

I've never in my life slept so well, so deeply, so dreamlessly. I would wake up each morning with a warm contented bliss washing through me, and the desire to never ever move, to burrow more deeply into bed, into the warmth, into Reagan. Sometimes I'd have a moment of panic, thinking it was all a dream, a new kind of nightmare. I'd jerk awake, seeking her. And I'd find her. Naked. Silk-smooth and beautiful and wrapped around me.

She clings to me in her sleep. It took some getting used to, as I've never shared a bed before, but it was something I absolutely cherished getting used to. I would wake up in the middle of the night, drowsy and bleary and confused, and Reagan would be curled up on the other side of the bed, at the very edge. And just as I was about to reach for her, she would murmur and mumble, roll toward me, grab my thigh and pull me closer, tucking her head against my chest, and nuzzle against me. She'd fling her arm across my waist, run her hands sleepily over my hip and stomach again and again until she was satisfied I was there. I'm guessing that was it—confirming that I'm real, and there with her. I know that feeling. It's how I wake up every morning.

Is she real? Am I here, in her bed? In...*our*... bed? I get to touch her? Hold her, kiss her? Yes, I do. Thanks to god or whatever powers may or may not exist. Whatever concatenation of events led me to this place, this time, wherein I get to bask in the bliss of waking up next to Reagan every morning....

Thank you.

Because it's the best my life has ever been.

And it's all because of what happened to Tom.

I'm not sure I can be thankful for *that*. I can't go there, mentally. I can only be thankful for now.

Usually I'm the first to wake up. This morning I've been awake for a few minutes, watching her sleep, memorizing her features. Inscribing in my heart and mind the feel of her in my arms. And then she'll make this little noise in the back of her throat, a stretching kind of moan—*mmmmmmmmm*—and her lovely pale blue eyes will be slits through her eyelids, and she'll arch her back, sheet falling away to bare her lush, round tits. She'll stretch her arms over her head, fists clenched and shaking as she tenses every muscle. I'm powerless to do anything but watch, and drink in her endless beauty. When the stretch ends, she somehow winds up molded to me, hair tousled and tickling my skin, her lips grazing my chest.

Of course, by then my hands are exploring her, and her lips find mine, and our bodies meet and merge. I slide into her, and she moans. Then she'll straddle me, but she doesn't sit up, doesn't ride me. This, in the mornings, is about closeness. She presses every last millimeter of her body against mine, lips to lips, until we can't keep the kiss going and she has to seek purchase on my body, toes scrabbling against my calves, mouth on my collarbone to muffle her moans, hands in my hair and fisting in the pillow.

It's not until we've found mutual release in each other—always protected—that we exchange "good morning" and "I love you," and get up for coffee and breakfast and the day's work.

Fifteen days.

On the sixteenth day, nearing three months from the day I walked out of the hospital in San Antonio, things change. I walk into the farmhouse, sweaty from building a deck on the back of the house. It's late afternoon. I hear a phone ring, once, twice, three times.

I hear Reagan's voice: "Hello?" I hear the shift in her tone as she responds to whatever was said on the other end of the line. "I—Yes. Yes, he is. Okay. Okay, thanks. 'Bye."

I lean against the kitchen counter, watching Tommy stacking Duplos as high as he can, then knocking over the tower. I feel heaviness in my chest. That wasn't a good phone call.

She comes into the kitchen, and she's pale. Her hands are clasped in front of her stomach. Her eyes on mine are fearful, worried. "That was an officer from Camp Lejeune."

"Shit."

"They're looking for you. They asked if you—if you were here. I told them you were. I'm sorry, I just I couldn't—"

I cross the space between us in two strides, grab her, and pull her against me. "Of course you couldn't lie. I wouldn't expect anything less from you, Reagan."

"They're coming here. What do they want, Derek?"

"Me. Guess they want me back." I try to sound casual.

"Will they—" She stifles a sob. "Will they send you…back?"

I can only shake my head and shrug. "I don't know. I'll do my damnedest to get out of it, but… if they say 'go,' there ain't much I can do except go."

"You can't. You *can't*." Her fingers claw into my back. "I can't—I can't send you off, too. Not you. Not again. I did it for eight years with Tom. And I lost him. I can't lose you, too. I just *got* you, Derek. You can't go."

I have no words of comfort. "I don't want to go."

"How can they make you? After what you went through, how can they make you?"

"I'm a United States Marine. They own me." Truth is a bitter fucking pill sometimes.

Heaven is a delicate, fragile thing. A brittle cocoon spun of ghost-thin dreams and ethereally faint hope.

So easily shattered.

They didn't waste any time. They arrive the next morning at nine, in a Humvee. I see the dust of their arrival and wait for them on the front porch. I'm wearing a pair of jeans and nothing else, no shirt, barefoot. Drinking a beer. Stubborn.

I'm not a Marine anymore is the message.

Reagan is inside, sitting on the couch. Curled up, a yellow legal pad on her thighs, a black ballpoint pen scribbling frantically. She won't look at me. Tommy is watching *Jake and the Neverland Pirates*. I know the names of his favorite shows now.

As they pull up to the house, I rise to my feet, lean against the post of the front porch, and swig my beer. I run a hand through my hair as the four doors open and four men emerge. Two hard-looking MPs and two officers—Captain Laughlin and a lieutenant colonel I don't recognize.

"Corporal West." Captain Laughlin, his voice sharp as ever, hard eyes raking over me. Tall, whipcord thin, angular features and a nose that's too long for his face.

"Alex." I don't move.

The colonel bristles and steps forward. "You're still an active-duty member of the United States Marine Corps, son. You'd better—"

Captain Laughlin just laughs and waves the colonel off. "Relax, Jim. I've got this." He moves up the steps, leaving the other three men behind. He gestures to the front door. "Can we talk inside, Derek?"

"We can talk right here."

He sighs. "All right, then." Sweeps his hat off his head, takes a seat on a chair, and leans back. "Don't make this harder than it has to be, Derek. You're AWOL. You left the hospital without being discharged. You left without being assigned a sponsor. You left without any further debriefing. Could be said you're in dereliction of duty. I could put you behind bars. Strip you of rank, make you a PFC all over again, and send you back to the FOB. I could dishonorably discharge you. You catching my drift so far, *Corporal?*" He emphasizes the word to remind me of my rank, I guess.

"Sir."

"But I'm a nice motherfucker, okay? I've got a heart of fucking gold, so I haven't done any of that yet. I've given you time. I'll be honest, of all the places I expected to find you, this wasn't one of them. But I get it. You're not getting any judgment from me. All right? You're a damn fine Marine, Derek." He shifts forward, elbows on his knees, dark eyes on mine like chips of obsidian. "You went through hell. You suffered. I get that. I respect the shit out of you for coming out of that with even a speck of sanity left in you. But I got orders, and you know as well as I do there ain't a goddamn thing I can do about that."

"I can't go back, Alex." I set my empty beer bottle on the railing and turn to face him. "Can't. *Won't.* To be totally honest, I don't think I'm fit. I'd be a liability. Soon as shit hit the fan, I'd be a mess. A while back, some punk little fucker set off some firecrackers, and I hit the deck, shaking like a leaf. How do you think I'd do ducking RPGs and avoiding IEDs, Alex? Huh?"

"You're preaching to the choir, Derek." He stands up. "They're not asking you to go back to patrols, all right? They're not trying to send you back into combat. They're not *that* stupid—" He breaks off with a grin, and, despite myself, I can't help laughing because, yeah, they usually are that stupid. He sobers and continues. "I can't say much, not here, not now. I've got to get you cleaned up and on a transport across the pond."

I frown. "So they want me back over there, but not for combat?"

Captain Laughlin nods at the screen door, at Reagan and Tommy, who are standing inside, watching and listening. "Like I said, this is not the time or place for a full rundown. But I can give you the bottom line. They're counting your time as a POW as another term of duty, so you're going to receive special pay for it, and credit for time served. Which means you've done three years out of a five-year term. Do this for me, and we can work something out. Get you a desk job. Recruiting in Houston, maybe. Something easy, possibly even close to here, if that's what you want. Something to finish out two years, get your walking papers, and do whatever the fuck you want with the rest of your life."

The idea of leaving has my stomach twisting. My heart is being ripped out of my chest. Seems I made a promise I couldn't keep. "I served my time. I did my duty to my country, goddamn it. Haven't I paid my fucking dues, Alex? Haven't I? It's not enough I watched a dozen of my closest friends get fucking *slaughtered*? It's not enough I held my best goddamn friend in my arms and watched him die? It's not enough that I spent *three years* enduring torture and beatings and interrogations? I never gave 'em shit but name, rank, and serial number. I didn't give 'em shit, Alex. But yet, none of that's enough? I gotta go back? Just one more mission. Fuck you, Alex. *Fuck you* for asking."

He stares out at the pasture, at Henry shaking his head and trotting along the fence line. "I'm sorry, buddy. I'm not asking."

"I'm not your goddamn buddy, *Captain*."

"I'm sorry. I wish there was something I could do."

"Fuck your 'sorry.' Fuck all of you!" I shout past him, at the colonel, at the MPs, who step forward, ready to bust my ass.

Captain Laughlin extends a hand, palm out, stopping them. He turns to me, all sympathy, humanity, and friendship gone. Nothing left in him now except the commander, and an expectation of obedience. "Get your shit, Corporal. The jet is wheels up in twelve hours. You're on it, or you're in cuffs."

I remain still for a moment, chewing on my rage. Eventually, the knowledge that there's nothing left to do but comply sinks in. Better to do the job, take the offer. Prison will kill me. I straighten my spine. I stand at attention. Snap a salute. He just narrows his eyes, and I can see a faint trace of regret lurking deep somewhere in there. I about-face, each move stiff and angry, and go inside. I slam the screen door behind me so hard Reagan jumps and Tommy drops his blocks, his little face screwing up, ready to burst into tears.

God, that kid. So sweet.

He lumbers to his feet and runs over to me. He grabs my leg and reaches up. "De'ek."

I lift him up. Hold him. "It's all right, little man. Sorry I scared you."

He touches my face. "Sad?"

I force all emotion out of my features, bring up a smile for him. "Nope. I've just gotta—I've gotta go."

"Go where?"

How do you even begin explaining this to a three-year-old? "I...I've got some work to do. I have to go be a Marine."

I hear Reagan choke.

Tommy tilts his head, looking deep into my eyes. Holy hell, this kid looks *so* much like Tom it's eerie and painful. Eventually he just wiggles, and I set him on his feet. "Okay," he says, sober and far too under-standing for his age. "Bye-bye. See soon."

God, my throat is tight. "Yeah. I'll see you soon. I'll be back. Okay?"

He goes to the wooden toy chest and digs in it. He brings out a little plastic figure that he hands me. It's a character I recognize as Cubby from *Jake and the Neverland Pirates*. It doesn't escape me that Cubby always has a map, always knows the way, how to find the path. I take it from him.

"Cubby," he says.

"Cubby," I repeat, putting the toy in my pocket.

Reagan still won't look at me; she's focused on the notepad she's still writing in, focused on not crying. It's a failed effort, because I can see tears on her chin.

I need a minute to gather myself before I can say goodbye to her. So I go up to the bedroom, our bedroom, taking the stairs three at a time. Pull a shirt on. Socks. Lace up my boots. Leave everything else. I leave it here, because I'm coming back. With my head down, I clomp down the stairs, slowly this time. Reagan is still writing, not looking up at me.

I stop in front of her. Kneeling down, I reach up and brush a lock of hair behind her ear. She turns her head away from my touch, and then she sniffles and nuzzles her cheek into my palm. She finally looks at me. Her blue eyes shimmer and shine. They're wet with tears. She's in agony, and she's terrified.

"Don't go." Her voice breaks.

"I have to." I swallow hard. "It's this or jail."

"I heard."

"I'll come back."

"Yeah." Bitter, sarcastic, angry. "If I had a dollar for every time I've heard that…."

"I *will*." Touch the corner of her mouth with my thumb. Run the pad of my thumb over her lips. "I will."

"You'd better."

This is the ritual. This is how you say goodbye: You use words like *you'd better* to cover up how you really feel about *goodbye. You'd better*—as if not dying in combat is a viable option.

She's shaking and trying to hold in the sobs. Tilting her face up to mine, she kisses me with salt-stained lips. Reagan pulls away first and stands up straight. She takes my hands and pulls me to my feet, then hands me a folded square of paper. "*Read* it, Derek. Just…read it."

I put the letter in my hip pocket and pull her against me in an embrace. Her arms wrap around my neck; her face wets my shoulder. "I'm sorry, Reagan. I know I promised you—"

"I love you," she cuts in over me, her words muffled in my shirt.

"Love you, too."

She tips her face up to mine, kisses me softly, then backs away and shoves me toward the door. "Go."

I go.

The inside of a Humvee is one place I never wanted to see again.

The lieutenant colonel, a man in his late forties with a square jaw and intelligent eyes, stares me down for long minutes. Finally, he speaks. "So, you and Barrett's widow?"

I'm a heartbeat away from throwing the limp-dick pencil pusher out of the truck with his teeth in the back of his throat, but Alex speaks up for me. "Jim?" His voice is razor-sharp. "Shut the *fuck* up…sir."

It's silent all the way to Ft. Worth.

Dawn comes early the next day. I'm now clean-shaven, hair cut high and tight, geared up and buttoned down, sitting in the back of a rumbling, echoing troop transport. I'm destined for Kandahar, and I'll get my orders as soon as I'm boots-down.

Oorah.

CHAPTER 18

Derek,

You changed me. You gave me my life back. Until I met you, I never thought I'd love again. Never thought I could, or even should. But somehow, love came to me, in the form of you.

So, that being said, I hope you understand when I say I HATE that I'm writing another goddamn letter. I hate writing letters. It's the loneliest thing in the world, but I'm really good at them. I've had enough practice, after all.

This time, though, I'm at a loss. I have no clue what I'm supposed to say. All I know is that I haven't had enough time with you.

This is my fourth attempt. There are three wadded-up balls of paper in the trash in the kitchen. Most of them were ruined by crossed-out sentences and tear stains. I never sent a letter to Tom that had a tear stain on it. I'd rewrite them, several times, if I had to. The messed-up letters all say the same basic thing. How much I love you. How much I'll miss you. Blah blah blah. But I can't write any of that. I just can't. I have to write what's in my heart. I can't hide it, and I can't keep it in. I'm sorry.

I can't be a good supportive Marine Corps wife anymore. I don't want you to go. I'm angry that you're going. I'm angry at you for being a Marine. I'm angry at the government for sending troops over there. I support the Corps. Of course I do. My brother is a Marine. My husband was a Marine. You're a Marine. But I just can't understand why you—all of you, any of you—keep having to go. And I'm angry about it. I'm angry with myself for falling in love with ANOTHER soldier. I let myself think they'd let you stay at home this time. Considering what you went through, you'd think they'd cut you some slack. But I guess not. And I have to go and fall in love with you. So I get to stay here, on this FUCKING FARM, by myself. Again. And I'm angry about it.

I'm so angry, Derek. And I just don't know what to do or how to handle it. It's eating me up inside. And if you don't come back, Derek, I'm just going to lose it. I'll never recover if you don't come back. So you have to, okay? I don't care what you have to do, but you have to come back.

I need you.

WE need you.

CHAPTER 19

Derek

Afghanistan, September 2010

THE HUEY CONTAINS EIGHT MEN: ME, A FIVE-MAN fire team, and the pilot and co-pilot. The side doors are open, the barren, rugged terrain flying by a few hundred feet below. No one speaks. The fire team is relaxed and ready, watching outside, scanning. I'm scared shitless and trying not to show it.

Apparently, some SEALs captured several high-ranking Taliban operatives. Most of them clammed up and wouldn't say shit. They ended up in Guantanamo. Whatever. But one of them...he didn't just sing, he talked shit. Bragged about missions he planned, IEDs he personally planted and watched blow us up. His biggest brag, though, concerned me.

The American soldier he captured and tortured. He talked about all the videos he shot using me, and how they recruited hundreds more terrorists using those videos.

They want a positive I.D. Seems if he is who they think he is, he's one of those operatives no one's ever seen or even gotten a good picture of, wanted in a dozen countries for countless crimes against humanity. So if he's the one who captured me, I'm one of the only people in the world who can I.D. him. Of course, he could be talking shit, making things up, trying to buy time or make himself seem important. A shitload of people saw those videos and could use them to describe me, but this guy's been talking in detail about things they did to me. Clearly, the best way to make sure he is who they think he is—a big ol' fish in the Taliban sea—is to bring me across the world and put me face to face with the man who tortured me for shits and giggles.

So here I am, in a helo en route to some remote outpost in the middle of the fucking Afghani desert.

Hopefully, this'll be easy. Fly in, I.D. the guy, and go back stateside. Never see this fucking country again.

I've read Reagan's letter easily fifty times. It's odd, that letter. Unfinished. As if there was more she wanted to say, but she didn't have time to finish it, or maybe she just couldn't bring herself to write the rest of it. Something. I don't know what, but I have my suspicions, idle conjecture. But I don't know. All I do know right now is that I need to do this shit and get back to her. The letter is in my chest pocket, along with the Cubby figure.

I'm officially a noncombatant, but I'll be damned if I'll go boots down in Afghanistan without a rifle, sidearm, frags, and spare mags. My heart is palpitating, throat thick, palms sweaty inside my FR gloves.

"Two minutes." The pilot's voice comes over the headset, a brief update.

I watch the ground, wiggle my fingers, and pretend they're not shaking. The helo flares, touches down. Two members of the fire team jump down, take a couple of steps, and then drop to one knee, scanning, rifles up. I jump down, jog toward the single building in view. It's a rude and crude hut, hastily assembled for this purpose in the middle of nowhere, accessible only by air. Remote, secure. There's a SuperCobra orbiting around us. I track its pattern as I approach the door to the hut and pound my fist on it. It opens, revealing a sweating face, a man in blue jeans and a black T-shirt, gray eyes colder than ice.

"Corporal Derek West, sir." I salute, although I don't know who this guy is. If he's here and dressed in civvies, I don't think I want to know.

"C'mon in. This won't take long." He doesn't emerge, just shoves the door open wide enough for me to slide through.

The helo is idling, rotors still turning. The fire team is positioned outside the hut and on either side of the Huey. I can hear the SuperCobra somewhere off in the distance, the sound of its rotors echoing off the mountainsides.

It's dark inside the hut. Hot as fuck. I pull my balaclava down, let my rifle dangle from the strap, holding on to the grip with one hand. I wipe the beads of sweat off my nose. My eyes adjust to the faint light, and I can make out a folding table with a couple of bottles of water, a liter of whiskey. Ashtray, smoldering butts, a few unopened packs of Marlboros. Coffeemaker, powdered creamer. MREs, both unopened and loose empty wrappers. They've been here a while.

A chair. A man, hands cuffed at his sides to the rungs beneath his thighs. Ankles cuffed to the legs of the chair. Shirtless, swollen cheekbones, puffy lip, bruises. Trickle of blood from his nose.

"The classification level of what you're seeing is off the charts, West. You get me?"

"Sir." I signed a whole bunch of shit. I can't say dick to anyone about this. Whatever. I just wanna go home.

"Take a look. Recognize him?" I register the voice of the spook or whatever he is, but I don't look too closely at him. I don't want to know what he looks like, don't want to know his name or what branch he's from. Don't want to know what's going to happen after I leave, or what happened before I got here.

I step forward, closer to the battered figure shackled to the metal chair. I swallow hard and pretend the sweat sliding down the back of my neck is from the heat. He's in shadow, and I can't make out his features.

A light is flicked on, and directed at the prisoner. He tilts his head away, eyes narrowed.

Look at him, pussy, I tell myself. *Fucking look at him.*

I finally take a look.

I blink, shake my head, stumble back, and swallow hard to keep my lunch down. It's him. Fuck.

Then the flashbacks hit me.

Rapid Pashto, or Arabic, or whatever. Black eyes like empty space, darker than holes in the earth. Scarred upper lip curled into a sneer. Thin beard, long and graying near the roots. Pockmarks on his forehead and cheeks from childhood illness. He kneels in front of me, a red Bic in his hand. He chatters to me, as if I understand him. Laughs at his own joke. But the humor doesn't reach his eyes. Nothing does. No light escapes the black holes of his pupils, no humanity reaches through. He grabs my middle and ring fingers, bends them back to the breaking point. Flicks the lighter; a flame spurts and wavers. Touches my skin. I grimace, grit my teeth. I can keep from screaming for a while. Until I feel the flesh charring, scarring. And then I cut loose. Scream. He moves the flame down to my palm, holds it there for a few moments, then cuts the flame and watches me heave for breath. Flicks the lighter to life again, but this time he holds the tip of a knife under the yellow heat and keeps it there till the blade point glows red. He rips open my shirt. Presses the flat of the blade to my nipple. Skin and hair sizzle. I don't bother trying not to scream. Seeing my agony, the black eyes show humor.

My back hits the wall. I'm gasping.

"Yeah. You remember, don't you?" His voice is raspy from thirst, low, evil. He only ever spoke English when he wanted to make a point. "Bet you like to kill me, huh? Try. Kill me."

He's the one who broke my finger, tortured me. Never asked questions, just the torture for the fucking pleasure of it.

I'm unaware of moving, but somehow I've got my sidearm out and the barrel pressed to his temple. I'm gasping, sweating, seeing double. He's laughing. He knows the effects he's left on me.

Brutally strong hands pull me away, and I let them strip me of my sidearm. The hands shove it into my holster at my chest. I'm pushed out the door into sunlight so bright it hurts. Dust blows, grit crunches in my molars.

"So that's him." The guy in civvies. The spook.

"Yeah." I turn away, back to the wind, spit, try to breathe.

I vomit, and when my stomach is done heaving, I straighten. Wipe my mouth on my sleeve. He hands me a bottle of water, and I rinse my mouth. Drink. He hands me the bottle of whiskey, and I take a slug. Chase it with water.

"He ever tell you his name?"

"No. He was the one who did all of the torturing, though. Let others do the beating. But he saved the fun stuff for himself."

Spook nods. "He's a sick fuck." He drags on the whiskey, then digs in his hip pocket for a pack of Reds. Lights one, hands it to me.

I was one of the few in my unit who never picked up the habit. I'd smoke one every now and again when we were all drinking, but it was never a habit. This is a unique circumstance. I inhale, cough, and the thick, unfiltered smoke stings my throat and burns my lungs. It makes me lightheaded, but the nicotine pushes the flashbacks down, down.

"Done with me, sir?" I crush the butt under my heel.

"Yeah." He blows a stream of smoke out of his nostrils. Turns away from me, takes a few steps, then stops and glances at me. "Sorry to bring you all the way the fuck out here for that. But we had to know for certain."

I can only nod. But it's not okay. I'm not fine with it. "Good luck with that fucker." It's all I can think to say.

"I'll make a call when I get back to Kandahar. See if I can get you rotated out sooner."

"I'd appreciate that."

"I'm sure you would. I read the debrief reports."

"The reports." I laugh, a bitter bark. "I couldn't bring myself to talk about half of what he did to me."

"Figured as much. Most of what we know about this piece of shit is from the bodies he leaves behind. You're still alive. Says something."

"Yeah. Its says I was fuckin' lucky." I scuff my toe in the dirt. "Or unlucky."

"You're breathing. You're going home. Got a girl. A piece of dirt to call home. Makes you lucky in my book."

I just nod, give a two-finger salute, fit my bala-clava back over my nose. I hop into the helo. I just traveled eight thousand miles to look into the eyes of the man who spent three years torturing me.

The flight out of the desert and through the mountains passes in a blur. I'm lost, trying to keep the flashbacks from surging up like hot puke. It's not working. I keep seeing his face, the scar, the lip curl-ing, the absurdly white teeth and the beard, the evil dark eyes. The lighters burning me, his fist snapping my finger again and again, just for the joy of watching me suffer.

"INCOMING! *INCOMING!*" The pilot's frantic voice over the headset jerks me back to reality.

The helo is banking hard, the rotors whining to full pitch as we accelerate. I catch a glimpse of a white trail, a dot of yellow. It feels like everything is in slow motion. The first trail streaks by, and the helo rolls, nose slewing around, rocking us in the opposite direction. I don't see the second trail, but I hear the pilot yelling "mayday!" and feel the chopper banking so hard we're almost tossed out, and then the craft jerks, judders, spins. I feel a blast of heat past the open doors, flames billowing. There's a deafening roar, so close and so loud my ears can't fully process the noise.

We go into a flat spin, dizzying, smoke black and thick following us in circles as we plummet. Sharp ridges and vertical rock faces flash past. I'm disoriented, and all I can see is ground-sky-mountain-flames-smoke-mountain.

Our impact is sudden and so deafening it's almost silent. I feel forward momentum and pain. I'm thrown clear, tumbling. Hit the ground, feel something break in my leg. The pain is like the noise, too intense to process.

*CRUMP—SILENCE—**BOOM***

Heat crashes into me as the Huey explodes somewhere close. A god-sized hammer hits my right leg, the one I felt break when I hit the ground. I catch a glimpse of something black and metallic whirling away.

The force of the detonation sends me rolling across the ground, rocks ripping at my face, elbow, and knees. I feel the ground beneath me tilt, vanish, and I'm falling again.

I wanted to make it home. The thought flits through my head in an instant of weightlessness.

SLAM. Breathless, wheezing agony. The sky above is a peaceful blue, a wide bowl of endless blue the exact shade of Reagan's eyes.

Reagan. Looks like I'm breaking my promise.

I'm lying on my rifle. I can't breathe. Right leg is starting to hurt. I can't move.

Quickly the pain becomes a hurt so bad words are useless to convey the enormity of it. I think I'm screaming, but I can't breathe, so it can't be me. Breathing hurts. Moving hurts. My ribs feel broken.

A bloody face appears in my line of vision. American, at least. My ears ring, and I can see his mouth moving, but I can't hear what he's saying. He points, emphatic gestures at the mountain face above us. He lifts me, pulls my rifle out from beneath me. Unclips it from my webbing. I feel my hand being lifted and a pistol is put into my palm. Gotta fight? Shit. I look blearily at the weapon and thumb off the safety. I peer in the direction indicated. Searing pain lances through me at each twitch of muscle. I can see no movement, and I glance at my companion. He's one of the guys from the fire team. Young fella, probably was a handsome sonofabitch once, except now he's missing the left side of his face. Ear gone, skin... not skin anymore. I can see the bone at his jaw. Fuck, that's gross. How the hell is he upright? Jesus, he's a tough motherfucker.

Crackcrackcrack. He's firing. The sound of my M4 in his hands breaks through the ringing in my ears. I follow his aim; puffs of rock dust spurt from the mountainside. Then I see a turban, white against the stone. I squeeze off a single round, and I miss. I try to get my other hand around the butt for a better grip. Can't shoot for shit one-handed under the best of circumstances. I see movement; I fire again. Blood sprays.

I'm dizzy.

God, the agony. I don't want to look at my leg. It's so, so, so fucked.

And then...the welcome sound of a helo, the distinctive rotor signature of a SuperCobra. Rockets flash and whoosh. The hillside crumps and bellies out in fire and smoke and rock chunks. A disembodied leg flies past us. The AH-1W angles sideways, hovering, sliding horizontally, and raking the mountainside with M197 rounds.

Thank you, sweet baby Jesus.

He rotates in midair, floats toward us. He pivots, and I can see him looking at us. Reporting our location, hopefully.

Finally, I make myself look down at my right leg. It's gone from the knee down. Just gone. I let my head thunk back to the dirt, wheezing, moaning. Breathe, breathe, breathe. I lift up again to make sure I didn't imagine it. Nope. Still missing half my leg. Why isn't it bleeding? I should be dead from blood loss by now. And then I remember the piece of metal flying by after the explosion. If it was hot enough and sharp enough, it'd just pinch and sear the vessels closed instantly. Or maybe I am bleeding out, and that's why I'm so dizzy. So cold.

The sky narrows, a squeezing cone of darkness closing in upon me. What's happening to the sky?

I'm passing out, I realize. Good. That's good. It hurts too bad to be awake right now.

Then darkness.

When I wake up, the sky is rotating. Helo rotors dopplering overhead. A helmeted head peering down at me, lifting me up. The jolting on the floor of the helo hurts like fuck. Someone is doing something to my leg. I look around me. My buddy, the one missing half his face, he's there, getting a shot of something to the upper thigh, then treatment to his face, or what's left of it. I manage to lift my hand toward him, fist closed. He touches his knuckles to mine. Our eyes meet. He nods. I fumble at my stomach, my chest. I locate my pocket. Cubby. Where's Cubby? There it is. I clutch the plastic figure in my hand. I can't even form the thought, the prayer, the hope to go home. All I can do is hold the toy and cling to life.

Darkness again.

Reagan....

CHAPTER 20

Reagan

San Antonio Army Medical Center, October 2010

I stand with my back to the wall beside the door to his room and gather my courage, my strength. *I can do this. I can do this.*

I can't do this.

But I have to.

I breathe again, deeply, and let it out. Then I open the door, trying for a smile. He's awake, sitting up in the bed with the sheet across his waist. Dressed in a black T-shirt stretched across his broad chest and molded to his thick arms. Stubble darkens his jaw. Hair is grown out a little. He's watching Sports Center, replays of the Cowboys losing to the Vikings. At the sound of the door, he glances up, sees it's me, shuts off the TV, and tosses the remote onto the bed beside him.

Staff Sergeant Bradford told me what had happened, injury-wise. Derek lost his right leg from the knee down, and he's got broken ribs and a concussion. There's some hearing loss, temporary, they think. He was in a hospital over there for several weeks before he was stable enough to be moved to the States. He's only been here a few days. He called me, and the conversation was short and tense. It amounted to me assuring him I was on the way, and then we hung up. Too much between us to say any of it over the phone. So I packed a bag and drove to San Antonio.

He looks healthy. Gorgeous, vital. But the sheet...I can clearly see the outline of his left leg, thigh, knee, toes. But, beneath the sheet, his right leg ends abruptly. My heart seizes at seeing that.

"Reagan." His voice is hesitant, soft.

"Derek." I whisper, finding it hard to speak. I cross the room, arms hugging my waist.

I stand beside the bed and look down at him. His green eyes search mine. I feel wetness, stinging tears, vision blurred. I reach down and touch his cheek with my palm. He cups his hand over mine and sucks in a sharp breath, eyes narrowing.

His lips move, press thin, then open. "Reagan, I—"

I cover his mouth with my hand, lean down over him, and put my head to his chest softly. "You came back." I find his jaw with my palm. Slide it up past his ear, thread my fingers in his hair, the way I know he loves. "That's all that matters."

"I made it back. Close one, but I made it." He holds me for a long moment. Then nudges me up. Twitches the sheet down. "Wanna see my leg?"

I don't. I really don't. But of course I do. He kicks the sheet off with his left toe. He's wearing khaki shorts. His left leg is thick and muscular and hairy. His bare toes wiggle. The right leg? No knee, just the rounded end of his thigh, scar-pinched, sewn shut. I touch his thigh, just beneath the hem of his shorts and slide my fingers down the muscle and short dark hair. I touch the end. He just watches, wiggling the toes of his left foot.

He goes for casual, but I can tell he's nervous, emotions roiling deep. "Funny. I wiggle my toes, and I still feel like I should see my right foot moving. I can almost feel it still." He looks up at me. "Pretty ugly, huh?"

I sit beside him, perched on the edge of the bed. I leave my hand on his stump and touch his cheek. "Derek. Every part of you is beautiful."

He just smiles. Then the smile fades and looks at me. "I read the letter. Soon as I sat down on the jet to Kandahar. I read it so many damn times."

My heart pounds, beating so hard it almost hurts. "Yeah?" It's hard to breathe or swallow, let alone speak.

"Yeah. And you know what, it felt like you hadn't finished it. That's the thought I had anyway. Is there something you want to tell me?"

Not here. I don't want to do this here. "I—yeah. I hadn't finished it. There was too much—too much I wanted to say, and—and…I just couldn't write it all down."

A doctor comes in just then, and I'm given a brief reprieve. The doctor is short and wide and balding, and bustling with busy efficiency.

"Corporal West. Or, rather, Mr. West, I should say. How are you?"

Derek shrugs. "Ready to get the hell out of this hospital, doc."

"I know, I know. You need months of physical therapy, though. You have to relearn how to walk, essentially, using the prosthetic. It's going to take time."

"I know. I'll do it. Can't I just go home and find somewhere to do the therapy closer to there?"

"Well, you're healthy, aside from that. Ribs seem to be on the mend, although I'm assuming you're still a bit stiff and sore?"

"Yeah, nothing too bad. Had worse playing football on base."

"Any headaches? Dizziness?" Derek shakes his head, and the doctor continues to examine his chart. Finally he nods, and does a thorough examination of

Derek's leg. "It's looking good, and I think you are in decent shape there. I suppose you're ready to go, physically, if that's what you want. We have a list of doctors who can provide the post-care you'll need."

Derek just nods. "Got it. I just need to be out of here. I can't stand it."

"I suppose that's understandable, son." He closes the chart and whacks the file with his pen. "I'll get your papers together, have you out of here in no time."

Another nod from Derek. The doctor leaves, and silence settles over the room. Our conversation has been put on hold, it seems, an unspoken agreement. I just hold his hand and rub my thumb on his knuckles.

Eventually, he reaches to the other side of the bed and produces a prosthetic leg, one of those metal, curving ones you see the athletes using. Derek rolls a type of sock over the end of his leg, fits the cup of the prosthetic over the stump, fastens the blade in place. He pivots on the bed and sets his foot on the floor, then moves so he can get the foot portion of the prosthetic on the tile. He takes my hand, smiling at me gratefully as I move to help him.

"Been practicing a little. It's hard." He shifts forward, tries for his feet, pushing on the mattress.

He gets up, wobbles, and then falls back. He tries again, and makes it. He stands, balancing uneasily. I stand in front of him, both of his hands in mine. He takes a step with the prosthetic, frowning in concentration. Another step. He grins at me hesitantly, *I'm doing it!* clearly written on his face. And then loses his balance and topples backward. I pull him forward over his center of gravity again.

Now he's focused. Step, step, step, pause, step, step, step. He's sweating; his lips are tight.

"Derek, do you want to sit down?" I ask.

He shakes his head. "Been lying down or sitting for a fucking month and half. Fuck that. I want to walk." He makes his way to the corner of the room, where a pair of crutches lean against the wall. He takes them, fits them under his arms, and tries walking again.

I follow him step by step around the room, seeing the pain on his features, the stubborn determination. I think he thinks he can master this right now, here, and be running PT again in a few days. I watch him carefully, aching for him with each step. He sets one of the crutches aside and tries a step with only one. He stumbles, falls, and he's too heavy for me to catch him. He lands against the wall, clutching my hand in a crushing grip, his good foot braced out wide and the prosthetic sliding out in front of him. He regains his balance and gets his feet under him. Feet, or foot? I don't know.

He bumped his head against the corner of the bedside table, and he's bleeding from his cheek.

"Goddammit, Derek." I help him to the bed, snatch a Kleenex from the box, and touch it to the cut on his cheekbone.

"I'm sorry," he grunts, easing down into a lying position, gasping, sweating. "Harder than I thought. Overdid it. I guess I wanted to impress you."

"You have to take it easy. Take it slow."

"I know. That's not how I do things, though." He wipes at his forehead, smearing the sweat away.

"Well, now you do."

A nurse must have heard the racket, and she comes in, sees Derek's cut, and tisks at him. "If you're trying to leave, Mr. West, this is not the way to go about it." She puts antiseptic on the cut, and a Band-Aid. "Now, stay *off* the leg, or you'll be stuck here for that much longer."

"All right, all right," Derek growls. "I get it. Damn."

The hours pass. Derek turns on the TV again, and I sit close to him, my hand in his, content for now to simply be near him. Eventually a nurse returns with the paperwork. Derek signs, takes a folder full of informational brochures and packets, and a list of doctors and physical therapists and support groups. It all takes another hour before I can bring the truck around to the front entrance. I set Derek's crutches and personal things in back, and then help him in.

I point us toward Houston, and we settle in. He twists the volume knob on the radio, and "Smoke a Little Smoke" by Eric Church comes on. We listen in silence, Derek staring out the window.

There's tension.

Finally, he turns to me. The volume goes down, muffling Gary Allan. "Reagan? The unfinished letter. Was there…was there more?"

I keep driving and don't answer. I sniffle. Bite my lip. A little dirt side road forms a T-intersection, with a wide shoulder at the apex. I pull over. I crank the window down and hang my hand out.

"My purse. It's by your feet," I say. "Can I have it?"

"Foot," Derek mumbles. "Only got the one, now."

He hands me my purse, and I unzip an inner pocket. I withdraw the folded square of yellow paper. I hand it to him. My eyes lock on his. "I love you, Derek."

He fiddles with the corner of the paper, folding it, unfolding it. Then he looks out the window, watching a turkey vulture soar. After a long moment, he turns back to me. "Love you, Reagan." My heart swells at the emotion in his eyes as he says that. "When the Huey went down, I got thrown free. Thought for sure I wasn't gonna make it. My first thought was…." He pauses, then, "Ah, shit, got dust in my eyes. My first thought was you. That I'd broken my promise. To make it back. To come back. My other thought was, the sky up there, in those mountains. Same color as your eyes."

"Dust in your eyes, my ass," I say with a laugh and a sniff.

He wipes at his face. "Fine, fuck. I'm crying about it. Happy?"

"That you're back, yes. You're alive. You're coming *home*. Home, Derek. You're home. You kept your promise." I kiss him.

Slow, but deep.

Finally, he pulls away and stares down at the letter in his hands and unfolds it. I can read it sideways or upside down, because I've got it memorized. I rewrote that letter ten times before I could write it without crying all over it.

Derek,

My sweet and amazing man. I was too weak and too scared to write this while you were still here. I knew if I wrote it, you'd be able to sense what I was feeling. I knew I'd lose it, and you'd get in more trouble. You had to go. I know that. I know you'll never be able to tell me what you did over there, and I don't think I want to know. It doesn't matter. All that matters is that I love you.

That I'm missing my heart while you're gone.

Every time a woman sends her lover off to war, she's sending out her heart. She lives, left alone there at home, with a hole in her chest. It's a big, gaping, numb wound. Yet it still hurts when you let yourself feel anything. I assume it's the same in many ways to send a son, or a brother, or a best friend. But nothing can touch the pain of missing or losing or fearing for the life of the man you love, knowing he may not come home.

Damn it. I'm avoiding the issue.

There was something I should have told you. I was going to, but then the phone rang. The captain came and took you away from me, and I couldn't tell you. I couldn't send it in a letter. I'm weak, you see. Selfish. Like you keeping it from Tom while he was dying. I think I understand now why you didn't tell him. And I forgive you.

I can only hope I'll be able to hand this letter to you in person and watch you read it yourself.

Let me write the words again: I love you.

I must be the luckiest woman in the world to have found the love of a man like Tom. And then, again, the love of a man like you. I'm also the unluckiest woman, having sent both of you into combat. I lost Tom, and now I don't know what your fate will be.

For the second time, I commit my truth to a simple piece of paper.

I'm pregnant.

I have no way of knowing how you'll react when you find out. Or what I'll do. What we'll do. I just don't know. I just…I love you. And if you're reading this, please, don't be afraid. Having your baby is an honor, Derek. Having a part of you growing inside me is a privilege. Loving you is a privilege.

I'm not going to sign this letter, either, because there's no good way to end a letter like this.

Except, maybe,

I love you.

His hands shake as he reads the words, and when he gets to the end, he lays the paper on his knee, turns to look at me. His eyes slide down to my stomach.

"I'm not showing yet," I say. "I'm not very far along."

His expression is impossible to read. "But you... you're sure?"

I smile. Why do men always ask that? "Yes. I—I had blood work done." Another long silence from him, in which he alternates between staring at me and at the letter, at my belly, out the window. "Say something, Derek."

"What? What do I say?"

"Anything!" It comes out in a hysterical shriek, and then my voice drops to a whisper. "Are you happy? Angry? Are you—will you stay with me?" I can barely ask that question, so thick is my fear that he's going to leave.

"Stay?" He says the word slowly, as if he can't fathom what it means. "Reagan, I *love* you. Where would I go?"

"I don't know." My voice is small, high, taut. "Anywhere but here?"

"Why? Why would I leave? You're carrying my— my child."

I can only shrug. I try to blink and keep breathing. My eyes burn, stinging from tears I've held in since the day he left. "I don't—don't know—" The words aren't even audible. Breathless sobs are stuck in my throat. My shoulders shake.

I unbuckle my seatbelt, lean forward, breathe, keep trying to hold it in, but I can't. I can't. I come apart. Derek unbuckles and reaches for me, pulls me to him. I crawl onto his lap, and I bawl. The Texas fall heat blazes, and a long wind blows. A sparrow wings past, trilling. I keep sobbing, and sobbing.

He just holds me, cradles me against his chest. "I'm here, Ree. I'm here. I'm not going anywhere. I love you. I'm here."

He repeats this, *I'm here, I love you, I'm not going anywhere,* over and over again, and eventually I hear it, believe it. Feel it, deep inside. He's not leaving. That was my worst fear—that he'd find out I was pregnant and not want me anymore. That he'd be scared and bolt. He's a better man than that, and I knew it, but the fear remained. It was an easier fear to hold on to than the terror of imagining that he wouldn't come back, like Tom.

Eventually, I manage to calm down. I sit up, but Derek doesn't let me go. He wipes his fingers beneath my eyes, smearing salt on my cheeks. He slides his finger over my ear, brushing my hair out of my face.

"Ree, listen. I don't even know what I'm feeling. So many things. I'm crazy fucking scared, mostly. I'm not—I'm not father material. Shit, I'm not even *boyfriend* material. *Before* I went back over there, I was messed up. But now? Baby, I don't even know which way is up. I'm a goddamn *cripple*. One fucking leg. What am I gonna do? I can't help you on the farm. It's gonna be months before I can even walk on my own. You have a baby, and I'll be waking you up screaming just as much as the kid will."

"*We.*" It comes out strong.

"What?"

I run my hand over his scalp, over the inch-long blond fuzz. Again and again, relishing the feel of him really, really here with me. "*We* are having a baby. Not me. We. And you *are* father material. You're husband material. You're *my* material. That's all I know. You're missing a leg. All right. You've got PTSD, and nightmares. Okay. You need physical therapy, psychological and emotional therapy. Fine. Shit, so do I. But you know what? We can do it. Just…stay with me. Okay? I don't mean just physically staying, as in not leaving, I mean…I mean you have to believe in yourself. In me. And in us."

"Of course I believe in *you,* it's just—"

"Do you?" I cut in. "Do you really? Because that means believing in my ability to love you and be your girlfriend or your lover or your wife or whatever it is we are or could be. You have to believe that I can and *will* love you, and be there for you, and be what you need, no matter how scary things get."

"Oh." He breathes in slowly, as if inhaling the scent of my hair. "That…that might be a little harder. I believe in you. I do. But I'm not sure what else I believe. If I'm being honest, I'm not sure if I—"

"Derek." I take his face in my hands. "All I'm asking is that you give me all of you. Just give me *you,* one day at a time."

He lets out a shaky breath. "That I can do."

"That's all I'm asking."

He nods, and I climb back into the driver's seat, get us going again, homeward. The silence is less tense now. Eventually, we start talking. He asks questions about being pregnant, and I answer them. It's funny, actually. He knows *nothing* about pregnancy. So I fill him in. Morning sickness, which is starting to get pretty bad. The first ultrasound scheduled for twelve weeks is not too far away now. Then we can find out the gender if we want.

I can tell he's trying to figure out how to ask a particular question, so I answer it for him, save him the trouble. "And yes, we can have all the sex we want. It won't hurt me, and won't hurt the baby." I grin at him, taking his hand.

He glances at me, and the look of relief on his face makes me laugh out loud.

CHAPTER 21
Derek

THE FIRST MONTH IS FUCKING HARD. REAGAN IS BACK to trying to work the farm on her own again, and that makes me feel impotent. I do finally, after the first week of trying on my own, head down to Houston and find the physical therapist. Turns out the therapy is exactly what I need. She pushes me. Hard. Makes me feel like I'm accomplishing something. Gives me something to work for.

The weird thing is, Reagan and I haven't had sex yet. I'm not sure of myself, I guess. Not sure of her desire for me as I am now. That sucks. The doubt comes from me, though, and I know it. I know she loves me, and I think she's starting to get frustrated. But, for some reason, until I can walk on my own with no crutches—shit, I'd even settle for a cane—I don't think I want to make love to her.

She's going crazy trying to keep everything running, and I feel increasingly useless as I watch her get up at five and bust her ass till dark, on top of taking care of Tommy as well as my sorry ass.

Lying in bed, late one night, I watch the moon and a million stars twinkling in the sky out the bedroom window. I can't sleep. Nightmares keep getting me as soon as I close my eyes. So I put on my leg and a pair of shorts. Using the crutches, I hobble carefully down the stairs, outside, to the dock. I take off my leg and set it aside. I dangle my foot in the warm water and lie back and watch the stars, watch the moon move across the infinite sky.

I don't hear her until she's padding up behind me on the dock. She sits sideways to me, pulls at me, and I sink backward and lay my head on her lap. Crazy, beautiful woman that she is, she's in nothing but a T-shirt.

"Derek?" My name is a question, and is all the emphasis she needs. She's referring to everything.

"Can't sleep. Keep having bad dreams. The crash. That other guy, what happened to his—his face." I close my eyes and shudder, pushing the image away.

Her fingers slide through my hair. She traces my nose. My eyes, cheek, chin. Lips. "What else? You know what I'm asking."

"I feel useless. It's hard to feel like…like a man, when I can't do a damned thing to help you. You're drowning out there, Reagan. You can't do it all, and I can't help you. Maybe I'll be able to someday. But I can't, not right now." I stare up at her, into her pale blue eyes. "And that helplessness, it makes me feel like…like, what good am I?"

She runs her hand down my chest, up and down my sternum. "You haven't so much as touched me since you've been back." She looks away, out at the water, green ripples in the silver starlight, moonlight. "Is it me? I'm starting to show, I guess. It might be hard for you be attracted to me as I get bigger."

"Ree. God, no. You're more beautiful than ever."

"Then why? It's been a month, and—I *need* you, Derek. I need to feel close to you." She presses her lips together, looks up, struggling. "I *am* drowning. It's so hard, doing it all. And I know you hate feeling useless. I don't know what to do. I'm trying to be strong, but I'm not. The more pregnant I get, the harder it will be. And then when I have the baby, it'll be…it'll be impossible. And the only thing that's getting me through it is that I love you, and I know you love me. You're going to therapy, and you've come really far. You can move around almost on your own, and god, Derek, that's just amazing. I'm so proud of you. But… Jesus, how do I say this without sounding needy? I need to feel close to you. It's not just…I don't just want to have sex with you. I do. But I need to *feel* you. I need to know you're…*here*. With me. That you're mine. That I'm yours. I need to feel like a woman, and not just…Reagan. The woman working a farm. The mother. The whatever else I am. I know it's hard for you, harder than I could ever imagine. But all you have to do is show me—show me you want me, and that you need me, too."

So I touch her. I reach up, caress her face. Placing my elbows beneath me, I lift up and kiss her.

And Jesus, that kiss, it sucks all the fear right out of me. Her words ring in my head. *All you have to do is show me.…*

But then, as we lose ourselves in the kiss, she starts to cry. I try to ask her what's wrong, but she shakes her head and pulls me back into the kiss. She lays me down on the wood of the dock and moves to straddle me. She's kissing me, crying. It's confusing, the tears mixed with the fervor of her need. She runs her hands on my chest and grinds into me, kisses, cries, lets our mouths fall apart, and sighs, moving on me.

"Derek, I need—*please*. Touch me. Put your hands on me. Make me feel. I need to feel."

My hands slide up under her shirt, over her spine. I feel my chest open, my heart—cracked, bleeding, unsure, and dry—and then I drink in the feel of her, drink in her need, soak up the way she writhes on me and whispers my name as I let my palms glide on her flesh. A slide and a tug, and her shirt is off, and she's pushing at my shorts, taking me in hand. She puts one hand to the dock, lifts up, and I palm her breasts. Her face is wet, and she still has tears sliding down her cheeks, not wiping them away, just watching me, staring down at me from between the curtains of her hair. She lifts her hips, guides me in. Sinks down around me. Breathes out, an almost-sob that becomes a whole-body shudder, eyes wide and lips trembling.

This isn't bliss or pleasure or ecstasy. No. This is reunion. Finding each other once again. It's me finding myself within her. A realignment of our souls.

Gasps float on the night air. Whispers of each other's names, pleas to God, pleas to not stop, don't ever stop.

I love you. I love you so much. She says it, I say it, we both say it.

Another month passes. I can walk unaided now, but not far. I've got a cane—a cheap one from Walgreens. We find comfort in each other after that night on the dock. It gets me around.

What also gets me through is the memory of the twelve-week ultrasound. My god. Sitting in that room, in the dim light, hearing the distorted *thump-thump…thumpthump* of a heartbeat, a life. Seeing the head and the limbs, the sheer reality of a child. It made it real. So very real.

I'm a father.

I spend a lot of time with Tommy. I'm stuck inside for much of the time, so I've taken over a lot of the care of him. He was curious about my leg, and a little afraid of it at first. Didn't know what it was or how he was supposed to feel about it. As the weeks passed, though, he learned to accept it as just a part of me.

Ida is around, making sure I don't fuck up anything, and she gives me pointers on the basics of raising children. Who knew there was so much to think about? She and Hank have been a godsend. They come over every day to help out and lend support. From the odd look I get from Hank, I think he figures I'm doing a halfway decent job of getting my shit together.

I've been thinking a lot, too—about three things in particular. What am I going to do once I've regained full mobility? What are we going to do about the farm? And Reagan. Is being here and loving her enough? I ponder and ruminate. I work out hard to build muscle, learn to walk without a cane, although I think I'll always feel more stable using one. I can jog on a treadmill by using the handrails. Yet, despite all this progress, I continue to think, and think some more.

Finally, another month later, I make a few decisions. At least, I decide how to best decide. Reagan is showing now, a bit of a bump to her belly. I love it, just fucking love it. Every time I'm near her, I run my palms over her, picturing the little peanut inside, growing and developing. I still have moments when I doubt I'll ever be even a halfway decent dad, but I'm gonna try. I'm going to do my best.

I sit on the front porch, Reagan's cell phone in my hand, and a scrap of paper with a phone number on it in the other. Finally, I begin dialing.

It rings, once, twice, three times. "Hello?"

"Hey, Hunter? This is Derek."

"Derek? Holy hell. Good to hear from you. How are you?"

"I guess you heard?"

He hesitates. "Yeah. I heard. You holdin' up?"

"Eh. Some ways, yes, some ways no." I swallow my pride. "I could actually use your help."

"My help?" He seems surprised. "Derek, brother. Anything. Say the word."

"Can you make it down here for a bit? You and Rania and the little ones?"

"I think so. I can take a week or so off. I'll work something out. Where are you?"

I hesitate again. He's probably heard scuttlebutt, but he deserves to hear it from me. "With Reagan Barrett. Outside Houston."

"Heard about…heard you and her had—"

Here comes the part that'll have him on his ass. "Fallen in love," I interrupt. "Which is part of why I need your help."

"Fallen in...good lord, son." He laughs. "You really did? *You?*"

"Came back different, Hunt. The first time around, I mean. After they yanked me out of that shithole."

That sobers him up. "I know. Trust me, brother, I know." I hear a child crying in the background, and I hear his voice address the kid, his voice muffled. "I'll be there in one second, sweetie. Daddy's on the phone. Yeah, look, it's fine, see? Daddy fixed it." His voice returns to normal volume. "Sorry about that. Okay, so what's the address?"

I give him the address, and we chat for a moment, but it becomes clear he has to go tend to his daughter. I say goodbye, hang up, and think about the next step.

That night Reagan is just out of the shower, towel clutched loosely to her chest, another around her hair. She sits on the bed, pulls the towel off her head, lets the other one drop to the floor. She brushes out her hair, and I watch quietly for several minutes.

"So, I was thinking about the farm." I trace the line of her shoulder, down her arm.

She stills, sets the brush down, and holds the towel over her boobs. Probably for the best, because it's impossible to concentrate on anything with those lush tits visible. "Yeah?"

"What if you sold it?"

She sags, puts her face in her hands. "I've thought about that so many times, Derek. I just don't know if

I can. It's all that's left of—of Tom's family. And what would I do? This is all I've ever known."

"I'm not sure I see much else by way of options, Ree. I think maybe you have to. For you. For Tommy. This isn't...*your* place. It's all you've ever known, sort of by default. But it's never been what *you* wanted."

"No. You're right about that." She breathes in a sigh. Rubs her face. "But then what? What do we do?"

"We start over. For us."

"For us." She repeats the words. Nods. "I need time to think about it, Derek."

"Think about it. We'd figure something out."

"Okay." And then she's brushing her hair again, but the towel slips, and so does my ability to resist.

I've still got my leg on, so I slip off the bed. I stand with my back to the wall, the side of the bed in front of me. She's facing away, cross-legged, naked, long blonde hair cascading damp around her shoulders, brush sliding through it over and over and over. I lean forward, wrap my arm around her middle. Pull her backward.

"Derek, hey! I'm in the middle of—" she starts to protest, then looks back at me over her shoulder. Sees me, sees the hardened evidence of my desire. "Oh."

"Yeah. Oh." I keep pulling her, but now she's got her knees under her, letting me pull her.

I bring her to me. Her feet touch the floor. She stands up, back to my front. I plaster her against me. She turns her head and finds my mouth with hers. I'm using the wall for balance and letting my hands roam as our mouths move. My heart soars, love for this incredible woman welling up inside me. She deserves more than this. More than endless chores and back-breaking work. And I'm going to give it to her. Give her more...of everything.

For now, though, all I can think of is her, wanting her, needing her. Showing her how much I need her.

My fingers slip between her thighs, finding her wet and waiting. Her lips fall away from mine as I touch her, finding her rhythm. Slow, gentle, but steadily building. She starts to moan, grinding against my hand. I tweak her nipples, cup her breasts. Let her ride my fingers, bring her to gasping completion. And while she's writhing and moaning, I take a handful of her hair, push her down so she's bent over the bed. I take my cock in my hand, find her damp shuddering core with my fingers, and guide myself in. Legs wide, balanced, I slide in, slide home. And she just moans, cries my name, and pushes back into me, taking me, taking all of me and giving back all of herself.

I hold her waist, keep her moving, show her my rhythm. She sinks back into me, turns her head to look at me, eyes wide and glazed with bliss, mouth falling open. When we're moving, I palm her ass, smooth and gentle, and circle my hand around and around the perfect globes. And then I pull out slow, plunge in hard, and smack her taut, plump, perfect ass cheek at the same time.

Reagan bites the blanket to muffle her scream, and then lays her face against the bed. "God, god...*damn*, Derek. Do that again."

So I do it again. Pull out slow, caress her sweet ass, the other side this time, give her a few teasing flutters of my hips, and then, without warning, slam in deep and spank her. I feel myself jerk and twitch. It's hypnotizing, watching her ass quiver as I smack it. I spank her again, plowing deep into her. And she takes it, cries out, loves it.

When she feels me come, she does, too. And god, I love that more than anything, knowing she can't help but come with me.

Finished, she crawls away from me onto the bed, and looks back, expectant, waiting for me to follow. I climb up, and she pushes me down, takes off my prosthetic, and massages the stump. Lays her head on my shoulder.

"I'll find a way to take care of you, Ree," I whisper to her as we settle in for sleep.

"Promise?"

"I promise."

"Will you do that again? The spanking thing?"

I laugh. "Babe, you have *no* idea."

"Good." She smiles, a secret smile of bliss. "And you'll love me forever?" She's looking at me, levered up over me, hair tickling my shoulder.

No laughter now. "Longer than forever."

She lies down, nuzzles into my chest. "Then we sell." A moment passes, her breathing evening out. "I trust you."

That's heavy, the weight of her trust. She's going into this blind, willing to sell the only home she's known for her whole adult life, and follow me, go with me.

Only issue is, I've only got some half-formed ideas as to where we're going and what we'll do. But I won't let her down. I promised.

But there's one more step to my plan before we go anywhere.

Hunter and Rania arrive, and it's so damned good to see them. They brought their little kids—two daughters aged five years and four months. Rania and Reagan bond instantly, like freaking Krazy Glue. They take off together and leave the kids with Hunter and me, which is really, really fucking weird. Hunter and I, two fucked-up ex-Marines, bouncing babies and playing dolls and trucks. We're sitting on the floor, my fake-leg prosthetic extended out to one side, Hunter and Rania's little baby, Emma, sitting beside it, slobbering on the flesh-colored plastic. The women have been gone for an hour; Reagan's showing Rania the horses. Hunter finally pulls Emma off my leg and shows her the blocks.

"So, what's up, D? Why'd you bring me down here?"

"What? Just visiting my ass isn't reason enough?" I joke.

"Watch your language around the kids, dude. Their age, they repeat everything." He glances at me. "And you know what I meant. You wouldn't come right out and ask for help unless it was legit."

I breathe out. "All right, fine. Look. I want to propose to Reagan. But I got no idea how. So I need a ring, and an idea." I stack the wooden blocks, not looking at Hunter.

"Damn, dude. You're serious?" Hunter rolls Emma to her stomach, and she lifts her head up off the floor, grinning proudly at her accomplishment. "Shoot. Okay, well, let's make a plan."

The women come back eventually, laughing, Rania's hand through Reagan's arm. We barbecue. Hot dogs and hamburgers and beer, Tommy and Maida—Hunter's and Rania's five-year-old daughter—running wild through the front yard, screaming, laughing, chasing Hank's old blue Heeler, Baker, who somehow got out and came to play. I'm at the grill turning the hot dogs and holding Emma on my hip. It feels weird, but not in a bad way. Never thought I'd hold a kid this way, on my hip like I've done it a million times. She's got Cubby, who stays in my pocket all the time now, and she's gnawing on his head, looking up at me, head wobbling on her neck. She just had a bottle of milk, or formula, I guess they call it, made from water and some powder. She's got it on her chin, along with slobber.

"Babababa—BABABA." She hits me on the chest with Cubby.

"Baba, huh?" I glance at her. "You think so?"

"Bababa. Ba." And then her eyes go vacant, her mouth falls open, and she grunts.

A wet, ripping sound fills the air, along with a stench worse than death.

"Oh." I feel my stomach revolt. "Oh my god. Holy shit, Emma." I toss the tongs on the table and bring Emma to Rania, who is barely restraining her laughter.

"No. I think *you* do this." She lifts her beer. "I am busy. See?"

I turn to Hunter, who leaps up from his seat on the porch steps. "The dogs are burning. Better turn 'em." He grabs the tongs and starts rolling the hot dogs, unnecessarily. "That one is all you, bro."

Last resort. "Reagan. Here, babe," I say, trying to hand Emma over.

She just shakes her head and stands up. I feel relief soar through me. Combat? Bring it on. Shitty diapers? Hell no. But instead of taking Emma from me, she walks past me to Hunter and Rania's car, grabs a satchel of some kind out of the back seat.

She hands it to me. "Go get 'em, soldier."

"Marine," I correct her in a mutter. The bag dangles from my hand, and I balance Emma on my hip, probably smearing shit all over me. "What am I supposed to do?"

Hunter chokes on his laughter. "Change her, man. It's not hard. Gross, but not hard."

"My god, you men." Rania sounds disgusted. Fakes a deep voice, thick with sarcasm. "'It's so *grooooooss*, Rania. I am going to puke, Rania. You do it, Rania.' Or, no, my favorite one. 'How can such a little baby make such big messes, Rania?'" She laughs. "It is only poop. You think, with all you big tough men have done in your lives, that a little bit of shit would not bother you. But you act so silly about it."

Affronted, I toss the bag to the grass. I get down and lay Emma on her back in front of me. "Fine. Jesus. It can't be THAT bad, right, baby girl?"

Emma coos and babbles, kicks her feet. I find the snaps of her little one-piece shirt thing and undo them. Rolling the garment up lets the smell waft up to me.

"You cannot change her on the grass!" Rania says, indignant. "There are bugs! Use the pad under her."

So I find the change pad. Unfold it, slide it beneath the baby. Try to breathe through my mouth rather than my nose. I unfasten the tape holding the diaper closed and pull it away.

"Oh god. I'm gonna be sick." I've never in my life seen anything like it. A sea of tan goo, speckled liberally with what looks like seeds of some kind. What the hell? How does this substance even come out of a human? "Is this normal? Is she, like, sick or something?"

Rania, Hunter, and Reagan all just laugh. So now I've got an open diaper, shit from Satan's own asshole assaulting my nostrils, and...no clue what to do next.

"Now what?" I ask.

"Wipe her ass, man!" Hunter's advice.

"Wipe down, from the top to bottom." This is from Rania.

"Wipe with what?"

"With the...*wipes?*" Hunter snickers, gesturing at the bag with the tongs. "In the diaper bag, dude. White package. Says 'Pampers' on it."

I hold on to Emma's ankles, which are kicking wildly, except the diaper bag is on the other side of me, so I have to reach over my body, grab the bag, set it on the other side. By now Emma is wriggling and twisting, and she's got the khaki-colored poop all over her butt and it's dripping everywhere.

Everyone is laughing hysterically.

"I don't think I can do this." I try to hold the squirming child in place, but it's like trying to wrestle an alligator one-handed.

"Sure you can." Hunter comes over, standing near me. "You're a grown-ass man, D. She's a four-month-old baby girl."

I finally find the package of wipes, get it open with one hand, and manage to pull a wipe free. But six of them come out all strung together. I try snapping my wrist, and the bag of wipes goes flying.

Rania is laughing so hard she has to put her beer down, and Reagan is covering her mouth with her hand, watching me with humor shining in her eyes.

"Baby, you can do this." She speaks from behind her hand, clearly trying not to laugh. "Just look at it as practice."

Hunter's head snaps up. "Wait. What do you mean, *practice?*"

Rania gives her husband an incredulous look. "For the baby? That they are having?" She points at Reagan, who turns sideways and pulls her T-shirt taut against her gently rounded belly. "You cannot mean you didn't notice?"

Hunter glares at me. "How did you not tell me this, you asshole?"

Maida, a tall, brown-haired girl with Hunter's eyes and the Arabic cast of Rania's features, tugs on Hunter's shirt. "Daddy. *Daddy.*"

"What, stinker?" He glances down at her.

"You can't say 'asshole.' Mama said. 'Member? Now you gotta give me a dollar, 'cause I'll just say 'asshole' at school and then I'll get in trouble, and it'll be your fault for teaching me bad words. Like 'asshole.'"

Hunter stares down at his daughter, struggling between laughter and sternness. Laughter is clearly winning. "Maida. You just said 'asshole,' like, four times."

"Three, Daddy. Three is not as many as four."

"That's right, baby. Good job."

"Now gimme my dollar. And don't say 'asshole' anymore."

"MAIDA. Stop saying it!"

"I'm *not* saying it. I'm telling YOU not to say it."

"But you're still saying it—"

"Hunter," Rania cuts in. "Stop arguing with your daughter. Maida—" And here, Rania spews a rapid string of Arabic.

Maida hangs her head. "Yes, Mama. Sorry, Daddy."

Apparently their daughter is bilingual.

I've gotten most of the poop off Emma's bottom during this exchange, but it's taken a good dozen wipes. I move her legs around and lift her butt off the pad, making sure I didn't miss any. Oops, there's a big smear of it, halfway up her back. Once she's finally clean, I stick a diaper under Emma. Except now I can't figure out which way it goes. There's the tape, so maybe....

"It's upside down, D." Hunter spins his finger. "Turn it around. Tape goes by her back." I get the diaper fastened around the squirming little poo-monster, but Hunter makes a sound. "Nope. Too loose. It'll just come off, or the sh—the *poop*—will leak out the sides. Tighten it up a little. There ya go. The tape usually goes right up to the pictures."

I snap the buttons in place and hold Emma up triumphantly. "Bam. BAM. Say *what* now?"

"Now throw the diaper away." Hunter tapes it closed to itself in a practiced move, hands it to me. "Good job. You changed your first diaper. Did better than I did my first time. Learned the hard way what happens when you don't put a diaper on an infant tightly enough."

I bring the diaper inside, toss it in the trash can. Hunter is behind me. "You probably want to wash your hands." He's silent for several beats. "So Reagan is pregnant?"

"Yeah."

"Is that why you're thinking about proposing?"

"Partly. Not entirely." I take longer than I need to at the sink.

"I want you to be happy, man. You've been through some serious shit, and I know how hard it can be to assimilate. It just seems like this all happened really fast, you know? I don't want you to rush into anything."

"It did happen fast. My head spins sometimes, thinking about it." I dry my hands and lean back against the sink. "I sometimes wonder if I have any clue what I'm getting myself into, you know? Like, I'm honestly worried it's all too much, too fast. I mean, shit, you know how I used to be. A different girl every weekend. Sometimes more than one in a weekend—"

"And sometimes more than one at a time."

"Yeah, that, too." I laugh, then let out a sigh. "And now suddenly I'm gonna be a father, and I'm thinking about *proposing?* How did I get here?" I drop my voice to a whisper. "And…will I be able to handle it?"

"Little late for that, bro. No choice but to handle it now." He grabs my shoulders and shakes me, hard. "Listen, Derek. You got this. You *got* this. Do you love her?"

"Yeah. Shit, yeah, I really do. I wouldn't know what to do without her."

"Then you'll be fine."

"I don't know. Sometimes I think it won't be fine. I'll fuck it up. The shit that goes on in my head—"

Hunter grabs another pair of beers from the fridge. "You are more than the sum of your experiences, Derek. When I first got home with Rania, I was having all these dreams, all sorts of nasty shit. It didn't hit right away, though. I thought I was cool, I thought everything was fine. But after a few months, shit started to get gnarly. I'd get angry for no reason. Snap at Rania. Started some fights with guys on the road crew. Finally, my boss cornered me after work one day. He took me out for drinks. He was in Desert Storm. Army, but he's a solid guy despite that. Told me I had to get my shit together. Hooked me up with the lady who helped him work his bullshit out. And that's the first thing she told me that really stuck with me: You are more than the sum of your experiences. I had to chew on it for a while, but what it means to me is that I'm not *just* a veteran. Not *just* a Marine." He hands me a beer, and we clink and drink. "I'm not *just* the poor fucker who went through all that shit in Iraq, you know? That doesn't define me. It happened. It has had some serious and lasting effects on me, obviously. Can't escape that. But it's not *who I am.* I had Rania depending on me. I had to work it out. So I did. Wasn't easy, still isn't. But you deal. You *have* to deal. For her, you have to."

"But I—"

He's not done. Cuts in over me. "You were a POW. That happened. You've seen and done some ugly shit.

That happened. You lost your leg. That happened." He stabs my chest with a finger. "I can't fix your shit in one conversation, Derek. No one can. You gotta start somewhere, though. Shit happened. Bad shit, granted. But the question is, are you gonna puss out and let it own you? Or are you gonna man up and be what Reagan needs you to be? Reagan, and that baby of yours you didn't tell me about."

"I guess I thought you'd figure it out on your own."

"Shoulda told me, dumbass."

"Sorry."

"You know if it's a boy or girl yet?"

I shake my head. "No. We're letting it be a surprise."

"Gotcha."

There's a radio suspended from underneath a cabinet beside the stove. It's always on, the volume turned low, tuned to the local country station. I always thought I hated country music, but it's just a part of life here somehow. I don't even think about it. It's just there, background noise. Sometimes I'll find myself humming along to a song, but usually I hardly notice it. Now, though, the end of a Dierks Bentley song fades out, static crackles, and then the fiddles start. The guitar joins. Tim McGraw's voice fills the kitchen, singing "Where The Green Grass Grows," and my head spins. Suddenly, I'm in the Humvee again, Barrett's beside me, chewing me out for humming the song. Blink, breathe, hands on my knees. Try to block it out.

Nope.

I can hear the *whoosh-BOOM* of the RPG that takes out the first truck, and I'm hyperventilating.

Dizzy.

I hit the floor, gasping for breath. Hunter is talking to me, but all I can see is Reagan pushing through the back screen door, falling to her knees beside me, cradling my head in her lap. Whispering something to me. It's just buzzing at first, but it evolves into her voice, telling me it's okay, it's okay, it's okay, it's not real, I'm okay....

Finally, everything settles back to normal. The tight ache in my chest fades, and my breathing slows. I struggle up to my feet. I grab my cane from beside the door and push past everyone. "And *that*, people, is why I'm worried about being a father."

After a while, Reagan finds me out at the pond. "I'm not worried, you know."

"You should be."

She sits behind me, rests her cheek on my back. "But I'm not. Flashbacks, panic attacks? They don't make you unfit to be a father."

"What if that had happened while I'd been holding Emma? I'd have dropped her. What if it happens when I'm holding our child? How are you gonna explain to a kid that I freak out for no reason? I've woken Tommy up more than once already."

"It's not for no reason, Derek. And we'd handle that, if it came to it." She pulls at my shoulder, and I pivot in place to face her. "I trust you. And I believe in you. Watching you with Emma? It's making me crazy. You're so fucking hot and adorable and sweet, it makes me crazy. You'll be an *amazing* father, Derek. You just have to trust me, and trust yourself. I wasn't ready to be a mother when I had Tommy. I had no idea what I was doing. And I did it alone. I had to figure it all out by myself. I thought for sure I'd screw him up. But, the thing is, babies are simple. Not easy, but simple. Keep them fed, keep their butts clean, and love them. That's all they need. It's hard raising a kid. I'm not gonna lie. You wake up a million times a night, trying to figure out what they want. You think for sure you're fucking up somehow, because they just *won't...stop...crying*. But you figure it out. You love them, hold them, feed them. And they forgive you when you mess up." She touches my face. "And so will I."

And goddammit, there are the emotions again, shit going haywire. But she just kisses me like it doesn't bother her that I'm a mess, that I'm grabbing her like I'm scared I'll lose her. She just holds me back, just as tight, and eventually we go back up and rejoin our friends.

And they understand, too.

Knowing you've got people in your life that can take the worst shit you've got and not judge you? It's the best feeling in the world.

CHAPTER 22
Reagan

THE FARM IS OFFICIALLY UP FOR SALE. THERE'S AN agent, a list price, a whole slew of things to do to make the house, especially, sellable. It's overwhelming. And I still have no idea what we're doing if it sells. *When* it sells. I'm trying to hold it together, trying to be tough, but it's hard. So hard. This is all I've known since I was nineteen. Tom's family has farmed this land since the eighteen hundreds, and I'm just going to sell it off like nothing?

And I have zero other skills. I'm very literally following Derek on blind faith. But I know this is the only real option. There's no way I can keep the farm going, not for much longer anyway. Not without Derek's help. God, he's working his ass off getting his mobility back, learning to function with as much normality as possible. But his ribs are still stiff, and he's spending too much time moving around, so it takes a toll on him. This just isn't a workable life for us anymore.

And, if I look deep down inside myself, I'm tired of the farm. I'm just exhausted. I can't do it anymore, emotionally. I need a change. But the problem is, change is damn scary.

Rania's been helping me sort things out. She and Hunter and the kids made a return visit to give us a hand. She and I have been packing up things I don't want to get rid of yet, but don't know what else to do with them except pack them. We've been cleaning areas that probably haven't been thoroughly cleaned in decades. Derek and Hunter are touching up the paint inside, patching holes in the plaster, pulling down wallpaper in rooms that haven't been touched since the sixties.

A week goes by quickly. Rania and Hunter are staying in Hempstead, in a little motel, and I can tell they're ready to go home. But god, it's been wonderful having them around. I haven't had a friend like Rania in…probably ever. Not since I was a little girl in Oklahoma. And Hunter has been great for Derek, kicking his ass to stay positive, pushing him physically, keeping him busy.

I wouldn't mind moving somewhere closer to them.

It's a Friday afternoon, and the house is so clean and empty of clutter that it's unrecognizable. I've been avoiding one room, though. Tom's room. I'm standing outside the door, a stack of Rubbermaid storage bins in my hands. Rania is beside me, holding a broom and dustpan, rags and a bottle of Pledge.

"Perhaps…maybe this is not my place, Reagan," Rania begins, glancing at me, assessing my obvious hesitation. "Perhaps I should do this myself."

I shake my head. "No. I have to do this."

Taking a deep breath, I place my hand on the doorknob and push it open. A double bed along the far wall, a hand-sewn quilt. A desk beneath the window, a Mason jar full of pens, a stack of *Sports Illustrated*. Baseball and football posters on the wall, as well as *Sports Illustrated* Swimsuit Edition centerfolds. I shake my head at that. Boys. A bookshelf between the desk and the bed, stuffed with old science fiction novels, westerns, some Tom Clancy. I pull out *Patriot Games,* open the hardcover; yep, it's Hank's.

God, Hank. He's been really sick lately, in and out of the hospital. Derek and I visited them the other day, and Ida and I stood outside the door, trying not to listen as Hank and Derek passed idle chatter, but eventually the conversation turned serious. To Korea, and Afghanistan. Coping with life after war.

I shake my head. I can't think about Hank right now.

I place the book, along with the rest of the novels, in an empty storage bin. Soon the shelf is empty. All the books are old, dog-eared, read a thousand times. Most have Tom's initials on the inside flap. Rania takes the bin full of books and wrestles it out into the hallway, and we move the shelf. I laugh, finding a stash of *Playboy* magazines stuffed between the wall and the bookshelf, within reach of a certain boy when he's lying in bed. I throw them away, struggling desperately against the image of a teenaged Tom, jerking off to some model on a centerfold. I end up half-laughing, half-sobbing as I check the other spot, between the mattress and box spring. There's more porn there, along with a flattened pack of Camel Lights and what looks like a twenty-year-old half-smoked joint. God, Tom. What a little troublemaker.

Rania stuffs the clothes from the dresser and the closet into several bags, tying them closed before I can see them. We peel the posters off the wall, strip the bed of the sheets and the quilt. The sheets get tossed; the quilt I save for Tommy. Tom's great-great-grandmother made that several decades ago.

I'm crying by the time the room is cleaned out. The floors are vacuumed, the bed and dresser and shelves moved and cleaned under and behind. The bins we leave at the top of the stairs for the men to move out to the barn. Finally, I stand in the doorway once more, looking into what is now just another bedroom.

"You are a strong woman, Reagan," Rania says.

"It's just stuff."

Rania shakes her head. "No. Our possessions, things like what is in those bins, they are not just blankets and books. They are memories. They hold pieces of us, I think. Little pieces of our souls. So it is not easy to see them, or to feel the spirits of a lost loved one that live in those possessions."

"You sound like you know from experience."

"Oh, yes. Before I met Hunter, when I was little girl." She stares off into space, thinking, remembering. "The first war was going on. My Aunt Maida, she was all the family my brother and I had left, and she was not well. She is whom my daughter is named for, just for you to know. She died. My Aunt Maida, I mean. She died, and Hassan and I were alone. She had few possessions. There was only a comb, I think. A little hand mirror, maybe? When the bomb destroyed the house, everything I owned, everything I had left of Mama and Papa and Aunt Maida and Uncle Ahmed, was all gone. Then, I was too concerned with staying alive to think about it. But now? I wish I had something of theirs. Aunt Maida's comb. I can remember her, before Uncle Ahmed died, combing her hair. She would comb and comb and comb, until her hair shone like the night sky, black with shining stars. I wish I had that comb." She shakes her head, clearing the memories. "It is not the same as this, I think, but it is similar."

"I wonder where the boys are?" I ask, by way of changing the subject.

Rania shrugs. "Off somewhere, being men. Who knows? They'll be back soon, I think."

We go back downstairs. Tommy and Maida are watching TV, Emma sleeping in the pack and play. Rania and I take a break, because there's really not much to do except actually sell the place, and pack up our things.

It's past six when Hunter and Derek return.

Hunter goes immediately to Rania, kisses her. "So, babe. How would you feel about staying here with me and all three kids while Derek and Reagan get some time alone?"

Rania narrows her eyes at her husband, but reads something in his gaze, some message only the two of them can decipher. She nods and shrugs. "Okay."

Derek takes my hand. "Come on. Let's go for a ride."

Something is going on. "We can't just—"

"Sure you can." Hunter waves his hand. "We'll make some dinner and watch a movie. Go."

I want to, so badly; since Hank has been sick, Derek and I haven't had any time alone. I feel bad about wanting Derek to myself, especially as it becomes more and more clear that Hank doesn't have much time left.

"Come on, babe," Derek whispers in my ear. "Just an hour or two."

"Okay," I sigh. "Let me get cleaned up."

Derek just pulls me by the hand, dragging me outside. "No point—we'll just end up smelling like horse. Come on."

I sigh again, and let him pull me to the barn. I saddle Henry; he saddles Mirabelle. Somehow, I know where we're going: the clearing. I settle into the ride, letting Henry pick his path at a walk, enjoying the cool of the evening, Derek riding beside me, grinning at me every now and again.

He's definitely planning something.

My heart ratchets as I try not to hope he's planning what I think he's planning.

Nope, nope, nope. Don't go there. You love him, he loves you. That's all you need. But it's not.

So I ride, and watch his back sway as he rides. I let him lead me to the clearing, keeping my mind blank of hopes. Yet when he pulls Mirabelle to a stop in the clearing, dismounting slowly and carefully, taking the weight on his good leg and hopping for balance, I know something big is up.

There's a huge blanket on the ground in the center of the clearing. A picnic basket. A bottle of sparkling grape juice, two goblets. There's a camp lantern instead of candles, since this is a forest.

"Derek?" I slide off Henry. "What is this?"

"A picnic, babe." He takes the reins from me, pickets both horses where they can graze. "Have a seat."

I sit. He leaves the horses saddled and moves to sit beside me on the blanket. He grins at me again, and digs in the picnic basket. "This was put together by a couple of dudes, so there's a limited spread. Some Brie and crackers, summer sausage, some fruit…." He lifts the bottle of grape juice. "And this instead of wine, since you can't drink right now."

It's too soon to be emotional, right?

We eat, talk about the random things that come up. Eventually, he gives me a look that says he's about to say something important. My heart clenches, lifts into my throat. "So." He pours us each some more juice, scratches at the skin where his leg meets the prosthetic. "Been thinking a lot. I want to make a career of physical therapy. Do what the guys at the gym did for me. I've got to take some classes to get certified, but that won't take too long."

I shouldn't feel let down, but I do. "That's good, Derek. I'm glad you have a plan."

"Well, it's a start. My CRSC benefits give us a little wiggle room. We can't live off it for long, but we should be okay." He takes my hand, rubs my knuckles with his thumb. "The thing is, it's a job I could do in a lot of different places."

I get where he's going with this. "You want to talk about where we'll move if the farm sells?"

He nods. "Probably should come up with some ideas, at least."

I swallow hard against the lump in my throat. This wasn't the conversation I thought we'd be having. "I don't know, Derek. I've never lived anywhere but Oklahoma and here."

"Well, here's the thing: Part of the reason Hunter and Rania could spare the time to come down here again was that Hunter had an interview with the Bexar County Public Works department, managing the road crews in the San Antonio area. And I made a couple of calls myself this week. Talked to some people at the medical center over there. I could work at the hospital as an orderly until I have my physical therapy degree."

"What—*ahem*." I have to blink hard, think. "What would I do?"

"Anything you wanted?" He rubs his cheek with a knuckle. "This is a chance to…I don't know. Start over? Find something you enjoy? You've been busting your ass, dawn to dusk, for a fuckin' decade, babe. Just to keep shit going. You never asked for it, and I kind of gather you never really wanted it. But you did it. And you never complained. Now we got a chance to find something just for you. For us. With my CRSC and the job at the hospital, we should be able to make it fine. You would have time to figure it out. Stay home with Tommy, if you want. Tommy and the baby, I guess it'll be. I don't know. My point is…." He trails off, seeing that I'm having trouble.

Meaning, I'm not looking at him, blinking hard and fast, breathing slowly. "Yeah. That—that sounds like a good idea."

"Shit. I fucked this up." He turns away from me, wipes his face with both hands. "This was supposed to be this romantic picnic in the woods, in our spot—"

"It is, Derek! It's perfect. I'm sorry I'm so emotional right now, I'm just—"

"I wasn't supposed to make you cry." He runs his hand through his hair. "At least, not like that."

That gets my attention. "What? What do you mean?"

He seems at a loss, as if he's bursting with a million things he wants to say but doesn't know where to start. Finally, he growls and leans into me, kisses me. It's a breathless kiss, a thought-stealing kiss. A distraction, a fake-out. He's got me down on my back, and we're getting lost in each other. I'm clutching his back, scratching my fingers down his spine.

Just when I think he'll take us where I suddenly want us to go, he pulls away. He's levered up over me, staring down at me. Touching my cheek with his palm.

"I love you so much, Reagan. Sometimes I still don't even know how it happened, but I'm thankful every day that it did. And I still have moments where I think you must be crazy for loving a guy like me. Moments where I doubt whether I'm good enough for you. I want you to be happy. That's all I was thinking about, when I was talking about plans just now. Where we could go, what we could do. I just want you to feel like you have a future you're happy about. I want that for us, even if I'm still sometimes wigged out by the fact that there *is* an 'us.'"

"I'll go anywhere, Derek. I'm trusting you. I'm following you." I stare up at him, let him see my sincerity. I *do* trust him, and I *will* follow him wherever he goes. It's scary, but he's worth it.

"And that's—the fact that you trust me like that? Reagan, it scares me. I don't want to let you down. I *won't.*" He swallows hard. "This has all happened so fast. A matter of months, you know? My life changed when I was taken prisoner by the Taliban. Changed for the worse. But then those Raiders rescued me, and I ended up in Texas, and I met you. You captured me, and my life changed again. For the better this time. And now I can't—I don't even know how to live my life without you in it. That's crazy, to me. That, in literally just a handful of months, you've become…shit, how do I put it? You've become part of me."

Oh, shit. Here we go. My heart is hammering in my chest again, and I have to hold on to his shoulders to keep my hands from shaking. I can only look up at him and drink in his words and hope, hope, *hope*.

"I love—" The words stick in my throat, and I try anyway, try to whisper them. "I love—"

"Ssshhh. Just listen." He touches my lips with a finger. Reaches into the picnic basket and pulls out a little black box. "I hope I'm doing this right. I'm so nervous. Never thought I'd do this, but here we go."

He starts to sit up, like he's gonna do the one-knee thing, but I hold onto him. "No. Here. Like this." I keep him in place, leaning over me. He's perfect here. *We're* perfect here.

"Reagan…will you marry me?" He's got the ring, a little thing, but beautiful. Simple, white gold, a princess-cut diamond, a single tiny diamond on either side of the larger center one. I'm crying, nodding. Holding up my finger. "Come on, baby. Let me hear the word."

"Yes." I choke it out, squeak the word he wants to hear. "Yes, yes. *Yes*. Please, yes."

"Dear god, thank you," he breathes.

He takes my left hand in his and slides the ring down onto my fourth finger.

"Did you really think I'd say no?" I ask.

He shrugs. "Like I said, it doesn't always make sense to me that you could love me, and I—I want to make you mine. So you can't change your mind."

I just laugh. "I was yours already, silly. I don't know how this happened any more than you do, Derek. But I'm grateful, too." I hang on to his neck and lift myself up for a kiss. "And I'll never change my mind."

"Swear?"

I push him; we roll so I'm on top. "Derek. To me, that's what getting married is: a promise that I'll never change my mind."

"Oh."

I kiss him then. Deep, long, and hard.

But again, before I can really get lost in it, he pulls away. "There's one other thing, Ree."

"What?" I breathe, kissing his jaw, aching for him, hungry for him.

"Tommy...I want to adopt him." He drops this bomb in a calm voice, as if it's not going to rock my world. "But I want him to—to keep Tom's name. I want you to take mine, and keep...keep the Barrett. Hyphenate. So Tommy has...so Tommy knows exactly where he came from."

"God, Derek." I'm bawling suddenly. Even without pregnancy hormones making everything go haywire, this would have me in pieces. But both? I'm a wreck, instantly. "You mean—you mean it?"

"I love that boy, Ree." He swallows hard. "And I loved his dad like a brother. I want Tommy to know, when he's old enough, who his father was. Where he came from. I want him to know that Tom was one of the best men I've ever known."

That makes me cry even harder. I can't stop. The proposal, and then this? I can't breathe.

Derek lets me cry, holding me tight.

When I get hold of myself, I'm still full of so many emotions I don't know what to do with them all. I'm overflowing. Boiling over. The only thing I know how to do is crush my mouth to Derek's and devour his breath, taking his strength into me. He holds me, and we kiss, and kiss, and kiss. And then his hands wander, and I moan into his mouth to encourage him.

We roll and paw at each other, peel clothes off, try to keep our lips connected while stripping each other. I reach for him, and when I've got him naked, he is hot and hard, and I'm wet and aching, and this is so perfect, him beneath me, his body a pillow, a rock, a shelter. I taste his tongue and impale myself on him, sinking down onto him. I fill myself with him.

I moan his name and begin to move.

I take everything I need from him, gasp his name and take and take. And between every breath, he says my name, and takes all I have. I take, he takes. It works, because I'm giving, and he's giving, and we're both complete.

CHAPTER 23

Reagan

I'M WEARING A WHITE WEDDING DRESS, HOLDING A
bouquet of pink roses, white lilies, and lavender. We're
not in a church, though. We're in the Brenham hospital. I'm walking down the aisle, which, in this case, is
the hallway of the hospital leading up to Hank's room.
Ida is pushing his wheelchair, and I've got my hand on
his arm.

Hank had a stroke last week. He was doing okay
for a while, but then he got a cold, the cold led to
pneumonia, and then a stroke. Now the right side
of his face is pulled down, his lip drooping. But his
left hand, clutching mine, is as strong as ever. He's
giving me away. The nurses and doctors are all lining the hall, piled into doorways, watching. They all
love Hank here, because how can you not? Hank is

amazing. Ida is blinking hard, fighting tears, like I am. Tears at Hank's deteriorating condition, tears for me, tears about me getting married.

The wedding march is coming from an iPhone, played over a mobile speaker. Rania follows me, holding the train of my dress. Tommy? Ohhh, Tommy. So damn cute in his tux, walking in front of me beside Maida Lee. Maida scatters flower petals, and Tommy holds a pillow with the rings. He practiced for days at home, walking from the barn to the house and back with the pillow from his bed and a toy of some kind.

We move through the doorway into the room. The bed got moved flat against the wall for the ceremony, and someone found a lectern or a podium from somewhere. The hospital chaplain stands behind it, flipping through the pages of his Bible. Derek stands to the left of the podium, dressed in his best blues. The right leg of his uniform slacks is pinned up, showing the athletic prosthetic. He's so gorgeous in his uniform it's hard to look at him, but impossible to look away. Hunter is beside him, in his blues.

I stop in front of Derek, and Ida turns Hank's chair so he can see us both, so he can hold my hand. He won't let go. So I stand facing Derek, my right hand in Derek's, my left clutched in both of Hank's.

I'm half-listening to the chaplain say the words—*dearly beloved, we're gathered here*—as I alternate my gaze from Derek to Hank and back again. We were going to wait to get married until the farm sale was finalized, but then Hank's condition started worsening to the point that he couldn't leave the hospital. A wedding without Hank was unthinkable, so we scrambled. I found a dress, Hunter and Rania and the girls drove down, making it in one marathon drive. They helped us find tuxes, flowers. It had to be a real wedding, even if it was in a hospital—that was Derek's only request. So here we are, me in my backless, strapless dress gown with a short train. Ida, ever skillful, managed to alter the dress to accommodate my growing belly.

We come to the vows.

Derek looks me in the eyes. "I stayed up all night for days, trying to figure out how to write these vows. I must've scrapped a dozen attempts. None of it was right. So I'm going for simple. Just say what's in my heart, right here, right now. And really, it is pretty simple. I love you. I'll fight for you. For us. I'll never give up, and I'll love you more every day. I'll always be faithful. I'll always be there for you, for Tommy, and for whoever this" —he touches my belly— "little person in here turns out to be. That's my vow, Reagan: to love you forever, no matter what, through everything and anything."

"Derek…I never realized it, but I didn't believe in second chances. Especially when it came to finding love. I don't think you believed in love at all. So we both learned something when we met. And now, here we are. I could tell you I love you right now, and of course it would be true. But it's not enough. It's not good enough. I know we haven't come to this part yet, but I'm going to say it anyway: I do." I squeeze his hand, blinking back tears. "I do. A million times, I do."

The chaplain glances at Derek. "Son?"

"I do." Two words from his lips, but I hear three, I see the *I love you* in his eyes.

"Then, by the power vested in me by the state of Texas, I now pronounce you man and wife. You may—well, ahem. I guess you know what to do."

We're kissing, a deep, slow kiss that's inappropriate for a wedding or a hospital, much less a wedding *in* a hospital, but everyone is cheering and clapping, and there are tears on many faces.

Hank pulls my hand, and I break away from Derek. Hank's other hand struggles up off his lap, gesturing to Derek, who takes it. Hank places my hand on top of Derek's, and then sandwiches our joined hands between his. He wants to speak, wants to say something, but he can't. His lips move, and his eyes go from mine to Derek's and back, full of thoughts and intelligence and emotion.

Ida speaks up, speaking for her husband of fifty-odd years. "We love you, Reagan. We half-raised Tom. We kissed him and gave him money when he left for boot camp. We sent him care packages everywhere he went. We stood with you at his funeral. We cried with you. We've helped you raise Tommy." Her voice falters, and she looks to Hank for strength. Somehow, she finds it. "We've raised six children of our own, and we have—oh my, what is it now?— more than twenty grandchildren, and at least three great-grandchildren."

There are cheers from the crowd around the door where those children and grandchildren and great-grandchildren are gathered.

"Yes, my loves. Now hush." She takes a shuddering breath. "We love you, Reagan. And you, too, Derek. Be each other's—"

"And me, Gramma Ida? And me?" Tommy pipes up. He climbs up on Hank's lap. Hank's eyes waver, and he squeezes Tommy. "You love me, too, Gramma Ida?"

Ida has to fight for composure. "Yes, Tommy. Dearest, sweetest Tommy. You most of all, my boy." She caresses Tommy's head. "Reagan, Derek, be each other's happiness. Life hands you a lot of lemons, which means you have to be each other's sugar, so you can make lemonade. That's the essence of love, if you ask me. The determination to be sweet as sugar when everything around you is lemons."

Hank nods. Reaches past Tommy for me. I keep hold of Derek's hand, pulling him with me. Hank's once long and strong arms, now trembling and straining, wrap around us three, binding us, blessing us.

In that same hospital room, Hank passes the next day, surrounded by his family. Which includes, of course, Tommy, Derek, and me.

Ida cries, but she's holding it together as the family, one by one, kisses Hank's face, saying goodbye for the last time. They cling to each other and file out of the room. Finally, everyone is gone. Everyone except Ida and me.

"Hank was my second husband, you know." She's lying on the bed beside him, her head on his chest, now forever still. I suppose she's fallen asleep like this every night for…whatever three hundred and sixty-five times fifty-seven is.

I'm startled by her sudden admission. "Really? I never knew that."

"Only Hank knows. Knew. My first husband, William, was a fighter pilot. I was sixteen, he was nineteen, and so handsome. I ran away to marry him. This was nineteen-fifty, and everyone knew the Korean War was coming. We were married in a little church in Tupelo, Mississippi, on February eighteenth.

"He'd just finished training school. I think he'd told them he was older than he was, but I honestly don't know. He was a very talented pilot, I do know that much. We had three months together. Three wonderful, amazing months. We were just kids, you know, he and I both. Me especially. My parents were so angry, and I ran away. I thought I knew better, the way teenage girls do. They sent me letter after letter to the little apartment where Will and I lived, outside Langley. They begged me to come home."

She's speaking quietly, eyes closed, as if so, so tired. "I didn't. Oh, no. I loved Will, and he loved me. He was going to war and we both knew it, but we thought our love was enough to bring him back. And it was, for the first two and a half years of the war. He flew hundreds of missions. He was an ace, and I was so proud. He sent his money back to me. I made us a home in that little apartment. I was ready for him to come home, ready for the war to be over so I could be his wife. Well, the last time he came home, in January of fifty-three, we conceived a child. I knew it by the time a month had passed. I knew it then, that night. I just knew. And I told him, I said, 'Will, you just put a baby in me.' He was proud. Like it was…like he'd won a race or something. He started talking to my stomach." She sniffs, laughs.

"He was shot down a month later. Killed instantly. I mourned for months. But I was pregnant and alone. So I went home to Mama and Papa. And they took me back. I miscarried, though. I was too upset, I think. Later, after the war, I was in Jackson with my parents, and I met a dashing young soldier named Henry.

My Hank. And we fell in love. He knew about Will. He loved me enough—throughout the years—and he always understood that a piece of me still belonged to William. He loved me anyway, and he loved that missing piece. I had three months with Will, and fifty-seven years with Hank. But your first love? There's something there that you can never replace. But you have to let Derek love you. You have to let him love that missing piece, Reagan. You have to let him."

Silence.

"Ida?"

She opens an eye at me. "I'm just going to rest now, Reagan. I'll be all right. I just need to rest."

I cross the room, kiss her cheek. "I love you, Ida."

She just smiles at me, eyes still closed.

Ida ended up never leaving the hospital. After Hank died, she just never woke up again.

And that's how I want to go. In my sleep, with the man I love. After sixty years together.

EPILOGUE
Derek

San Antonio, 2013

"PUSH, YOU PUSSY!" I SHOUT. "GET IT UP! GET IT UP! You better push harder than that, you little bitch! Yes! There you go, a little more…and down. Good."

PFC Michael Helms is missing both legs from the waist down. Stepped on an IED. He's a buff motherfucker, though, and he's got heart. Real heart. Never gives up. That's what kept him alive when the medics couldn't get to him for nearly ten minutes, pinned down by a sniper.

Everyone in here has a story. Buddy over there lost most of the skin on his face in an explosion. And he's the funniest guy I've ever met. He can make anyone laugh, no matter how shitty their day. They're all my clients. I started out in the Army hospital where I did my own recuperation…twice. Busted ass night and day to get my therapy license, and opened my own gym for guys like me. Guys and girls, I should say. Seen a few women come through here, combat vets like everybody else, missing pieces, with stories they don't want to tell. I push them, squids and grunts and jarheads alike. Force them to live. Force them to *want* to live, despite the losses they've all suffered. I'm damn good at it. And they identify with me, knowing my story. Seeing the evidence in my missing leg, in the Paralympics medals on the wall.

Quitting time comes around, the guys showering and filtering out, leaving me to close the gym. I wipe everything down, stock the cooler, shut off the computer, the lights. Drive home.

Well, I head that way, at least. I stop at a certain bar on the way. Hunter is there, has a round waiting for me. We talk about the day, about his and Rania's third kid, a boy this time. Victor, after Hunter's dad. He just turned one. *Big* trouble, but cute as hell.

Not as cute as Hank, though. Never has a three-year old boy been as cute as Henry Thomas West. He's all me, and all Reagan. Blond, green eyes, sweet as sugar and ready to cause a hell of a ruckus if you take your eyes off him for a split second.

"How's Reagan coming along?" Hunter raises a finger for a refill.

"Oh, she's in the *I hate my body, I hate being pregnant, why did you do this to me, I'm a whale phase.*"

Hunter chuckles. "Fuck, I hate that phase."

"Me, too. Why d'you think I'm here?" I jerk my head toward the outside world, meaning home. "Soon as I get home, Tommy's gonna want to play LEGOs and Henry will need a diaper, and Reagan will need pretzels and peanut butter and diet root beer."

"Quit complaining, douche. You love it."

I nod. "Fuckin' right, I do. But it's my right as a man to complain about it now and then."

Hunter laughs. "True shit, son." He swigs at his Buck Wit. "So. Y'all done?"

"With kids?" I clarify. "Ain't had this one yet, so I'm not sure. Ask me when the baby's a month or two old, and I'll probably say hell yes, we're done. Ask me again later, and I'll probably say maybe. I'd like a daughter."

Hunter chuckles, shakes his head. "As a man with both, I can tell you girls start out easy, but they only get harder as time goes on."

"Guess we'll have to see."

We each have one more, exchanging baby and work stories, and then I drive home. I had a big ol' Chevy Silverado rigged up so I can do everything from the steering wheel, gas, brake, all that. No way I could drive with my right leg the way it is. Took some learning, but I'm used to it now.

Rania is there, along with Maida, Emma, and Vic. It's a fucking zoo. Five kids, all yelling, running around. Tommy and Maida have toy lightsabers, and Tommy is on top of the back of the couch, swinging at Maida, who is dancing across the cushions. Each one yelling "I GOT you!" Emma and Hank are on the floor, whacking each other with a doll and a truck, respectively, and laughing about it, for some reason. Vic is crawling around on three limbs, using one hand to keep a binky stuffed in his mouth.

There's my love, sitting in her favorite chair, nibbling on Triscuits, talking to Rania and overseeing the chaos.

"Has he gone home now?" Rania asks me as I enter.

"Yeah. He'll beat you there, though." I give her a one-armed hug, and she squeezes my waist.

Rania has, throughout Reagan's pregnancy with Hank and this one, too, been here every day, helping with the cooking and cleaning and childcare, so Reagan can work.

My girl writes books. Who knew? She writes these kinky, steamy novels about military men and the women who love them. They make me blush like a schoolgirl, but they sell like hookers on a two-for-Tuesday.

She'd smack me for saying that.

I'm proud as hell of her, though. She's good at it. Works hard. She's talented, and she has a mind for the business aspect, which is tricky, it turns out.

Plus, when she's writing *those* scenes, I get booty. Like…*mad* sex. Crazy, swinging-from-the-ceilings fucking. "Research," she calls it. My goal, usually, is to see how many times I can make her come before she begs me to let her sleep. So far, my personal record is six. She couldn't move after that, though. And that night led to the current burgeoning belly.

And, judging by the look on her face as I approach her, I'm in for one of those nights.

It is *good* to be me.

Rania and the kids leave after a few minutes, and we have dinner. A sit-down family dinner is a nonnegotiable for us. Reagan quits writing when I get home, and we cook together. The kids goof around, and we have a glass of wine or two, providing Ree isn't preggo. And we have dinner. Seven days a week. And as the kids get older, I'm going to continue insisting on it, no matter how mad they get. I grew up without sit-down dinners, and I'll be damned if they will.

Dinner, sit and read through Ree's latest chapters while the kids play. Get the boys to bed.

Get the boys to bed. Five words that make it seem a shitload easier than it really is. Tommy wants to finish watching his show, and Hank is just…Hank. Quirky and difficult. Sleepy, but refuses to sleep. And when he does, he wakes up as soon as I leave the room. Which leads to finding Reagan asleep in her chair, *Nineteen Kids and Counting* repeats playing on TLC.

I shake her gently. "Babe. Wake up, Ree."

"Mmm."

"Come on, babe. Wake up." I kiss the corner of her mouth, shake her thigh. "Time for bed."

"Sleeping."

"Yeah, but not in bed."

"Nite-nite."

"Come on, sexy. Time for bed."

"Sex?" She perks up at that. "You get Hank asleep?"

"Sure did."

"Then what are we still doing here?" She holds her hands out, and I help her to her feet.

We head upstairs, and I "help" her up them by way of groping her ass. The thing I like most about Reagan pregnant is that her tits and ass get bigger and squishier, and if you're me, that's a damn good thing. So I take every opportunity to "grope and molest" her, as she puts it. Whatever. She loves it. She knocks my hands away and says, "Not in front of the kids, you horny caveman," but when the kids are down and we're alone in bed, she sings a different tune.

Loudly.

Tonight she's sleepy. Dragging. She barely makes it up the stairs, fumbling at her shirt and bra on the way. I help. Hehe, help. Getting her naked is my favorite kind of helping. She pees, steps out of her pants and panties, crawls into bed. I shed my own clothes, resigned to a nookie-free night. It's fine, though. Cuddling up to her is almost as nice and, in some ways, even better.

And then, when I'm almost asleep, she angles a bit, turns her head to talk to me. "Well, Caveman? What are you waiting for?"

So I push up against her. She moans. I nudge some more. And then suddenly she's on her hands and knees, her favorite position, especially when she's pregnant. She stuffs a pillow beneath her face and reaches back for me. Guides me in. God, she's tight. I don't know how she manages it, but she's so tight, even after two natural births. She squeezes me as I slide in, clamping down so hard I can barely move inside her, but it feels so, *so* good.

We find a rhythm; we move together in a familiar bliss that never, ever gets old.

Except this time, I falter and slip out, accidentally poke a little too high.

Reagan gasps and bolts forward, and then, when I start to pull back, calls out. "Wait. Oh god….hold on. Just wait." She hangs her head between her shoulders, arches her back, and pushes back against me. "Try it. Slow."

"You sure?"

So I nudge, ever so gently, and she moans. She pushes back, gasps. Pauses. I hold still, and she arches her spine and pushes back again, and I'm in, just a hint. Just the tip, but *fuck,* so tight.

"You write about this?" I ask, breathless, groaning.

"Oh, god…holy shit, Derek. Yeah…."

"I'm not hurting you, am I?" I can't help flexing my hips, just slightly.

"Oh…*oh*…. No." She pauses, stills, and then moves so I slide in a bit deeper.

This time, her moan is the breathless whimper that tells me how close she is. I lean over her back, reach down between her thighs, and find her core, find the touch she likes best. Barely touching, feather light. Slow circles around her clit, never quite touching. And then, when she's writhing and shrieking, I press down in quick movements. She comes, screaming, and I sink in deeper, and she bites the pillow, muffling a loud wail of ecstasy.

And that's when I explode, groaning, gasping, cursing, praying her name.

Moments of silence pass between us as we both fall back to earth from the dizzy heights. Finally, when I'm starting to wonder if she fell asleep like that, on her stomach, knees under her, fine ass up in the air, she stirs.

She flops to her side, pushing at me. "Cuddle me."

I cuddle. "I love you. So much."

"That's 'cuz I'm awesome."

"Yes, you are."

"So are you."

"Yes, I am."

A few moments of silence, and I think she's asleep. I almost am. "Derek?"

"Mmm?"

"If it's a girl, can we name her Ida?"

"Of course, love."

"Ida…what's her middle name?"

I take a long time to respond, fighting sleep. "Dunno."

"*Derek.*"

"Babe. We got five months."

"Derek."

"Jesus. Fine. Elizabeth."

"Why?"

I groan. "Dunno, babe. I just like that name." I yawn. "Ida Elizabeth West."

"'Kay."

Reagan

OhmyholyshittingJesus. Giving birth never hurts any less. All of me is being ripped apart. I think I broke two of Derek's fingers. Not the bad one, fortunately. He doesn't complain, wonderful man that he is. Just holds on, kisses my sweaty forehead, and does the count for each push.

"One...two...three...four...five...six...seven...eight...nine...ten. Good, babe. Almost there." His voice is low and soothing, right in my ear.

"Can you see her? Is she coming?" I'm frantic. Nine hours of labor, and I'm ready for this little girl to be out.

"Almost, love. Almost. One more push." He peers down between my legs. "Yep. I can see her head, the top of her head."

"Then one more isn't going to do it. Several more," I pant.

"You're almost there, babe. Just think about the push."

"DON'T LIE TO ME!"

"You're almost done, babe. For real. Couple more pushes, and she's out." He pulls his hand from mine, flexes to restore circulation, and then takes my hand again. Starts the count. "One...two...three...."

I stop thinking about the count and focus on pushing. Every single ounce of everything inside me—*PUSH. PUSH. PUSH.* Don't breathe, don't scream, nothing but the push.

Breathe, gasp. Rest. Ignore everything and gather my strength. Once more. I can do it. One more time. One last time.

PUSH.

I feel something give—something inside me breaks and escapes, and the pressure is gone, the cramping searing pain lessens, and there's a moment of silence, muttering from the doctor and nurses, a call for scissors. The cord? Is the cord?—But then I hear that sound, that sweet sound. A newborn wail, thin and high and angry and delicate.

A weight on my chest, the smell of blood and something else. I open my eyes and there she is, held by the doctor, birth-smeared and beautiful.

Ida Elizabeth West.

Sister to Tommy and Hank.

I'm crying. "Ida. Hi, baby girl. Welcome to the world."

Derek, blinking hard, voice cracking. "It's a beautiful place, this world. And there's some beautiful people waiting to love you."

Our eyes meet, and a lifetime of love passes between us, transmitted in a single glance.

THE END

SNEAK PEEK AT *BETA*

WAKING UP HAS TURNED INTO ONE OF MY FAVOR-ITE games. The first question is always whether I'm up first, or Roth. If I'm up first, it's my job—self-appointed—to make sure he wakes up in the best possible way. Meaning, with my hands and mouth around his morning wood. And if he's up first, he pretends to be still asleep, so I can wake him up that way. The second question is where in the world we are, because it's different every week or two. Last week, I woke up in Vancouver. I still had one of Roth's neckties knotted around one wrist, remnants of a long and scream-filled night spent tied spread-eagle to the bed. Roth didn't untie me until I'd come…god, like six times? Seven? And when he did finally untie me, well, let's just say I don't think he'll play the "torture Kyrie with multiple orgasms without letting her touch Roth back" game again any time soon. I literally attacked him. The claw marks raking down his back are still healing. I fucked him so hard I think I nearly broke his cock, actually. I think that's possible. Pretty sure it is, and I'm pretty sure I nearly accomplished it.

I woke up and took stock. A little sore between the thighs, but nothing too bad. Roth was snoring, real snores, so I knew I was up first. I breathed in, sighed, stretched. Cracking my eyes open, I caught a whiff of salt sea air, the crash of waves. The bed rocked gently from side to side. We were in a small room, low ceilings, an open window. Just room enough for the bed and a small chest of drawers. But the bed was moving. Why was the bed moving?

Where were we? It took a few minutes for memories of the preceding day to bubble up. A week in Vancouver…a long, *long* flight to Tokyo. A week in Japan. God, what a week. So many tours, so much hiking, so much sushi and sake. I wasn't sure I'd ever drink sake again, that was for sure.

Tokyo, Nagoya, Osaka, Kyoto….

Then where?

A seagull cawed, and I heard voices off in the distance, chattering rapidly. Not Japanese. I remembered the flight out of Kyoto, the flight attendants all dressed identically, down to their hairdos and the little scarf-tie thing knotted just so.

"*Nhat nó lên!*" The angry voice echoed across the water, faint and distant.

Vietnam. That's where we were. Hanoi. Roth bought us a houseboat, paid for it in cash, and he piloted it himself up the Red River from a little village on the Gulf of Tonkin to Hanoi. We stopped often, took it slow. Ate, drank, slept, fucked. We parked the houseboat and checked out temples, hiked out into the farmlands, into the hills, and hired an interpreter and guide to show us the best places off the beaten path. That's the thing about Roth: He never seems like a tourist. He always seems like he belongs wherever we are, and always makes sure we're safe.

We arrived in Hanoi last night, and Roth found some little old lady to cook us a huge dinner on the houseboat, and he paid her enough in U.S. dollars that she left looking a little faint from shock.

After dinner, he uncorked a bottle of some local wine or liquor—I wasn't sure what it was, except *strong*. A couple of small glasses, and I was hammered. Roth took full advantage, laying me on my belly and drilling me until we both came. That was it, because I passed out after that.

Once in a night isn't anywhere near enough to sate my Valentine, so I owe him.

Roth was on his side, facing away from me. The sheet was low around his hips, showing me his broad, rippling back. His blond hair had grown out over the last few months, enough that it brushed his collar when he had a shirt on and hung down past his cheek-bones. He'd grown a bit of a beard, too. Being fair as he was, he didn't grow a thick beard, just a fine coating of blond hair on his cheeks and jaw. Sexy. Oh, so sexy. I cuddled up against him, pressed my lips to the back of his shoulder and kissed, ran my hand down his thick bicep. I found his hip, pushed the sheet away. Peered over his body to watch myself as I cupped his balls in my hand. That, I'd found, was the best way to get him hard if he was still asleep. Massage slowly, gently, maybe a little pressure to his taint, and the sleeping giant would respond. Sure enough, within a minute or so, his cock was engorged and his breathing was changing. He groaned, his abdominal muscles tensing, arms raising over his head. He rolled to his back, stretched, flexed his hips to drive his dick into my fist.

I glanced up at him, found his eyes on me. "Morning."

He grinned at me, a slow, sleepy smile. "Good morning, my lovely."

"I passed out last night, huh?"

"Yes. Snake wine does you in rather quickly, it seems." He watched as I stroked him slowly, one hand sliding from root to tip and back down in a smooth glide.

"Guess so."

"You passed out before we got to do the one thing I'd been wanting to do to you on this boat."

"Which is?"

"Mmmmm." He closed his eyes and lifted his hips. "Would you like to find out?"

I just gave him my small, secret smile, the one that meant I wasn't going to argue either way. The *do as you wish* grin.

Roth growled low his in throat and sat up, pushing me off him. Grabbed the blanket, a big, thin piece of dark green fleece, and draped it from his shoulders, wrapping the ends around both of us as I stood in front of him. He gestured at the door leading from the cabin up to the deck, and I ascended, squeaking as Roth's fingers traced up my ass-crack. He just chuckled and kept fondling and fingering me, making the trip up the ladder a little difficult, but fun. On the deck, Roth kept the blanket around both of us and guided me to the bow, which curved up elegantly to about waist height. Hanoi was spread out before us, dim in the early-morning haze. There was another houseboat some two hundred feet away, and a third the same distance on the other side, but there was no motion from either. A fishing scow plied the water about a thousand feet up-current, nets spreading and being hauled in, voices echoing now and again.

"Grab the bow," Roth whispered in my ear. I took hold of the bow with both hands, turned my head to watch him, but he made a negative sound. "Act like you're just staring out at the city. And try to keep your voice down."

I took the edges of the blanket and held on to it for him, keeping it pulled around us as Roth's hands slid around my belly and descended between my thighs.

Oh, shit. Staying quiet is not one of my strong suits, it turns out.

He had me writhing and moaning, pressing into his touch and biting my lip to keep from screaming. It didn't take long before I was coming for the first time, and then he was bending at the knees, fingers of one hand on my pussy, the other around his cock, feeding it into me. I bent forward over the bow, legs spread wide, and took him.

The fishing scow was getting closer, floating downstream, angled slightly so they'd slide right by us.

"Oh, god, Roth. Hurry. I'm so close."

"Don't come yet. Not yet."

"I can't help it. I'm about to—"

He slowed his pace immediately. "Not yet, Kyrie. Not yet."

The scow neared. Faces turned to regard us, eyes narrowed, suspicious. Roth just waved, and I heard the fishermen exchange comments, laughing. At that exact moment, Roth flexed his hips and drove into me. I wasn't expecting it, and I let out a loud whimper, and all the fishermen guffawed. But at a glare from Roth, the steersman gunned the engine and they were past, and then Roth was moving again and I was coming apart despite his exhortations to wait, wait.

"Come with me, Valentine!"

He came. Oh, dear god, did he come. So, so hard. He filled me with his come, and then kept driving, coming and coming, and I could only clench around him and bend over farther and keep taking him, gasping.

Two weeks later, we were in a chateau in the hills of southern France. I was waking up, playing my game. Taking stock and guessing at our location.

Only, this time something was wrong.

I sat up suddenly, totally awake. Roth wasn't in bed. He never, *ever* left me alone in the mornings. I glanced at the bathroom, but it was dark and silent.

My heart was pounding, sweat beading on my forehead.

"Roth?"

Silence.

The bed beside me was rumpled, still warm from his body heat. The pillow was indented where his head had been.

There was a note. A white scrap of torn paper pinned to the bed with a long, thin knife. The words were written in neat, feminine, looping handwriting, red ink:

He belongs to me.

About the Author

NEW YORK TIMES, USA TODAY, WALL STREET JOURNAL and international bestselling author Jasinda Wilder is a Michigan native with a penchant for titillating tales about sexy men and strong women. Her bestselling titles include *Alpha*, *Stripped*, *Wounded*, and the #1 Amazon and international bestseller *Falling Into You*. You can find her on her farm in northern Michigan with her five children, a menagerie of animals, and her husband Jack Wilder, author of *The Missionary* and co-author of *Captured*.